# THE HOUSE OF FIVE GATES

*Alexandra Martin*

ISBN 979-8-9866779-1-0

# CONTENTS

CHAPTER 1: *Mr. Augustine On Fire* .................. 6

CHAPTER 2: *Blood and Wine* .................. 19

CHAPTER 3: *The 21ˢᵗ Precinct* .................. 33

CHAPTER 4: *Coming Home* .................. 48

CHAPTER 5: *A Soul for Serapis* .................. 60

CHAPTER 6: *Breaking and Entering* .................. 75

CHAPTER 7: *Family Traditions* .................. 89

CHAPTER 8: *A Necromancer Walks into a Bar* .................. 103

CHAPTER 9: *Prosit* .................. 118

CHAPTER 10: *Evergreen and Wheat* .................. 133

CHAPTER 11: *Father Cosmatos* .................. 143

CHAPTER 12: *Milk and Honey* .................. 159

CHAPTER 13: *The Ballad of Maren and Henry* .................. 176

CHAPTER 14: *Io Saturnalia* .................. 186

CHAPTER 15: *Fractio Panis* .................. 201

CHAPTER 16: *Burning Up* .................. 210

CHAPTER 17: *The Library of Irene Lucanus* .................. 226

CHAPTER 18: *Patéras, Anakaléo* .................. 247

CHAPTER 19: *Thais at the River* .................. 264

CHAPTER 20: *Hunger* .................. 278

CHAPTER 21: *Sesheta Maren Nykara* .................. 291

CHAPTER 22: *A Golden Wedding* .................. 307

CHAPTER 23: *Coin* .......................................................323

CHAPTER 24: *The Third Gate* ...................................338

CHAPTER 25: *The Lake of Life* ..............................352

CHAPTER 26: *Hall of Ma'at* ...................................367

CHAPTER 27: *Dies Wadi* ...........................................376

CHAPTER 28: *Three Lives* ..........................................398

CHAPTER 29: *A Knife in the Dark* ...........................410

CHAPTER 30: *Hecate Trimorphe* ...........................429

CHAPTER 31: *The Gardener's Daughter* ..................441

*Privately owned and operated since 1919, The House of Five Gates strives to offer excellence in all areas of the funerary process. Our goal is to guide your loved ones from their last earthly breath to their first in the afterlife with the utmost care, decorum, and splendor. Our team of talented embalmers, administrators, and priests are here to make sure that your family's wishes and wants are met and that your loved ones are treated as the Pharaohs and Emperors they once were. By offering full mummification and funerary services under our roof, we can deliver levels of quality and discretion that other Funerary Houses are unable to meet.*

*- from* About Us, *houseoffivegatesny.com*

# CHAPTER 1

## *Mr. Augustine On Fire*

Somewhere between Sunday night and Monday morning, the gods open the skies above New York City. The subway is a sodden, packed mess, damp commuters jockeying for position with umbrellas and elbows. Dog walkers, normally some of the more intrepid citizens of the city, are absent from the slick, gray streets. The small shrines to Janus punched into niched walls of skyscrapers and brownstone alike are dark and empty, no little old ladies to tend to the abandoned incense cones and springs of wheat.

Tumbling through the onslaught, umbrella creaking in protest under the storm, Maren Nykara careens around the last corner of her commute. Normally simple and brief, today the last leg of her trip from the Christopher Street subway station to her Funerary House has been an agility course through puddles, over curbs, and around taxi wash.

She has never wanted anything more in life than the inside of a building. She'll take anything at this point. She can't even hear herself think over the punishing drone of the unceasing raindrops.

The House of Five Gates materializes ahead of her, the front steps of the brownstone appearing through the roiling steam billowing from a nearby open manhole. Bypassing the front entrance, she hurries down the smaller side steps to the garden level of the House, shouldering the door open and wrestling her now-lopsided umbrella closed.

"You need to see something."

Maren freezes just inside the basement vestibule, dripping on the tile floor from the hem of her coat. Turning around slowly from the door, she nearly canes the person standing there across the shins with her umbrella — the House's administrator, Henry. He's much closer than she expected, his dark eyes wide behind his glasses. Taking a startled step back, she catches herself with her umbrella.

"Henry," Maren says, after she's swallowed a few times. "Why on Gaia's green earth are you lurking in the hallway in the dark?"

"Panicking and waiting for you," he says tightly as Maren transfers her umbrella from her hand to the stand near the door. She shrugs out of her coat, more than happy to separate herself from the water-laden garment.

"What's happened?" Maren asks, frowning. There's a tight, unhappy energy around Henry this morning that's starting to put Maren on edge.

"I'll need to show you." He turns on his heel, into the dark.

"For fucks sake, the dramatics," Maren mutters, flipping the hall light on and then squelching after Henry in her rain boots.

They pass the House's prep room — doors still closed, no light spilling from beneath them — without incident. Maren's about to stop Henry for answers when they pass the morgue storage drawers in the hall next to the prep room.

One of them is open and empty. Maren does not remember that one being empty of a body yesterday.

"Henry," Maren says, a nervous edge creeping into her voice.

7

Henry doesn't answer. Instead, he throws a shoulder into the french doors at the end of the long hall. The glass-paneled doors swing away to reveal the inside of the brownstone's former greenhouse.

The heavy raindrops rattle the glass roof and fill the space with the incessant buzz of the late fall Nor'easter. At least the bone-deep chill of the outside world is shut off, the warmth wafting through quite pleasant. She takes a deep breath of the hot dry air, and then freezes.

"*Henry,*" Maren says, more urgently.

The air in the greenhouse — the *crematorium* — should not be warm. And yet, standing in front of the immense metal maw of the cremation machine that had long ago taken the place of ripped out flower benches and beds, Maren can feel a bead of sweat roll slowly down her back.

There hasn't been a cremation in a solid month, and there absolutely was not one scheduled this morning. Maren would remember, the fiery final choice as destructive and rare as it is.

"It was on when I got in this morning," Henry says, smoothing down the front of his sweater vest again and again, watching his hands and resolutely not meeting Maren's eyes.

"It was just on?" Maren asks slowly.

"Yes." A vigorous nod from Henry, although still no eye contact. "Just finishing a cycle."

Maren very slowly moves towards the machine, twisting the strap of her bag in a white-knuckled grip.

The rain is an impossible din, but Maren's heart is beating hard enough to be heard clear across the Hudson. With extreme trepidation that she hopes she masks as dignified concern, she reaches for the handle of the retort door, hand almost imperceptibly shaking.

Her eyes take a moment to adjust from the rainy half-light of the greenhouse to the smoldering dim of the retort, an unrelenting grayscale broken up by pockets of hot orange. Still, there is no mistaking the heap in it. A body. What very little remains of it, anyway. The soft tissue is boiled away, the hair and nails and bits of recognizable human all stripped off, leaving only a pile of brittle bones caught between a bleached white and a charred brown. The burnt, cloying smell of fresh cremains swirls around her, the heat and scent resting at the back of her throat.

She is dully aware of Henry hovering behind her, looking over her shoulder. His own breathing is clipped and fast. Hearing it so close to her ear, she settles into herself with a deep breath before turning to Henry. Releasing her bag strap, she reaches up to wrap her hands firmly but carefully around his upper arms.

"Do we know who this is?" She asks, keeping her voice even.

"I think so," Henry says with a quick, too-tight nod. "I checked, and everyone is accounted for except for Mr. Augustine."

The bottom of Maren's stomach drops out. Hysteria bubbles up in its place. In a show of remarkable restraint in the face of an unsanctioned cremation performed by neither her administrator nor herself, she somehow manages to tone it down.

"Did you check the security tape?" Maren asks. Her eyes slide sideways to where the cheery, unblinking eye of the camera above the door is mounted. It's still on, the little blue light glowing through the gray haze of the room.

9

"Your office is locked," Henry points out.

"Right," Maren says.

They beat a hasty retreat back into the House, heading up the stairs at a strange pace somewhere between restrained and terrified.

Maren draws up short in the front hall when she sees faces bobbing through the glass of the front door, distorted by the rain sluicing down the panel. Henry bowls into her, and it's only thanks to his resemblance to a green bean that they don't go toppling over.

"Is that–" Henry says.

"Yes," Maren says darkly. When it rains, it pours. And not just outside.

Standing on the stoop in the downpour is Phaedra Augustine — the daughter of the late Casper Augustine, one of the richest men in Manhattan, and current non-sanctioned resident of their cremation retort. And, horribly, she's brought a guest.

"Crap," Henry breathes.

"*Yes*," Maren says. Without taking any more time to think, she digs into her bag, produces her keyring, and half throws it at Henry's face, sending him scrambling backwards. "Go pull the tape, I'll deal with this."

Henry gives her a look that she assumes is supposed to be serious but instead comes off more unhinged in the current circumstances, before swinging himself around the polished oak banister of the grand front stairs and taking them by two. The minute he's out of sight, Maren drops her bag behind a small side table and strides for the door.

"I am so sorry, we didn't hear the bell," Maren says, ushering Phaedra and her plus-one inside. "Come on in."

The first time Maren had met Phaedra, when her father

10

had been brought to the brownstone for his intake a few weeks ago, Maren had thought there was something familiar about her, although she couldn't quite put a finger on what it was. Considering the wealth and status of her father, Maren had just assumed that she'd seen a photo of her in passing before. Now, with the other person standing next to her, Maren realizes exactly what's familiar about her. There's no doubt that the similarly damp person is her sister — a bit pointier, a bit less round, hair a bit darker, but undeniably a sibling. A sibling Maren knows.

"Ariadne," Maren says in open shock.

"Hi," Ari says, sporting the same gob-smacked expression. They square off for a moment, both eyeing the other like they're seeing a ghost, before Phaedra delicately clears her throat to snap the brittle tension.

"Let's take a seat in the parlor," Maren says, sweeping an arm open to indicate the direction of the room, very much excited to move away from this space where she's locked gazes with Ariadne Augustine on a morning that is already awful and bordering on disastrous.

Coats are hung and towels offered (and refused) before Maren ushers them into the sitting room. Cars flash by on the street outside, headlights glancing off the ceiling and walls where the old wall sconces don't quite fully light. She watches from the doorway as the two sisters perch on opposite ends of a couch.

"I'll be right back, but please let us know if you need anything," Maren says.

"We're just here to drop off anointing oil. If you're busy we can always come back," Phaedra pipes up sweetly. "We were meeting our mother for breakfast around the corner and thought we'd stop by."

11

"Let us know if this is a bad time, clearly something is... afoot," Ari says, and Maren fights every instinct to freeze in shock before she realizes Ari is pointedly looking at her feet.

She's still wearing her damn rain boots.

"We can always accommodate all needs," Maren says smoothly, starting to slide the pocket doors shut. "Just one moment."

She reclaims her bag from behind the table in the entryway before getting up the stairs as quickly as she can without making a squeaky racket in her boots. The door to her office is cracked open, the glow of a computer screen slipping into the hall. Maren opens the door fully and turns the lights on with a savage *click*.

"You have *got* to quit hanging around in the dark," Maren sighs before dropping into a visitor's chair and tugging her boots off.

"It's causing a glare," Henry murmurs, his nose mere inches from the computer screen. Maren chucks her boots behind the desk in response, before liberating her sensible mules from her bag.

"My ex is downstairs," Maren says.

"I'm sorry, what?" Henry asks, glancing around the monitor with a raised eyebrow.

"There's a second Augustine sister. I dated her in college. This morning is just on *fire*," Maren says, and then, after a pause and a look of horror from Henry, "oh Gods, sorry, poor choice of words. Also, just tip the monitor a bit."

"No, it's–" with a small noise of extreme frustration, Henry flips the monitor around and Maren's stomach drops.

The security footage is ruined. Not in a way that suggests the recording hadn't worked, or that something like a hand or cloth was covering it. Not even static. No, what's on the screen is a kaleidoscope of popped color, stars skittering across the screen, leaving it impossible to see what's happening in the greenhouse.

"I didn't even know it could record in color," Maren says, otherwise at a loss for words.

"It can't," Henry says. "Look."

He scrubs back, and the galaxy of mismatched shapes and colors recedes to show a perfect picture of the crematorium, silent and dark in the small hours of the morning. Everything looks fine, and the machine certainly isn't on. Then, slowly, that popping distortion starts creeping around the edges of the frame. Right before it swallows the recording whole, a shadow falls across the floor. Someone must have opened the greenhouse door.

And then nothing. Well, nothing useful at least.

"Did you try redownloading it?" Maren asks.

"Twice," Henry says with the most somber nod the world has ever known. "It came straight from the system like this."

Hunching over in her chair and letting her messy, loose curls fall across her face, Maren lets out a small *fuck* in the direction of the floor. Maren has never had something like this happen. She'd apprenticed at this House, had taken over when the old owner retired. The House of Five Gates is hers to preside over, and she takes that duty seriously for the sake of the souls in the basement awaiting their journey into the afterlife.

If that is truly Mr. Augustine in the retort, his soul is lost, his earthly body destroyed by fire before he's been

13

prepared to be ferried to the afterlife.

"This is not ideal," Henry says after the silence stretches on just a bit too far.

"This is a full bore clusterfuck," Maren says sharply before sitting back in her chair. The security video is still up on the screen, taunting her with its destroyed image.

"What do we tell his family? Phaedra and — who was the other sister?" Henry asks.

"Ari," Maren mutters.

"You rang?" Someone asks from the open office door.

It takes all of Maren's fortitude to not jump out of her skin. She spins to face the door, only to find the last two people in the world she wants to see.

"Can we help you with something?" Maren asks, trying to relax her fingers where they're digging into the arms of the chair.

"We thought we'd drop off the oils and be on our way, we don't mean to intrude," Phaedra says. Maren can see her give the back of Ari's jacket a yank, but Ari remains unmoved, framed in the old, polished wood of the door frame, hands on hips.

"But we'd love to hear what you have to share," Ari says.

There are several ways Maren could do this. She could tell the truth. *Someone broke in and cremated your father's body.*

She could lie. *The coffin he wanted is back-ordered and the burial will be delayed.* She could just get rid of them, taking the time to think of a better answer, although that possibly leaves them stewing in suspense and suspicion, which can only end poorly.

"What's that?" Phaedra asks with wide eyes before

Maren can say anything, pointing to the computer screen over Ari's shoulder.

The security video is still up on screen, front and center, the image kaleidoscoping for all it's worth. The world comes to a screeching halt. Maren cannot get her treacherous brain to produce a single useful thought.

"Nothing!" The word is wrenched out of Henry as he leaps up, practically hugging the computer screen to wrestle it back to him, turning its face from the sisters. Unfortunately, this is the most suspicious avenue of action Henry could have taken. It is, very clearly now, *not* nothing. Far from it.

Ari slides into the room as if it's hers, hovering by the edge of the desk. Henry eyes her up, giving her a quick once-over and pressing his lips into a thin line.

"That's private, Ms. Aug–" Maren starts, moving to stand.

"Shh," Ari says, flapping a hand in Maren's general direction.

With a growing sense of absolute and total doom, Maren watches as Ari starts to scrub through the footage. Traveling on almost silent feet, her flats soft on the carpet, Phaedra comes to stand with her. The sparks and bursts of color illuminate their pale faces, reflecting in their wide eyes. Maren has to tear her gaze from this horror show of a slowly unfolding car crash. She fixes her gaze on Henry instead, watching as his face travels through several complicated emotions before landing on something that suggests he needs a vacation and alcohol post haste. Flanked by Phaedra and Ari, the whole trio lit in that unnatural light, they make an awful picture.

After what must have only been a minute or two but

15

feels like years, Phaedra draws herself up to her full height, chin pointed and proud, horror in her eyes.

"What," said so deliberately as to be a physical strike, "is going on here?"

—

There are police in the front hall, dripping on the same maligned rug that Ari and Phaedra had similarly abused a mere hour ago. Maren eyes them warily, feeling much too beat down for it not even being noon yet.

Because there wasn't much turning back to be done after Henry's frantic embrace of the computer and what they'd seen, Maren had felt duty-bound by the truth. Phaedra and Ari, to their credit, had listened very carefully, not interrupting while Maren and Henry had gone through as much of the horrible tableau as they were able to.

Unfortunately, it had ended with Ari cracking up hysterically and Phaedra diving for her phone to dial 911 with so much force that Maren swears she had heard the screen creaking under the onslaught of her fingertips.

And now they're here, all four of them, carefully sequestered in the front room while a small army composed of NYPD detectives scrounge up whatever horrible clues they can. Maren has never seen the police react so quickly and so overwhelmingly to anything, but she supposes desecration of a corpse is extremely illegal. Desecration of a very rich corpse is probably even more illegal, with the way things go in the world. With all the various cults, offshoots, and Catholic sects floating around, they're always very careful to embalm bodies exactly as a family requests. The Augustines had asked that their patriarch get the full, classic suite — embalming, mummification, anointing, entombment by a priest of Serapis.

Cremation has achieved the exact opposite of what they were aiming for.

"Maren," Henry murmurs.

"Mmm?" Maren replies, deep down a rabbit hole of awful *what ifs*.

"What if it was one of them?" Henry hisses, *sotto voce*. A dramatically timed slice of lightning illuminates Henry's face in a series of hard planes as he says this. "They were here very early."

The thought had occurred to Maren, although she'd dismissed it quickly. The one silver lining to the raincloud currently pummeling the outside world is that it would be easy to tell if anyone had come in sopping wet, and, as far as Maren can tell, the only trails of water dropped sadly through the halls are from those presently assembled.

Well, and now the police, unfortunately.

"No," Maren says, shaking her head. "I can't see it from them."

"What, because they're rich?"

"My thinking was more rain-related, but sure. You think either of them has ever done a second of dirty work in their lives?"

The two turn as one to stare at where the sisters are seated on a chaise across the coffee table. Phaedra is sitting rigid and coiled, typing away on her phone with such tightness in her shoulders that they look about ready to pop from her torso. As her fingers fly across the screen, the almost garishly large sapphire ring she's sporting flashes in the lamplight.

In contrast, Ari is long-limbed, spread out on her side of the couch and picking at a thread on the arm with such little interest that it's almost enviable. If she wasn't unfortunately acquainted with Ari already, Maren would assume she's not thinking of anything at all. But she is unfortunately acquainted, and knows that the more disinterest Ari is showing, the faster her brain is spinning.

"I kind of hate all of this, for the record," Henry mutters. Maren lets her eyes slide his way, and she turns her body, angling herself to him as a barrier to the Augustines.

"I know," Maren says with a sigh. "I do too."

"I don't want anything to happen to the House," Henry says, and he looks absolutely miserable.

"Nothing's going to happen to the House," Maren says, vigorously shaking her head and sending her curls flying. This is her House, and she won't allow anything to jeopardize its future. Henry blinks — once, twice — at her, his eyes sharp behind his glasses.

Maren takes a deep breath in, closing her eyes for a moment. No use getting upset about something she has no control over. She takes in a few more measured breaths, deep and slow, before looking back at Henry.

"The House will be fine," she says, voice even and strong. She has to believe that, because there is no other option for her. There's no other option for the House.

# CHAPTER 2
*Blood and Wine*

Maren has just taken Dremel tool to temporal bone when the doorbell rings. It's hard to hear over the pitched whine of the spinning blade, and it takes her a few seconds to pick the sounds apart. She looks up to find her two assistants, Oscar and Tad, watching her. She can't blame them for their deer in the headlights approach to someone at the front door, considering the day they'd had yesterday. The police had strongly suggested to Maren that she call all employees in to be questioned and they'd all been stuck, trapped in the House in a swirl of badges and flashing lights, until mid-afternoon. Everyone had alibis, because of course they had. Maren would have been more shocked to find out that one of her staff had done this than she had been at the actual cremation.

Now, with her own spike of trepidation, Maren peers through her face shield at the tablet they have propped up in a stand next to the prep room sink. The grainy video shows a man and a woman standing at the door, jacket collars tugged close and pulled up against the cold. Although the rain had finally broken early this morning, the pervasive chill most certainly has not.

"Should I, uh... go get the door?" Tad asks. He's been restocking the cabinet with cleanly rolled new linen wrappings and is therefore the only one of the three not currently speckled with small bits of Mrs. Colvard, the ancient, wizened woman on the steel table. Oscar has his hands held up like a surgeon, although in this case it's less about germs and more about the tacky, decaying blood that's coating his gloves.

"Please," Maren says.

Tad straightens his tie and his back, and then gives Maren a quick nod before striding out with perhaps more purpose than Maren had given him.

"They're cops," Oscar murmurs, jerking his head towards the tablet.

"We don't know that," Maren says. She lets her eyes slide towards the video feed again — they're both dressed smartly, but not uniformed.

Oscar makes a non-committal noise at the back of his throat before Maren returns to grinding through Mrs. Colvard's skull. Bone crunches and resists, the smell of unpleasant burning wafting over the thick, loose smell of decay that will always hang around the basement, no matter how many candles and sticks of incense they light to ward it off. Oscar dutifully peels back scalp as they go, keeping skin and hair out of Maren's way.

"Did you see what was in the retort?"

Maren stops the whirring blade for a second time, letting her hand come to rest on the table and looking up at Oscar.

"After the cremation?" She asks.

Oscar gives a curt nod.

"I did," Maren says. "It was a normal cremation. Mr. Augustine was reduced to bone fragments."

"Do you think his soul is lost?" Oscar asks. In the bright, sterile light of the prep room, she can see the shadows under his eyes thrown into sharp relief. She wonders if he'd gotten any sleep the prior night, or if the question — and she's sure, others — had kept him up. Maren believes in the afterlife for her clients. Oscar believes in it for himself.

"I'm not sure," Maren answers honestly. Something shifts in his face, but behind his mask it's hard to tell exactly what. He turns away, carefully and gently pulling a bit more of Mrs. Colvard's forehead away from the smeared white surface of her skull. His hands work with such care that it makes Maren sigh. She'd like to say something to make it better, but nothing reassuring comes to her. Oscar is young, fresh out of school, and Maren can only assume his emotions are still too raw, not yet dulled by years of standing on the close side of life to death.

Tad chooses this moment to stick his head back into the prep room with a small knock on the door, saving Maren having to come up with an empty platitude or two.

"They've requested you, Ms. Nykara," Tad says. "Urgently."

"Cops," Oscar reiterates.

"Please finish up with the skullcap, Oscar," Maren says instead, handing over the Dremel before stripping off the various bits and pieces of PPE she'd strapped on a mere half an hour ago.

The woman and man from the video feed are fully realized in the front hall, removed from monochromatic grain into the real world. She can tell now the man is young-ish, around her age, perhaps somewhere in the nondescript years of his twenties or thirties. The woman is approaching middle age, her black ponytail shot through with a few strands of silver. Maren has to admit that Oscar might have been onto something. Although they're not wearing NYPD blues, there is still something about their

21

clothes that suggests a uniform.

Oscar's suspicions are confirmed a minute later.

"Chief Embalmer Maren Nykara?" The woman asks, tugging a badge on a chain from inside her coat. The unmistakable shield of the NYPD blinks brightly back at Maren.

"That's me," Maren says, wondering what could have possibly brought the police back.

"We're Detectives Choi and Perry," the woman says, hooking a thumb at her own chest before indicating the younger man standing at her side. "We just have a few more questions for you."

"Of course," Maren says with a tight-lipped smile. This has to be quick, considering all the questions she answered yesterday. "Should we talk in my office?"

"May we see the crematory, actually?" Perry asks, finally speaking.

Maybe her hope that this would be fast is misplaced. She doesn't let them see the twist of her expression as she turns, leading them into the depths of the House and through to the greenhouse.

Even though a small nation's worth of police had trampled through the brownstone yesterday, the scene of the crime is remarkably intact and calm. There wasn't much to do in here except dust for fingerprints — nothing was amiss or out of place. Although the nature of the crime was heinous, the cold truth of the matter is that it appears to have been done quietly, with minimal fuss.

"This is where it happened?" Choi asks. Maren just nods in response, knowing that her tight smile is probably slightly suspicious but caring little. As much as dead people will wait forever, Maren has learned over the years

22

that their living families will not, and they're already a whole day off schedule.

"If you have other things to attend to, please don't feel like you need to hang out with us," Perry says. Maren wants to jump at the chance to get back to Mrs. Colvard, but there is zero chance that she's letting these two out of her sight. Her House has been besmirched enough lately.

"We're not particularly busy at the moment," Maren lies easily. "Let me know if I can answer those questions."

Choi and Perry exchange a quick glance before Perry shrugs.

"Ok," he says, and then with a practiced fluidity pulls a golden bowl from the satchel he's carrying. Maren watches in confusion as Choi rolls over the spare gurney in the corner, placing it in the center of the empty space in front of the hulking machine. The bowl is placed on the stretcher with a resounding gong like a hand bell, before more strangeness continues to come out of Perry's pack and pile up on the gurney.

"Wish we didn't have to do this in here," Choi mutters.

"I want to be close; the world's so wet right now I might not get a good hook on him from too far away," Perry says. "The dead don't cross water well."

Maren frowns at Perry, trying to make heads or tails of whatever had just come out of his mouth. He ignores her. Coals go into the bowl, then small containers of a few substances that Maren can't necessarily identify. One might be wine, another is honey-thick and golden, yet another is a dull, sluggish red. Well, that one is blood. Maren's fairly articulate in the language of bodily fluids at this point in her life.

The substances are set around the bowl at the four

compass points, left in their little jars, and then Perry pulls a long-necked barbecue lighter out of his bag.

"I don't know if open flame is a good idea," Maren says, and she can feel a furrow forming between her brows. "I mean, it's a great idea for this," Perry says. "Or nothing's going to happen."

Maren is about to ask what on earth he means by that, what *exactly* is going to happen, when he snaps the lighter on and thrusts it into the coals. The coals spring to life, a roiling flame spreading across the bowl like a wave.

Nothing happens. Maren is starting to feel like she's having an elaborate prank played on her.

"Excuse me," she starts, crossing her arms.

"Hush," Choi admonishes her, tight weariness in her voice.

The hairs on Maren's arms stand up, her skin prickling as the previously still air in the crematorium starts to shift. A few pieces of paper blow from the desk in the corner, falling to the floor and dancing in the unnatural breeze like autumn leaves.

The flames drop to the coals, glowing a deep red, and then burst forth once again. This time, they are molten gold.

Maren stares, transfixed, as Perry inclines his head over the bowl, eyes closed. His lips move, murmuring low, liquid, unclear words into existence. Although Maren's first instinct is to run, her second is to move closer, to hear whatever spell or prayer Perry is weaving. She finds herself rooted to the spot, arms clutched around her, hair lifted by the preternatural wind that's been called into the greenhouse. It all feels so incredibly wrong to her, alien and from somewhere far beyond the world they're standing

24

in.

With a grace that he shouldn't possess, Perry raises his head, swiveling to face Maren. His eyes are open now, and they are the same molten gold of the fire. The metallic shine swirls where there should be white and iris. A sharp, electrical taste rises in the back of Maren's throat, replacing the hold of the burning bone from downstairs. It reminds her of the moments before a summer thunderstorm.

A great weight slams into her back. Her breath is punched from her body, replaced by a bone-deep chill that curdles her blood and sends her tumbling to knees and hands on the concrete floor, shivering and gasping for air. Her vision narrows, tunneling into dark channels. Behind her, the doors rattle on their hinges with such a vengeance they shriek with it, threatening to come apart.

From somewhere above her head, as if in a dream, Choi's weary voice speaks a single word, shot through with something ancient and powerful.

"Felix."

The wind abruptly stops. The chill is pulled from Maren, from her skin and gut, torn from her skull like a tooth with a suddenness that leaves her shaking and weak. Pressure pops in her sinuses and starbursts replace the tunnel vision before fading, leaving her staring at the floor and feeling like she needs to sleep for a week.

A pair of hands take her by the shoulders, pulling her back to kneeling with a kind strength. She takes a deep, shuddering breath, then another. In and out. Over and over. Her body gulps it down, as if she's just surfaced from too long spent below the water.

"You're alright," Choi murmurs near her ear. Maren

25

nods, clinging to the words.

Maren spits once on the floor, trying to get the strange summer storm-taste out of her mouth, before she stands on shaking legs. Choi offers out a hand but doesn't press Maren to take it as she rises on her own.

Perry is sitting on the gurney next to the bowl, swinging his legs back and forth. His eyes have returned to looking human. The bowl is clear of flame, the coals dark and dead. He doesn't meet her gaze.

Her whole body shakes violently, stress and fear consuming her from the inside out as she stares Perry down.

"What the *fuck*," Maren says hoarsely.

"Our apologies," Choi says pointedly. At first Maren thinks the snipe is directed at her, but when she turns her face to the side, she finds Choi glaring at Perry. "The feeling will pass, perhaps after a good night's rest."

Maren can't even wrap her head around the idea of sleeping for a full eight hours right now. At this very moment in her life, she assumes that she will never again know a full night's sleep.

"I thought you knew what we were doing," Perry says conversationally after a beat, jumping down from the gurney and starting to round up his collection of odds and ends. He holds up the bowl last, waving it around, causing a few bits of briquet dust to trickle from it and onto his hand, leaving a sooty smudge. "People see this and know."

"Only people who know necromancy," Choi says with a weary sigh. "Pick up the pace, Felix, let's let Ms. Nykara get back to work. We've been in her hair too long already."

*Necromancy.* It's forbidden, awful, dark stuff — *death magic.* The word rings a hollow in her chest, pushes the chill in her body further into her bones.

"Alright, alright," Perry murmurs, shouldering his bag.

"Out," Maren says. She wants them out of her crematorium, out of her House, and away from her person. Something inside her feels like it doesn't fit anymore, and she's afraid when she takes a step, she might shatter away into nothing.

Luckily her legs carry her back to the front door in one piece, although still quite shaky and weak, as if she's been running sprints for the better part of an hour. Choi and Perry offer up one last soft *our apologies* and then they're out into the midday light, Choi slipping Maren her card on the way out. Maren stares at it as she tosses the door shut, appreciating the cessation of noise from the outside world, leaving her in the quiet of the front hall with her skin still crawling and her mind jittering around in her skull.

The business card in her hand is a simple one, just plain white with a splash of blue at the top emblazoned with the white NYPD logo. *Emerson Choi, Detective* appears on it, plus a collection of various reachable phone numbers and their precinct number — 21. But that can't be right. As the House is registered with the city and the police, Maren knows for a fact that they're located in the 6th precinct. She can't even figure where the 21st would be; somewhere far up north, hugging the park or perhaps even above it. There is zero reason why these two should be this far downtown.

Maren frowns at the paper in her hand. She stares past it, glaring into nothing. None of this is right. Nothing fits, nothing makes sense. A body had ended up cremated, there's no proper footage of it, and now cops from way uptown are poking their noses into her House and doing sacrilegious rituals. Maybe once upon a time, when she was younger and hadn't spent so much time pacifying herself to be fit to be around the grieving, she might have torn up the card, flinging the bits of paper to the floor. Instead, drawing herself up to her full height, she takes a deep breath, taps the card against her palm a few times, and forces her thoughts into order.

Whatever Perry had done back there, it hadn't been a cheap trick or a charlatan bone reading in a corner shop — that was real death magic. Maren can still feel the echoes of it in her core, yawning and horrible.

Possibly even worse, someone believes this case requires necromancy to solve. Maren has never heard of that in all her years, even standing as close to death as she does.

Neither of these realizations sit correctly on her shoulders, in her mind, around her heart. They're both wrong — angular bits that don't fit into the world in which she's cocooned herself. They crystallize and shatter, sending fragments bouncing around her skull as she tries to make sense out of all of it. She'd love to go home, go lie down, and try to remember what life feels like. Instead, she knows she has to descend back to the basement, back to the death that awaits her there. Her work does not normally weigh on her mind like this, but most days are not like these.

She closes her eyes for a moment, taking a deep breath in and filling her lungs to a point where her ribs seem about to give way, before letting that air out slowly. With a finality that she knows won't last, she pockets Choi's card and forces herself to move. She has to keep herself together to keep the House together. They have to survive this as one.

—

A good night's sleep does not quite seem to get rid of the feeling that something is *wrong*, that something within Maren doesn't fit correctly. It's a persistent, low hum at the back of her head, even though she nurses it in spits and starts with hot showers and hotter cups of tea, inviting the warmth back into her body. Not even clutching Miu, her cat, close to her chest seems to warm her. Whatever it is that had traveled through her in the greenhouse doesn't want to quite shake loose.

With no way of knowing what's causing the feeling, she pushes it as far down as she can, ignoring it to the best of her ability. If she's finding herself feeling colder, it's because the temperature is rapidly dropping off as they accelerate into winter.

At the end of the week Maren locks the doors to the House half an hour early, and herds Henry, Tad, and Oscar towards the bar a few blocks away. It's a designated celebratory bar, for things like birthdays and well-conquered long weeks, and the fact that they've all made it through this week of horrors calls for alcohol.

The place is homey and dark, laughter and conversation bouncing around, clusters of overstuffed and well-loved furniture orbiting small marble tables like especially lumpy and gilded solar systems. They colonize a space of their own in the back corner and send Tad to get the first round of drinks.

"I could have done with fifty percent less insanity this week," Henry sighs as he sinks into a chaise, leaning back and staring up at the dark ceiling. He blends in quite well, his hair and clothing melting into the same spectrum as the upholstery under his body.

"A hundred percent less," Oscar mutters. He half-heartedly kicks at Henry's legs so that he can join Henry on the chaise, hunching over and refusing to strip out of his heavy peacoat, instead choosing to stare at Maren owlishly with the collar turned up.

"The good news is that we've made it," Maren says, breaking away from Oscar's eye-line and staring down at the small flickering tea light on the table. It's a lie, full stop. There is a storm brewing at the back of her skull, threatening to batter straight through the walls she's carefully placed between herself and the need to yell and scream and sob.

"Have we?" Oscar asks. "The investigation just started."

"I believe we'll all make it through alright," Maren says. "I trust you all implicitly, or you wouldn't be working at the House. It wasn't one of us."

"Gods, no," Henry says, shaking his head violently. "We would never invite that dishonor or mess into our own House."

Tad returns with drinks, carefully placing them down onto the table one at a time with the same concentration as he finesses all his tasks.

Nursing her cider slowly, Maren allows herself to sink back into her chair, the conversation around her flowing like wine. Although Henry and Tad can't get Oscar to crack a smile he's at least a bit less of a raincloud than usual, a needed respite after this week. She cares about these three, who work by her side on this narrow spit of the world between life and death.

The cider warms her, her over-stuffed chair happily accepts her body, and for a few hours, everything is alive and *easy*. At the end of the evening she's somewhat disinclined to rise from her slightly tipsy nest, but the small, sober bit of her brain prevails, and Henry offers her a hand to help her back up to standing.

They stand clustered together on the sidewalk outside, breath puffing out in clouds. The city swirls on around them, bright lights pushing away the night, socking them in with the rush of wheels and the hurry of steps. All around them is the swell of humanity, unburdened and unbothered by the death that the four people on the sidewalk share.

"Thank you for this week," Maren says as the tip of her nose starts to chill. "You all really did so well."

"Anything for you, boss," Tad says, giving her a thump on the shoulder.

Oscar gives her a small nod with an even smaller smile before he and Tad float off in the direction of the subway, vanishing into a million other figures clad in similarly dark clothes on a similarly dark Friday night.

"Chin up, Nykara," Henry says.

"Oh, now you're giving me a pep talk?" Maren says with a sharp grin tossed his way.

"Don't get used to it," Henry says, raising his eyebrows before starting to walk backwards, slipping away just like the other two.

"Get home safe and say hello to Taner for me," Maren calls after him.

"Same to you!" Henry hollers, cupping a hand around his mouth, and then he's gone.

—

Her welcoming party comes in the form of a fluffy black cat, haunting the threshold of her apartment like the beast hasn't been fed in days.

"You know, if you grew thumbs you could do this yourself," Maren tells Miu over the chattering chorus of meows she's currently producing with every squeaky bit of her small body.

The minute the dish of food touches the floor, Miu is on it like a well-hunted meal. Maren smiles down at her, squatting down for a moment to scratch at Miu's back as she attacks her food. Sticking her other hand in her coat pocket, Maren's fingers come into contact with the worried edge of Detective Choi's card. Sitting down on the floor of the kitchen, still in shoes and coat and hat, Maren pulls it from her pocket, idly stroking Miu with her other hand. She flips the card over and over in her palm, dirtying the edges of the clean white paper with the oil of her skin more and more.

Nothing about this week makes sense, and, worse, it's all a threat to her House. It's a threat to the reputation they've cultivated, to the souls in their care, and seemingly to Maren's very person. Death magic is just the forbidden cherry on top of this awful sundae. What could come of this case, and what could happen, or has already happened to Mr. Augustine's soul, gnaws at Maren.

And then there's the cold in her veins and bones. It's getting harder to ignore.

Her House. Another flip of the card. Herself. The card scrapes across her palm. *Death magic*.

She can't leave something like this to chance alone.

# CHAPTER 3

## The 21ˢᵗ Precinct

The House of Five Gates is dark and silent when Maren slips through the front door on Monday morning. She knows no one will be here yet, the main door still locked up tight to visitors. Not even Henry is in yet, Maren having purposely beat him to work this morning.

When she'd first set foot in this Mortuary House, trailing on the stylish coat tails of *Hemet* Thais Cooper, Priestess of Serapis and guide to the souls that passed through the House, she had been uneasy. Not frightened — she'd seen death before — but uneasy. Raised in a faithless household that celebrated holidays because it was culturally dictated, not out of any religious obligation, it had been like stepping into another world. The golden hieroglyphs on the door, done in a clean, careful hand, had been as unfamiliar to her as Cyrillic or Katakana. Hieroglyphs were the alphabet of a world that Maren had not known at that moment, reserved for headstones and ancient texts.

Now, as she heads up the steps, moving through the early graying light of the morning, Maren feels strong, a captain at the head of her ship. This place has become her home. She will not let the last week shake her up so much that she is unable to feel at ease in her own House. She is going to fix this.

She unlocks her office, taking off her coat and setting her bag down, ritually shedding herself of the outside

33

world before perching on the edge of her chair and booting up the computer. Reaching for the mouse, she calls up the security footage from the other day when Detectives Choi and Perry had decided to darken their doorstep. Scrubbing through, she watches the screen as the three of them, awash in grayscale and slightly grainy, walk into the room on silent feet. She watches with rapt attention as the digital Perry starts the ritual all over again, watches as he carefully pulls item after item from his bag. The way his body moves with the objects speaks to an ease that she knows, although for another avenue entirely — he wields the bowl and coals like she does a scalpel and anointing oil.

She's so close to the screen that she nearly misses it when the edges of the video start to fizz and pop, color blooming in the corners. Pulling back, she takes in the whole video, widening her scope from what Perry is engaged in, to see the whole picture.

Perry lights the bowl, and with a sudden ferocity, the rest of the footage is buried under a galaxy of sunsetting stars, crystalline and chaotic.

Maren stares wide-eyed at the screen before rubbing at her face and rewinding to watch the whole thing again. But no, there's been no trick, no strange double playback. The same kaleidoscope effect that had invaded the footage of Mr. Augustine's cremation is here too, like an insidious bit of decay.

Necromancy had damaged the recording of the cremation too.

The thought of a necromancer in her House, performing unsanctioned cremations, makes her feel sick. In the quiet dark of the brownstone, she rubs at her skin despite herself. This is all wrong.

From somewhere in the cradle of the House, a door opens and shuts. The sound, as dull and muffled as it is, still shakes Maren from her reverie, and she closes out of the footage as someone makes their way up the stairs from the basement.

Making sure to cause as much noise as one normally would while walking, she heads down the stairs to find Henry in the hall, coat and bag still in hand.

"You're in early," he notes with an arched brow. "Burning the candle at both ends?"

"I just had some paperwork to catch up on." *Liar.*

"Don't overdo it, I don't need you expiring right in the middle of an embalming."

Maren tamps down on the overwhelming desire to roll her eyes, only just barely.

"I'm not planning on dropping dead any time soon," Maren says.

"Good, because I don't know if you could afford this House's services." Henry's expression clearly suggests that he's a little shit and he knows it.

"What?" Maren says, crossing her arms. "You wouldn't do pro bono for me?"

"This is a business," Henry intones. "Not a charity."

Maren gives him a shove in the shoulder in response.

"I'm glad you're feeling more up to life," Henry says with a soft smile.

"Trying to be more up to it, at least," she says.

They double check the calendar for the day, moving a few people around on the whiteboard in Maren's office before they take their leave of each other, separate in their duties. Henry is no doubt off to make sure the lounge is spotless before his first meeting with the grieving for today. Maren doesn't envy Henry, having learned across the years that while she's perfectly capable of dealing with the left-behind loved ones, she much prefers the conversation of the corpses a floor down.

Tad and Oscar trail in as Maren is wheeling Mrs. Colvard out of the freezer, who's scheduled to finish this part of the process this morning.

"Good morning," Maren says. "Let's finish up with Mrs. Colvard so that she can get out of cold storage and into some salt."

This is nice and normal, the rock and even rhythm of the world, in every roll of new linen they inventory, in every apron tied on, in every soul shepherded beyond the veil.

With Mrs. Colvard's cold skin under her hands, Maren lets out a long, steady breath, banishing everything from her mind that is not her job.

Or, at least, she tries. But there, at the base of her skull, the chill in her body still buzzes.

—

"Are we going to get Mr. Augustine back?"

They're standing in front of the whiteboard in Maren's office again, another morning of another day much like those before it. Henry has been moving magnets with names scrawled on them, shuffling people around as they move from *intake* to *phase 1 embalming* to *salt*, all steps in their post-mortem adventures.

Maren looks up at Henry from where she's picking through a file, frowning. Although the case — or, more specifically, the necromantic bit of it — has been on her

36

mind near ceaselessly, she's embarrassed to realize she hasn't given Mr. Augustine much thought. What little remains of him.

"I haven't heard one way or the other," Maren says. The police had taken the cremains into evidence, something that Maren had found somewhat ghastly. "I would hope so, however. We still have a duty to him."

"Is there a 'him' anymore?" Henry asks, sorrow ringing in his voice.

"I would certainly hope so," Maren says. "I'll give the police a call and see when we can expect him back."

Even though there's precious little they can do at this point, Maren does want to see Mr. Augustine all the way through. They can still anoint and bejewel and wrap him, can still say the correct prayers and have the right spells painted on the inside of his coffin. *Hemet* Thais will still be able to guide *something* into the afterlife, Maren hopes.

Plus, she has an ulterior motive for calling the police.

After they've sorted through that week's clients, Maren fishes the now quite worn business card out of her pocket, liberating her phone from under a stack of paper.

Although the 21$^{st}$ precinct doesn't seem to exist online, it certainly does on this business card — there's a phone number for Choi, and even an address. She'd looked the address up the other day to find a familiar, squat mid-century ramble of a building in the middle of an otherwise lovely West Village street, only a few blocks away — the 6$^{th}$ precinct. Maren's best guess at this point is that the 21$^{st}$ is some special operations unit tucked into the otherwise normal 6$^{th}$.

She punches in the number, listening to the tinny ringing on the other end while she half-heartedly scrolls through her emails, slouched against her desk. Not particularly shockingly, the number rings through to voice mail. Maren's trying to figure out what kind of message to leave when the pleasant greeting message wraps up with a cheery *this voice mailbox is full*. The line goes dead. Maren frowns down at her phone. She'd simply send a text, but she's fairly sure that this number belongs to the kind of good, sturdy, old-fashioned phone that requires a hard line into a wall.

Maren has precisely zero interest in just walking into a police station for fun, but she unfortunately has a contradictory abundance of interest in both having Mr. Augustine returned and making sure this case can be quietly put to bed.

"Maren!" Henry hollers from a floor down. "Come help me bring in this shipment of canopic jars!"

"I thought those weren't getting here until next week," Maren answers at a similar volume as she pushes back from her desk and heads for the stairs.

"I guess we're just blessed," Henry intones. "Although not too blessed — they're those special-order ones with the president heads instead of gods."

"Those are so weird," Maren mutters. The things people feel they need to be buried with will never cease to amaze her.

—

The rather harangued-looking young officer working the front desk of the 6th precinct seems like he might be on the verge of flipping a desk over and storming off to Cabo.

Maren can get behind that. She'd like to level with him that yes, sometimes life *really* sucks, especially when dealing with the living on a day-to-day basis. Instead, she puts on her best tranquil smile, softening her face so that she is a placid, masked figure of absolute agreeableness and support.

The young officer looks back and forth between her ID and her face a few more times before sliding it back across the desk and turning to his computer.

"Do you know where you're going?" He drones without looking at her, savagely hitting the *ENTER* button before swiveling in his chain in a clearly well-known pattern.

"I don't," Maren says as he twists back around, slapping a visitor badge down where her ID had just been.

"Elevator is down that hall–" a thumb is jerked in the general direction, "–go up to the second floor–" two fingers are held up, as if in case she's suddenly lost her hearing, "–and it's the last door straight ahead of you."

The second floor turns out to be exceptionally boxy, offices tacked on around bullpens full of drab metal desks and various uniformed officers. Overhead, sickly yellow government-issue lighting flickers slightly, illuminating the equally government-issue linoleum floor. It paints a rather dreary picture.

True to the young man's word, she finds her quarry tucked into the far corner of the second floor, in what's possibly the quietest corner of the building. A dull, flat-faced wooden door with a tiny window set into it bears two names — *Detective Felix Perry* and *Detective Emerson Choi*. Raising a hand with a degree of caution, she gives the door two quick raps and then scoots half a step forward, listening for any motion. She hears nothing, the room as silent as a tomb.

"You can just wait inside," a voice says.

Maren turns to find that the occupant of the office

across the hall has appeared, half in and half out of both his coat and his door.

"Pardon?" Maren asks.

"Morticia and Gomez are pretty hard to track down in their own office," the man says. "Did you check in?"

"Of course." She taps her paper sticker of a visitor badge.

"Someone will have paged them for you. Good luck finding a clean couch or chair out here; I recommend theirs," he says, jerking his chin at the door.

"Thank you," Maren calls as he walks away, shoulders hunched. He just flaps a hand over his shoulder.

Even though she's just been given carte blanche to saunter into the office, she's still surprised when she finds the door unlocked. Even more surprising is the sheer normalcy of the office that forms up around her as she flips on the lights. Realistically, there's no reason this cramped space would be any different from any other office on the planet, but some part of her had expected something slightly more sinister.

The back wall is taken up by bookshelves, holding things so average in their banality that Maren doesn't even take that much time reading past the first shelf — procedure manuals, annual reports, crime logs. The two desks pushed front to front in the middle of the office are the same as those in the bullpen, although the chairs have been swapped out for a mismatched set of more modern ones that perhaps were brought in by their occupants. One of the smallest and blandest couches Maren has ever seen is wedged between the door and the far wall. A cushion in the shape of a slice of watermelon is its only trapping.

Travel photos dot the wall behind one desk. A novelty

mug bearing the image of someone's dog's head pasted into a photo of a eighteenth-century military man is full of pens, the name *Vice Admiral Taco* printed in overwrought calligraphy under the image. There's a spare pair of sneakers under one of the desks. The still air smells a bit like old furniture and banana. The fact the small space is so disturbingly average sits worse with Maren than if she'd waltzed into a den of veil piercing and prognostication.

She's about to squeeze herself onto the small couch when something on one of the desks catches her eye. A black and white photo-booth strip is tucked into the corner of a computer monitor, showing a young man and woman laughing, kissing, tucked together, the woman on the man's lap. It's a sweet image, until she notices who the people are.

One is undeniably Perry. The other is an Augustine sister. With the small, grainy photo not much to go on, she can't be sure which one, their face turned to the side, hidden in Perry's collar a bit.

"What–" Maren breathes, inching closer to the photo.

With a clatter of blinds on the small window, the door swings open, and Maren catapults herself backwards, arranging her body on the couch so quickly she feels like she might have given herself a minor case of whiplash.

"Ms. Nykara," Detective Perry says, closing the door behind him and slouching into one of the desk chairs, an impossibly large takeaway coffee cup clutched in one hand. "Thanks for stopping by. What can I help you with?"

"Well–" Maren starts.

"Actually, let me just say first," Perry interrupts her, "I really am sorry about the other day."

"It's fine," Maren says with her quiet smile.

41

"So if it's not about that?" Perry says, raising his eyebrows.

"Well," Maren says delicately, figuring she'll lead with something else. "I'm here about Mr. Augustine. Or, his cremains."

"Ah," Perry says, slouching a bit further in his chair and taking a long drag of coffee. "I myself was asking about that earlier this week... the coroner claims that we should be able to return the remains to you within a week."

"Intact?" Maren asks.

Perry gives her a look over the top of his cup, tilting his head and raising an eyebrow.

"Define 'intact,'" he replies, dry as a desert. Maren gives him a look that she hopes is reproachful while also not strong enough to get her thrown out of the office.

"In the condition they were given to you," she says.

"I mean, yeah, hopefully," Perry says as he leans forward to put his cup down on his desk, making his desk chair squeal in response. "There's no reason they would have done anything with them that would destroy them, except to take a sample or two of something small. You'll have Augustine back as fragmented as he was when he left the House of Five Gates. Gnarly name, by the way."

"It's a truthful name," Maren replies.

"Yeah, but just because to get to greener pastures you have to pass through five gates guarded by, I don't know, piranhas and alligators, doesn't mean you need to be reminded about them in life."

"Well luckily, no one in our care is living," Maren points out. "You're not much of a believer I take it?"

"I have to be," Perry says. He leans on his desk, stares her straight in the eyes with an extremely unnerving gaze.

42

Maren is suddenly very aware that whatever slouchy, disorganized cop facade Perry has built is merely paper thin. His eyes are deep, stormy — a brown-blue that Maren struggles to meet without blinking or looking away.

"But what about personally?" She asks.

Perry just shrugs in response. It's a practiced ease, a movement he's clearly used to answering a multitude of questions with.

"We'll get you Casper back. I'll hand deliver him if you want me to," he says.

"I don't think you need to go that far."

"What can I say, I'm a public servant," Perry intones. "Might as well serve the public. You know you could have called to ask, right?"

"Detective Choi's mailbox was full, and I didn't have your number," Maren says.

"You could have called the precinct and asked for mine," Perry points out.

"Oh, I suppose I could have," Maren murmurs, rubbing a hand over her chin.

"Yeah, I'm sure you never thought of that," Perry says, raising his eyebrows. His voice has gone back to desert-dry. "Why are you really here, Ms. Nykara?"

Maren looks away from him finally, setting herself a bit further back into the tiny couch, staring at the wall behind his head for a moment to gather her thoughts.

"I want to know how the case is progressing," she says.

"Slowly and without much progress," Perry says. "I can't share details with you, however."

"You're aware of the level of client that we serve?" Maren asks.

"Well aware," Perry replies. "You worried about your

43

reputation?"

"Absolutely." There's no sense in lying.

Perry shifts in his chair, making it squeak, and sighs.

"I'm not going to accuse you of trying to interfere with a police investigation, because I'm going to assume you're smarter than that," Perry says.

"Theoretically."

"Hah. But I can assure you that our motives probably mostly align. The House of Five Gates will hopefully sail right through this, unharmed."

They square off for a moment, Maren with her hands clenched tightly in her lap and Perry jingling one foot under his chair.

"Thank you," she says finally, standing with a relief she hasn't felt in days and days.

"You own the House?" Perry asks.

"I do," Maren says with a nod. Perry gives her a one-sided smile and stands as well, crossing to the door to open it.

With one hand on it, he hesitates, turning to her.

"I am honestly sorry about what happened the other day. Are you feeling ok?" He asks.

"Fine." It's out of Maren's mouth before she can stop it.

Perry reaches out to her, his hand almost brushing her upper arm before she surges back, pressing her legs up against the couch.

"I can feel the cold coming from you," Perry says quietly, his eyes suddenly full of that intense focus again.

Maren just stares at him with wide eyes, at a loss for words. She's breathing hard, like Perry had chased her down a hall instead of just reaching towards her. Her pulse is so loud in her ears she's wondering if Perry can hear it as well.

"I'm still having... chills. From the ritual you performed," she says finally, quietly.

"Spell," Perry says quickly. Maren blinks at him for a moment, frowning.

"Fine, spell. Why is this happening?"

Perry chews on his lower lip, looking away from her for a moment.

"You were in the way, unfortunately," Perry says at last. His bottom lip is worried red against his pale skin.

"Of?" Maren has a feeling she knows what this answer is going to be, and something cold settles at the base of her spine, raises the hair on her arms.

"The echo of a spirit." Perry pauses, and then suddenly dives back in, like someone's pulled the cork out of him and there's no stopping the flow of words. "What I did was a spell to call a spirit echo back into a place, so that I could see its last steps, or actions, or what have you. In the absence of security footage I felt it necessary, especially since the tape had clearly been damaged by necromancy. It leaves a pretty obvious signature. It's not a real spirit, exactly, but enough. And you were standing in its path, so it went through you."

Maren swallows hard. She wants to rub her arms, wants to curl up the couch and ball herself up in her coat. She stays still though, hands folded neatly on her lap, even if her knuckles are paling under her own grip.

"I see," she says at long last. "You admit to the necromancy?"

"Yeah, duh," Perry says and he's closed up again. Whatever loose, liquid boyishness he'd shown before is suddenly gone, the stopper back in. "That's the whole point

45

of our precinct."

"Will it pass?" Maren asks. "This cold."

"I... I'm not totally sure," Perry says. "I could introduce you to some people who might be able to help, however."

"What, death magicians?" Maren says, squaring her shoulder.

"I know you guys are all major league uptight about this—"

"For good reason, it's forbidden."

"Do you want help?"

Maren can feel a glare breaking through her features, hardening her face.

"Not from death magic," she says.

"Necromancy," Perry corrects, scowling. "You're quite the devoted piece of work."

"At least I'm devoted to something," Maren says, reaching for the door and wrenching it open. She never drops Perry's gaze, lets it bore into her.

"Anything else I can help you with, Ms. Nykara?" Perry's voice is the very picture of pleasantries when he finally speaks.

"No, thank you," Maren says. "You'll be in touch about Mr. Augustine?"

"Like I said, hand delivery," Perry says flatly before she leaves as quickly as her feet will take her without raising suspicion.

Maren doesn't realize her lips and fingertips are buzzing until she's halfway down the hallway to the elevator. She shoves her hands in her pockets, licks her cold lips.

"Shit," she murmurs, a soft sound under her breath. Then, slightly louder, "*shit*."

This has to pass, she's so sure of it.

# CHAPTER 4
## Coming Home

More and more desiccated leaves pile up on the sidewalks, brittle and brown-red. They huddle in the corners of the steps up to the House and down to the basement. One gets stuck along the edges of Maren's office window and it flaps anemically in the wind for days, just out of the corner of her eye, before it finally vanishes between one evening and the next morning.

Maren pulls her boots down from the top of her closet and sentences her sandals to the upper shelf instead, their turn to gather dust for six months. Miu uses an impressively athletic jump routine to inspect this change, sticking her face into a flip flop, never mind that the exact same shoes had just been on the floor.

"They're not new," she assures the cat.

Miu ignores her and moves on to making sure that nothing is amiss with the strappy heels next to the flip flops. Maren rolls her eyes and leaves the closet door cracked for Miu's eventual escape.

Tad and Oscar rescue the throw blankets for the parlor from the storage room on the top floor, a home for miscellaneous things like coffee makers and folding tables that always seem to be a good thing to have on hand but rarely get used. Maren watches them shaking them out on the front steps from the hall staircase, Tad's laughter bouncing through the open black-lacquered door.

"At some point we should probably clean that room out," Henry says with a sigh, tromping down the stairs behind Maren and coming to rest a step above her.

"The minute we do, we'll have a funeral that requires putting tables out in the back garden," Maren says, and takes another sip of her coffee.

"That has never happened," Henry points out.

"It could," Maren counters, and Henry just sighs again.

A breeze kicks up again, scattering a few leaves into the front hall.

"Oh, for — Tad, Oscar, come in or close the door!" Henry hollers.

"We're coming," Oscar says, giving his blanket one last savage whip to get any lingering dust out before he and Tad trundle back in, kicking the leaves out and shutting the door behind them. Fall is left to go on outside while they arrange the throws on the back of the couches.

"These candles are all sea breeze scented," Tad says, picking one up from a side table and sticking his nose in it. Oscar flops down on a chair, clearly not interested in any kind of candle journey that Tad might currently be on.

"I'll order something a bit more seasonally appropriate," Maren says.

For a moment they exist in easy silence, Oscar and Tad in matching chairs and Maren and Henry bracketing the door, Maren leaning against the frame and Henry standing ramrod straight.

"Who do you think killed Augustine?" Tad muses to the ceiling, his head tipped back over the edge of the chair.

"Excuse me?" Henry asks.

"He was murdered," Oscar supplies. "We figure."

"We don't know if he died a second death," Maren points out. None of them are priests — that's not a call they can make.

49

"Yeah, but no one ends up in a crematorium by accident," Tad says. "Someone deffo put him in there to cover up evidence of regular, good old-fashioned murder."

"That's horrible to speculate on," Henry says, and he's crossed his long bony arms so hard that his wrists are looking more skeletal than usual.

"They might not be wrong," Maren says softly before taking another sip of coffee. Three sets of eyes swivel towards her.

"Nykara." Henry sounds exasperated. "You cannot seriously be entertaining this idea."

"Maybe not seriously," Maren says with a one-shouldered shrug. "But burning a body at a high temperature would be a great way to get rid of it, now that Tad points it out."

"We examined Mr. Augustine when he came in," Henry points out. One of his eyebrows seems to be twitching.

"Visually. As far as I'm aware, no tox screen was run. There are a plethora of ways to kill someone without doing damage to their outsides," Maren says, and then follows it up with one more sip of coffee.

"What a macabre line of thought," Henry grouses.

"We deal with dead bodies for a living," Tad points out.

"That's different," Henry says.

"I fail to see the difference," Oscar says. "There's no way he'd be the first murder victim to come through the House."

Oscar's not incorrect. If Mr. Augustine was murdered, he wouldn't be a pioneer. Because of the privileged cache of their usual clientele, they perhaps see fewer murders than other Houses, but certainly not none. Maren knows the cause of death of most of the bodies that have passed

50

through her care — they ask on the intake paperwork. The family can refuse to share (except in cases of communicable diseases as mandated by the state of New York), but most do. It's cathartic, as much as any other information they decide to divulge to Maren.

She tends not to share when someone has been murdered, however. If Oscar or Tad were to ask what had killed someone she wouldn't lie, but she doesn't volunteer the information. There's something cloudy and heavy about working with someone whose life has been cut short, ended at the hands of another person. Not to say that other deaths aren't gutting to Maren — they are plenty. Children, young adults just starting out, new parents. But murder is, as Henry had put it, especially macabre. It's a weight around her neck for as long as that person is under her roof, in her House.

"There have been murders," Maren says simply.

"But that's not something we need to examine right now," Henry says. "Let's get back to work, come on."

Henry herds Tad and Oscar back towards the basement, leaving Maren to trail behind, quietly thinking to herself.

She wonders, if anything about Mr. Augustine's case had been normal, if she'd be musing more on it. But no, there's a set of papers upstairs in her office emblazoned with *Cause of Death: Myocardial infarction,* which is Mortuary House for *it was Tuesday.* Nothing about Mr. Augustine's intake would have raised her brow. His skin had been clean of wounds or discoloration (at least, outside of the usual livor), and his family had seemed appropriately equal parts shell-shocked and in mourning, considering his sudden manner of death.

It would be so open and shut Maren never would have

51

spared it a second thought. If he had been murdered, he'd been offed in a way that raised no suspicion. There would be no reason to destroy the body and any lingering evidence.

Now, his death is being speculated about by the whole House and an NYPD precinct. If this whole mess is because someone was trying to cover something up, they've sure done a wonderful job of the exact opposite.

—

Mr. Augustine returns to the House of Five Gates on a sleepy, quiet Monday, the world still working on getting back into the swing of normalcy after a long Augustalia weekend. The holiday had fallen on a Thursday, leaving everyone with four long days of exactly zero work. Maren, being profoundly unreligious, had spent the time at home, catching up on housework and marathoning TV with Miu curled up on her lap. She'd consumed a lot of take out and it had been mostly lovely, outside of the strange, listless chill that refuses to quit dogging her steps.

The knock comes when she's in her office, answering a few emails and ordering some apple cider-scented candles. With a deep sigh and a stretch, she shoves her feet back into her shoes and heads down the stairs. There are two familiar faces beyond the textured glass, half-obscured by the golden letters and glyphs. She makes sure to plaster on a pleasant smile and line her shoulders with some approximation of good posture before she opens the door.

Detectives Choi and Perry are on the front stoop. Perry is cradling what looks to be a large coat box, except rather plain and antiseptic. Maren knows what, or rather *who*, it is immediately.

"The long-awaited return," Detective Perry says in a tone usually resolved for funeral dirges and processionals as Maren ushers them in.

"I appreciate it," Maren says, accepting the box from Perry. She peeks under the lid and finds a thick plastic bag sheltering in the gloom of the box, kept closed with a bright red bit of tape emblazoned with *EVIDENCE*.

"The remains are in good order," Choi assures with a small jerk of her chin towards the box. "We made sure of that."

"Thank you," Maren says. "I'm sure they had to do some testing, but as long as he's the most in one piece as possible at this point."

"We'll leave you to it," Perry says.

"Please," Maren says before she can stop the word.

"Joyous Augustalia to you, Ms. Nykara. Uh, belated, anyway," Perry says with a quirked eyebrow.

"And to you two as well," Maren says as they take their leave. She watches them halfway down the block before taking Mr. Augustine back down into the dark of the House. She very much hopes this will be the last time she'll ever have to see Perry or Choi.

With no funerals scheduled this close to the holiday the prep room is silent, the other three staff members of the House busy catching up on work a couple of floors above her head. Maren likes the quiet. It seems correct, the silence of a temple as she brings a lost soul back Home.

She hopes, anyway.

Placing the box gently on the cold metal of the table in the middle of the room, she fully removes the lid, revealing the sad contents of the bag. She'd been so shocked, so blindsided as she tried to work her head around everything on that day, that she hadn't registered much about Mr. Augustine's remains except that he had, in fact, been burnt to a horrible crisp. Now, as she scoops the bag out the box, she can't help cataloging the sad weight of it — easily lifted — and the lack of remains present. It's not a shock, logically; she knows what a body is reduced to after cremation, or she'd be a rather terrible Mortuary Director. But emotionally it's something else. This is a man who had been in her care, reduced to femoral heads and pelvic crests by a pyre of human-made fire. Little now remains of the skull that had supported a face she had first looked upon a mere month ago, mostly just bits and pieces of the bottom half and the lower jaw, the bulky bones that supported a man of industry, once.

Although everyone ends up a corpse eventually, Maren has never been particularly pessimistic to that tune. Everyone makes a different corpse, as they'd been different people in life. Cremations are always different for her though. For the few they perform, they always end the same way. Bone and ash. Fragments of the same bits that hold everyone up.

Maren knows that some people find cremations a relief, or religiously preferable. She doesn't. Tad had once opined that he'd happily be cremated, not seeing the point of making sure his body hung around for centuries just to take up space as a husk. Truthfully, Maren wishes sometimes she felt that way. Burn her and be done with it. But she's so entrenched in this place now, this House where one day her body will be pulled meticulously apart and then put back together, dried up and desiccated, that anything else seems wrong.

She has no desire for anyone to ever have to gaze sadly at her bones as she's doing now with Mr. Augustine.

"Well, we failed you rather profoundly," Maren sighs, her voice taking up space in the empty room.

Ripping the *EVIDENCE* sticker, she starts pulling out fragments one at a time, bone by bone, with a set of long forceps. When there's nothing left in the bag but dust and ash, she fetches a small, standard canopic jar from the basement storage room and carefully pours the ash into the urn. In the silence of death, Maren's own breath is quiet to her ears, and there is reverence in her movements. If she was *hemet* she would have prayed. She's not willing to cock up Mr. Augustine's journey into Duat any more than she has, however, and so she says nothing. All she can do for him now is be gentle and careful.

Laying out what's left of the bone is easy in number and hard in practice. She has to peer at certain bits and chunks, puzzle over whether she's looking at tibia or ulna. Skeletal anatomy is not her strongest suit, she's much better with soft tissue. Still, she has enough to get by, enough to delicately lay him out into some approximation of what he once was.

So:

A handful of cracked molars. The pock-marked curve of either the parietal or occipital, in several shards. Enough of the mandible to be recognizable right away.

Vertebrae, in various states of ruin, perhaps what was once a fourth of the man's spine. Shanks of long bone. A crack of rib.

The core, pelvis in multiple pieces that will never fit together correctly again. A patella with spindly, spun outer edges. Most of a femur, now damaged and charred.

Ankle bones, perhaps — just a few.

All that remains of Mr. Augustine is transferred from box and bag to table and jar. Maren only finally sits back when it's done, the box stored away on the counter and the table clear of everything that isn't skeleton. She hasn't realized how long and how far she's been leaning over until she straightens her own spine, wincing when it pulls in soreness and cracks.

Standing up carefully, she surveys her work under the bright lights of the tiled room, all white and chrome, gleaming and clean, a nest of perfection around the decidedly imperfect remains on the table.

"We'll protect you from here," Maren says, and places a hand on the table, near where a shoulder may have been.

She'll have Tad and Oscar anoint the bones, bundle them up and adorn them. She'll call *Hemet* Cooper and let her know that finally, a month delayed, Mr. Augustine can be shepherded into the afterlife.

If such a thing even exists to accept his soul. If *that* is even still extant to be accepted.

—

Knowing that she can't shut herself up in her apartment every night sitting by the fire with Miu on her lap while nursing her fourth cup of tea of the day, when one of her friends from college reaches out to invite her to drinks after work, she gives in to going out.

It's a group of them, the strange ones who all met in gross anatomy and still hunker together over drinks when they all happen to be free, a rarity these days as they get busier and busier with careers and families.

The bar is crowded and loud, people packed in around high tops. The crowd is mostly college students, probably half of them with fake IDs, a side effect of being so close to the university that sprawls through most of this neighborhood. When it's Maren's turn to buy a round she has to push and shove through the mass of bodies, all slightly damp from the misting rain that's dogging the outside world. Holding her wallet above her head like a beacon, she scoots and side-steps her way up to the bar, finding a path mostly by virtue of her height.

This technique works until the last second, when someone who's just finished ordering turns around right into her, knocking their drink into her side and sending it sloshing half onto the already-sticky floor under their feet.

"Fuck–" the person mutters at the same time that Maren jumps back.

"I'm so sorry!" Maren says, immediately going for a napkin on the bar to help the person mop up.

When she turns back with napkins in hand, she finds herself face to face with Ari Augustine.

"No way," Ari says dryly, never mind that she's currently got half of a beer all over one sleeve. "What are the odds of us bumping into each other twice?"

"Slim," Maren says, pursing her lips and handing over the napkins. She watches Ari mop half-heartedly at her shirt for a moment before pinching the bridge of her nose and breathing out into– "can I get you another drink?"

"You don't have to," Ari says.

"What do you want?" Maren says, leaning against the bar with one hip and crossing her arms.

They stare each other down for a moment. With Maren slouching and Ari wearing heeled shoes they're closer to

57

the same height, and it's unfortunately easy to meet Ari's gaze. It's a hard thing to do, finding herself staring down the barrel of a hazel, wide-eyed gun that reminds her of college, reminds her of being a kid when she didn't know she still could be, reminds her of what they once meant to each other.

The breakup had been awful.

*This* is awful now, she realizes, and finally looks away, searching instead for a bartender.

"Bel Air sour," Ari says.

"Ok," Maren says, just to keep Ari from saying anything else, absolutely not wanting to engage in conversation with her any more than they need to. In the rush of the crowd they're too close together, and it sets Maren's teeth on edge.

And then Ari has the gall to reach around her, setting her half-empty glass down next to Maren, moving her body even closer. Maren licks her lips, tips her chin up, silently pleads with the bartender to notice her, take her order quickly, and then get the fuck away from this particular space and time. She wants to be back with her friends, not boxed in against a bar by Ari.

"I expected a sarcastic comeback," Ari says, and her voice is close to Maren's ear to be heard over the music that's thrumming and thumping through the air.

"All out of those tonight," Maren mumbles.

"That seems impossible," Ari says.

"Ari," Maren says, letting out a long breath and turning towards her with a pinched look.

They're closer than Maren realized. Facing each other, this close, Maren finds herself able to catalog everything about Ari's face, even in the half-dim of the trendy Edison

58

bulb lighting.

She's exactly the same in a way that Maren hadn't quite had the presence of mind to notice when they'd seen each other last month. Impossibly wide eyes, moles cresting her cheeks like heavy freckles, bushy eyebrows, pointed jaw. Her hair is even still wrangled up into a messy bun that she'd worn most of the time in college.

This girl. This stupid, gorgeous girl.

"Maren," Ari answers.

"Sometimes even the impossible comes to pass," Maren says in response, and then takes a step to the left, finally turning to find a bartender ready to take her order. She shuts Ari out behind her, takes a deep breath, and plasters a smile on her face. When she speaks to order a handful of beers, it's in a voice much more chipper than she feels.

The last drink the bartender puts down is the Bel Air sour, because of course it is. Maren doesn't bother picking it up, her hands already full of the four beers for her own group.

This time, Ari waits until Maren moves away from the bar to reach for the drink, hefting it up.

"Cheers, Ren," Ari says, a cut grin plastered on her face. "Shall we plan on running into each other for a third time?"

"Perhaps not," Maren says, and practically jumps back into the crowd, putting as much space between her past and the current as she's physically able to.

# CHAPTER 5

## *A Soul for Serapis*

When she puts her mind to something, she's very good at getting it *done*, and getting it done well.

So she pushes Ari from her mind like a bad dream. She convinces herself that the lingering chill in her blood is anxiety.

Instead, she throws herself further into work. Now that Mr. Augustine is back under their roof, they have two funerals that need scheduling. Negotiating for the time difference across the ocean she places a call to Thais, to figure out a schedule for not only Mr. Augustine but also Mrs. Colvard. With the important bits out of the way they slip into chat about nothing in particular, and it's a breath of fresh air, a sea breeze across her cheekbones as a smile breaks there.

Thais is such an easy constant, even on the other side of the world. Priestess, mentor, call her whatever. Maren is privileged to call her a friend.

Henry ropes her into joining Taner and him for dinner, and she makes the pilgrimage to Queens for them. There is wine, and good food, and they laugh and joke and everything is warm and jocular.

The House takes in two new clients, a middle-aged woman who had died of breast cancer and a young man who had taken a tree on headfirst in a skiing accident. Those are both hard, people snatched from life painfully, leaving behind large, grieving families that don't know what direction to turn to try to make anything feel correct again.

She goes to the movies with friends. She takes her father and stepmother out to brunch. They ask her about death and dating — the usual topics.

Another new body joins the first two a week later, an elderly gentleman who had slipped away in his sleep at ninety-three. That one doesn't hurt like the other two.

A box is found in storage, a sturdy upgrade for Mr. Augustine from the police-issue box the cops had crammed him in.

(There is a pull under her sternum like a hook on a reel when she transfers his remains, the bones buzzing under her hands. It doesn't go away for hours.)

The trees shake bare branches in the cold breeze. The leaves curl in on themselves, brown and dry and deader than dead. Frost blankets what's left of the greenery one morning.

They prepare for Thais' arrival, and Maren forgets the bar, forgets how she'd suddenly found herself unmoored and facing down Ari.

She'll put Mr. Augustine to rest, and finally this will all be over.

—

"For your stash," *Hemet* Thais Cooper says with a wink, presenting Maren with a pale green-blue tin in the way one might present a proffered, ritualistic object.

Then again, incredibly overpriced tea from an ocean away might certainly be ritualistic depending on how you stack it.

"You *did not* need to do that," Maren murmurs, running

a thumb around the copper edge of the tin. *Wedding Breakfast Blend*, it's called. "From the royal wedding?"

"Of course," Thais says, grinning and throwing her hair over a shoulder. "I thought it might cheer you up after the horror that was committed under this roof."

Thais, being a priestess of Serapis, believes in the whole damn thing, from soup to nuts. Maren had been horrified for a client's mental health and concerned about the decorum of the House that awful morning, but Thais was deeply concerned about the sin that had occurred. Burning a body was high on Thais' list of unspeakable crimes. Really, any kind of desecration of a body was.

"Thank you," Maren says, and hugs the tea to her chest for a moment.

She deposits the lovely tin in her office, and then Thais joins her in the basement as she carefully removes Mr. Augustine from cold storage. There's absolutely no reason they need to store a few splinters of bone in sub-zero temps, but truthfully, Maren wasn't sure what to do with the remains otherwise. It had seemed strange to leave them out, or relocate them to a place where Mr. Augustine would be divided from the other souls under the roof of the House. So she'd set him on a low shelf, almost on the ground, one she doesn't normally use.

She pulls the top off the box and the scents of cedar and cloves coil into the air, wafting past them and getting stuck at the back of Maren's throat. They had anointed whatever part of his skull they could find, before wrapping him up by segment of body — or what little remains of it. They've been left with four small, unhappy bundles in the box.

Maren reaches in and takes one out, tugging at the end of the wrapping with long fingers, carefully unraveling the linen enough to get a better look at the bone. A ruined ball joint peeks over the edge of the fabric and Thais sighs, closing her eyes and cupping her palm around the cracked head. Her eyebrows are drawn together, unease written in every fine line on her face. Maren stays totally still, afraid to move. She wonders if she should even breathe.

For one silly moment, she wonders if Thais is trying to call the spirit back, if it will rush through Maren again. But no, *Hemet* Cooper is no necromancer — the very opposite, really. Maren would be shocked if she even knew a single bit of death magic.

Instead, Thais replaces the bundle, and lets out a long sigh.

"What a fate," Thais murmurs.

"Do you think his soul is still clinging to the skeleton?" Maren asks.

"I have no way of knowing," Thais says, pressing her thumb down into a corner of the box hard enough to leave an indent. "I hope and pray that his soul is still with us, so that I might release it into Duat in a way that prepares him for what's to come."

Maren hopes so as well. If his soul had been thrown from his body immediately upon application of fire, or if it had faded away later, before they could perform any rites, he's dead a second time over. His soul won't survive a single gate in Duat without protection or needed spells.

"We have no way to tell?" Maren asks finally, and Thais just shakes her head.

"A necromancer might. But we're not in that dark business, so we'll have to go on faith," Thais says, a honed edge peeking through in her words. "We'll put him to rest, one way or another."

Maren would very much like if things were normal, if she didn't have to fight back a small flicker of panic at Thais' mention of necromancy. She would very much like if the strangeness of death magic had never come into her life.

They check in on Mrs. Colvard next, which requires a trip all the way up to the attic. The salt cellar is horribly misnamed — they get off the elevator on the very opposite floor to anything that could be considered a cellar. It's a name that's always put a small twist of a grin on Maren's face, a relic from when the whole of their religion was practiced in climates where you could indeed have a cellar underground and not have it end up damp and dripping. Now, in New York, the basement would be a horrible place to try to preserve anything. Houses had moved that particular bit of the process up into the dry heat of attics a century and more ago, squeezed under eaves, bright sun slanting in through squat, rounded windows.

Walking into the salt cellar is a bit like stepping onto a different planet. The perfectly temperate air of the outside hallway is replaced at a startling speed by air so dry that it seems to suck the breath from your lungs. It's a gorgeous room, the wide wooden planks of the floor bright in the sunlight streaming through the low windows and the skylight. Nine stone plinths of sandstone sit in three neat rows, four of them currently occupied by simple wooden coffins, not too dissimilarly colored from the floor. The whole effect is of leaving Manhattan and stepping into a strange room a world and an eon away. Here, in this desert-colored space, the air smelling of sand and cedar, Maren has always felt closer to what the House stands for, what it is built on, than anywhere else.

The door closes behind them with a soft sucking sound, sealing them into the heavily controlled dry climate. Grabbing a long-handled brush from a hook by the door, Maren leads the way to the body on the very middle plinth. Tucking the brush under her arm, she and Thais are able to heft the top of the coffin off. They set it down, a heavy thunk of wood on wood, and then Maren straightens up, peering down into the box.

A desert of stained natron greets them. What had once been off-white has gone multiple shades of yellow, brown, and gray, roughly in the shape and size of a human body. The cloying scent of decay rises to them, even choked by salt and heat. Maren doesn't mind it too much — she's smelled decomp much worse from bodies left out too long, bodies that should have been embalmed long before she got her hands on them. This almost sweet smell, mingled with the sharp tang of salt and various oils, isn't particularly bad.

Maren hands the brush over, and Thais carefully brushes away the grains over where a head might be. For a moment, all she gets is stiff, clumped natron. Then, part of a face.

Mrs. Colvard's left eye and forehead appear. Her skin, rather pale in life, has gone a dark, leathery brown, as if she'd spent a lifetime under the sun. The lid is shriveled, covering a desiccated socket. Her eyebrows are thin, the same color as her wizened skin.

"She looks good," Thais says pleasantly. "How long has she been in?"

Maren checks the toe tag that they had tied to a small protrusion in the plinth.

"Thirty-six days," Maren says.

"Perfect," Thais says, nodding more to herself than anyone else.

They leave Mrs. Colvard recovered by sand and wood, and head back downstairs. Thais rubs her hands absentmindedly, and Maren knows she's feeling the dry air of the salt cellar still.

"I'll make the arrangements, then?" Maren asks.

"Yes, please," Thais says with a soft smile. "I'll be glad to see Mr. Augustine safely on the other side, especially."

Maren has seldom agreed more with a statement in her life.

———

Arrangements are made with Phaedra, and Maren is exceedingly grateful that she's the point of contact and not Ari.

The funeral is set for a week later, a Tuesday far away from any upcoming holidays.

"My mother assures me that it's an auspicious date," Phaedra had said very seriously, and Maren had agreed.

"Yes, of course, very sensible."

Maren has no clue as to what day might be more or less auspicious. Every cult and sect likes to interpret innards and bird flights in radically different ways, and tends to come up with wildly varying dates. Maren has a rule of just always going along with what the family wants, based on their particular cult.

The Tuesday in question rolls around with an anemic blue sky, the air thin in the cold. They all assemble early, Tad and Oscar making sure that the House is in order, and Maren and Henry making sure that Mr. Augustine is as ready as he can be. They're all dressed nicely, in dark shades of grays and blacks and blues for the occasion. Oscar has been banned from wearing sneakers, and Tad warned against a brightly colored sweater, something that Henry likes to tell them before every single funeral, even though the two are more than aware of proper procedure at this point. Maren doesn't stop him though; knows that it's part of his process to prepare for a funeral. Tad and Oscar seem to know too, always dutifully nodding along as if this is brand-new information.

Candles are lit, incense cones are placed in the small shrine above the fireplace in the parlor, and fruit and springs of wheat are laid out on the side table in a lovely stone bowl, should anyone feel a calling to make their own offering. Downstairs, tall metal lanterns are filled with candlelight, and temple offerings are prepared.

When the house is like this, full of spiced air and earthy foods, it feels like the outside world vanishes. Maybe, just maybe, they could be transported back into the past. It's a comfortable feeling, and they gather in the staff kitchen on the second floor to share a pot of dark tea before anyone else arrives.

"An offering from this House, Serapis Lord." Maren holds her cup up and out, watching coils of steam lazily curl out of the amber liquid.

"An offering from this House," the other three murmur in assent, their voices slightly off from each other like a harmony in the round. Their cups clink together with a nice clean, final sound, and then they all take a moment to just drink deeply, banishing the chill in the air.

"Thank you for all the work you've done on this case," Maren says after she knows her gathered employees have settled into the heat of the tea, calm and still. "I know it hasn't been an easy one. But today, Mr. Augustine will complete his journey into Duat, and we'll move onto the next client, and the next, and the next."

"Hopefully," Oscar mumbles, but Maren chooses to ignore it.

"Ditto to Maren," Henry says between sips of tea. "Let's pray that those next clients are a bit easier."

"We'll take whatever they can throw at us," Tad declares, looking fierce over his tea, despite his rather innocent mop of golden curls. Maren smiles softly to herself, staring down into her tea.

"I know you all can. But still, an easy client every once in a while is far from a bad thing," Maren points out. "It'll be nice to have an open and shut case next."

A car door slams somewhere outside.

"That'll be *Hemet* Cooper, I presume?" Henry asks, and Maren nods.

The woman they let through the front door is not the Thais that Maren looks up to, who buys her tea and sweets and is always ready with a quick smile. No, the priestess standing in the front hall is *Hemet* Cooper, from tip to toe. She holds herself with the same poise she always does, but now her fashionable togs have been stripped away in favor of her black, gray, and cream robes, belted up with a sash of golden embroidery. Her braids are carefully done up on the top of her head, a constellation of gold accents clasped at various places in the updo.

This Thais always takes Maren's breath away, no matter how many times she sees it. She is a sight to behold, a holy statue sprung to life.

"Welcome, *Hemet* Cooper, to this House," Maren says,

with an incline of her head, and Thais mirrors it. It's an old, ancient thing.

"I bless this House, *Sesheta* Nykara." A call and response from a deep past that will probably last long into the future.

Maren leads the way down the hall, trailed by Thais, Tad, and Oscar. They leave the two junior embalmers in the basement to collect Mr. Augustine, and she and Thais continue on. The silence that descends on them as they walk down the last flight of stairs to the very deepest level of the House is total and complete. The sheer emptiness of noise weighs heavily in the air, their footsteps sharp on the stone floor.

The candles had been lit earlier, and now they stand in the low, flickering glow of the antechamber of the temple carefully sculpted into the earth. The floor is a polished flagstone, the walls covered with frescoes meant to invoke the mortuary temples and tombs of the old world. Some Houses have garish, modern paintings, but these were put in over a hundred years ago by a team of artists with incredible skill. The floor lanterns with their giant beeswax pillar candles are antiques as well, the whole effect one of leaving New York behind and entering another world. If the top floor of the House is a strange liminal space, the deepest space is as well. The night to the day of the salt cellar, the chilly and rock-hewn to the warm and wood-lined.

Tad and Oscar appear with Mr. Augustine, having transferred him to his cedar coffin. They help Maren open the heavy, carved doors to the temple, Thais waiting patiently as the antique hinges protest.

Inside, the frescoes and fluted columns have been lit by

69

more lanterns, two stationed at the base of each pillar like sentries. The domed ceiling is painted a dark, rich navy studded with golden bursts of stars. A view of the heavens, frozen very specifically in time and place, telling the story of night in the Nile Delta sometime mid-February. The sky for Dies Wadi, a sky that has hung over the valleys and mountains and river of the home of the gods for thousands of years, the stars watchful wardens of the dead.

The soles of their shoes and their breathing seem impossibly loud in the grand space. As always, the dull thump of the coffin being placed on the delicately-carved stone altar at the center of the temple has a note of finality to it. It's a lighter sound than usual, as they've used a child's coffin for what little remains of Mr. Augustine. They'd wrapped the bundles of bone best they could, laying them out on top of the neatly-folded suit that he was to be buried in. His portrait, finely done in neutrals and golds, has been laid at the head of the coffin, unattached to a mummy as it would have been in any normal circumstance.

Tad and Oscar remove the top of the coffin, the whole tableau flooded with candlelight. Mr. Augustine's wide, muddy green eyes stare up at them from his portrait, and Maren lets out a long sigh that would be almost inaudible had they been in any other setting.

Taking her cue, Thais sweeps into the temple last, her robes floating behind her on a wind none of the rest of them can see or feel. She takes up her place behind the altar, setting her tablet down next to the coffin among various offerings. Maren hasn't seen Thais ever forget a single word of the ceremony, but she's a traditionalist, so she always comes armed with a digital copy of whatever funerary text she's reading from that particular day.

"Do you present this soul to Serapis, *Sesheta* Nykara?" Thais asks. Maren looks up from the portrait to meet Thais' dark, impassioned gaze. It is a look that had taken Maren in years ago for the first time, and continues to, every time Thais turns it on her. Giving a small nod, Maren swallows heavily.

"I present this soul and these offerings to Serapis," Maren responds.

"Then let us begin," Thais says, and one quick rap of her knuckle brings her tablet to life. Paying it no attention anyway, she raises her hands, palms up, and begins a ceremony that Maren has heard hundreds of times before. Somehow, it hasn't gotten old. She hasn't grown tired of it. There is something almost lyrical about Thais' voice in this space, saying these words.

"Serapis, everything that is hateful has been carried away for thee," Thais begins. She raises a ceramic bowl of purified water, dipping the fingers of her other hand in it before flicking the drops into the open coffin. They catch the light as they fall like raindrops, shining like gems.

"The evil which was spoken, Thoth has advanced and carried it to Serapis. I have brought the evil which was spoken, and I have placed it in the palm of my hand." Thais' voice rises and falls, strong, shot through with steel and conviction. "I have placed it in the palm of my hand. I have placed it in the palm of my hand. I have placed it in the palm of my hand.

"The fluid of life shall not be destroyed in you, and you shall not be destroyed in it. Let him advance, advance with his *ka*. Horus advances with his *ka*. Set advances with his *ka*. Thoth advances with his *ka*."

71

*Does he?* Maren finds herself thinking.

"Thoth advances with his *ka*."

She wants to believe that Mr. Augustine's soul still lives, that he has not died a second, permanent death in the fire.

"Thoth advances with his *ka*."

He must still be out there somewhere, ready to begin his journey into Duat.

"Thoth advances with his *ka*."

The ceremony progresses along at a familiar rhythm, almost like a song. Thais lights incense over the coffin, pours the bowl of purified water across the contents, recites well-traveled passages. The smell of the incense is a sharp spice overlaying the mellow, thick scent of the candles surrounding them. It's one of the most familiar smells of Maren's adult life. She closes her eyes for a moment, breathing deep, letting it roll across her tongue, rest against her skin.

"There shall be no stoppage to your heart with it, and there shall be a coming forth to you through the word which is spoken."

A strange feeling snakes up Maren's spine, raising the fine hair on the back of her neck. She frowns, opening her eyes and looking around. Tad and Oscar are so still as to be almost statuesque, their posture straight and heads bowed. Thais is directing her words to the stars swirling over their heads. Nothing seems out of the ordinary. No one moves, gives any indication that something is wrong.

And yet–

"There shall be a coming forth to you through the word which is spoken."

A few of the lanterns are rattling against the polished

stone floor. The candlelight flickers wildly. Maren finds herself getting colder and colder, like she's being crushed under a block of ice. She finds it hard to breathe, her eyes wide. She's felt this horrible feeling before, once, what feels like a lifetime ago.

"There shall be a coming forth to you through the word which is spoken."

Maren's hair lifts, swirls around her head. The hem of her dress moves in an unknown wind. When she lets out a shaking, raspy breath, it comes out in the fog of a chilly day, and on the inhale a sharp taste snaps at the back of her throat.

"There shall be a coming forth to you through the word which is spoken."

For the second, awful time in her life, Maren feels a specter of death spike through her body, striking her bones like a wave of ice. This time, she knows what it is. Can name it, can try to stay anchored to this life.

A spirit, a soul. A *ka*. She has a good idea who it belongs to as well. She grits her teeth, squeezes her eyes shut, balls her hands into fists at her side, and tries to root herself to the spot. Imagines herself a tree, impossibly old and dug deep into the earth. While she stays stationary, she does not fight the soul passing through her own, lets it pass, lets it swirl within her body. The cold recedes, stripping itself out of her core, her limbs, rolling off the ends of her fingers.

She takes in another deep breath of the incense and candle and opens her eyes. They're wet, tears collecting along her bottom lids, and her breath is coming in ragged gasps, but she has weathered the storm.

None of the other three seem to have sensed anything.

To them, nothing has gone amiss during this ceremony. It's progressed exactly the same way as every other one before it.

"Right," Thais says, clapping her hands together, almost as if she's breaking a spell that has fallen over the temple. "Let's get everything put together and bring Mr. Augustine upstairs to his waiting family."

The ceramic bowl and incense join the suit and portrait and linen-wrapped bits of bone before the top of the coffin is replaced. This time, Maren's junior embalmers run paint brushes thick with pine tar around the outside edge, sealing the two pieces together for as long as eternity will let them be joined.

Maren lingers in the temple after the other three have departed with Mr. Augustine, blowing out candles and collecting a few left-over items — matches, the jar of pine tar, Thais' tablet. She takes deep breaths, three count in, three count out.

Mr. Augustine's soul has survived. Even though she feels cold still, knows now that she'll feel chilled for days, the confirmation that not all is lost warms her from the inside out.

# CHAPTER 6
## Breaking and Entering

The Augustine family, both immediate and extended, plus miscellaneous friends, are gathered in the parlor of the House. They're dressed in muted, dark mourning colors, and they all talk in hushed, careful tones. Maren hovers by the door, people-watching. It's a habit during funerals — especially those of the ultra-wealthy.

Irene Lucanus, Casper Augustine's wife, is seated under a window, next to the coffin. It's been fitted into a sturdy, polished wooden outer one. Once, years and years ago, it would have been stone, but wood is commonplace now. Easier to lift, easier to carve.

The light shining through the windows lands on Irene like a spotlight, making her carefully-placed dark bob shimmer with each tiny movement she makes. She has a water glass clutched in her lap, and every so often she taps at it with one deep red lacquered fingernail. A hunched older woman Maren doesn't know sits to one side of her, eyes wet and nose red, one hand on Irene's shoulder. The other is occupied by a mountain of tissues that seem to be in infinite reserve in her small handbag.

On her other side, body placed carefully behind the coffin, angled as if almost to protect it, is Phaedra. Unlike her mother, who's doing a good job of looking as blank as possible, Phaedra is a jumpy, mixed bag of unhappiness. Her eyes are red, bags under them. Her hair is slicked back, her gaze darting around the room like a cornered animal trying to make an escape. Everything about her posture and expression is unsettled. She keeps looking at the far wall, and then snapping her eyes away from it, as if being caught looking at a blank wall will get her in trouble.

It's a strange picture, the three of them, all seemingly in wholly different stages of mourning, all swathed in black and pearls. Mother, maiden, and crone.

The maiden's sister is nowhere to be seen. Maren's in no hurry to go looking for her.

Drawing back, she shuts the door, sealing the conversation inside. As she turns to the front hall behind her, two people slip through the front doors.

"Mention the cat, and he will come jumping," Maren murmurs to herself as she locks eyes with Ari Augustine.

However, the other person with Ari is more surprising — Detective Perry has accompanied her. Maren briefly wonders what god or goddess she has to make an offering to for an assurance that she'll never have to see these two ever again.

"I thought we agreed not to meet again," Ari says, tugging her peacoat closer around her and looking perfectly miserable.

"I'm not interested in trading barbs with you right now," Maren says tiredly. Something in Ari crumples a bit at that. "You're a bit late."

"Being late is fine," Perry says. "We're here, aren't we?"

"Don't sound so put out about it, it's my father's funeral," Ari says back, narrowing her eyes at Perry as the three of them come together in the middle of the hall, drawn to this point by some gravity.

"Apologies," Perry says, and he does actually sound

kowtowed. Maren notes that Perry looks rather out of place, his black suit not particularly well fitted, and his shirt and tie two totally different shades of black.

"So good to see you again, Detective Perry," Maren says, all smooth silk and simpering smile. "News about the case?"

"No. I'm here on personal business," Perry assures her, waving a hand in the general direction of the receiving room behind her.

"I wouldn't want to be in your way," Maren says as she steps aside. Perry hustles past her, and although Maren expects him to drag Ari with him, instead she takes her sweet time, stopping in front of Maren first.

"I don't know how to stop this," Ari says. Maren has no idea what that means nor what to do with it.

They stand tersely still and silent for a moment, Maren hoping that the muffled words beyond the doors behind her will draw Ari in, pulling her away from Maren. Instead, Ari leans in closer, hands in her coat pockets and a cut, broken grin on her face. It's work to hold her gaze, to not drop her own eyes to the floor.

"Coming with us to Staten Island?" Ari asks.

"No," Maren answers. "I'll join the procession to the piers, but after that you're in the very capable hands of *Hemet* Thais."

"You know my father didn't believe in all of this?"

"Plenty don't."

"And yet we still do this to our dead."

"It's a tradition. It's easy to contend with when people are dealing with a terrible moment in their lives."

"I'm well aware," Ari says, eyes clear and bright. "Well, you'll be missed on what I'm sure is going to be a rather dull sea voyage."

"I'm sure it will be exactly what it needs to be."

"Always have a diplomatic answer, huh?"

"I am here to serve." Maren's never said that particular sentence with as much barely concealed venom as she does now.

Ari leans away, seismograph grin still fixed to her face. There's something a little confused behind it, a little strained and lost. Maren almost wants to reach out and brush the expression away. The sudden thought rocks her, and she tucks it down and away, her hands firmly clasped at her back.

"In that case," Ari starts, and then trails off, leaving the sentence unfinished. Maren tilts her head to the side, leaving room for Ari to continue the thought. She doesn't, her voice staying mute. Maren doesn't prompt her.

Finally, when Maren's about to break, tell Ari to *just say whatever you want to*, Ari opens her mouth.

"I take it my family is in here?" She asks.

Maren nods, and Ari pushes around her, brushing their arms together. Maren watches her go, watching her until the door has clicked softly shut at her back. The moment she's alone in the hall again she sags, letting out a long breath.

She can't wait for Ari to be a distant memory again, smoke and mirrors, something that may never have been real. Having her around just isn't a calming option.

—

True to her word, Maren accompanies the funeral to the river. Four attendants bear the small wooden coffin down

78

the street and over the pedestrian bridge to the piers. She hangs near the back with Henry, hired mourners and Thais leading the way.

Even though the sky is a clear, clean blue, Maren's cheeks and nose sting with the miserable cut of wind that blows off the water. When she looks at Henry out of the corner of her eye, she finds that the high points of his face are as red as Maren's skin feels.

They watch, silent sentries in their black armor, as the coffin is loaded onto the waiting boat. While there are plenty of for-hire boats that work the Hudson, ferrying the dead from the city proper to Staten Island, this one is clearly not an average rental. The black sailboat bobs quietly in the river, a void of color in the bright mid-day sun. Even the sails are black, the edges done up in gold and green embroidery. Maren recognizes some of the pictographs as being from various funerary texts. No, this boat has been made for this moment.

"Ah, to have so much disposable income that they build you a boat after you die," Henry murmurs next to her.

"The pharaohs would be pleased," Maren replies.

"Indeed. Come collect your man, Serapis," Henry says. Maren can't help the brief clip of laughter that she cuts as quickly as possible.

After everyone is safely loaded on the sailboat — dead and alive alike — Maren and Henry start the trek back to the House, hands in pockets and chins tucked into turned up jacket collars.

"Funerals during the winter," Henry says with a heavy sigh once they're back inside, stripping his scarf away from his neck. "This religion was not invented for this climate."

"Not at all," Maren agrees. "You should go home."

79

"I will, just need to get a little bit of paperwork done," Henry says. "And you'll be leaving too, correct?"

"Correct," Maren says with an easy smile.

This is a lie. Maren is still there a few hours later, when Henry is long gone, and the sun is starting to set. The House is mostly dark, a few scattered lights left on in the yawning emptiness of the halls and rooms. Although she knows she needs to get home, Maren hasn't really found it within herself to get up yet, swaddled in a blanket at her desk as she finishes up answering some woefully belated emails.

She takes another sip of the water sitting by her left hand, munching on a piece of ice that comes with the sip. The shadows have started to grow long in her office. Eyeing the light switch, she wonders if it's worth it to get up and turn it on, or just throw in the towel for the day and leave now, chased home by the coming evening. It's a hard call. Both require standing up and ditching her very cozy blanket.

The front door opens so quietly Maren doesn't hear it. The only reason she's even aware of it at all is thanks to the front door alarm chime beeping at her from the security app on her computer. She frowns, tabbing through windows until she pulls up the camera. The front door is indeed slightly open, cracked just wide enough to slip through. However, there's no one on the camera. Either someone hadn't closed the door fully on their way out and the wind had been pushing at it for hours only for it to finally pop open, or–

Voices, almost imperceptibly low. Maren feels like someone's dropped a block of ice into her stomach, the chill is so immediate. Someone is here. Someone who doesn't want anyone to know that they are. Staying still as a stone, her breath shallow and rough, Maren strains to hear. She can't make out words, can barely hear the clip of shoes. Whoever it is, they're sticking to the carpeted parts of the hall.

The soft, intruding sounds trail off towards the back of the house. Maren stands up immediately, stealing out of her office and down the stairs on stocking feet. She holds her breath as much as she can, although she's sure that the thunder of her heart must be loud enough to hear outside her chest.

Peeking around the banister, Maren is just in time to catch the crown of a head vanishing down into the basement. She scoots forward, almost skating along the floor, afraid that one wrong move will make the old wood under her feet groan in protest at being trod on, giving her away. Distantly, she wonders if she should have grabbed some kind of weapon, but they don't exactly keep anything around that could be used that way. No bats, no golf clubs. Certainly no guns.

Maren is going to die, like the idiot in a horror movie who creeps towards the sound instead of fleeing. She glares into the gloom of the staircase, wondering if she should just beat a hasty retreat out onto the sidewalk, where there are witnesses walking by and she can safely call 911.

Unfortunately, simmering anger wins out. Her House has already been defiled once recently, and she's not in a big hurry for anything so garish to happen again.

When she gets to the bottom of the back stairs, she expects to find lights on, or perhaps the doors to the prep room open. The room has plenty of stores of natron and canopic jars, neither of which are cheap, and would probably fetch a tidy sum on some horrible black market of back alley embalming supplies.

Instead, she stands in the dark for a moment, seeing no sign of any other human in the House. Then, the voices from a moment ago float out of the door to her right, almost behind her.

The greenhouse. Whoever tried to make sure Mr. Augustine suffered a second death is back. Most probably a necromancer. The correct, sane thing to do would be to peel out of here so hastily she leaves skid marks.

"This is breaking and entering," a voice says. It's louder in its urgency, pitched up, and Maren realizes with a lurch that she recognizes the voice.

"No it's not," a second voice says.

Maren knows that one too. She glares into the darkness, fear replaced with anger. Pulling her body up to her full height, back ramrod straight, she marches to the crematory doors and throws them wide open. Like deer caught in Maren's headlights on a dark road, two heads swivel to face her in open surprise, eyes wide and mouths soft.

"Hello there," Maren says to Phaedra and Detective Perry. "Can I assist you two with something?"

"Oh Gods," Phaedra says, voice small and almost hysterical. They're both still wearing their black ensembles, clearly having come straight back here after laying Mr. Augustine's earthly remains to rest.

"Yes, yes you can," Perry says, clearing his throat and straightening his tie. Maren notes that his hands are shaking, clearly having not expected Maren to make such a dramatic entrance out of nowhere.

"With?" Maren prompts after neither of them speak for a moment.

82

"Well," Perry starts, and Maren can see the moment he gets his cover story in order and his detective mask descends onto his face. "Phaedra left her shrug here. She was wearing it earlier, and it's real fur, so we didn't want it to get misplaced."

"Did you," Maren says, voice as dry as desert.

"I — I did," Phaedra says, tipping her chin up, clearly trying to play into Perry's lie. "Have you seen it? It's... it's black."

"I haven't seen anything, but I'll keep an eye out for it," Maren says. "May I show you out?"

Please, for Gods' sake, may she.

"Yes, let's go, please," Phaedra says, starting forward. Perry doesn't move though, and she whirls on him, wrapping a hand around his wrist and giving it a tug. "*Felix*. We need to leave."

"I mean, shouldn't we look for the shrug?" Perry says. He avoids Maren's eyes.

"No, you shouldn't," Maren says. "Unless you'd care to tell me why you're actually here."

"Just for the shrug, we're going, we promise," Phaedra says, trying to tug Perry along again. He seems to be very interested in a spot on the floor, clearly wrestling with something.

"Listen," he finally says, and the sound bursts out of him as he looks up at Maren, wide-eyed like a child. "*Listen*. Or, wait, let me show you–"

"Felix, no, let's go and get out of Ms. Nykara's hair," Phaedra says, almost pleading.

"She saw me, once before," Perry says, turning back to Phaedra. He takes her hands in his, eyes soft. "Let me show her."

83

"This is over," Phaedra says with force.

"Officially, but–" he takes his hands back to stalk over to Maren, pulling something up on his phone as he goes, raking a hand through his hair with his other hand. Maren is thinking about taking a step back, away from the man advancing on her. Instead of him bowling into her though, he stops an acceptable distance away and shoves his phone into her face.

It's a video. A large play arrow obscures a decent amount of it, but Maren can see enough to trigger a visual that's been on her mind more often than not, lately. The now-familiar galaxy-glow static of necromancy glitters across the screen of the phone, frozen in time on pause.

"Hit play," Perry says, and now he's the one who sounds almost like they're begging. His eyes — perfectly normal and human, not dripping gold like he appears in her mind's eye in memories — are wide, boyish.

Maren should just throw them out, say something like *you're lucky I'm not reporting you to your precinct*. She should put this behind her, hammer that final nail into this coffin and send it to the underworld, dust her hands off and move on.

Instead, she hits the play button, her nail making a clean tap sound on the screen of the phone.

The video lurches to life. As Maren watches, the static starts to warble and recede, slowly and jerkily. Enough of it vanishes that it goes from totally obscuring the frame to semi-transparent, like a badly taped rerun on VHS. Underneath the static a familiar image forms, showing the very spot they're standing right now, only in grainy black and white. With narrowed eyes, Maren tracks the opening of the door behind them, and then the strange movements of a person as they lumber into the room. Something about the person is off, as if they can't quite remember how to walk, or they're very drunk. Perhaps a head injury. They're in shirtsleeves and slacks, totally ordinary. Had a banker wandered in here after too much to drink?

Maren inches closer, her nose almost touching the phone. After wanting to know who dared set foot in her House so long, it seems anticlimactic that this is what she's seeing. There's no intrigue here. The person moves around the edge of the retort, most likely to turn the machine on and set it to the right temperature for the correct amount of time — a hard enough thing to do when sober.

The figure comes swaying like a marionette back around the edge of the retort.

Maren's world drops away. She grabs the phone from Perry, clutching it so tightly that her knuckles go white.

"That's impossible," Maren whispers as Casper Augustine starts straining at the handle to the retort door, swaying from side to side. She'd done his intake personally, had cataloged the broad, flat planes of his slightly jowly face and receding hairline. She'd spent an hour with him, after his body had been dropped off. She'd carefully arranged the cuffs of that club shirt and removed his loafers from under those slacks, so that his feet wouldn't swell so much his shoes couldn't be removed.

With a growing revulsion and horror, Maren watches as Mr. Augustine clambers into the retort, ungainly as can be, slamming his head into various metal lips and edges a few times and not even wincing in the slightest. Watches as he pulls the door most of the way shut with jerking motions, and then, with one awkward hand, reaches up to slap the witness cremation button before slamming the door shut.

85

The room spins. Maren practically throws the phone back at Perry before finding her way to a folding chair, as clumsily as Mr. Augustine had been on the video. She's breathing hard, heavy. Her heart is slamming against her ribs, trying to get out. She wants to throw up, to go back in time.

"That's not possible," she grinds out, voice like swallowing broken glass. "The video has been doctored."

"I swear it hasn't," Perry says, words rushed and urgent.

"It *has* been," Maren says. She looks up sharply, glaring at Perry from behind her curls where they've fallen into her eyes, a curtain to divide her from a world where the video isn't a fake. She can feel a twitch in her forehead, the edge of a snarl on her lips. Can feel anger blooming in her gut, hot and red and ugly.

"I had a guy I trust in digital forensics work on it." Words are pouring out of Perry. "He was the only one who had his hands on it, was the only one who worked on it. We've had a few cases over the years where we had to do reconstruction on videos damaged by necromancy. This was the worst we've ever seen, but he did it. He did this, he cleaned it up. I trust this guy with my life. It's real, Ms. Nykara. This is real. Some kind of powerful — incredibly powerful — necromancy did this."

Phaedra has crept up behind Perry, a hand clutching his shoulder, her face as white as clean bone. Something haunted lurks in her wide eyes.

Maren wants to rail against him. Wants to shame him right out onto the street for daring to play this kind of prank. Wants to curse everything.

But two sets of eyes are looking at her — one horribly earnest, and one incredibly scared — and Maren can't fully form that rage, can't get it to materialize enough to burst forth from her chest. Instead, her ribs feel like they're caving in, her heart a sluggish void of ice.

"That's a nightmare," she chokes out. "That's a scary story you tell children. That kind of thing doesn't happen–"

"What, outside stories? Outside myth? Where do you think the stories and the myths came from? They had to come from somewhere," Perry says.

Maren looks down at her shaking hands. She grips them together, palm to palm, fingers interlaced so hard that her stacking rings press painfully into the skin of her other hand.

She takes in a deep, horrible, shuddering breath. It feels like breathing in splintered wood and broken glass. The world spins and tips. Her mouth tastes like unholy blood.

Maren gulps down air, trying to get her vision untunneled and her heart somewhere down below tachycardic.

"*Leave,*" she grinds out.

"Absolutely," Phaedra says.

"Absolutely *not,*" Perry says, right as Maren topples out of her chair. He lunges to catch her, but they're too far apart, and she takes the brunt of the fall on one shoulder. Curling into a tight ball, she wonders dully, through the pain and the haunting coldness, if she's dying.

What had she done earlier? She tries to remember, tries to let this horrible feeling go.

But it doesn't make any sense. There should be no spirit lurking in this house anymore, they took him away.

There are two sets of hands on her. From one she feels something strong, something strange, that pushes at what's inside her.

It seems to pierce her heart. She gasps, voice impossibly raw, the sound strangled.

The feeling withdraws, slowly, bit by bit, until she's shivering on the floor but fully aware of the world.

It's dark, here in the greenhouse. The night has never bothered Maren. Now she's afraid it's going to swallow her home.

"You're ok," Perry says. When she struggles to a sitting position, she finds both Perry and Phaedra looking caught again, terror in their eyes.

She wants to haul back and punch Perry, wants to slam her hands to the ground, wants to sob. Wants everything to go back to normal.

She needs this to end.

"I–" Perry starts.

"You're going to fix this," Maren says. "You — your people. You're going to fix this."

"Ok," Perry says, still looking like a scared animal. He drags a hand through his hair, tugging strands loose, letting them splay across his forehead. "Yeah, ok. We can do that. I'll text you. I'll — your number is in the file, right? I'll send you a text."

They help her to her feet, shivering and wavering, and then she helps them right the fuck out of her House.

Maren is left in the dark of a House that's off-kilter, strange, desecrated. She feels empty, a horrible, hollow sensation as she slides down the front door. She lets the House cradle her, lets the cool of the wooden floor seep into her skin, into her bones. She stares at nothing as her world tries to rearrange itself right there, right now, and is unable to right itself.

# CHAPTER 7
## *Family Traditions*

The minute she walks into her apartment, she makes sure that both door locks are done up tight and that the deadbolt has been slid into place with a satisfying thump.

Her skin feels like it's crawling, as if something about her body doesn't fit right anymore. She turns on all of the lights, and then fires up some candles for good measure.

Miu, as if sensing something is wrong, sticks close to Maren, weaving between her heels and occasionally offering up a helpful, bolstering meow from down below. It's oddly comforting, this black void of yellow eyes and dark fluff following her around, a soft shadow that squeaks.

The last thing she does is sit down at the small table crammed into the very tiny space between her bitty kitchen and only medium-sized living room. Maren never has people over — her apartment could most kindly be compared to a shoebox, would more aptly be called a postage stamp — and she always eats on the couch, or standing in the kitchen, so the table has actually gotten dusty.

Tonight though, she feels a need to do something she hasn't done in a very, very long time.

Between the years of moving out of her father's house for college and buying her current place, she never had access to an altar in her own space. They'd so rarely used the one at home after her mother died that it hadn't made any sense to Maren to bother with one, and her various roommates over the years had agreed, either passively or actively. The day she'd gotten the keys to this apartment though, her very first place both without roommates and with her name on the deed, her father had met her at the door with a small box.

There had been three items in the box. Anhur had pulled them out, one by one, almost reverently. Maren had instantly recognized them as pieces of one of the smaller altars her mother had used.

First came a simple piece of wood, polished and pretty with rounded edges and corners. It was a lovely deep color, and it caught the light from the lamp over the table. Next came an incense dish that perfectly fit one of two excised depressions in the wood, painted with a deft hand in the bright turquoise of the Turkish style. Lastly was a *lar*. Maren had watched with a twist to her mouth as Anhur set the little bronze statue in the other depression, taking it all in. The *lar* was extremely traditional, no modern flourishes or fashions, just a small figure of indeterminate gender, wearing a crown and carrying a loaf of bread in one hand and carefully carved sprigs of wheat in the other.

Although Maren has left the assemblage on her bistro table for the past two years, she hasn't touched any of it. It's a comforting presence, a gentle reminder of her mother. But she has no strong belief that drives her to sit at this table night by night, light the incense, and give thanks to this tiny representation of a household deity.

Now though, she feels differently. In the face of so much that she can't explain — that she shouldn't have to explain — she sits down heavily in one of the chairs with her back to the dark windows of her living room. Miu jumps up with her, installing herself next to the *lar* and wrapping her bottle brush tail carefully around her small feet. She blinks once, lazily, as Maren slides open the small drawer in the side of the wooden plinth and fishes out one of the matches stored there.

She takes a deep breath, ready to strike the match against the edge of the drawer, and then pauses, frowning. She realizes, with a startling clarity, that she can't remember a single prayer that her mother used to say. It's been so long that those paths of memory are overgrown and wild, a tangled mess with no clear way through.

"Shit," Maren exhales, and wakes up her phone with her free hand, doing a quick search and feeling like an absolute idiot for not remembering the prayers her mother had said every day for the first twelve years of Maren's life.

Miu chirps helpfully, butting her head into Maren's shoulder.

"I know," Maren mutters. "Who forgets this shit, right?"

Her voice hitches slightly. She tries not to dwell on it.

It takes her zero time to find what she's looking for, considering the commonality of her search. It's something a child would search for under the table at a family gathering, having realized that they were old enough to pay attention but unable to remember anything.

"Ok," Maren says, and takes a deep breath before striking the match. It springs to life with a joyful sizzle and Maren touches it to the dusty incense cone, watching as sweet-smelling smoke starts to curl up towards the ceiling.

"Ok," Maren repeats, and then, reading from her phone, "may this incense cast out all impurities, as from lead to gold. Purify my body. Purify my mind. Purify my heart. It is so."

She takes a second to take another breath in, and then frantically blows out the match when it burns too close to her fingers.

Maren does not feel purified. She is pretty sure the apartment doesn't feel purified either.

None of this is right. She slumps forward, head in her hands and her breath shallow and worn. What she would give to have this be any other old moment in time, any other Tuesday night like the hundreds she's had before. This feels like she's been thrown from her body, from her universe, into some strange place where dead men walk and her only hope lies with death magicians.

Scrubbing at her face, she looks past her curled fingers to where Miu is looking at her. Miu squeaks.

"I hate this," Maren tells Miu. Miu headbutts her again in response, and Maren slowly reaches out, scratching Miu behind the ears, sending her into a trilling purr. Over the years, the hurt of losing her mother has stuck with her, the grief like the tide — ebbing and flowing. Right now, she finds herself desperately wishing that she could pick up the phone and talk with her. Selene would have known what to do. She would have taken it all in stride. Maren wishes she could rise to that challenge as she's sure her mother would have.

It takes Maren a while, surrounded by the dense smell of the lit incense, but eventually Maren does stand up. She strips off her tights, balling them up and throwing them in the direction of the door to her bedroom, and then makes for the couch. Miu dutifully drops to the ground to follow her, a *thump* and then a drum beat of tiny taps.

They curl up together on the couch, Maren wrapping

them up tight in a blanket. She keeps her phone close and turns on the TV to be a distraction more than anything, the volume low enough to be soothing. Staring out the window, she absentmindedly runs loose fingers through Miu's fur. The cat settles closer against Maren's chest, her purring a deep vibration that Maren can latch on to.

Maren wants to think that everything will be alright. Wants to speak it into existence in the world, wants, wishes, *needs* it to be true. She knows it's not though. Knows that the minute she stepped through the doors to the greenhouse, following a concerned Henry, her world had tilted on its axis and changed.

———

There is a bird outside cooing. Maren cracks one eye open and finds herself staring at a pigeon on the windowsill. It stares at her, in the strange unseeing way that pigeons have a habit of doing, and she takes a deep breath, opening the other eye.

She's still in the living room, still wrapped up in a blanket, the TV still on low in the background. With a groan, Maren forces herself to sit up, unsticking one drool-covered cheek from a throw pillow. She blinks in the bright light of morning, and slowly takes stock of her apartment. It's later than she would have wanted to wake up. Candles that had been burning last night are melted down, black soot halos at the bottom of pretty glass containers. The incense cone on the table has been reduced to almost nothing, leaving a small heap of white-gray ash and the smell of cedar hovering in the background of the room. Miu is fast asleep on the back of the couch.

Maren's dress is rucked up, pinching under her arms, and she can feel the smeared, dry crust of makeup on her face. With a wince, she extends her legs, shaking her body out of the blanket, and takes a slow walk to the bathroom.

A tired face looms in the mirror when she switches the light on. Her normally warm brown skin has taken on a distinct tone of gray, bags underneath her dark eyes. Her mop of deep brown curls is mashed flat against one side of her head and her eye makeup is skewing towards raccoon-like. Not to put too fine a point on it, she looks like crap.

When she peels her dress off, she finds fine, red lines across her torso from where the creases and fabric pressed into her skin overnight. Letting the black garment drop to the tiled floor, she steps into the shower. For a long time, she turns her face into the spray, letting the water heat up and take her body from goose bumps and teeth chatter to smooth skin and warmth. The water peels away her makeup, mats down her curls, and sluices down her arms and chest and back, swirling around her feet before vanishing down the drain.

She wraps herself in a robe and a towel, hunkering down into the terrycloth, and then goes in search of her phone. She finds it knocked down next to the couch, the screen showing the disturbingly late time of *8:44* and one missed text.

*Fiona Avenne*
*I'm coming by with a drop-off before work!*

She texts a quick affirmative reply to her stepmother, and then blazes through an abbreviated version of her usual morning routine, throwing on clothes and mascara and tying her hair back, only half blow-dried. Close enough. She's positive there's no universe in which she would feel

94

or look put together at this point, and the only people who are going to see her today are Henry, Tad, and Oscar. They've seen her covered in viscera — dressed down is nothing.

Miu is staring at her with narrowed eyes from the back of the couch. She yawns, displaying all her pointy white teeth, and then follows this up with a pointed squeak of a meow.

"Oh Gods, Miu, I'm so sorry, I'm such an ass." Maren has already started for the pantry. Miu thumps down to the floor and happily trots to the kitchen, positioning herself in front of her bowl while Maren fills it up. It occurs to her that she should probably feed herself as well, but she can't quite find the motivation at the moment. Instead, she flips her kettle on and figures tea will have to suffice.

Fiona calls her twenty minutes later, and, armed with a travel mug containing boiling hot water and two tea bags, Maren salutes Miu and heads out. She'd bundled up, sporting both coat and scarf. Something about the heavy, comfy clothing feels safe.

There's an alarmingly orange hatchback idling in front of her building, with Fiona's bright red head just visible through the window. Maren raps on the glass with the travel mug and Fiona rolls it down, a sunny smile ready.

"Good morning!" Fiona coos as Maren leans through the empty window, eyeing the bags on the passenger seat. There are three, and they're all large.

"This is a lot," Maren says.

"I know, I know," Fiona says, brushing the comment away with a waved hand. "But I figure you could bring them to work!"

"For all three of my coworkers," Maren says.

95

"And yourself. I mean, this isn't even a bag a person! I could have brought more."

She could have, Maren doesn't doubt that for a second. She's seen it happen. And she's honestly just giving Fiona a hard time — Maren can smell the round, homey aroma of the various breads and bagels in the bags. Flicking one of the bags open, she takes in a deep breath. Even though they're a few days old they still smell amazing, reminding Maren of the year in high school when she worked at Fiona's bakery.

"Thank you, Fi," Maren says. "I mean it."

"I know you do," Fiona says. "Want a ride to work so you don't have to sully my wares with the subway?"

"Please," Maren says, unlatching the door and sliding into the seat carefully, gathering the bags up in her lap as she goes.

"You look frigid," Fiona says, cranking the heat as she pulls out into traffic.

"I feel it," Maren says with a sigh. Fiona gives her a quick glance out of the corner of her eye but doesn't say anything. Digging around in one of the bags, Maren pulls out a scone to tentatively nibble at. The sharp taste of cranberry greets her.

"What's been up with Anhur?" Maren asks through a mouthful, licking sugar off her lips.

"He's decided to start a podcast," Fiona says. Her ability to say this straight-faced and even rather supportively is testament to her love for Maren's father.

"I'm sorry, what?" Maren asks, arching an eyebrow.

"I know," Fiona says, merging onto the West Side Highway with the furious concentration mixed with offhand flippantry of a lifelong New Yorker in possession of both a license and a car. "He wants to use it to do a sort of interview format, where he has two people on every episode, one an old entrenched academic and another a grad student working in the same area. To play them off each other, I would guess, while also educating everyone."

"How very Anhur," Maren muses. Her father, a professor in a rather cliché way, has always loved holding gatherings and salons and really anything he can do to get as many people talking about art history as possible. The fact that he does not wear tweed with elbow patches is honestly a shame.

"Indeed," Fiona says. "But what about you? Things going well?"

"I guess," Maren says with a deflecting shrug before scooping her tea up from the holder and taking a long drag of probably too-hot liquid. She grimaces and swallows, can already feel the burn scalding up on her tongue and roof of her mouth. At least she can feel some kind of heat. Still, in the interest of preserving her mouth, she pops the top off and lets the steam swirl up and out and dissipate a bit, blowing on it.

"You guess?" Fiona prompts.

"Sorry, tea's the temperature of the surface of the sun," Maren says. "Uh, yeah. We had a funeral yesterday. Couple of new intakes over the last month. Thais is back in town. I guess obviously, if we had a funeral."

"That sounds decent!" Fiona says pleasantly. "I mean, perhaps not decent for the poor person's family, but decent for you all."

That is the problem in her line of work — if business is booming, she can't exactly be excited about it in polite company.

Fiona waits until they're almost to the House, Maren suckered into calm complacency, to pounce.

"So," Fiona says, the indicator beating out a *click click click* as they wait to turn onto 11th. "Are you getting enough sleep? You're ok?"

"Where's that coming from?" Maren asks, scooting around in her seat and stretching out her legs.

"You look…" Fiona seems to be chewing on various words, trying to find the best one to deploy. "You've looked livelier."

"I've looked livelier," Maren repeats deadpan, staring out the windshield and not meeting Fiona's eyes.

"I just want to make sure you're well, you're eating enough, and you're getting enough sun."

"Fi, it's about to be winter. *No one* is getting enough sun. And I work in a basement."

"Your office has that lovely west-facing window."

Maren doesn't point out that the ratio of time spent in the basement to time spent in her office is heavily lopsided in favor of the darker, more subterranean option.

"I'm fine." A lie. Add it to the pile. "It's been busy lately, that's all."

Another lull, another silence. Fiona pulls the car to a stop next to the line of cars parked up and down the block, nowhere for her to idle against the curb.

Drumming her fingers on the steering wheel as Maren gathers the bags up, she heaves a deep sigh. Something about it makes Maren tense up and freeze with a hand on the door handle.

"Oh no," Maren says.

"I only ask because your father was worried, and that of course makes me worried, and we just want you to be happy–"

"Oh Gods, Fiona. Please. I promise I'm fine."

"No, no, I'm not starting in on that again. Anhur wanted me to ask you if you're seeing anyone."

It takes a moment for the words to register in Maren's tired, scrambled brain, and when they do, she has to take a moment to pinch the bridge of her nose and let out a long breath.

"I know I am old and yet still unwed," Maren intones somberly.

"Oh no, that is not what I mean, and you know it," Fiona says. "I was once *actually* old and unwed."

"No, I'm not seeing anyone," Maren sighs. "I have too many dead people on my hands to worry about the living."

"Maybe find it within yourself to worry about one living person?"

"I don't even want to date anyway."

"I mean you. Worry about you. You're alive. I hope, anyway. If not, good show, walking and talking and all."

Maren freezes.

Fiona's voice is light, a laugh at the edges of her words. Maren is sure that if she turned to the older woman, she would find a twinkle in her eye, a small grin. It's a joke. It's harmless.

*Breathe*, Maren tells herself. She can feel her shoulders hunching up towards her ears, wants to clasp her hands together. Fiona does not know. Does not know that Maren is wondering if that border between life and death is much looser than she'd ever given much thought to, wondering how to contend with a new reality that includes necromancy.

She has to breathe. She sucks in one deep breath, then

another. When she finally uncoils her body, letting her shoulders drop and swiveling to face Fiona, she finds that there is no grin there, no bright eyes. Instead, there is worry, drawn and wan, and Maren instantly feels horrible.

"I'm... I'm just not feeling up to going on dates, all of that," Maren says. She sounds like she's a world away to her own ears. "Maybe in the spring."

"Ah, a new beginning, how lovely," Fiona agrees, bobbing her head. The concern has vanished from her face, carefully packed away. "Well then! Sorry for being horribly parental and poking at your soft underbelly. Let me make it up to you by kicking you out of my car with a lot of delicious baked goods?"

"You know me so well," Maren says. She puts forced levity into it, weaving it around her words. She can do this. She has no other option.

Fiona sends her off with another sunny smile, waiting until Maren waves to her from inside the front door to drive off. Maren watches her go for a moment before pressing her forehead to the glass, taking in several shuddering deep breaths.

Turning around, she finds the front hall yawning around her, something sinister and awful even though she can hear music from downstairs and Henry walking around above her head. This is her House — she has to remember that. She controls this space. No one and nothing can take that away from her.

—

She triple-locks herself in again that night.

Next, incense and a prayer for the little *lar* on the table.

100

A new pattern is forming for her evenings. This time however, she does force herself to eat after subsisting on a bagel and a scone all day. The food tastes strange in her mouth but she forces it down, swallowing hard and knowing that she has to do this. She can't just stop eating, can't waste away to nothing just because her House has been invaded by something unholy.

She will not let herself be consumed.

Although sleeping on the couch with the comfort and safety of the watchful TV and kitchen light is enticing, Maren pushes herself past that as well. She actually changes into soft shorts and a ratty t-shirt and slips between the covers of her bed. Miu joins her, circling around on the plush comforter a few times, inspecting various folds and creases for the best sleeping spot.

No matter how hard she tries, sleep doesn't come easy. At first she leaves her desk light on like a small child afraid of a monster under the bed, but the light finds its way into every corner of the room, the brightness making it impossible for her to sleep. She's a born and raised New Yorker, she's always assumed she can sleep through anything the world would see fit to throw at her. And yet, here she is defeated by a small desk lamp.

The light has to go off. She's left in the dark, and it constricts her throat and makes her feel like something is lying on her chest, slowly sinking deeper and deeper, suffocating her.

In. Out. In. Out. Forces the air into and from her body.

"I hate this," she tells the dark ceiling, eyes wide. She needs Perry to text her now.

Miu takes this as her queue, and slowly picks her way across the comforter until she's staring down at Maren, eyes a very strange green-ish color in the deep blue of the night. Then, with all the grace of a toddler, she flops down next to Maren, shoving herself into the small space between Maren's arm and the side of her chest.

With a sudden start like a pull-cord motor, Miu starts purring. The vibration simmers through Maren's body, and she finally closes her eyes.

"You're a pretty great cat, Miu," Maren murmurs. Finally, she can feel sleep tugging at her edges.

Miu just purrs even louder in response.

# CHAPTER 8

## *A Necromancer Walks into a Bar*

Waiting for Detective Perry's text is borderline impossible. She moves around the House as if she's concerned a zombie might spring from the second-floor bathroom and terrorize all of them right there in the upstairs hall. Every time her phone buzzes she finds herself itching to pick it up, no matter if it's under a mountain of papers on her desk or on a counter in the prep room while she's up to her elbows in cadaver. She's extremely concerned that she might be turning into a crazy person.

"You seem concerned," Tad says one day.

"Do I?" Maren asks archly, not even bothering to look up from the incision she's making.

"Not about this," Tad says, tapping the table between them. The still body of a middle-aged woman is resting on it. "More just sort of in a general way. Is there anything I can help you with? You know I'm more than happy to take up more work."

Maren does know this. Tad is horribly helpful in all things. She looks up from the body with a sigh, letting her hands rest on the cool metal of the table. Everything in the prep room is cool — the prep tables, the tile floor, the air piped in by the humming ductwork. Sometimes Maren wonders what it would be like if she cut into live people, instead of dead people. She supposes it would be warm, the skin under her gloved hands rising and falling with heartbeat and breath alike. The air would probably smell like blood and sweat, the lights bright. Instead, it's cold and there is a vague smell of decay permeating through the air. Occasionally, when they do an intake of a rather decayed corpse, the smell is so thick and cloying that Maren is afraid that it might never leave the back of her throat and nose, remaining a heavy, dead weight there.

There have been days where she's walked out of the House knowing that she reeks like death. Perhaps it never really leaves her, she's just gone nose blind to it in all but the most severe cases.

"You don't need to take up more work, Tad," Maren says kindly. "You're incredibly helpful already, and I don't want to overwork you."

"Ms. Nykara," Tad says, steepling his fingers in front of him as Maren just barely succeeds in not rolling her eyes at the formal title, "you know that there is no universe in which I can be overworked."

"Careful," Maren says. "I'll try to find the one universe where that's not true. And for the love of all the Gods, Tad, *please* call me Maren."

"You're my mentor," Tad says. A frown creases his brow, as if he can't figure out why he'd address Maren as anything but Ms. Nykara.

"We've worked together for over a year."

"A year in which I have remained an apprentice," Tad says sagely. "And as long as I am your apprentice, you'll be Ms. Nykara."

"Don't make me have to start calling you Mr. Archer-Manius," Maren says as she returns to working her blade down the chest of the body on the table. This is another difference — no blood wells from the wound she's making, as it would in surgery. Instead, the woman is long dead, her blood pooled down along her back, leaving none to be pumped to the surface by the pressure of her heart. The skin peels back slightly as Maren forces the scalpel down into the waxy skin, subdermis and fatty tissue revealed, periosteum below that.

Tad holds the skin flaps back as Maren continues her work, creating a large enough opening in the woman's torso to allow for the removal of her organs. They'll dry them separately, the body cavity packed to the gills with natron. Eternity and entropy are harsh mistresses, so they do all they can to stall them for as long as possible.

Maren's just set her knife down on the tray by her elbow when her phone lets out a rumbling vibration. She slides her gaze sideways, staring at where the screen has lit up on the counter a few feet away. She can't tell what the notification is from this distance, and she can feel her fingers twitching, her mind wanting to propel her up and scrambling towards the phone.

Carefully rising, as to not seem rushed, she strips off her latex gloves, depositing them in the trash.

"A break, perhaps?" Maren suggests.

"I could go for some coffee," Tad says. "Should I make a whole pot?"

"Sure, thank you," Maren says with an easy smile. Tad answers her with a blinding one of his own before ditching his gloves and apron and vanishing through the doors into the hall.

Very suddenly alone, Maren lets her smile drop as she whirls around on her phone, her back hunched against the emptiness of the space she's in, hyper aware of every noise. She really wishes she'd stop checking shadowy corners like a six-year-old in need of a night light.

There is one notification on the phone, the little white pop-up cheery against her mostly black background — a photo of Miu, hanging out upside down on the back of the couch. It's a text. Maren's breath catches, her fingers shaking as she hurries to unlock her phone.

*Detective Felix Perry*
*are you free thursday night at 7pm?*

Two days. She only has to wait two more days. She lets out a long breath, letting her head drop and hang, her shoulders bunched up around her ears. Her curls dangle around her face, her chin, and she closes her eyes, just breathing. Relief washes over her, slow and careful, like the first wave on the way to high tide.

The creaking sound of the prep room door opening is so sudden and so outside her current world that it makes Maren finally give into the staticky nervousness that's been circling around her mind for weeks. She jumps straight up, her heart pounding, phone clutched in her hands as she whirls to look in the direction of the door. For the briefest of moments her treacherous brain provides her an image of horror — a flash of a stumbling body, skin sloughing off in decay and torso clumsily sliced open, guts hanging out. Her eyes widen, and Tad, carrying two mugs, stares at her with open concern in the place where the imagined body had been.

"You're sure you're alright?" Tad asks as he crosses to her, handing her one of the mugs of black coffee.

"Absolutely," Maren says, embarrassed at how breathy she sounds. Her hand shakes slightly as she raises the mug to take a sip, distantly wondering if putting caffeine in her adrenaline-amped body is the smartest idea at the moment. If nothing else, the strong, warm smell of coffee is a lovely grounding compared to the floaty feeling she's experiencing.

"I didn't mean to scare you, sorry about that," Tad says.

"No, no, I'm just jumpy," Maren says, waving him off. Tad gives her an extremely concerned look in response, head slightly tilted to one side. It's quite possible that he smells that for the bullshit it is the minute Maren drops it. She's been ribbed by her staff on more than one occasion for acting like a robot.

"Alright, well if that's true, shall we get back to it?" Tad asks.

"We shall," Maren says, taking another long pull of coffee.

———

In the same way that Detectives Choi and Perry's office was incredibly bland considering their jobs, this gathering of necromancers she's attending seems to be held in a rather normal location. Maren's had so much time to let her imagination go absolutely hog wild, she'd figured that they'd been meeting in some horribly cliché location — like the vault of an abandoned turn of the century bank, or perhaps a warehouse near the docks in Brooklyn where they'd all stand in a circle around sketchy marks on the floor, hemmed in by the stalwart, hulking protection of shipping containers.

Instead, the address Perry had sent her with a quick brief about the group he belongs to has landed her in the lobby of a rather hip hotel low down on the East Side. It's tucked up close to the river and seems to be caught somewhere between hipster and hypebeast in terms of general style and vibe.

Putting on her usual air of serene calm and armed with an answer for everything (even if half of that is deflection), she strides across the polished concrete floor, past the front desk. Her blocky heels click against the floor with purpose, her eyes on the elevator bank on the far wall. She makes the barest eye contact with the man working the front desk — nonthreatening, a simple exchange. He smiles in response, and she warms her face for him.

Taking a moment to shake herself out and then recompose her face in the elevator, she checks her hair and outfit in the dully reflective walls, making sure that she looks perfectly ordinary. She can't imagine what this group is going to look like, but she figures they'll probably look like New Yorkers — dressed primarily in dark colors not for any occult reason, but rather that it's November in Manhattan.

The elevator dings. The doors slide open. Maren looks up, and into the eyes of the second necromancer she's ever known herself to have met in her life. Assuming this person is one.

He's a young man with a bushy beard and a clipboard.

"Hello!" He says, waving with his free hand. "Welcome! I haven't seen you around. I'm Max."

"Nice to meet you, Max," Maren says, stepping out of the elevator and offering him a small wave back, unwilling to close the distance between them. "I'm — I'm new."

"Name?" Max asks, clicking his pen into action with gusto.

"Nykara. Maren."

108

"Ah ha, found you," he says, crossing her name off a list before looking back up at her with a warm grin. "Come on in, grab a drink, mingle. If you've got any questions, I'm happy to answer them."

"Thank you," Maren says. Max just grins even brighter. It's weird. She has a brief flash of fear that she might be accidentally joining one of the extreme mystery cults that the more conservative news channels are always warning about.

The bar is as hip as the lobby, and the floor-to-ceiling windows on three walls offer a breathtaking view of the city. Before she can even worry about getting a drink, or even taking stock of the rest of tonight's crowd, she finds herself drifting towards the glass as if possessed.

In the thin darkness of twilight, the city is lit up like a glittering galaxy, coming alive in the gathering night. Lights simmer and twinkle in windows, down streets, at the edges of buildings and bridges. She can see from downtown to midtown, the city spread out at her feet fifteen stories below. Maybe it's not particularly cool to be gawking like this, but she grew up in Brooklyn, so this view will always mesmerize her. When she and her high school friends had gotten old and stupid enough to combine weed and high places, they'd started having parties on various people's rooftops with ratty folding beach chairs, wild dreams, and bright eyes turned towards this incredible skyline. She'll always be enchanted by it, by the promise the city has for her.

"Isn't it a cool view?" Someone gushes near her right hip. Maren reluctantly turns her face down and to the side. A teenage girl is looking up at her with stars in her eyes. She's squeezed onto a plush sofa with two other girls.

Sitting in chairs on the other side of the low table at their knees is another girl and a boy. They're all wearing various bits and pieces of uniforms, sweater vests and plaid skirts. There's no way on earth they're old enough to drink, and Maren spies bright orange paper wristbands on each of their scrawny arms. While the bar won't be serving them tonight, evidently there's no lower age limit on necromancy.

It puts a weird taste in her mouth to see teenagers turning out in force for death magic.

"It is," Maren hedges.

"Are you new?" One of the other girls asks. "Are you from here? What sub-field are you interested in? I'm really feeling bone casting right now."

"Uh," is all Maren can figure to get out.

"There you are!"

They all swivel towards the approaching voice. Detective Perry has made his grand entrance, striding over towards the group with a disarming smile.

"What do you say, drink time?" Perry asks, looping his arm through Maren's and then tugging her away from the gaggle of teens, that smile still plastered on his face. The minute they've disengaged, on a path for the bar, Perry lets her arm go, instantly dropping the smile.

"That was aggressive," Maren notes dryly.

"You know the only thing worse than a bunch of teenagers?" Perry asks, leaning against the bar.

"Necromantic teenagers?" Maren grouses.

"Catholic school teenagers," Perry says.

Maren frowns at him for a moment, his words working themselves over in her head.

"No shit, really?" She asks, peeking over her shoulder

110

to where the group is back to chattering at each other all at the same time. "Is Catholicism more willing to deal with all this shit?"

"Depends on who you ask," Perry says, posting them up at the bar and looking at Maren expectantly.

"Uh, just a glass of white wine," Maren says.

"Old fashioned," Perry says.

While Perry pays, she takes a moment to get a better look around the bar and the people crowded around tables and sofas. All the furnishings are bright and bold, blocky shelves and brocade couches. People of every kind are tucked into the comfy cushions, from the Catholic kids to a trio of ancient — bordering on decrepit — old men sitting off to one corner, regarding the goings-on as slightly suspicious. There are finance bros, jackets unbuttoned at the end of the long day, Uptown moms in hip jeans, and a large assortment of very normal people. More groups are clustered close to each other on the outdoor patio, heads bent and collars turned up, the cherry glow of cigarettes smearing spots of light through the dark air.

"Not what you expected?" Perry asks as he hands Maren her drink.

"Thank you," she murmurs, staring down into the drink for a moment before looking up to meet his gaze. Despite his sandy hair and pale skin dusted with moles, he has dark eyes, not unlike the deep brown of Maren's own. "No, it's not. You think these people can help me with whatever this death magic problem is?"

"Necromancy," Perry says, a correction so quick it seems automatic.

"Necromancy," Maren corrects herself, even as the word makes her hair stand on end. "I just need it to fix me.

111

I expected something more... occult. Magical, I guess."

"It is, sometimes. Those guys–" Perry points to the suspicious old geezers in the corner, –do a mean bit of cleromancy."

"That's not necromancy."

"Au contraire, young padawan — it is when the *sortes* are carved from bone and you're calling on the connected spirit to tell a future."

"That's desecration of a body." Maren can't keep the distaste from her tone.

"Boy, we're going to have to get you past that if you're going to survive among these people long enough to figure out what's wrong with you." Perry sighs, pinching the bridge of his nose and taking a beat before continuing. Maren waits patiently, tapping a thumb against her wine glass. "Look. I invited you here for a somewhat self-serving reason. I'm not interested in your turning up dead due to whatever supernatural bullshit is going on with you, because then I'll have to deal with it. Whatever happened that morning in your House, it was an incredibly powerful bit of magic, and it clearly screwed you up. You wanted to come. You wanted help. That means you play by our rules, ok?"

Maren gives him a long look over the edge of her glass.

"Ok," she says, because she does want to fix this. She wants to heal her House, and protect her employees from the open, festering wound of necromancy that has seen fit to enter their lives. That starts with curing herself of the horrible chill that has a hand around her heart. She is, however, one hundred percent ready to turn her back on it the moment this is fixed.

"Good," Felix says cautiously, studying her with that

strange, intense gaze of his. "First up, I introduce you to Roger and Juni. They started this salon ages ago, and they still run it."

"Lead on," Maren says, toasting with her wine. With one last glance, Perry turns and leads her into the crowd mingling in the space.

They wind past people and through groups until, with zero fanfare, the crowd parts and Maren finds herself facing one of those glorious floor-to-ceiling windows. Sitting in front of it on another couch is an older couple. The man has a pair of reading glasses perched on his nose, and he's tapping away on his phone while one of the teenagers from earlier leans over his shoulder, pointing things out from time to time. The woman is doing, of all things, needlepoint. As they draw closer however, Maren can see that the design carefully being dipped in and out of the fabric isn't flowers, or trees, or anything so bucolic. It's a familiar scene from an illustrated funerary text: a smiling man with warm skin, dressed in rich white robes, bracketed by Thoth on one side and Horus on the other, both of them in their animal-headed forms.

"Hunefer," Maren says. The old woman looks up at Maren slowly. Her short, wispy silver hair falls around her face like a gilded frame for her wide eyes. They're a strange blue color, pale and arresting, magnified to an unnerving size by her thick, round glasses. There's something young about those eyes, despite the deeply inscribed wrinkles circling them.

"You know it?" The woman asks. Her voice is sweet and rough — the kind of grandmotherly voice that might normally be offering cookies up to anyone and everyone.

"Yes," Maren says. "It's the version of the Book of

113

Coming Forth By Day which I know the best, probably."

"Smart girl," the old woman muses. "You're *hemet*?"

"Not even remotely," Maren says, shaking her head.

"Uh, actually," Perry says, popping up over Maren's shoulder. "Juni, this is Maren. She's a chief embalmer."

"Ah, *sesheta* then." A confident nod as the woman puts her needlepoint down in her lap. "Welcome to our little salon, Maren. I'm Juni, and this is — Roger, would you–"

"Logan is showing me how to fix my autocorrect," the old man — presumably Roger — says.

"We have a new person," Juni says gently, reaching out to put a hand on Roger's arm. He looks up at that, soft surprise in his eyes.

"My, my, we do — welcome! What's your name?" Roger asks. He sounds perfectly grandfatherly to go with Juni. Maren is having a hard time imaging these two as necromancers. The most supernatural thing about Roger is that he has all his hair still, a shock of white that he clearly takes time to style. Otherwise, he looks like he might be simply passing through here quickly before heading out on a Florida golf trip.

"Maren," she says.

"*Sesheta* Maren," Juni interjects.

"Oh, excellent," Roger says, nodding to himself. "We don't get many members of the priesthood here, but you're always welcome."

Maren doesn't point out that she's technically not part of the priesthood, nor that no member of the priesthood should ever be in a place like this.

"Sit here for a moment, my dear," Juni says, patting the seat on the couch next to her. Maren darts a quick glance at Perry, but all she gets in return is a wholly unhelpful shrug.

114

Giving him a small glare, she lowers herself to the heavy velvet, letting her body sink into the sofa.

Juni looks Maren over with those arresting, wide eyes, expression neutral. Then, transferring her needlepoint to the table in front of her, she pulls a small pouch of something out of her breast pocket with knobby fingers. Pulling it open, she unceremoniously dumps five finger bones out of the bag. They bounce across the glass tabletop, taking odd, angled paths, skittering almost like bugs before Juni wrangles them back into a pile.

With one deep breath, Juni passes a hand over the bones. When she lets her breath out it's as frosty air, as if the temperature in the bar has suddenly dropped below freezing. A buzzing sensation creeps across Maren's shoulders, down her arms, setting her hair on end.

Maren knows her eyes have gone wide, her mouth open. The air in the bar is still warm, and yet somehow Juni seems half into another place, where it's frigid and icy. Maren has never seen anything like it before.

Lifting her hand up, Juni closes her palm and whispers something so low, so under her breath, that Maren can't make out her words. Then, on the table, the bones start to move. They drag themselves across the glass top in jerking, slow motions. Watching with wide eyes, Maren notes that there are marks on the bones, circles in circles, designs carefully incised. She can feel her heart in her throat, seeing this in front of her like it's nothing.

For a moment, all is silent, Maren and Juni tied together in a bubble of space, shut off from the hubbub around them. Then, turning to Maren, she blows out her held breath. Barely visible in the air, fine and light and bright, there is gold. As quickly as it had appeared, it's gone,

115

leaving only the slightest taste of something metallic in the air. Maren has no idea what to do with any of this, and she finds that she's torn between fear and wonder.

"Hmm," Juni says. "You have a fractured future."

"What does that mean?" Perry asks. Maren had almost forgotten he was even there.

"Who knows," Juni says, voice round and unconcerned. "Well, the dead do, I suppose. But I don't."

"That's cryptic," Perry grouses. "But I guess that's your MO."

"So impatient, Felix," Juni says, shaking her head. "Not to worry, *Sesheta* Maren. You have many futures."

She follows this up with a quick wink before she sweeps the bones back into her small pouch with a surprising speed and grace for someone of her age. This is not the soothsaying and fortune telling that happens on boardwalks — this is magical, glittering and golden.

Maren has no idea what to say. She presses her palms into the soft material of the couch, steadying herself on her hands. Juni watches her, blinking slowly through her bottle glasses.

"Is that easy?" Maren asks finally, licking her dry lips.

"I suppose," Juni muses. "I'm glad you're here. Let us know if we can help you with anything."

Juni smiles pleasantly at both of them, and then picks her needlepoint back up. It's a clear dismissal, and when Maren looks to Perry for guidance, she realizes that a small line has formed behind him. Juni seemingly has others who would request a moment of her time.

She lets Perry place a hand on her shoulder, lets him guide her to a table a few groups away. They take up places in overstuffed chairs that face a low table, and beyond that, the twinkling skyline. Maren runs a finger around the smooth lip of her wine glass, staring out into the night.

"Did you grow up here?" Perry asks after they've been silent for a while, wrapped up in the low ebb of others' conversations.

"Yes," Maren says. "Well, no. Not here. Brooklyn. You?"

"I went to high school in the city, but I grew up in Westchester," Perry says. He takes a long sip from his drink, not meeting Maren's eyes. "Juni can give weird predictions sometimes. The first time I met her, she said that my future would be lawless."

"She wasn't wrong," Maren points out.

"No, but when you're seventeen and you hear that you assume that you'll be the one committing the crimes, not the one stopping or solving them."

"Does she predict everyone's future when she meets them?"

Perry takes another sip, gives a quick nod, and then sips again.

"It's kind of a rite of passage, a sort of test," he says.

"And I passed?" Maren asks.

"You passed the minute you said... what was it? Hugh something?"

"Hunefer," Maren says.

"Yeah, that dude. Juni's always working on a quilt or an embroidery or something, but I don't know if anyone's figured out her subject matter that fast."

Maren focuses on her wine and tries not to think about that exact funerary text that she's currently thumbing her nose at. It's a means to an end. Hopefully a very quick one.

117

# CHAPTER 9

*Prosit*

Maren goes back to the next gathering. And the next. She tags close to Perry still, watching with careful eyes as people drift through this space, normal and friendly. People seem to like her, and if they read her distrust of the whole mess she's found herself in, they let it go or choose to ignore it.

She learns about wards from an excited middle-aged lawyer. They won't seem to help her much, can't dig the frost out of her veins, but they can protect the House. Perry comes by the next day to help her set up the symbols and salt required to keep vengeful spirits at bay. They carve tiny ones into the baseboard just inside the front vestibule, down on their knees and elbows against the elegantly-done wooden inlay floor. Maren finds herself strangely exhilarated by the concentration and the strength she feels in her hands as she works, and she feels safer when it's done. They repeat the process twice more — once leading into the greenhouse, and once out the basement door.

That night though, sitting in her dark apartment, she feels like she's done something unholy, and she tosses and turns into the early hours of the morning. All she can do is keep telling herself that she's protecting her House.

On the night of salon number four Maren dashes across the 9th Avenue cobblestones in heels, carefully dainty on her toes as she dodges a cab and a few puddles. The air is thick and almost claustrophobic with moisture, hovering dangerously close to freezing. Tad and Oscar had agreed on a twenty-dollar bet that it would snow tonight — Tad in favor of, Oscar against.

She finds Perry, and they order their usual drinks before installing themselves at a high two-top close enough to the bar that they can judge drink orders. Despite her initial hostility towards him, now that he's started to help her, she's warming to him. She knows that at each of these salons he's been asking careful, leading questions, trying to figure out if anyone has ever dealt with anything similar to Maren's current predicament. If nothing else, it's probably nice to have an actual detective at her side for this.

"Wait, check this out," Perry says, and points with the hand that's holding his cocktail, making the ice clink against the glass. Maren follows his finger to the bar, only to roll her eyes when she sees the bright orange paper peek out from a sleeve. It's one of the high schoolers. He's swaddled himself in someone's borrowed coat, the collar turned up and the sleeves long enough to reach down to the backs of his knuckles. For some inane reason, he's got a pair of wayfarers perched on his head, even though the sun set hours ago. Perhaps he's laboring under the delusion that this makes him look any less dewy and fresh-faced.

"Oh no," Maren says, shaking her head. "Don't do it."

"He's going to do it," Perry says.

"Are you going to have to arrest someone?"

"No, no." Perry's eyes are alight with glee as he watches the kid stumble through ordering some local IPA.

The bartender leans forward on the counter, regarding the kid with a raised eyebrow. Perry leans a bit to the side to catch their conversation, leaving Maren with a clear view towards the elevators.

119

A woman emerges from one as the doors slide away. Despite the cold, she's wearing jeans that are more rip than denim. Her coat is open, revealing a sweatshirt with some enigmatic design of unknown origin that probably cost a fortune. It's the kind of look that's meant to be clearly fashionable while also carrying an air of *oh, this old thing? I just threw it on.*

It's the kind of look that people spend years perfecting. It's also currently being worn by Ari Augustine.

"*How*," Maren says, pinching the bridge of her nose.

"Hold on, the bartender is playing dumb about what an IPA is—" Perry says, clearly distracted.

"Ari Augustine is here," Maren mutters.

"Whoa. Weird," Perry says, spinning around to look into the crowd. Ari has stopped to chat with someone, head thrown back in a laugh.

"Weird is one way to put it."

"She's *never* where you expect her to be. I haven't seen her at one of these things in ages," Perry says, and then, with a simple move that drains the color from Maren's face, he cups a hand to his mouth and shouts across the bar. "Augustine!"

Ari's head swivels towards them, her eyes narrowing in suspicion for the briefest moment before she plasters on an elated smile.

"Hello!" she calls back as she strides towards them. She and Perry exchange a quick hug, and then, continuing Maren's horror, she pulls up a bar stool from a neighboring table. "Maren! Gods above and below, are you stalking me?"

"No," Maren says, pursing her lips, because she can't think of anything she'd be less likely to do.

"Could have fooled me," Ari says with a small shrug. Then, catching the eye of a passing waiter, she throws her hands wide, her smile just as encompassing. "Drinks! Drinks on me, let's get something good."

"We're not getting drunk at a salon," Perry sighs. It rings as something that he's said before.

"You might not be, but I am," Ari says, accepting the drink menu that the waiter has handed her. "Maren, what do you say? Get drunk and come home with me?"

Ari is staring at her like she's trying to read the very things written on Maren's soul. The frivolity in her voice isn't matched by the storm in her eyes.

"No," Maren manages to get out. *Absolutely not on your or my fucking life.*

"You're both boring," Ari says, although there's no heat in it. She states it as a fact, not an insult. "I'm going to go order something from the bar."

"I'm so sorry about her," Perry says the minute that Ari's out of earshot, voice low. "She grows on you, I promise."

"No she doesn't," Maren says.

"I like her," Perry says with a shrug. "And Phaedra has me keep an eye on her."

"You and Phaedra are pretty close."

Perry gives her the strangest look, confusion written across his features.

"Uh, well… yeah," he says finally, the words halting and just as perplexed as his face looks. Maren gets the feeling that she's missing something, that she's overlooked something obvious, and she frowns. It's not a feeling she likes, and it sours her stomach.

"Forgot my wallet!" Ari has returned to the table, where

she's now digging around her giant bag for the aforementioned item. Her words are a sudden crack of sound, her words burnished and bright.

"You'd forget your head," Perry says.

"Yeah, yeah, I know. Luckily–" Ari points to her head "–it's attached."

"Truly, a blessing for us all," Perry deadpans. Ari flicks him good naturedly in the forehead before turning on her heel.

"Ow," Perry mutters, rubbing at the spot. "What a child. I can't believe anyone trusts her with any kind of responsibility. Like, major responsibility."

Maren stares after her, hands knit in her lap, body still.

"I don't know how she got like this, Phaedra's so sensible. And their parents are, too. Or… were. Are. Both," Perry says.

The mention of the Augustines shakes something loose from the back of Maren's mind.

"What was the end result of that investigation?" She asks, turning back towards Perry. She hadn't followed up, had taken him at his word that their interests were aligned.

"Mr. Augustine's?" A nod from Maren. "Nothing. We had zero evidence of anything — absolutely no forced entry, all of your people alibied out, as did Phaedra and Ari. All that we had was a destroyed security video. Which, while suspicious, can't prove anything on its own. Case closed. As you wanted."

"But the video — you cleaned it up. And what was on it…"

"Still case closed. I thought you of all people would be relieved by that."

"There are just a lot of awful questions left."

"Unfortunately," Perry says, leaning back in his chair, "I didn't have any say in the indeed very unexplained manner. I was pulled off the case, and they closed in. No one wanted to bring up the weird facts with the wider force. We get brought in when shit gets weird, to insulate everyone else."

"So it just stays in limbo like that?" Maren asks.

"Yeah. A lot of our cases do, when things defy explanation and we can't make any arrests," Perry says.

"What if someone were to try to reopen it?"

"Not a chance."

"I hope you're right," Maren says.

"I wouldn't worry about it. We were told to stop poking at it, so we did," Perry says, with one of his patented shrugs.

Maren hopes to all the gods and goddesses that no one else will try to poke at it either. She hates that they don't have answers, but if it keeps her House open and besmirched, she'll take it.

Even with the wards and catches that they'd set up in the House, sometimes Maren finds herself checking over her shoulder, afraid that something — or someone — is lurking behind her, a dead figure that wants to take her down with it.

She lets a small shiver ripple down her body at the thought, starting in her jaw and shoulders. She shakes it away, squeezing her hands tightly together for a moment, letting the energy release between her palms.

"So," Maren says finally, keen to change the subject. "What's up next?"

"Well, I've actually been thinking about that," Perry says. "I've been asking the people who know the most about what might be up with you, and so far I haven't gotten much, but someone did suggest a cleansing ritual."

"Ok, how do we do that?" Maren asks, leaning closer to the table.

"That, I'm still figuring out. They're used for spaces, not people. So we may have to do some adaptation," Perry says.

Ari returns before Maren can say anything further, double-fisting some very fruity-looking drinks.

"Ari, we're here for a reason," Perry says with a heavy sigh.

"Yeah," Ari says, and for a second, something drops away from her face. Her eyes shine hard like twin stars, her mouth a slash of red lipstick. "So am I."

She holds Maren's gaze for a heartbeat too long, those muddy eyes sharp enough to cut. Then, just as quickly as it had come the expression vanishes, and it's replaced with an eyebrow and a quirked-up smile.

Outside, beyond the windows in the dark of the city, the first snow of the season starts to fall.

—

The only thing dryer than the salt cellar in the summer is the salt cellar in the winter. Maren swears she can feel her lips chapping and the heels of her hands cracking after spending just a few minutes in the attic room.

She checks out a few of the current attic denizens, all in various states of mummification. She brushes the salt aside with careful strokes of the rough brush, revealing a hand here, a hip there, the upper quadrant of a head. Each one smells of arrested decay, sickly and cloying, overlaid with

124

the pine and tar of the coffins, the sharp tang of the salt, and the various oils with which the dead are anointed. It's all known and comforting — the smell, the salt, her own dry skin.

Mrs. Colvard is the last one to be checked on. When Maren brushes some of the salt away from her brow, she finds a fully-desiccated corpse. According to photos her family had provided, Mrs. Colvard was a round-faced woman in life, cheeks high and full and lips plump, even in her old age. Maren has no doubt in her mind that a fair bit of surgical intervention was employed to keep her looking younger. However, now in death her carefully-lifted cheeks and cupid-bowed lips have given way to little more than a dry husk. Her cheeks are gaunt, her lips flat and thin. Maren supposes that Mrs. Colvard would approve of how sharp her cheekbones and the bridge of her nose have gotten, but perhaps that's it. Maren reaches down with a gloved hand to carefully scoot a few rough grains of natron away from where they've come to rest against the edge of Mrs. Colvard's nose. Her skin is leathery, darkened by salt and oils and desiccation, and Maren knows that she'll be ready for her final journey soon.

A knock on the door announces Henry's arrival. Maren looks up to find that he's stuck his head in through as narrow a gap as possible, not wanting to upset the climatic equilibrium that keeps their clients carefully drying.

"Just about wrapped up?" Henry asks.

"Yeah, I can be done," Maren says, rising to standing on slightly tight and sore knees. Kneeling has gotten a bit harder in the last couple of years, in a way that makes Maren know that her own body is starting to lose its inexorable battle with time. It's not something she likes to think about, but she can't outrun the fact that her age has started with a three for a couple of years now.

Stripping off her gloves and hanging the brush back by its hook on the door, she follows Henry down a floor. He clearly wants to talk about something, Maren can read it in the hard set of his shoulders. Also, he's sent Oscar and Tad home, which means all prying, eavesdropping ears have been removed from the premise.

Expecting Henry to show them both into Maren's office, she's thrown for a loop when Henry holds open the door to the bullpen instead. The large front room has been the home to various administrative staff and apprentices over the years. When Maren had first started she'd had a small desk under the window in this very room, where Oscar sits now.

Henry holds court on one side of the wide room, his desk set up in front of the fireplace so that it can frame him like an especially lively painting when he has visitors. Two plush chairs that sit further into the room beyond the edge of his desk provide a perfect view of the whole picture. For a Mortuary House in a historical brownstone, the three denizens of the room have made the whole place rather warm and friendly, each side in a different way. Tad and Oscar's portion of the room, mostly carefully hidden behind a few rolling cubicle walls and hemmed in by wide, low filing cabinets covered in knick-knacks and house plants, is a riot of color, paper, and character.

The carefully positioned furniture on the fireplace side of the room is all plush, rendered in dark, but gentle, colors. Henry's desk is sparsely populated with personality, but only in a way that makes it seems respectful, not antiseptic — a few framed photos of his family, a matte black mug with an acceptable number of matching pens, his leather glasses case. Tall pillar candles in a soothing off-white dominate the brick inlay in the fireplace, cleanly unlit, as if waiting for the perfect match and the perfect hand.

It's when Henry goes for the bottom drawer of his desk that Maren realizes what's happening. Sure enough, as she drops into one of the visitor chairs, Henry pops back up with a bottle of tequila and two shot glasses. The clear glass catches the yellow light of his desk lamp, throwing shards and sparkles across the leather blotter.

"I can't believe I forgot," Maren says.

"It's because you've got forty-eight hours," Henry says. "But I thought I'd get you before, instead of after."

"Prudent," Maren says.

The cork comes free of the bottle with a round pop in the quiet of the room. Maren watches, as raptly as if they were assisting in a funeral, as Henry pours out two rather generous shots.

She accepts the cool glass he holds it out to her, staring down into the liquid with a deep sigh.

"*Prosit*," Henry says, raising his own, and Maren mirrors it, like they've done more than half a dozen times before.

The tequila is the good shit — Henry sees no reason to skimp on fine alcohol — but it still burns a bit going down. Maren's gotten used to it, used to the cut of it in her throat, the warmth in her stomach, the instant looseness of her shoulders that comes from her being a giant lightweight.

That first year, it had not been the good shit. It had been left over from some funeral at some point, something that a mourner had brought and then forgotten. The whole thing

127

had been improv, from the moment it started, because Henry was just trying to be helpful and Maren was being incredibly, unendingly morose in a way that she's learned to publicly smooth over as she's aged.

Giving a little sniff at the burn of booze and then swiping the back of her hand over her mouth, Maren deposits the glass rim-down on the desktop. It clinks cleanly on the surface, a nice finality that will never be quite final enough.

"I'm glad you forgot, I suppose," Henry says, turning his own glass upside down with a concentrated furrow between his brows. "Or is it just because I was early?"

"It's because you're early," Maren says. "I don't really forget it, unfortunately."

"No, I don't suppose you would," Henry says.

He can only suppose, because as far as Maren is aware, Henry has never lost someone particularly close to him. Maybe all the grandparents he ever had, he's old enough that they'd have to be fairly ancient, but his parents are both still alive. His husband's parents are even both still upright and walking as well, and Maren has never heard about any kind of death in the family.

They all come to have a certain understanding of death after working in this House, but it's just that — an understanding. Maren did not gain an understanding of death from her mother's passing. She still hasn't, all these years later. There's nothing to be *understood* about it. It's too messy, and Maren is too close. The dead that pass through these halls are not their dead, and therefore a bit cleaner, a bit tidier. Easy, even, although Maren hesitates to ever use the word easy in relation to anyone's death.

Her mother had been ripped from her life in a way that

can never be recreated by any of their clients.

"It's ok though," Maren says with a shrug. She leans back into the chair, letting her body sink into it. "It was a long time ago."

"You say that every year," Henry says, cracking a grin.

"And every year, you pour us tequila shots," Maren says with her own answering smile. "We're very good at ritual."

"I suppose we are," Henry says. "What do you think, should I renounce this vocation and decide to live the priestly life of a *hem*?"

He says this with a carefully raised dark eyebrow, and Maren can't help the brief snort of laughter that it tugs out of her.

"You'd make a miserable *hem*," she says. She means it. Henry's no priest, and they both know it.

"Gods, the absolute worst," Henry says. "Thank the gods, honestly. I don't know how anyone lives that life. Well, except maybe Thais. She's very good at all of those peculiars."

Thais is a strange example of a *hemet*. Every other priest or priestess devoted to Serapis and his underworld Maren has met has been either incredibly fanatical about death — which is always a strange look on anyone — or a dour geriatric who seems to have one foot in the grave themselves. Thais, in the prime of her life, with her beautifully tailored clothes and trendy, giant jewelry, is a bit of an enigma by comparison.

"Thais would be good at any life she chose," Maren says, interlocking her fingers over her stomach, feeling the easy rise and fall of her breath.

"She would be," Henry says. "If only we could all know

129

what that's like."

"I think we did ok," Maren says.

"I suppose," Henry says. He leans forward onto his desk, his forearms braced, and looks so seriously at Maren that she's momentarily afraid that he's lured her here not to get her drunk in remembrance of her long dead mother, but to reprimand her. His glasses catch the light, his eyes luminously dark behind them, the pale frames riding the top of his thin nose.

"Henry?" Maren asks. He licks his lips, takes a hard swallow that looks like it might have hurt.

It's fear. There is fear in his eyes, something alien. Henry doesn't scare, he doesn't startle, he's not one to ever say that he's afraid of anything. Now though, she's seen that look in his eyes in as many times in two months. The first time, a very wealthy man had been mysteriously cremated. Maren is not afraid of what Henry's going to say. No, she's downright terrified.

She keeps her face neutral, meeting his gaze. She doesn't want to scare him out of spilling whatever words he's about to.

"Can I confide something in you?" He asks. His voice has dropped a register, a quiet rasp, and Maren has to scoot forward in the chair, tipping towards the desk to catch the edges of his words.

"Always," Maren says, frowning.

Henry scoots around in his own chair for a moment, looks down at his hands, and then back up at Maren.

"It cannot leave this room," Henry says. Maren nods mutely, if only because her mind has immediately gone into overdrive, sprinting through a million possibilities that may have either befallen the House, Henry, or both.

They're all over-reactive and awful.

Henry takes a deep breath. Clutches his hands together tightly, palm to palm, as if in supplication.

"This whole thing with Mr. Augustine has stuck with me," he says. "I know you said the police closed the case, but Gods — the whole thing is so *strange*. It's so unnatural. I hate it. I can't believe that they'd look at an accidental cremation with no perpetrator, where the footage had been vandalized and say *oh yes, sure, that's normal*. Case closed. That's alarmingly shoddy, even for the NYPD."

Maren does not speak. Henry takes this as enough of a sign to continue plowing onwards.

"I did some research." A breath, a break, silence loud enough that Maren can't even hear her own heartbeat in her ears, even though she knows her blood is roaring. "Into the security tape. I discovered that kind of data corruption happens from one source only. But... it's something that shouldn't exist."

*Necromancy.* The word is on Maren's tongue before she can stop it, her lips going as far as to start to round out the first syllable of the word. Henry takes this for confusion, Maren's mouth open in a soft sound.

"What do you know about death magic?" Henry asks.

"Necromancy." The word finally leaves Maren's body. Henry bobs his head in a nod, some of his hair flopping down over his forehead with the motion.

"Yes, exactly. I know — I know *so well* — that it's a forbidden domain and it's unholy, and I can't believe I even looked into it. But I wanted to know."

"You're not a believer."

"In necromancy?"

131

"In the faith."

"No," Henry shakes his head. He and Maren are similar in that way, fervent in their devotion to their clients' religion, to their mourning. It's cultural, ingrained in the very stitches and weaves of their lives until it would be unthinkable to turn their backs on it fully. But Maren would be shocked to find an underworld existed or that gods had ever walked this earth, and she knows Henry agrees.

"Then why call it unholy?" Maren asks.

"Because we work here. We serve Serapis, as much as Thais does. If someone brought necromancy into this house…"

He leaves something unspoken, although Maren isn't quite sure what. He shakes his head after a moment, as if at himself, and sits back into his chair heavily, letting his arms drop and hang. They're quiet for a stretch, long enough that one, two cars pass by on the wet street outside.

"I had similar misgivings," Maren says at long last, and her voice is smaller than it usually is.

"Ok," Henry says in a long breath, released in relief. "Ok. That's good. What are we going to do?"

Maren wants to have an answer so badly, not only for Henry, but for herself. But she feels like even though the process of fixing this all has at least started, it hasn't gotten particularly far.

"I don't know," she says honestly, and Henry looks grave.

# CHAPTER 10
## *Evergreen and Wheat*

Maren follows her father up the swell of the hillside, her jacket buttoned up tight and her chin dipped into her scarf. The road they'd just turned off of has been plowed, but now they're crunching through a few inches of icy, days old snow. It blankets the gray world surrounding them — the dying grass, the stone edifices, the skeletal trees. The only green comes in the form of the evergreen trees lining the road. Someone, an age or more ago, had decided that stone pines were needed in every possibly funerary space, as if the plain blacktop they'd just left was the Appian Way itself.

Even though Anhur is something of a windbreak ahead of her, Maren's cheeks and nose still sting in the cold. The wind whipping off the bay is cruel and sharp, even though the sky overhead is a pleasant semi-overcast. Her throat is raw, and her breath comes in hard, short jags.

Fiona brings up the rear of their solemn procession, carrying a small sheaf of wheat and pine sprigs. After Maren's mother had died, pre-Fiona, Anhur had always done the carrying. Fiona had offered her first year married to Anhur, and that was that. Maren didn't mind, she's always been glad that Fiona has cared enough to want to be included in the funerary traditions of a family who are honoring her direct predecessor.

They pass small mortuary temples, holding anywhere from two to a dozen mummies, past obelisks bearing the names of the dead on plinths of marble, granite, nondescript gray stone, the named spirits buried in vaults below them. There's always an ongoing debate over the proper way to do it — below ground, to be returned to the earth, closer to Duat, or above ground, so that technically the body is no longer *in* the city proper. One of the rare cases where the two distinct halves of their syncretism come into direct clash. It seems to mostly just break down to personal preference now. No city government has dared step into that mess in a century or more; the only rule these days is to just make sure the body makes it into a designated cemetery.

Selene Hatt is buried at the base of an old oak that spreads its boughs far over the ground it grows through. In the summer the shade afforded by it is cool and soothing. In the dead of winter, the skeletal gray-brown arms seem spidery and brittle. There are seven graves in total around the base of the tree, all in clean gray stone, the tops of the sarcophagi still holding their carvings and artistry despite the elements. The obelisks at the foot of each one are short and small, nothing too gauche, and perfectly suited to the low hanging spread of the tree. Three sides have epitaphs in English. The fourth bears only cartouches.

This was the first proper place that Maren had ever seen hieroglyphics. There was no reason that anyone outside of the mortuary or religious world really needed to come into contact with the ancient writing. It wasn't something that Maren thought of, until they'd buried her mother. It hadn't been her first funeral — she'd lost a grandmother when she was a kid — but certainly the first she remembered.

She'd learned how *Hatt* was written that day. It was carved into every single one of the stone pillars standing guard at the feet of the graves. Relatives of hers on her mother's side, most of them long dead. The last grave that had been open was supposed to be for an elderly aunt, but she'd abdicated the space graciously when Selene had died before anyone had expected her to.

Maren presses her gloved thumb into the frigid chill of the carved stone, tracing the familiar shapes. A folded-over bolt of cloth, a stately lion, and rough peaks of water for Selene, and the blocky square of a house, a proud eagle, and a risen loaf of bread for Hatt. If Maren wanted to be buried here with this side of her family, in the new temple just slightly uphill from their current position, she wouldn't be a Hatt. She'd be a Nykara — a group otherwise buried clear on the other side of Staten Island in a different cemetery that they rarely visit. Anhur's parents, gone for three and eleven years, had decided to die and enter the eternal life of Duat in Florida, much to Anhur's chagrin. He had vehemently promised one night in the kitchen, the smells of an enjoyable dinner still lingering, that he wouldn't retire to Florida. He'd stay here, and let death claim him in the city in which he's lived his whole life.

It was a very Anhur thing to proclaim. Fiona had just patted his hand and said *that sounds perfect*, which was true. Perfect for Anhur. Maren can't imagine living in this cold, long-blocked city, full of stairs in walk ups and subway stations, with creaky joints and an aging mind. Perhaps she'll retire somewhere warm one day.

For now though, the three of them stand in the biting cold on either side of Selene's grave, and look down onto the frozen, stone face of Maren's mother. She'd been quite pretty, a petite woman with bird bones and large eyes, and the stone carver had gotten all those parts right — the

135

delicate upturn of her nose, the dainty line of her brow, the pointed chin and wide eyes, now forever unblinking. It's not quite as gracile as the portrait mask that lies below the stone lid, permanently entombed with the body it rests on, but sarcophagus reliefs never are.

It takes them a moment to clear the snow out of the divot where her carved hands rest over her torso. Once the space is clear of crystallized drifts of snow, Fiona passes the pine and wheat around, so that they all have a bit.

"Everyone ready?" Anhur asks. It's the first thing that's been spoken since they piled out of the car to tread this well-worn path up to Selene's grave site.

"Yep," Fiona says, her round cheeks rather red in the cold.

"Right," Anhur says, and then takes a deep breath before dropping into prayer. "An offering given to Serapis, the great god, the Lord of Duat, that he may be given an invocation of pine and wheat, and all pure and good things upon which he lives. For the spirit of Selene, beloved of the gathered."

It's the same prayer as every year. Even after they started including Fiona, who of course could never love a woman she had never known.

One by one, they slip golden and brown stems through the small holder, so that the stone relief of Selene holds them tightly. It's a small, simple gesture, out here in the frozen cemetery, but not too small to stop doing. So they come every year to mark the date of her death, making this pilgrimage to the oak tree that stands sentry over Selene and her family.

—

They take the ferry home, the deep green boat slicing cleanly through calm waters, returning them from the island of the dead to the city of the living. Technically, there are people who live on Staten Island, but their whole lives revolve around the death industry in ways that not even Maren's quite does. To live and work within the bounds of a necropolis is not Maren's idea of an enjoyable life.

The passenger decks are not particularly crowded on a blustery winter Sunday, so after they stash the car down below the three of them find a whole row of empty bench seats and take it over with abandon. Fiona is deep into some kind of bookkeeping paperwork for the bakery, and Anhur is grading papers, tapping out an even beat on his knee with his red pen.

This leaves Maren to put her back to the window, and, in a flagrant violation of ferry rules that she's been flagrantly violating since she was a teenager, heft her booted feet up onto the seats. At some point in her early twenties, when the rebellious edges of teenager brain had finally matured, she'd felt bad about doing it, but now her attitude about feet on seats when there's plenty of space for everyone has swung back around to petulant. Not that she's of the mind that she, a full ass adult, really has it within her to be *petulant*. Perhaps lazy would be a better way to describe her attitude towards the feet/seat rule.

Neither Anhur nor Fiona have ever chided her about it, and they're certainly not going to start now, so Maren hunkers down against the cold wall of windows, the bay at her back, and pulls her phone out to wade through emails and updates. It's nothing much, as she'd done this exact same thing a scant few hours ago when they'd made their journey west. Really, it's a distraction to ease her back into real life, away from the time and space of the borough that belongs to the dead. Away from the pain of this day, as in every year before it.

"Maren," Anhur says.

Maren looks up at him as if surfacing from sleep, her eyes glazed over from the emails.

"Yeah?" She asks. Her voice is a bit rough from the cold.

"How are you doing?"

She lets her body swivel on the smooth plastic of the seat, dropping her feet to the floor so that she can face Anhur. He's tucked his pen behind his ear, a bright splotch of red in a low-contrast sea. Her father has always seemed a bit gray to her — not in personality, or in spirit, but in coloring. His skin doesn't quite have the warmth of hers, nor do his gray eyes, or his salt and pepper hair. Maren's long-limbed height comes from Anhur, and her smile and nose, but otherwise her color is all from the soft amber that Selene had possessed. Maren remembers her being warm like the sun, as if some of the rays were trapped beneath her skin, behind her eyes, shot through her hair.

Bracing her arms on her knees, she gives him a half smile. It's not a day for full smiles.

"Same as always," she says. Anhur puts his papers aside and comes to sit next to her. He pats the top of her hands in a slightly distracted way.

"We would have been married thirty-three years this year," Anhur says wistfully.

"Yeah," Maren says, letting out a low breath. It seems both too long and too short a time for her mother to have been dead, somehow.

"I appreciate you still coming out with us," Anhur says. "You don't have to."

"Yes, I do," Maren says, frowning. She can't imagine a world in which she wouldn't be standing by her mother's gravesite on this particular cold day every single year.

"You're very kind," Anhur says, and stands to return to his grading. Maren stares at him once he's ducked his head towards the printouts again, and wonders when her father started sounding so old, and so weary. Mr. Augustine had been around her father's age, and now he's dead. To think that her father is in any way old is a sobering thought, and it doesn't sit well with her.

As much as she protests when they dock in Manhattan, her father and Fiona decide to bother with driving her up the West Side Highway, dropping her directly at her door. Maybe she should have gone to dinner with them, but they'd done lunch, and now Maren just feels weary and chilled. She wants to be alone.

This is of course why there is a person huddled just inside the vestibule to her building, standing hunched in the cold, coiled like a spring that needs defrosting.

"No," Maren says as she opens the door, and she has never meant the word more in her life. "I love you, but *no*."

"You have no idea what I was going to ask," Henry says with a sniff. He looks like he's halfway to hypothermia already.

"You know it's–"

"I do."

They stand squared off for a moment, both with red-tipped noses and sheer stubbornness running through them. Henry, perhaps as he is the much colder of the two, wilts first.

"Tad and Oscar are around the corner at a diner," he says.

"Why didn't you just text me if you wanted to get dinner," Maren says, sighing heavily and reaching for the interior door.

"Because I knew you'd ignore it and not come," Henry says. "And you should come."

"Henry, I am so tired. I'm tired down to my bones. Let me have the evening, and we can all talk tomorrow morning."

"Here–" Henry strips a glove off with his teeth, baring them as he pulls his phone from his pocket. He fiddles with it for a second, frustration on his face, and then hands the phone to Maren. She has no idea what's going to be on the screen, but the minute it starts up, she knows *exactly* what it is.

Perry's somewhat-cleaned up security video from the greenhouse is on the screen.

"How did you get this?" Maren asks, her voice a rush.

"I was sent it. We have no idea who from," Henry says. "I got everyone together, although it did then occur to me that it could absolutely be a fake, but then of course, someone would have to know the situation and go to the trouble of faking it–"

"It's not fake," Maren says, practically throwing the phone back at him. Her head is spinning, her skin crawling. It feels like her heart is trying to escape from behind the cage of her ribs, and she can't get a single breath in. "I — I have to go–"

"Maren!" Henry says, looking alarmed, right before she slams the door in his face, rushing up the stairs and refusing to look back.

—

Maren doesn't sleep. She drifts, in and out, bouncing between a state of half-waking and one of nightmare haze. Every time she drifts back to something resembling consciousness her heart tumbles wildly into a staccato rhythm, fast and uneven enough to trigger a panic that just makes it worse until the nightmares snatch her again. In them, she sees Mr. Augustine over and over again, in her apartment, in the House, on the street, lurching and decaying and horrible.

Miu, who has never met a battle for a soft spot to sleep in that she is not determined to win, resolutely stays on the bed through the night. Maren is stupidly glad for it, because the comforting fluff and rumbled purring that Miu brings to the table are the only things that feel safe to Maren as she struggles for breath.

The next night is the same. And the one after that. And again and again and again. Every night, as the dark closes in, she finds herself seized with buzzing fear. Her bed has become hostile territory, and what little sleep she does manage is awful at best.

She exists on coffee and tea and lets Tad and Oscar do more and more of the cutting as her hands shake progressively more each day.

"I am going to give something to you, and you are not going to complain," Henry says late one day, appearing in the door to her office. He places two items on her desk — a cup of coffee, and a pill bottle. "Melatonin and decaf."

"Henry, I'm–" Maren says.

"If you say *fine* I'm going to trocar the decaf into you," Henry says rather nonchalantly.

"That's not even *remotely* how trocars work," Maren says in horror as her tired, jumpy brain swirls through those grisly logistics.

"I am highly resourceful," Henry says, and gives her a pat on the shoulder.

He pauses in the door, giving her a rueful glance.

"Is this... because of what I showed you?" Henry asks. "The video?"

"Yes," Maren says. A gross oversimplification but not a lie, particularly.

"I'm sorry," Henry says, and she knows he means it, deeply, and she tries to offer him the best lopsided smile she can conjure up in her present state.

Maren drinks the decaf and takes the melatonin. It's evidently enough, because she crashes at nine p.m. and sleeps for ten hours, which is something she hasn't done since she was in college. Unfortunately, she still feels like fatigued shit when she wakes up, this time with the addition of a sleep hangover. There's no winning when she's running on this much of a sleep deficit.

The only good news on the icy horizon is that there's a visiting speaker coming to the salon this weekend, some ancient little Greek man who's evidently one of the foremost authorities on waking the dead — not just spirits, but actual bodies. Maren is, understandably, intrigued.

She can make it to the weekend, she's certain. All she has to do is stay upright and not fall asleep on the train and accidentally end up at the end of the line.

# CHAPTER 11
## *Father Cosmatos*

Perry, begging a previous engagement, announces via text that he can't come a mere hour before that weekend's salon. Maybe if this was a month ago, Maren wouldn't have gone. She would have stayed home, put her feet up, candles blazing and Miu on her lap, and lived her life.

But now, in this present, Maren zips up her boots and tromps out into three inches of rapidly piling up snow, her scarf pulled high and her hood pulled low. It's a fat, fluffy snow, and it's accumulating fast. It deadens the noises and smells of the city, making everything seem strangely disconnected. Between the snow and the weekend the streets are mostly quiet, aside from the occasional dog owner.

The subway is wet and half-empty. Maren leans on a pole at the far end of the carriage, eyeing an advertisement on the other side of the car. Thanks to the sickly yellow cast of the light on the old train, the image of a smiling doctor and child emblazoned with *Have you gotten your flu shot yet?* looks downright sinister.

As bars are much harder to get a hold of for private events on a Saturday night, this is the first gathering that Maren's attended that's at someone's apartment. She's not sure who the benefactor is for tonight, but when the door opens Maren instantly knows they're rich as shit. The Soho loft is massive, full of a weirdly eclectic collection of furniture that all seems over-sized and lived in. A

143

hammock has been strung between two pillars in the wide-open space, and the kitchen, which runs along one bricked wall, has bright red cabinets and a white stove that's gone past vintage into straight up antique. The art is just as mismatched as the furniture, everything from movie posters to strange statues to paintings that seem like they've been pilfered from a museum. No one seems to be paying the odd art much mind, however. Small groups of people are talking and drinking like always, low music on in the background somewhere. Aside from the domestic setting, it's exactly the same as every other one of these Maren has been to.

Carefully unwinding and unwrapping herself from her damp layers, she leaves them hanging to dry by the door. Stuffing her hands into her pockets, Maren suddenly realizes that she's going to have to talk to someone at this thing, considering her usual human shield is MIA. She can deal with that. She talks to people every day. She's good at it.

Granted, it's not necromancers she's normally chatting up.

Drinks have been lined up on the kitchen island like a phalanx guarding the ancient stove. Maren eyes them with a wariness — they're all chilled items, beer and soda, bottled and canned things that are so cold they're sweating condensation in the heated warmth of the apartment.

"The La Croix can't hurt you," someone says. Maren lets her gaze slide sideways and finds Ari leaning against the island a few feet away.

"Perry told me once that you're always where you're least expected." *Or wanted.*

"Did he?" Ari sounds delighted by this. "I think I'm

precisely where I need to be right now."

"Protecting me from the La Croix?"

"Welcoming you into my home."

Ah. Rich as shit, indeed. Maren had been right on the mark.

"Your stove is a relic," Maren says in response. "It belongs in a museum. It could light the whole building up."

"It's a recreation, but thanks for the misplaced concern," Ari answers with a cut grin. "Speaking of, why don't I heat something up for you?"

"I'm not interested in being coddled, Ari," Maren says, sighing.

"I'm not coddling you. I'm keeping you from combusting cans of perfectly acceptable drinks with your mind. Tea or coffee?"

"Tea would be lovely, please," Maren says in a tone normally reserved for such phrases as *bite me* or *go take a long walk off a short pier*.

"Any particular kind?"

"Dealer's choice."

Perhaps leaving this choice up to Ari is a horrible idea, but Maren can't make her brain work much past the idea of *warm* at the moment. She's so sick of being cold. There's been a pervasive chill deep in her body for a while now, no matter how much she tries to purge it from her system. It squeezes her chest every hour of the day, rooted and suffocating.

Maren slips into one of the chairs at the island, leaning over the butcher block top and bracing her weight on her forearms. Watching Ari putz around the kitchen is a strange picture, domestic and simple, such a far cry from the Ari of Maren's memory. Maren doesn't even know how much of her internal narration regarding her time with Ari is true anymore, most of it clouded in a fog of college and alcohol and dark spaces.

They'd met at, of all things, a toga party. Maren had never really understood the point of them. But no self-respecting group of college kids would ever let an excuse to do keg stands go by without seizing the day. She'd been to a few before, dragged by various friends, and she'd gone because she was trying to do college properly. It was nothing less than a minor miracle that her father and Fiona had even had the cash to not only send her to a college her dad didn't work at, but also let her live on campus. Her whole senior year of high school she'd resigned herself to being a commuter student, struggling from Brooklyn to Manhattan and back every day. She'd never quite gotten over the relief of that reality not coming to pass, and so she'd jumped into the college experience with both feet, toes pointed and eyes wide.

Maren had been midway through her second year. She had a pleasant buzz going. She'd shown up in jeans and a t-shirt, so someone had slung a bed sheet around her shoulders, laughing drunkenly before vanishing into the undulating mass of partying bodies. The apartment was cramped and tiny, fairy lights strung up with prayer flags around the windows and doors. It gave the whole thing a slightly supernatural feel, like they'd left the world behind and had crossed into some new dimension, one where white-hot gold starbursts lit the path from the dance floor to the sticky corner with the keg.

Ari was holding court in the living room, standing on the couch and letting the music sway through her body. One leg was up on the arm of the sofa, and her toga — also

146

made of bedsheet — was slipping away from her tanned skin. Maren had stared, alcohol warm in her stomach and making her blood hum.

Her drunk, stupid, college brain had said *I want to lick that leg.*

Maren stumbled through the crowd and stared up at Ari in the dark. There were pops of light behind her head, and her hair seemed to be half void-black and half rich gold.

"I want to lick your leg," Maren had said out loud.

Ari had turned her face down to Maren. There were rings of light circling her irises, the curvature of her eyes showing the reflection of the fairy lights. She had been beautiful and unearthly in that space, a goddess from another age, a fury, a fate, a muse. For a long moment, whole stanzas of the thumping music, she hadn't said anything. Just when Maren was starting to feel like an utter idiot for saying an utterly idiotic thing, Ari had dropped to her knees on the couch, holding Maren's gaze with her own wild one.

The kiss had been sloppy. It wasn't particularly good. The fact that either of them remembered it at all had been a shock in the morning, and they'd laughed about it.

It was always like that, though, Ari always looking a little too sharp. Too lit by the sun, too edged, her head thrown back in laughter. She partied and ran hard, burning bright late into the night, a drink in each hand, and yet somehow, only with eyes for Maren. Ari had pulled her into her orbit, with her wide, intense eyes that were muddy enough that they'd go a dark almost-black in the low light of a bar or a club.

Maren remembers it all. Maybe she remembers it wrong. But she remembers the way Ari had danced against her, all tight dresses and high heels to boost her closer to Maren's height. She'd always worn her hair down when they were out at night, a thick sheet straight down her back, and she'd run her hands through it, the glint of her painted nails catching the light.

She remembers the way that Ari had kissed, alternating between playful darts and pecks that didn't seem like they were going to go anywhere, and all consuming, soul-sucking things. They'd been so hungry, starving for air, and hadn't stopped until their mouths had wandered from lips to necks to chests and lower.

Maren remembers Ari's skin against her own. The heat of her, the throb of her. The way they'd tangle themselves up in sheets and blankets, the way they'd knock things off tables, the way they'd upset the couch cushions.

They'd burned so horribly hot, so incredibly bright, until they were both blind to anything else that they could be.

And then with one phone call Ari had vanished from her life.

Maren hadn't seen Ari for a decade, her memories fading and twisting. They'd fallen out of contact. That had been it.

Now, Ari sets a steaming cup of tea in front of Maren, complete with a small bowl for the bag and a spoon to fish it out of the mug with. The tag that hangs out over the side of the mug says *Rooibos*. Her favorite.

Somehow, Ari has remembered.

"Thanks," Maren says, voice small, and she cups the mug in cold hands.

"Any time," Ari says with a shrug.

Maren just stares down into the deep red-brown of her

tea in response, the steam swirling up and around her face to banish the chill in the air.

—

Juni and Roger round people up like mother hens, carefully and skillfully shepherding everyone onto couches and into scattered dining chairs. As Maren tucks herself against the far edge of a couch, she finally finds herself with a clear view of their speaker.

He's an old man, far on in years that seem to weigh heavily on his shoulders. His olive skin sags, and he has a hawk's beak for a nose, of which Maren has an excellent view in profile from her vantage. He seems like any other old man whom she might pass without a second thought on the street, paying no mind to his wispy hair and protruding joints. Wholly average.

Except for the collar. He's dressed in crisp blacks, with one small square of white nestled at the base of his throat — the mark of a Catholic priest. Perhaps she should have known something was up when the usual gaggle of high schoolers had shown up in force tonight, all agog, despite the weather that must make getting to and from Jersey even more murderous than usual. They're now all clustered on and around the other sofa opposite Maren, sitting on the back and the arms and the deep pile rug at its feet.

Juni carefully wedges herself into the small spot next to Maren, patting her on the shoulder as she sits. The low, warm light of lamps and the candles scattered over various surfaces make her large glasses look plated and burnished, almost ancient.

"I didn't know the speaker was a priest," Maren says,

leaning close to Juni and keeping her voice low.

"Yes, yes," Juni says, bobbing her head. "Father Cosmatos is known in their Church for being quite the authority on exorcisms."

"What?" Maren murmurs.

Before Juni can answer, Roger clears his throat and the low rumble of chatter dies off, leaving a warm silence in the loft. With the snow outside socketing them in, even the sounds of Manhattan have been dulled down to almost nothing. Maren takes a deep breath, drawing her feet up under her body and letting herself sink back into the wide couch cushions, taking her tea with her.

"Thank you so much for braving the rather ghastly weather," Roger says, placing a wide, dark hand on the back of the chair above the weathered old man ensconced in it. "So that we can get you all home as soon as possible before we're all snowed in for the night and have to *really* take advantage of Ms. Augustine's hospitality, let's get right to it!"

Maren can't help the direction her gaze slips at the mention of Ari. She's placed herself on the low bookshelf that runs under the windows, seated cross-legged on a large, squishy pillow. A smile splits her face at the mention of her name, at the few low laughs that ripple through the assembled at the mention of them all bunking down on her floor due to weather. The expression makes her look young, an Ari from another age.

"Everyone, please welcome Father Cosmatos, Catholic priest and expert on waking and expelling the dead," Roger says. A smattering of applause follows this, and then the aged priest clears his throat, lets out a croupy cough, and begins.

150

"Thank you for having me," he says. His voice sounds like a road often, but well, traveled. Over top of it lays a heavy accent, stringing his words together. "As the esteemed Dr. Bisset said, I am Father Cosmatos, an ordained member of the Jesuit order. I'm here to discuss the dead, and the business of raising, removing, and quieting them. Not just in spirit, and I'm sure you're all quite adept at that, but also in body. Perhaps not even their original body."

He sounds like he's telling a story, speaking of demons and ghosts. Maren feels wrapped up in it, and she lazily reaches out to draw a long line down one of the fogged-up windows with her knuckle as she listens. It had never occurred to Maren that you could cram more than one soul into a body, especially creatures of an underworld that Maren has no knowledge of. There are certainly gods that no one wants to get on the wrong side of — no one is ever excited when Ammit is brought up — but demons, no. Still, the thought knocks around Maren's head lazily as the priest speaks into the silence of the loft. The idea that perhaps they didn't need to worry about Mr. Augustine's soul at all rises in her mind. His body could have been a shell, the bits and pieces of his soul decayed away, leaving room for someone else's to wedge itself inside his body and make it walk.

It's a comfortable thought. Maren wants to cling to it, but it's a hard thing. She knows that her priests believe that some parts of the soul stay with the body all the way through mummification, until they reach their final resting place and their mouths are opened one last time, allowing their spirit to recoalesce on the banks of the river in the underworld. They hadn't even gotten beneath Mr.

151

Augustine's skin, hadn't opened him up and started the process. His soul must have still been there — and therefore, gone into the retort as close to whole as a dead soul could be.

Maren takes another sip of tea. It's gone lukewarm, and she tucks herself a bit further into the cushions to force warmth against her skin, under it, inside her. Instead, she finds herself shivering and feeling like she may never be warm again.

—

After a brief Q&A, which mostly concerns how to banish the risen dead — honestly, the most helpful part of Father Cosmatos' whole speech, for Maren — people start trickling out. Perhaps on another night they would have stuck around instead, laughing and drinking. But with the snow piling up outside, people are in more of a hurry. They bundle back up, thank Ari profusely for offering to host, and then they're gone, out into the white, swirling flurry of the storm outside.

The last people there are the herd of Catholic school kids, gathered around the old priest with wide shining eyes and breathless questions and thoughts. They talk over each other like waves breaking on shore, and Father Cosmatos nods along, picking out pieces of conversation here and there to answer or engage with. Eventually though, Juni and Roger step in.

"You'll be sorry if the PATH stops running and you're stuck sleeping in a train station," Roger says gravely.

"And I'm sure you all have texts from your parents," Juni says pointedly, and more than one of the kids looks momentarily uncomfortable. Maren would put good money on none of them having told their parents exactly where they were going on this brumal night, instead going for broad strokes of *oh, just out with friends*. She'd be shocked if a single parent had given their kid permission to hop the train to Manhattan in the middle of a snowstorm.

The teenagers reluctantly start to scatter, departing in groups of twos and threes. Roger and Juni, with Father Cosmatos in tow, finally stand by the door, buttoning coats and pulling on boots. Maren hangs back with them, moving at the same sedate speed, wanting to talk to the trio a bit more, away from the prying ears of any other gathering attendees.

Especially the one currently playing host.

"Thank you so much, darling," Juni says, pecking a kiss to Ari's cheek as they slip out the door.

"Any time, you know my space is your space," Ari gushes, and Maren resists the urge to roll her eyes, instead plastering on a mask of pleasant neutrality for a quick goodbye. The minute they're out of the apartment and waiting for the elevator, she feels her body finally expel a breath she didn't realize she had been holding.

"Alright there, Maren?" Roger asks.

"Fine," Maren says out of habit, before shaking her head at herself. "I mean — I actually wanted to ask you guys a question, if you have a moment? I'll walk you to the subway, or a cab, however you're getting home."

"Of course!" Roger says. Father Cosmatos nods sagely in the background, looking even more stooped under his massive parka.

"Perfect," Maren says. "Great."

Awfully, she is suddenly acutely aware that she doesn't

exactly know how to broach this topic and all the absolute mess of divulging that comes with it. By the time the very slow-moving elevator has deposited them down two stories, the door rumbling closed behind them, she hasn't gotten any further than that *great*, even though the others have been making small talk.

Felix has been doing the heavy lifting on this. He's been asking around, talking to people, needling in on the hard questions. Or, she assumes he has been.

What if he hasn't been? She can't imagine why, but, still — she swallows hard as they open the door out into the polar vortex encapsulating the city.

"What was your question, Maren?" Juni asks kindly, taking her by the arm as they start their walk to the subway station at the end of the block.

"I uh… wanted to know about possession. Perhaps. I don't have a better word," Maren says, cold and full of dread, and fiddles around in her pockets for something to occupy her hands.

"By a demon?" Father Cosmatos asks, peering at her through the icy flurries that are making it hard to keep their eyes open.

"Shit," Maren says in answer, when she realizes her phone isn't in her coat pocket. Disengaging herself from Juni, she pats down her jeans, digs in her bag, the whole time fully aware of the others staring at her like she's lost her mind. Perhaps she has.

"Forgot something?" Juni asks helpfully.

"Yes," Maren admits morosely. "I think my phone is upstairs. I'm — I'm so sorry, I have to unfortunately go get it. I'll maybe send you an email?"

"We'll keep an eye out for it!" Roger assures her,

blinking frantically through the snowflakes falling against his ruddy cheeks.

"Amazing, thank you — and again, so sorry," Maren says as she starts to retrace her steps through the snow, her footprints already starting to fill in. Juni merrily waves her off, leaving Maren to hurry back through the swirling flakes to the vestibule of Ari's building. Her teeth chatter brutally, violent spasms of cold wracking her body. When she presses the call button for Ari's apartment, her hand shakes. A spike of panic tunnels into her mind, worry flooding her at the thought of how easily she found herself so incredibly chilled. She *has* to ask them, has to get to the bottom of this. Her body feels like it's sinking into a frozen pit and she's barely able to hold on.

"*Hello?*" A static-choked voice asks through the speaker.

"I forgot my phone," Maren says tersely.

"*Come on up, I'm cleaning, we'll find it,*" Ari says, right before the door clicks open. Swinging it back open feels like stepping backwards. She'd so much rather be standing on a subway platform with Juni and Roger right now, finally unburdening herself of the yawning horror currently weighing heavily on her.

Instead, when Ari opens the door, it takes Maren every ounce of self-control to not purse her lips or frown.

*Calm*, she reminds herself. She's very good at that, and she has zero interest in being in Ari's apartment alone with her for a second longer than it takes to find her phone. Getting in a verbal sparring match isn't something she currently has time for.

"Not in the kitchen," Ari says by way of greeting, stepping aside. "Where were you sitting?"

155

"I'll go look," Maren says, turning her back on Ari and doing a quick loop around the living room. Her phone isn't on the couch or the bookcases, so, with a deep sigh, she shoves a hand down into the cushions, rooting around and mentally bracing herself for strange hair and unidentified crumbs.

Instead, she comes up with her phone and the surprising knowledge that Ari keeps her couches quite clean.

"Cushions, always the culprit," Ari says, shaking her head from the far end of the sofa. "By the way, can I ask you a question?"

Maren would very much like to say *no* and sweep out of the apartment with a dramatic flare of her coat, but instead she pockets the phone and smiles anemically at Ari.

"Yes?"

"Are you feeling alright?" Ari asks. There's something detached but warm in her voice, almost clinically professional, and it makes Maren's mouth tug into a brief frown.

"Why the interest in my wellbeing?" Maren asks mildly.

"To be totally honest, because Phaedra told me about what happened the day of my father's funeral," Ari says.

Maren's veins turn to ice, her heart slowing and then suddenly lurching forward, uneven and unhappy. She swallows hard, trying to clear the lump in her throat.

"What specifically? It was a long day," Maren says. Her voice sounds pitiful and scratchy to her own ears.

"When you collapsed in the crematorium after they showed you the video of my reanimated father," Ari says.

It's so straightforward that Maren is momentarily thrown. She's been so used to broaching this particular

156

subject in milquetoast half-truths that hearing it laid out like this, so clean and sharp, nearly steals her breath all over again. She puts a hand out onto the couch to steady herself, not caring when she notices Ari discreetly cataloging the motion.

"You want to know if I'm feeling mentally well after seeing a zombie made of one of my clients?" Maren says tightly.

"Well, yes, but beyond that," Ari says. Her eyes are wide as always, but with a hard steeliness that is different from her usual look of wild disconnect.

Or maybe, she hasn't had that disconnected look since Maren last knew her.

Here, under the light, separated only by a loveseat, Maren can see bits of Ari that are new to her — lines at the corner of her eyes and between her brows, a seat of power behind her strong gaze that had not existed a decade ago.

"When did you grow up?" Maren asks before she can stop the words.

"Slowly, since the last time we saw each other," Ari says with a shrug. "Or, you know, since the last time before that morning."

*That* morning. A morning when everything in Maren's life had very suddenly gone horribly wrong. She hadn't known it would when she'd walked through the door, sodden and carrying a half-broken umbrella.

Ari doesn't drop her gaze. Doesn't try to see around her, as Maren has known her to do. Doesn't fidget, doesn't falter, doesn't toss off a clever comment. It's like now that they've seen each other a few times, that strange energy they'd both carried to each other has worn off, leaving just them.

157

"No," Maren says. "I'm not feeling alright."

"I figured," Ari says. She lets out a quick breath, scrubbing a hand across her face. "I would like to see if I can help."

"Why? You hate me," Maren says.

"No I don't," Ari says, frowning. "I mean, I think that the stick that was up your ass has been wedged in even further, but I could never hate you. I'm awful at hating people."

"I do not have a stick up my ass," Maren admonishes. "You really think that?"

"I know it," Ari says, and then follows it up with a scathing wink.

"You and I have very different opinions of me."

"That tracks, what with one of us being you and the other not. What do you think? Let me help?"

Maren takes a brief moment to look down at her feet, to wriggle her toes in her boots. They're still cold, and she finds them stiff and difficult to move.

"One chance," Maren says, looking back up at her.

Ari grins, that off-kilter smile she's always had, and Maren clings to it for no other reason that it's something she knows.

# CHAPTER 12
## *Milk and Honey*

Like so many New Yorkers, Ari lives in a railroad-narrow apartment, and the temperature and light level drop more and more as they venture down the long hall towards the back of the building.

"It's freezing in here," Maren murmurs, scarf still wrapped tightly around her neck.

"Sorry," Ari says with a loose shrug, a few paces ahead. "Old building, single-paned windows, the usual."

Maren assumes that they're heading towards the door at the far back of the hall, the darkness stretching around them, but instead Ari shoulders open a door to the right and vanishes into a room. Left momentarily thrown, Maren stands in the door, fidgeting with the end of her scarf and trying to reorient herself in the strange new space.

The bedroom is small but sparsely decorated — perfunctory at best and clearly a guest room. Ari grabs a decorative bowl off the low dresser before flipping on a table lamp. Even with the paltry amount of light, the room goes from dull blue-gray to warm amber and Maren lets out a breath, closing her eyes for a moment to reset herself.

"What's the bowl for?" Maren asks.

"This is a *psychí* bowl," Ari says, right before she kicks away the round rug at the foot of the bed, sending it slumping into a corner in a shower of dust. The motes drift lazily through the golden light, a sneeze threatening at the back of Maren's nose.

"Which is?" Maren prompts.

Ari holds the bowl up between her hands, spinning it a half turn and showing Maren that while the outside is a dull, brushed material of indeterminate color, the inside is a shining, hammered gold so brilliant it catches the light and contains it like flame.

She's seen a bowl like that fairly recently, unfortunately.

"Absolutely not," Maren says as her blood runs cold again. She's suddenly very aware of the difference between talking about necromancy and actually performing it.

"Ah," Ari says, staring down into the bowl. "You've seen Felix use one."

"Yes."

"This will be different, I promise," Ari says.

Maren doesn't trust that at all.

"Ari," she says, sighing deeply. "I'm leaving. I'm not doing this again."

"What happened the last time?" Ari asks. She's strangely serious.

There is no way for Maren to explain it, because she doesn't have that knowledge. Doesn't have the words to explain what had happened, what Felix had done and what had then occurred within her own body. All she can even attempt to replicate is how it had all made her feel, that horrible gnawing sense of dread and cold and horror that something was reaching up to pull her down.

That sense that's dogging her steps every day, closer and closer. A specter of something she can't even fully realize, it's so alien — a shard of soul, a segment of the *ka* of a man she never even met alive. But how it got there and what it's doing, or what Felix had done to accidentally

160

lodge it there, she can't explain beyond the very basic.

"Felix lit a fire in a bowl, and I ended up with an extra bit of soul in me," Maren says. "I think. After the talk tonight though, maybe I'm possessed."

"Well that's not good," Ari says mildly, and then stomps her foot twice.

There's something carved into the floorboards around her, Maren realizes, creeping closer.

It seems to be a thinly incised circle. The cutting in the wood has been cleanly done, and at four points around the circle brass caps have been placed. Maren squats down across the circle from Ari, brushing her fingers over one of the caps. It has a small handle in the top, which falls flush into a pocket in the metal. It takes a few tries to get her nail under it, but she finally does, and gives it a yank.

With a small scraping sound, it pulls loose and a brass canister roughly the size of a small drink can comes free. Stylized figures are carved all the way around in a style not unlike the type Maren has seen on ancient Greek pottery. It shows a parade of winged and helmeted figures in couples, carrying stiff bodies between them. With no start or end they're forever frozen in their parade, and Maren rolls it over in her hands a few times.

"Don't open that," Ari says, sitting down next to her. Maren hadn't even realized she had left, but now she's returned with small twigs piled in the golden bowl and a few extras clutched in her other hand.

"What's in it?" Maren asks.

"That's, what, north?" Ari says. "Milk. Or what was milk. If you open it, it's going to reek. And then some."

"There's old milk in here?" Maren asks, alarmed.

"Yeah, unfortunately," Ari says. "Luckily my mom

161

gifted these to me already full, so I've never had to open it. The other three are wine, blood, and honey, therefore less odorous."

Ari points to each one of the other three canisters as she names off their contents. Maren realizes them to be the same liquids that Felix had used in the crematorium.

With a level of care normally resolved for small animals or babies, Ari gently sets the bowl down in the middle of the circle. Maren slots the canister back in its spot, easing it back into the thick floorboards until the top is once again flush with the wood.

"Ok," Ari says, crouched over the bowl. She's brandishing a match in one hand and the box in the other. "I'm going to attempt to call up the *ka* stuck in you, if I can. If you'll let me."

Maren wants nothing less than that, knowing that it will mean pain that she's already had too much of for a single lifetime.

"Do I have another choice?" Maren asks. Doing this willingly feels like a betrayal.

"I don't know," Ari replies honestly, face open and stark. "Maybe nothing happens, and this is just your life now."

"My heart rate is never normal and I'm always cold," Maren says.

"Or, maybe something awful happens and you die," Ari finishes. "Trust me?"

The bitter laugh that bubbles out of Maren is unconscious and unbidden. She's not expecting it, but the sharp grin that Ari throws back seems a wholly appropriate response.

"No," Maren says. "I don't trust you. But I'll give you

162

one chance, because I'm not interested in dying."

"Sounds perfect," Ari says. "Don't move."

With a deep breath, Ari swipes the match across the striker strip and the cherry-red head springs to life with a sizzle and a popping hiss. She places it into the bowl and, after a moment, the twigs in the golden interior spring to life, a pleasing, warm flame in a perfectly normal orange-yellow color. As Ari takes the cardinal point across from Maren, she wonders if whatever Perry had been up to was just strange and had gone wrong, leading to the cold and horrible feeling that day in the greenhouse.

Ari slashes that thought down in its infancy the minute she opens her mouth.

"This is going to get bumpy and uncomfortable, just know that I've got you and you're safe," Ari says, and then, licking her lips and closing her eyes, "*anakaléo.*"

Instantly, the flame in the bowl burns half down, hunkering low and deep red, and starts to turn a metallic gold, liquid metal dancing to life where fire should be. The end of Maren's scarf and hair start to float, the air in the room rising in that strange way it had in the greenhouse, and then, in one sudden burst, the taste of a summer storm blooms on her tongue. Her nose twitches and she sucks in a deep breath, swallowing to get rid of the bloody, electric taste and finding no relief. It washes over her, a never-ending wave, and Maren feels like she slips below something, into a space that looks exactly the same as their own world but feels horribly different. Digging her fingers into her knees, Maren forces herself to keep her gaze on Ari, forces herself to keep breathing normally.

Ari's long hair has started to float on the invisible breeze, spreading out in a gracile static cloud. Her thin shirt

163

lifts away from her frame, showing a strip of the cool skin of her stomach, which Maren latches onto like a lifeline. Anything to combat the metallic taste spreading through her mouth and nose, the horrible growing feeling of *cold*.

The canisters rattle in their wooden homes, and Maren clenches her teeth so hard she's afraid she's in danger of cracking a molar.

Then, just in case everything wasn't terrible enough, something underneath her breastbone starts to *pull*. Not inward on herself, but out, like a hook under the bone and out through her skin, tethered to something unseen outside her body. Her breath runs ragged, and she finds herself huffing out puffs of steam in the rapidly cooling air, the hair on her arms standing up.

The hook gives another tug. In this cold room on this chilled floor, it's the worst feeling Maren has ever known in her life. She feels like she needs to move, needs to get away from the pressure, but both the thoughts of hunching over and leaning back seem an impossibility.

And then, across the circle from her, Ari opens her eyes.

Perry's eyes had been thin swirling gold, like metallic dust trying to cover as much of a pool as possible. When Maren meets Ari's eyes, all she sees is pure gold. It's a solid, perfect cast and cover of her sclera. She stares at Maren, unseeing and unblinking, her lips parted slightly. For a moment she is still, and then her face falls into a frown and she tilts her head to the side in one quick, inhuman motion.

"Huh," Ari says. It's more of a sound than a word, an exhalation, something in Ari's hindbrain doing the talking. The flame in the bowl reaches higher, the metal vessel clattering against the wood as it starts to rise a hairsbreadth

164

from the floor.

A memory slices into Maren like a shard of ice, the world around her swirling and changing with jagged edges and curling smoke.

Books around her, open and floating. The floor seems to breathe, rising and falling. The sun shining through the high window slants in and slashes across her face, making the world dance in a cacophony of broken color. She clutches at something that shines so brightly it seems to put the natural light to shame.

There are hands on her chest and she's falling backwards as her heart falls out of its rhythm, setting her chest on fire.

Pain crackles through her blood and she knows she is dying.

No — not her blood. Not her chest, nor her heart. Someone else's, someone whose place she shares in this strange dreamscape masquerading as one of her own memories.

Her own heart stutters. Her breathing is acidic within her lungs. She has to do something, to say something.

Only one word comes to her.

"*Ariadne*," Maren gasps, her teeth chattering. She feels like she's going to come apart at the seams, her skin flayed and her bones shattered, clutching at her chest in a desperate bid to make just one single feeling stop.

As if her name is a magic word, the unearthly wind and golden fire die as one, and the cladding over Ari's eyes vanishes. The bowl clangs back down to the floor and the canisters abruptly go silent. Maren lets out a heaving sob and then curls over in a hunch, gathering up as much of her body in as small a space as possible, her eyes squeezed

165

shut, aware of the chill and night around her all at once.

"Maren?" Ari asks. There's the sound of someone crawling across the ground, and then Ari's hands are on her, slowly peeling her up. Maren lets it happen because she has no idea how to make it not happen. "Open your eyes."

When she does, Maren is surprised to find her vision misted with tears. Raising one shaking hand to her face, she touches a cheek, and her fingertips come away wet. The world around her swims, and she looks up to meet Ari's gaze — wild with the unknown — right before she plunges into darkness.

—

Ari sits under the lamp in the corner, swaddled in a throw and seated on a leather armchair. Maren blinks at her, once, twice, trying to make sense of the scene. She licks her winter-chapped lips as everything slides into place cleanly. Ari's guest room. The summoning circle. The bed that the carving sits at the foot of is currently cradling her, bundling her up in bedding.

She takes a quick inventory of her body, a new and annoying habit she's developed the last few weeks — heartbeat still uneven and wan, fingertips and toes still cold and stiff. Reaching up to massage her jaw she finds it tender, either from clenching her teeth during the summoning or in her sleep.

At the movement, Ari looks up from the tablet in her blanket-covered lap. Maren watches as her eyes refocus from whatever she was looking at to Maren's form on the bed, her mind moving from one place to another.

"You're up," Ari says.

"Awake," Maren corrects, because she's not sure she can physically get up yet, her body wracked with cold, and muscles spun tight. "What time is it?"

"Almost midnight," Ari says.

"*Shit,*" Maren breathes. She forces herself to a sitting position as Ari watches, wrapping the covers firmly around her and fumbling for her phone where it's been helpfully left on the nightstand. "I have to get home."

"You're not going anywhere," Ari says.

Maren looks up at her, glaring from within her cocoon of sheets.

"You don't get to dictate that," Maren answers.

"I didn't mean it like that," Ari says, sighing and scrubbing a hand across her face. She sets her tablet and blanketry aside before crossing to and plopping down on the edge of the bed. Maren would love to move away from her, but she's not really in any shape to do so.

"I have to feed my cat," Maren says. She can picture Miu now, sadly walking the path between the front door and her food bowl, meowing at each terminus, waiting for Maren to get home so that she can look abjectly pitiful for the two minutes it takes Maren to feed her.

"You passed out, have an irregular heartbeat, and seemingly aren't breathing particularly well either. I'm extremely concerned about your wellbeing," Ari says.

"You don't know that," Maren says with a frown. In response Ari grabs Maren's hand and holds it up before Maren can yank it away.

Her pointer finger seems to be wearing a small plastic hat with a screen. Maren stares at it, brow furrowed. The little digital readout is displaying the numbers *89* and *91.*

167

It's the kind of thing she's seen in her doctor's office, once a year when she dutifully shows up for her annual checkup.

"I don't remember you having lung disease, so I'm going to go out on a limb here and say that O2 level is not great," Ari says pointedly.

"Why do you have this?" Maren asks.

"Work."

Strange, but not Maren's biggest problem right now.

"So you want to keep me here for observation, basically."

"Basically," Ari agrees, but then adds, not unkindly, "could you find someone to feed your cat?"

The older couple who live across the hall could certainly assist with that, if they're even still awake. Shooting them a quick half pleading, half apologetic text, she crosses her fingers for a response. She can't imagine having to haul herself back home in her current state.

"It hasn't hurt quite like that before," Maren admits, fiddling with the pulse reader. "And I haven't lost consciousness."

"It's getting worse?" Ari asks. Maren just nods in response, watching as Ari's lips twist into a grimace.

"Were you able to figure anything out?" Maren asks.

"Only that you're correct, and you do have a shard of someone else's soul in you. However, that raises two questions — how it happened, and how to get it out. I tried excising it out of you, but it wouldn't budge. Felt like trying to wrestle a splinter out of someone's foot using only your fingers."

"Ok, how do we fix that? Felix was asking around, but I don't think he'd gotten very far."

"He probably wasn't asking the right questions. Or at

least, not quite right. I love the knucklehead, but he's new to this. Anyone can do necromancy but that doesn't mean that they'll go about it correctly. I don't even have an answer for this yet."

Maren stares Ari down for a moment, searching her face for something and coming up empty handed.

"You love him," she says.

"I mean, sure." A pause, and then, with raised eyebrows, "Oh my Gods, not like that. I'm still gay."

"Sexuality is fluid," Maren points out primly.

"*Very* gay. I remain exceptionally gay. Extraordinarily, even."

"Congratulations, you are the most gay person to ever live."

"There's that sarcasm! You must be feeling better. But no, I love him like a brother — you really think if I had a sudden thirst for dude I'd go after my sister's fiancé?"

"Ah," Maren says, and instantly feels somewhat chagrined, but also relieved.

"You didn't know," Ari notes, tipping her head to the side. "They're not great at talking about it."

"Relationships can be difficult to talk about," Maren says.

"Yeah, they can be," Ari says, holding Maren's gaze.

Maren's phone vibrates in her clasped hands, drawing her attention away from Ari. On screen is a text from Maren's neighbors — an enthusiastic yes that they'll happily feed Miu.

"Ok, Miu taken care of," Maren says, letting out a long breath.

"You named your cat Miu?" Ari asks incredulously.

"I'm a traditionalist," Maren replies.

169

"Don't I know it," Ari says. "But that's good news. In addition to your present physical state, there's also that problem to contend with."

Raising a hand over Maren's shoulder, Ari points out the window behind them. Turning slowly, wincing when she becomes aware of the stiffness in her body all over again, Maren manages a glance at the outside world.

Every surface she can see is piled high with snow, and it's still coming down at an alarming rate. Below on the street trash cans and newspaper boxes are in danger of being swallowed whole underneath the fluffy onslaught, the flakes speeding and spinning through the pools of sickly yellow light provided by streetlamps and building sconces. The glass of the window itself is rimmed with heavy frost, all crystalline whorls and patterns. The world looks like something out of a storybook.

"Oh shit," Maren murmurs.

"They keep revising the totals, but we could have two feet by tomorrow morning," Ari says. "So unless you've got a death wish on two fronts, you should probably stay parked in this bed."

"Yeah," Maren says, nodding slowly. "Ok, yes, I'll stay."

Ari grins at her crookedly, and then pats the bed before getting up with a sigh, a stretch, and a crack of her back.

"I'll let you get some sleep," Ari says. "But if you start feeling like you're dying again, I'm down the hall to the right."

"I'll cry out dramatically," Maren assures, deadpan. "And, uh — thank you. I do appreciate it."

"Yeah, of course," Ari says, hovering in the doorway, as if it's nothing, and then she's gone, leaving Maren in the

170

dark of an unknown place alone, all over again.

—

Maren wakes to silence after a nightmare filled half-sleep. She opens her eyes to find herself staring at an unfamiliar beamed ceiling, and it throws her for a moment before she realizes where she is.

She sits up, scrubbing a hand over her face and up into her hair, trying to pull back some of the untamed wilderness going on in her curls. There's no telling how much of a mess she looks like for sure without checking, but she has a good enough idea that she doesn't want to go anywhere near a mirror.

Each movement pulls at muscles she didn't know she had, all of which are now sore. To the Gods, even her *bones* hurt. With a generous amount of wincing, she rolls her shoulders and neck out enough to carefully slide out of bed, testing each ankle as she goes. The minute her bare feet touch the ground she freezes up, sucking in a quick breath of shocked pain at the chill that shrieks through her body.

"Fuck," she murmurs, drawing her legs back up to her chest and perching on the edge of the bed, feeling like she's lost at sea. Around her, the room dawns muted and still, the light strange. Swallowing hard, she turns gently to take a look out the window.

The snow has stopped. The world, however, remains drawn in stark shades of white and gray. Snow is plastered to every conceivable surface, the sky arching above just as gray as the buildings on the ground. Plumes of early morning steam puff into the freezing air. Between the low

171

clouds, the thick snow, and the roiling steam, she almost feels inclined to check herself for earplugs — the ever-present sounds of Manhattan have been flipped off like a light switch.

When the door cracks open a moment later the sound is so clear and loud that it throws Maren for a second. Turning slowly, she has to reorient herself all over again.

Ari's poked her head into the room, her hair uncombed and piled on her crown in the messiest bun Maren has ever witnessed. Judging by the shadows smeared under her eyes and the puffiness of her eyelids, she seems to have slept about as well as Maren has.

"Oh good, you didn't die," Ari says, dry as the desert.

"Thanks for the concern. I'm sure you could have just resurrected me," Maren says dryly. "Do you have a pair of slippers I could borrow?"

"Sure, gimme a second," she says and vanishes once again.

Maren takes the Ari-free minute to swaddle herself in the duvet, pulling it free from where it's tucked into the foot board with a savage yank that makes her shoulders protest all over again.

"Just for the record, I can't resurrect you. Necromancy can kill but it can't give life, so don't do anything stupid," Ari says when she returns, dropping a pair of slippers on the floor. "Dig the burrito costume."

"Thank you," Maren mutters, carefully slipping her feet into the plaid shearling. The slippers look like something purchased at an outdoorsy store with their headquarters in New England and they're a size too small, but they're worlds better than having to feel that painful chill with every step.

172

Ari leaves again, and, feeling compelled to follow her, Maren gingerly sweeps into the hall, the duvet trailing behind her a bit like a cape.

"Can I make you breakfast?" Ari asks, flipping on the lights in the kitchen to banish some of the strange gray half-light of the wintery morning.

"You don't have to," Maren says, perching on a counter stool. "I should... I don't actually know if I should get to work."

"There are twenty-three inches out there," Ari says as she begins rooting through her fridge.

"Seriously?" Maren asks with alarm.

"Very seriously," Ari answers into the fridge. "You still a vegetarian?"

"Yeah," Maren says, and only gets a humming noise in response. Pulling her phone out of her pocket, she finds that she does indeed have a few questioning texts on the chain with Henry, Tad, Oscar, and herself. Considering they all live in outer boroughs, there's no way she's asking them to come in. Even though the subway is probably technically running, that means jack shit for any parts of the city that are a river away from Manhattan.

*Yes, please don't come in today, enjoy the snow day*, she texts back. Almost immediately, she gets a response from Tad that only consists of five separate thumbs up emojis.

"If I bought these eggs at the farmer's market from a guy who, and I quote, is 'very proud of his girls on grass,' does that make them vegetarian?" Ari asks. Maren looks over to find her awkwardly standing in front of the fridge, holding up a cardboard carton of eggs like they're something to be submitted to scientific study and

173

hypothesis.

"I eat eggs," Maren says.

"Ok good," Ari says. "Because otherwise I was going to have to renege on my promise of making breakfast and just feed you very sad toast."

"I will take eggs over sad toast any day."

"Excellent, I will make you at least halfway happy eggs."

The unnatural quiet of the apartment is soon replaced with the sizzle of cooking, wonderful smells drifting through the apartment and warming something in Maren's core. She finds herself leaning closer to it, leaning heavily on the counter, and taking in deep breaths. Cooking has never been her strong suit. Selene had loved to spin up incredible meals for the family, a tradition that Fiona has replaced with baking. Left to her own devices, she'll just get takeout or microwave something.

But this she remembers. Ari had shocked her twice in their first twelve hours of knowing each other — once by asking her to stay over, and then a second time when she made pancakes the next morning. They'd even had blueberries in them, if memory serves. At the time, it had seemed strangely domestic and motherly to Maren.

Over their months together, however, it had taken on a very different feeling. Something homely, yes, but something charged. Just like every piece of their relationship, there was an electric undercurrent of hunger and need and want.

Every once and a while Maren will reflect back and wonder when she let her edges be filed off. Inevitably, she'll remind herself that she didn't let it happen — she made it happen herself.

An omelet appears beneath her with a plume of steam, making the skin on her nose briefly damp.

"This looks amazing," Maren says, and tucks into it without much thought. "Thank you."

"Do you mean it?" Ari asks with a laugh.

"Yeah, of course," Maren says. She frowns as she stares up at the strange, conservative joy on Ari's face.

"Ok, good," Ari says, and then stabs her own omelet, smiling at Maren across the island.

# CHAPTER 13

## *The Ballad of Maren and Henry*

Outside is already a godsforsaken mess by the time Maren finally steps out onto the street. Even though she's given the House staff the day off, that doesn't mean the city has ground to a halt — far from it, in fact. Manhattan remains Manhattan. As much as she usually appreciates that resilience, it's currently causing slush puddles six inches deep and troublesomely brown to rise on every corner.

Riding the subway home is an exercise in abject misery. People are crammed in together again, all of them damp and chilled. It smells like wet dog and decaying dust, even after she sticks her nose into her scarf. Every jolt and sway of the train against the tracks sends more bolts of sore pain through her body.

Miu is there the minute she has her apartment door open, weaving in and out from between her legs in a very chirpy figure eight while Maren locks the door behind her. What she should do is feed Miu, go across the hall to thank her neighbors, and then perhaps make some more tea.

Instead, she lets gravity win out, and lets her body drop to the ground in a graceless cross-legged heap. Miu clambers into her lap, purring so loudly that she sounds like a lawn mower. Maren curls over her, making herself as small and as close to Miu as possible. The cat, Gods bless her, puts up with the extreme ministrations, hunkering down in Maren's lap and letting out one last beep of a

176

small meow before devoting herself to full-time purring.

Maren buries her hands and face in Miu's long fur, trying to take deep breaths and finding that she keeps losing the beat of her own lungs and heart, choking air in and out as if she's fighting for it. She has no idea if she's ever felt this wretched in her whole life. Maybe after her mother had died. That mental anguish that had squeezed its form around her body like a boa had caused actual pain.

She's cold, and fractured, and her own soul feels like it's been broken open to make room for part of the spirit of a man who she never even met alive. For him to do this to her in death seems incalculable. No matter how many bodies she's shepherded through the embalming process, none of them have ever reached back out and struck at her from somewhere beyond.

Eventually she straightens herself up when the dull throb of being hunched over gets too much. She leans back against the flat, dry texture of the wall, and idly strokes Miu where she's collected her in her arms. Miu is warm and whole. It's a needed comfort.

If she wasn't alone in her apartment with just her cat for company, perhaps someone would have told her to get up, to stand straight and stare this in the face, to figure out her next steps. She knows she should be telling herself those exact words. Breathe. Get up. Work the splinter of soul free. Easy, neat steps that she can follow faithfully. A path to walk. But there is no one else here, and she doesn't know what to do. She wants to, dearly. Wishes that she knew how to excise the shard. Even that Ari, or Felix, knew how to.

So she stays on the floor, and clings to Miu, and wonders if she should cry or not.

---

Maren suspects that even if she lives to be a hundred, she will never unravel the mystery of how she manages to make it through the week. Somehow though, she puts one foot in front of the other, walking a straight enough path that no one notices anything is wrong. No one but Henry, anyway. He's very good at sniffing out when something's gone wrong in Maren's life, and this is a very big thing to have gone wrong. He even pulls the tequila back out one night, when all four of them are still there.

"This is good," Tad says, after he's downed a shot. He sounds shocked.

"You'd be amazed what you can find if you don't buy your alcohol purely from the cheapest shelf at Duane Reade," Henry says, and pours him another shot.

"Relatedly, I'd like a raise," Oscar says.

"Put it in writing," Maren says. "You can email Henry and I with an outline of how you're feeling you're doing in your role as well as your contributions to the House overall. We'll sit down and chat with you afterwards."

Maren knocks back her own drink, not realizing that what she's said has been greeted by silence until she slams the shot glass down on the desk. She swallows and then looks around at three confused faces. Or rather, two confused faces, and one worried. Instantly, her own confusion is replaced with an extreme need to backpedal.

"I was kidding," Oscar says, frowning in confusion. "It was a joke. About nice booze."

"Yes, of course," Maren says with a lopsided smile. "I was joking as well. Perhaps my humor's a bit desiccated."

Tad humors her with a quick bark of laughter at her own miserable attempt at humor.

"Don't encourage her," Oscar grouses.

Henry shoos Tad and Oscar home eventually, leaving just the two of them standing in the front hall.

"Tired?" Henry asks, his tone amazingly pointed for a single-word sentence.

"Yes," Maren says. She goes for nonchalant, but knows she lands more somewhere in the vicinity of fatigued.

"Anything else?" Henry asks.

"No," Maren says. She's getting extremely good at lying, especially about this. The words come out smooth now, not tripped up on her tongue or tied up in her thoughts. If she needs to lie, she just does. It's cleaner, insulating her employees from the undulating mess of insanity that she's barely keeping at bay. She can't imagine what Henry would do if he found out she was carrying around a portion of someone else's soul, what he would do if he knew that they weren't the only souls in this hall.

"One day you'll stop telling me half-truths," Henry says. He usually lets it go, and it catches Maren by surprise. She blinks at him for a heartbeat, then another, before plastering on the most serene smile she can conjure up on short, tired, broken notice.

"I never tell half-truths," Maren says. "I'm either outright lying or telling the whole truth."

"Fine," Henry says. "Then stop lying, Nykara."

Maren turns away from him then, pressing her palms into her pant legs to stop the tremor she can feel threatening to run through her hands.

"I'm doing it to protect you," Maren says finally.

That's not a lie. She heads up the stairs after that, when

179

Henry doesn't speak for a few moments. She's almost at the top of the steps when he finally decides to rejoin the conversation, crossing to the edge of the banister to stare up at Maren.

"If this is related to the... *recording*," he says, "I'm looking into it. I want to fix it." He's gripping the newel post hard enough that Maren can see his clenched joints starting to turn white from constricted blood.

"I don't think you can," Maren says, her heart suddenly beating in her throat. The fucking video — she'd managed to purposely forget that Henry had it.

"And I don't believe there's a single problem that we can't fix together," Henry says.

"I... I don't even know where to start with that," Maren admits. Yes, there is an unholy nightmare in her own House. Yes, they should probably figure that one out. Mostly, however, she's currently occupied with the bit of Mr. Augustine trying to strangle her from the inside out.

"Then let's figure it out," Henry says. "It's really just the recording? I mean, not that the video was *just* anything."

"Yes."

"*Maren.*"

"*Henry.*"

They stare at each other for a moment longer before Henry's shoulders finally fall a fraction of an inch and Maren knows she's being dismissed, a problem child who insists on clouding the truth and not accepting help. It's a horrible posture to see on Henry's proud frame, horrible to see the defeat in his eyes and know that she's put that rare expression there.

"I'm sorry," Maren says, voice quiet, knowing that her

180

words will fall to Henry's ears.

"Ok," Henry says, but it's not ok, because now he's the one who sounds weary.

—

There had been a dead body in the basement hall when the two of them had stepped through the front door into a wall of cloying decay. Two men stood over it, one looking rather put out and the other with a hand over his mouth and nose.

"I'm going to leave a very stern voice mail for the hospital," one of them said. He was older, what hair he had left was graying, and Maren would put money on him having shrunk an inch or two from his full height. He hitched his suspenders up and headed further into the gloom of the basement, not paying the newly arrived Maren or *Hemet* Cooper any mind.

"Hello," the other man said. This one was much younger, tall and skinny, his clothes hanging off his shoulders. His dark eyes were ringed in horn-rimmed spectacle frames, and Maren could see that his eyes were watering a bit behind the glass. Maren couldn't blame him. The body smelled like a vile mixture of decay and hospital cleaner, all mixed up in something really quite putrid. It made her gag, and she had to keep swallowing to try to keep the deep, unrelenting smell out of the back of her throat. She wished they would move anywhere else that wasn't this cramped, small hall.

"Body transfer problem?" Thais had asked.

"Unfortunately, *Hemet* Cooper," the man sighed. "The body was left unrefrigerated and then dropped off this

181

morning before I could stop them. They didn't even leave me time for the proper paperwork, and we'll have to run it over to the hospital now."

"What a sad state of affairs, that treatment of a body," Thais said, had shaken her head back and forth and made her gold-capped braids swing around her high cheeks.

"New acolyte?" The man asked, gesturing at Maren.

"Not at all," Thais said. She had surprised Maren by reaching out to put a hand on Maren's shoulder, drawing her into the conversation with a warm smile. Maren had gone, carefully dressing her face in an expression of professional calm, despite the fact that she had almost zero experience with corpses, especially one as odorous as this one. At least the body itself didn't present a problem to Maren; it was just a dead person. A dead person who stank to the stars and back. Her own eyes were starting to water under the onslaught.

"Ah, another stray," the man had said. His smile had been thin but warm, and he'd held a hand out over the sheeted body on the stretcher.

She'd stepped up to him, reached across the body with a strong hand.

"I'm Maren. Maren Nykara," she said, hoping she sounded professional. "Pleased to meet you."

"You too, Miss Nykara," the man said. His smile warmed even further, his eyes bright behind his glasses. "I'm Henry Dawa."

They'd finally fled the hall after that, moving to the parlor to escape the smell of decay. It had been so easy to talk to Henry, to slot right into this strange world of a Funerary House. The other man — the aging Marcus Valentine — had needed a new apprentice to pass on his knowledge of embalming to after his last two had moved clear across the country for job opportunities. He'd hired Maren on the spot, leaving her slightly poleaxed on a brocade couch in the afternoon sun.

"You haven't even interviewed me," Maren said.

"Eh," Marcus had said, flapping a hand loosely in her general direction. "If Thais recommends someone, I pick them up. It's worked great with Henry."

"Thank you, Mr. Valentine," Henry had murmured demurely over the rim of his coffee cup.

Maren had wanted to say *but* Hemet *Cooper just met me as well*, but she hadn't. She'd zipped her lip, picked up her tea, and smiled nervously at Henry, who smiled back.

To celebrate after the tea, after Mr. Valentine had stuck paperwork under Maren's nose and she hadn't had enough time to start overthinking the idea that she was about to embark on what might be a lifelong journey among the dead, Henry had pulled out the first bottle of tequila. He had no idea what the day meant, the state that *Hemet* Cooper had found Maren in. He was just trying to be friendly with this brand-new employee who had evidently been hired in a very similar fashion to himself.

It was the shitty tequila that first year. He kicked the filing cabinet closed and held up the bottle and two paper cups. It had burned going down but Maren instantly took a shine to Henry. They'd grown close fast, bonding over shared upbringings in New York — Henry from Manhattan, Maren from Brooklyn — and their strange path in a world that had only recently started to accept them. Henry had shyly shown Maren a photo of himself and Taner on his phone.

"We'd like to get married soon, now that we can,"

183

Henry mused between bites of lunch. They had been sitting in the small kitchen on the second floor, Henry eating something homemade and rather adult and Maren slurping down a cup 'o noodles with enough salt that her nose itched a bit.

"You should," Maren said with a wide smile.

"We will," Henry agreed, bobbing his head in ascent. "One day."

Maren hadn't minded going back to her apartment alone. Technically she wasn't alone — she shared it with two other girls she'd met in school, a crammed railroad three-bedroom a little too far into Hell's Kitchen to be fashionable quite yet — but she didn't have a partner or a family. All she had was her bedroom that was so small that she'd seen closets larger. She hadn't cared a lick, back then.

Now, in the cold evening, it bothers her. Standing alone just inside her chilly, dark apartment, it smarts a bit. Something seems especially bad in this moment, something caught between fear and longing, and she deeply dislikes it.

She lights the fireplace, the gas flaring to life with a satisfying *foomf*, and leaves the lights off. Stripping clothes off, she trades her slacks and blouse for sweats, and then tops them off with a blanket cape. Her last stop is to grab Miu from the back of the couch, tossing her over one of her shoulders so that Miu can ride high, her bright golden eyes surveying her domain as she chirps out some story that Maren will never be able to understand.

They sit on the deep windowsill closest to the fireplace, the flames warming Maren's back while the single-paned window chills her face. Miu settles into her rumbling purr, and Maren strokes her, detached from it all.

184

Down on the street, against a backdrop of the anemic layer of new snow that had fallen this afternoon, a festival is spinning itself up. People laugh, drinks in hands and noses red, their breath fogging in the air. A few have laurel leaves wrapped around their crowns, and Maren even spots one who has woven their laurels around the stem of their earmuffs, a strange, tilted wreath. They travel in groups, no one alone, and Maren can hear giggling and singing.

Selene had been a big fan of Saturnalia, but she'd died a scant few weeks before the festival all those years ago. And so Maren has spent her whole life mostly celebrating the back half of the holiday week only. It's easier to ignore the first few days to keep the lingering grief at bay.

She is cold, and adrift, and she closes her eyes and lets her bare forehead press against the frosty window glass.

# CHAPTER 14

## *Io Saturnalia*

When the text comes in, Maren's momentarily thrown when she notices who it's from.

*Ariadne Augustine.*

A second later her brain catches up with her wide eyes and she realizes that Ari is merely the first name in a group message. Letting her shoulders fall from her ears, she unlocks her phone to find that the others involved are Felix and a number she doesn't have saved. Really, two of the numbers should be ones she doesn't have saved, but she's never cleaned out her contacts and her phone number has followed her from high school. If she still has Ari's number, she can only imagine what other skeletons are lurking in the graveyard of her phone's memory.

Evidently Felix has felt it prudent to invite her to the necromancy group's Saturnalia gathering — a paltry three hours before it's due to start. If it had been at any other time, had she not spent the day curled up on the couch with Miu, shivering under a blanket, she'd be tempted to ignore it.

Instead, after almost a week off work for the festival in a horrible liminal space where she's been convinced her death is coming any moment, she throws off her blanket in a fit of pique and goes to wrangle up an appropriate holiday party outfit. Miu watches her go with a small rumbling, inquisitive *mao?*

She tells herself if nothing else, she'll be able to

repurpose whatever gift she gets tonight for their work party tomorrow. The only gift-like item she has sitting around her apartment feels too crappy for a small, intimate gathering, but perfect for what's probably going to be a large mess of people she barely knows, at best. As she wraps layers of clothing around her, she tries to ignore the cold, setting her face in a steely frown.

Miu has vanished by the time she's ready to go, which means she's probably squashed herself behind the TV or on top of a bookshelf.

"Miu?" Maren calls, gathering up her coat.

No response. Correction: Miu has squashed herself somewhere small and *fallen asleep*.

"I wish I had your life," Maren murmurs. She's said it many, many times before, but this time something cold and hard twists between her ribs, her mouth contorting to match the feeling as she steps out of the warm embrace of her apartment.

—

"What'd you bring?" Ari asks the minute Maren walks in, having somehow installed herself right next to the door.

"*Shit–*" Maren bites out, scooting away from Ari and clutching at her jacket. "Why are you lurking by the door?"

"Waiting for the lovebirds to arrive so I don't have to mingle alone. Luckily, my new bestie is here instead," Ari says. Maren gets the distinct impression that were her hair not piled up in a bun, she would have flipped it over her shoulder.

"Get fucked, Augustine," Maren says politely, and Ari answers with a blindingly sharp smile.

187

"I won't respond to that in a way that will make you blush to the tips of your toes, as I am a caring person," Ari says. "In all seriousness though, now that you're here let's claim a table. I'll look like less of an ass than I would holding a space by my lonesome."

The restaurant is pretentiously French, the tables packed together and the general atmosphere one of warmth and pastries. Someone, either the group or the staff, has strung a deep green garland between the lights, letting it dip gracefully between the fixtures, woven through with golden ribbon. It all feels perfectly cozy and festive, and Maren eyes a plate of macarons that someone has set out in bright colors — orange, red, gold, purple — with the realization that she hasn't eaten all day. She snags two as she walks by, although the minute she has them in her hand something within her curdles, and instead they end up deposited on Ari's table, ignored and uneaten.

"Jacket staying on?" Ari asks after having shucked hers into a corner of their chosen booth.

"Of course it is," Maren says. "I'm constantly cold. It doesn't end, even when I'm standing under steaming water."

"Nice to be able to say that out loud?" Ari asks.

"Yes," Maren replies with raised eyebrows. "Why?"

"Just a hunch," Ari says with a small shrug. "Oh hey, look who finally decided to show up."

Maren turns to find two familiar faces weaving through the crowd towards them — Felix, towing Phaedra Augustine after him.

"Io Saturnalia, you jerks!" Ari says, bouncing up onto her knees in the booth to swing her arms around their shoulders.

188

"Io Saturnalia to you, too," Phaedra says with a pretty, small smile. "And you, *Sesheta*."

"You're more than welcome to just call me Maren," Maren says. She's in no hurry to be reminded of her title while surrounded by this particular group of people.

As she and Ari disentangle themselves from the booth to let the new arrivals slide in, she feels a tap on her shoulder. Half turning, she finds Juni looking at her from behind her thick purple glasses. She has a wreath of gold and green resting rather jauntily on her shoulders, tiny fairy lights strung through it.

"Io Saturnalia," Maren murmurs, smiling down at the old woman.

"I'm glad you've been able to join us so often," Juni says. "Although we didn't get to chat last time. What was it you were going to ask?"

"Oh — uh," Maren says, fiddling with a button on her jacket. "Honestly, I don't know if it's appropriate for the festivities."

"Nonsense," Juni says, waving it away.

Maren sneaks a glance back at Ari to find her in a heated discussion about something with Felix, Phaedra tucked between the two and looking rather serene for someone who's being argued over. They look so alive and wonderful, noses and cheeks flushed, hands flying. With a deep breath, Maren turns back, smoothing down the front of her coat and offering Juni the best tender smile she can conjure up.

"Maybe in a bit," Maren says.

"Well, whatever's troubling you, try not to let it bother you tonight," Juni says kindly, and then pulls the wreath off over her head. "Bend a bit, child, I'm losing height in

189

my decrepitude."

Maren does as she's told, tipping her head forward so that she can accept the wreath from Juni. She slides it home around Maren's neck. It's itchy, the fake greenery made of rough-edged plastic, but the lights are nice and it's over-the-top enough that Maren does feel a bit more festive while wearing it.

"Thank you," Maren says, and Juni winks at her.

"I like the new look," Ari says as Maren slides back into the booth. "The fake plants are hot."

"Could you not," Maren says.

"It is hard for me to not," Ari admits. Maren rolls her eyes.

Maren realizes as she stares across the table that she hasn't really properly met Phaedra yet. All of their meetings have been professional or awful, and Maren hasn't had much time to pay her attention beyond a shallow surface inspection.

Her resemblance to her sister is mostly passing. While they're clearly related, all of Phaedra's coloring is a shift of Ari's — she's paler, her freckles standing out further. Where Ari has the barest touch of red in her auburn hair and no more than a wash of green to her hazel eyes, Phaedra has a metallic red sheen to her hair and perfect jade eyes. There's something almost strange about her, a sharper version of Ari with a bit more ice in her eyes and a steely set to her shoulders.

Phaedra catches her watching, tilting her head to the side and making the long strands of her pin-straight hair sway. When she smiles, the expression doesn't reach the icy green of her eyes.

"Something on my face?" Phaedra asks kindly.

190

"Just noting the family resemblance," Maren says.

"Everyone says we look like my father," Phaedra says. "But I believe there's a bit of my mother in us in other ways. Did you ever meet her?"

"No, I just saw her at your father's funerary rites." Maren tries to remember the woman but comes up mostly blank — severe dark bob, heavily tailored black dress in a woven material.

"Oh, I assumed you had. Did you never meet our parents? Before?" Phaedra asks before turning to her sister. "Ari, did you–"

"I'm going on a mission," Ari says. She's halfway out of her seat already, tugging Perry with her. "We'll be back."

"Let's do this," Perry says, eyes already on the small mountain of wrapped and bagged goodies set on a table near the back. It's a riotous mess, the wrapping vacillating wildly in true Saturnalia fashion. Maren spots everything from a bag with cats in space shooting lasers from their eyes to plain, but alarmingly neon, blue paper, done up with an equally eye-searing pink ribbon. Someone has even gone for traditional golden wrapping with a fake laurel leaf bow on top. Maren would put good money on it being one of the older attendees of the party. Her grandmother used to do the same schtick for Saturnalia.

"You should just wait, you don't want to ruin the surprise," Phaedra says sweetly, putting a hand on Perry's arm. Her large sapphire ring sparkles in the candlelight against his pale skin.

"No, I *do* want to ruin the surprise," Perry says with a sharp grin. "And so does Ari."

"Of course I do," Ari says, draining the last of her drink

191

before they launch themselves into the crowd.

"Of course they do," Phaedra echoes. "Ari hates surprises."

"What were you saying?" Maren asks.

"I thought that when you two were dating, maybe you'd met my parents," Phaedra says.

Maren schools her features carefully, twisting the napkin in her lap.

"I didn't know you knew our history," Maren says.

"She only told me recently. I'm glad you two have reconnected. Something good in all of the bad," Phaedra says. "Although — you really don't need to do this."

"This?" Maren asks.

"This," Phaedra repeats, gesturing around them. Maren watches as something hardens in her face, almost imperceptibly, and when she turns her gaze on Maren there's a shrewdness hovering somewhere behind her eyes.

"Necromancy?"

"Yes. I know that Ari's a big fan of it, but you don't have to be for her. *Especially* you, *Sesheta.*"

She's not sure she's ever heard her title wielded so pointedly before.

"You're not a fan?" Maren says, keeping her voice light.

"No," Phaedra says distantly. "I'm much more into letting the dead stay dead and silent. I'd imagine you'd be the same way, as a member of the priesthood."

"I'm technically not part of the priesthood," Maren says.

"You are, though," Phaedra says. "The history of your profession is one of religion."

"That is true," Maren hedges. "You're worried about

192

the conflict of my job and necromancy?"

"I am," Phaedra says with a small nod, almost to herself. "I just don't want you to get caught up in a world that you don't need to, all because Ari loves it. I don't even know if she cares about it outside of using it as an excuse to be social."

"You're here," Maren points out. She wonders if Phaedra's bluffing, or if she has no idea about the summoning circle that Ari has literally carved into her floor.

"Felix is here for academic reasons relating to his police work. I support him at parties like these," Phaedra says.

Maren wonders if this conversation would be easier if she felt that Phaedra was pushing at her, trying to raise her hackles or get under her skin. But instead, there's something very motherly about her strange, misplaced support. Her face has thawed, and she's being kind. Maren wonders whose benefit she's being kind for.

"You'll think about what I said?" Phaedra continues.

"Yes," Maren lies. "Thank you for the advice. I'm going to go investigate the gifts with Detective Perry and Ari."

———

After food has been served and people are both rather full and rather drunk, they all pull up chairs and perch in booths to gather around the literal mountain of presents. The air is heady with the smell of wax, smoke, and spice, and it makes Maren a bit sleepy, lulling her into comfort. She might even be feeling a little bit warm for once, happier than she's been in a while.

193

Without thinking, she leans against Ari in the booth. The minute she does she finds herself freezing up, that yawning, icy pit opening back up in her stomach. She's about to sit back up straight when, against all odds, Ari slings an arm around her shoulders, keeping her tucked into her side.

Maren sucks in a small breath, lips pressed together, and bores into the gifts with an overly determined gaze.

The minute Roger and Juni are done with their toast and thanks, people rush the presents, sending those who have stayed seated into a joyful, undulating chorus of laughs. Maren has never been one of those people who leaps up first, determined to grab the present that's been calling her name all night. She figures that whatever's left at the end is meant for her.

"Alright, I'm going in," Ari says, and then practically throws herself over Maren's lap to head for the table.

"Yep, me too," Perry says, standing up and grabbing Phaedra's hand. "Come with me?"

"Oh, I suppose," Phaedra says with a smile, and allows herself to be led through the forest of chairs and people to pick a gift.

Once the first wave has cleared, Maren finally takes a luxurious walk to the table. Although the pile has been significantly reduced in size, there are still plenty of intriguing-looking gifts waiting to be claimed. Maren passes over a few smothered in glitter wrapping, decides against a package that's doing an admirable job of holding back whatever large, strangely shaped item is inside, and shakes her head at what is very clearly a wrapped ball of some kind — probably a bowling ball, considering how heavy it is when she tries to give it a roll.

In the end, she chooses a safe-looking gift. The box is roughly the size of a fat deck of playing cards, covered in warm burgundy wrapping — thankfully free of glitter. It's light enough to possibly be a gift card, which she'll gladly accept. People think they're being sneaky, getting gift cards to strange places, but Maren can always put them to use. She'd gotten one a few years ago that was thirty-one dollars to a hardware store, which the giver had assumed no one in Manhattan would have anything to do with. She'd used it to purchase several months-worth of masks, WD40, and a small can of paint for the fireplace molding in the parlor of the House, quite pleased with herself.

When she sits back down the other three are already back, sporting gifts of various shapes and sizes. Two of the Catholic school kids have also joined the booth, chairs pulled up to the edge of the table. Phaedra and Ari seem to enjoy their company, even though Perry looks a little alarmed.

Biggest and smallest?" She asks the teenagers as she sits back down, nodding at their chosen gifts. It's a rotating group who're constantly swapping in and out of uniforms, getting new piercings, and changing their hair colors, so she has trouble telling them apart, but she thinks these two are Chloe and Becca.

"Yeah," the one who's probably Chloe says, holding up her tiny box proudly. It's small enough to fit in her palm.

"We're hedging our bets," most-likely-Becca agrees with a very serious nod. She's resting her feet on her own gift, which is little more than a medium-sized moving box done up with a surplus of garish rainbow ribbon.

"We're up for swapping," Chloe says, just as seriously. They seem to think they invented the idea, and Maren

195

would bet on this being a first Saturnalia for them.

"We used to do that," Ari says, leaning around Maren with a grin. "But then Phaedra went and grew up and now we can't anymore."

"I've never stopped you from doing what you wanted," Phaedra says. "You can still pick the biggest or the smallest."

"Your lack of participation in this scheme means there's no point," Ari says with a sigh and an eye-roll.

The last group of people finally wander away from the table, the last two stragglers a couple of the finance bros who seem confused about which gifts they should take. They swap back and forth all the way back to their seats, and then once more after a beat once they've sat down, presumably for good measure.

"Alright!" Juni says, clapping her hands to get everyone's attention. "I'm going first!"

She grips the neck of whatever's in the bag she's holding. It's one of those tall, thin bags, normally reserved for wine. Most other nights of the year, Maren would assume it was a bottle of booze. Not so much during Saturnalia.

The item comes free with a flurry of bright orange tissue paper. Juni holds it up triumphantly, earning cheers and laughter when people realize it's the largest bottle of cough syrup one could possibly get.

"That's almost as big as you, love," Roger teases, before digging through the tissue paper in his own bag. It takes him a moment, because despite the bag's size, it turns out that whatever's in there takes up a much smaller amount of space than the bag provides.

"Ah ha!" Roger says at last, holding up his gift — Hello

196

Kitty hair clips. "These are perfect, thank you whoever brought them!"

While Roger adds two of the clips to his carefully coiffed gray hair, the group goes around like a wave, unwrapping, unbagging, unboxing. There are the requisite ironic mugs, Maren's personal favorite because they're actually useful. She's pretty sure of all the Saturnalia gifts she's kept over the years, three-quarters of them are mugs. Some people get tacky board games. There's an inflatable fake mustache that the recipient immediately blows up and sticks on her face, and a tiny plastic tiara that also gets instantly worn.

Chloe ends up with what seems to be just a normal travel-sized tin of mints. However, her eyes light up immediately, her jaw dropping open.

"Ohmygod," she gushes, holding them up like they're a piece of godhood. "These are discontinued! Everyone is going to be so jealous!"

"Man, I miss being a teenager," Ari murmurs. "Such a low-stakes time."

"You and I had very different teen experiences," Maren mutters back.

The big moving box with the rainbow ribbon is a cat bed shaped like a giant fur-lined Croc. Much like Chloe, Becca is beside herself, instantly snapping photos of it while babbling about having to show her mom. Evidently, her family has a cat. Somehow, their gifts have worked out amazingly well.

"You better send photos of Momo using the bed!" Someone shouts from across the room.

"Post them in the Facebook group!" Another voice agrees. Maren didn't even know there was a group, but

197

she'll join it purely for the cat photos if they're ever posted.

"I will," Becca promises, nodding up and down so hard that her teeth clink.

Phaedra finds herself in possession of a helmet with a can holder and straws mounted on each side, which sends Perry into stitches. The favor is returned a moment later, when Perry opens his own gift to find a bag of cheese puffs.

"No, this is a great gift," he tells Phaedra seriously, already opening them.

Ari gets a jar of tiny plastic hands, which can evidently be worn as small finger puppets on each finger.

"*Stupendous,*" Ari says, electric light in her eyes as she rubs her palms together.

It's very suddenly Maren's turn. She rips away the wrapping paper to find a small, natural brown box. Inside, nestled in bright shreds of paper, is a small dinosaur figurine. It's green, some kind of raptor, she guesses, and it's wearing a hand-knitted sweater and scarf.

"Oh wow," Maren says, setting it on the table so she can get a proper look at it. "It's so adorable."

"That's so fucking cute!" Says one of the finance bros at the next table before he digs into his own gift. Maren lets the party fade into the background, smiling gently at the small dino. It's perfect, snuggled and warm.

"You're welcome," Ari murmurs in her ear, and Maren turns to her to find that she's close enough that their noses nearly bump.

"You brought the dinosaur?" Maren asks with a raised eyebrow

"I did," Ari says, and her smile is a summer day.

"Your Saturnalia gift giving sucks, this is a good gift,"

198

Maren says. Ari's grin just takes on a sly edge that makes Maren look away.

Maren's gift — a pair of slippers that look like baguettes that are actually a regift from last year — go to a middle-aged woman who looks delighted.

"I'm going to wear these home and take off these horrible shoes," the woman laughs, tapping her heeled pumps against the legs of her chair. Once everyone has had their turn, and several important swaps have been made, the drinking and general merriment resumes. With the help of the restaurant staff, the group moves some of the tables out the way and Roger and Juni start dancing, encouraging others to join them out on the makeshift dance floor. Quite a few people take them up on it.

Maren lets herself sink into the booth, in no mood for dancing with her stiff limbs. Ari stays with her, and they watch the merriment together, Phaedra and Perry cutting a rug through the middle of the dancers. Chloe and Becca head out with giggling calls of *Io Saturnalia*! and they're left in the booth alone, just the two of them. The low light is warm and lovely, the taper burning low.

"How are you feeling?" Ari's voice is quiet enough that it gets caught up in the music and voices around them.

"Ok," Maren says.

"I'll take ok," Ari says.

Maren freezes when Ari reaches out to take her chin in her fingers but relaxes when she realizes Ari's simply taking stock of her face, her hand and gaze clinical.

"Take a picture," Maren murmurs.

"Don't need to," Ari says, dropping her hand. "What are you doing tomorrow?"

"Nothing, why?"

199

"Come stay with me tonight and I'll see if we can poke and prod at that splinter in you a bit more."

"We can't do that during the daylight hours?"

"Sure, we could," Ari says with a nonchalant shrug, and reaches for her wine, eyeing Maren over the top. The sterility in her gaze is gone, replaced with something that makes Maren's gut twist.

"Why are you helping me?" Maren asks. "And don't bullshit me this time."

"Because the scholarship isn't exactly bursting with papers and articles on what the hell having extra soul in you does, or how it can get there."

"So you're purely curious."

"Professionally curious."

Maren narrows her eyes at Ari, earning herself a grin in return.

"What do you do, professionally?" Maren asks.

"Does it matter?"

"Yes."

Ari takes another drag of wine, the deep red of the liquid glinting in the low light and drawing Maren's gaze to her lips and throat.

"I'm in the medical field."

"That's all you're giving me?" Maren says, frowning.

"And yet...?" Ari asks.

Maren hates with every last fiber of her being that she knows Ari's right.

# CHAPTER 15

## *Fractio Panis*

The darkness of Ari's apartment seems to cling to corners and hard edges, even after they flip lights on. Maren wishes she was in her own space, the one that she knows.

"I want to do what's called a PSG test," Ari says as she starts pulling various heavy plastic boxes out of a D'Agostino's bag sitting in her kitchen. Maren can feel her brow furrowing further with each thing that comes out of the bag, the whole mess radiating *medical*.

Maren has made it her habit to stay away from anything medical. Sometimes she wonders if her general good health comes from sheer willpower alone. Or, she supposes, her previous general good health. She'll admit that she's not in fighting form currently.

"PSG," Maren says dully.

"Polysomnography — which, say that five times fast," Ari says.

"Poly what?" Maren asks.

"A sleep test," Ari says, looking up from the bag, her arms laden down by the gods-only-know-what.

"Yeah. You know what would be excellent? Explaining how this makes sense," Maren says. She trails Ari down the hall, her furrow deepening to a straight up frown when they end up in the guest room again. Even though the rug is back in place at the foot of the bed, Maren swears she can feel a pulse under her feet from the summoning circle that she knows is still lurking there.

"Don't worry about it, you're in good hands," Ari says.

"Augustine," Maren says, and the steel rising in her words feels like an old friend coming home. She knows that Ari hears it too, watches as she carefully dumps everything on the bed before straightening and turning to face Maren.

When they face each other, Maren feels very much that they're seeing each other behind façades, carefully arranged and placed. Maren with her hands folded in front of her, shoulders back, that neutral pleasantness firmly in place. In the low lamplight Ari is turned towards her with a similar posture, although her face holds a clinical blankness that Maren knows she can't match.

*Sesheta* Nykara gives the woman she suspects is actually Dr. Augustine a quick once-over before tipping her head to the side, her curls swinging away from her face.

"Yes?" Ari asks.

"I see your Art History major has taken you places," Maren says mildly.

"Those who live in glass houses shouldn't throw stones," Ari answers. "Last time I checked marketing has little to do with the dead."

"You'd be surprised," Maren says. "If you'd like to keep me from walking straight out of your front door right now, you owe me at least some information. Informed consent and all, I believe?"

"I'm trying to inform you about what you're consenting to, but you insist on being so tweaked about doctors and hospitals that it's kinda fucking hard, Ren," Ari grouses, dropping her shoulders and her facade in favor of an eye roll.

"Wow, I wonder why," Maren bites back. "Great bedside manner, Dr. Augustine."

Ari narrows her eyes, crossing her arms across her chest.

"I'm not diminishing your mother's death or what she went through leading up to it," Ari says. "But I'm also trying to save you, so throw me a fucking bone here."

"Are you? Or am I a professional curiosity?" Maren asks.

"Can't it be both?" Ari asks, pinching the bridge of her nose. "Gods, how are you *still* like this? Would you please just roll with a single punch for once?"

"Fine," Maren snipes, shrugging out of her jacket and throwing it onto the chair in the corner. Her sweater follows after that, and then her jeans, until she's stripped down to a tank top and leggings that she'd worn under her pants so she wouldn't freeze to death.

"I'm about to be *extremely* inappropriate," Ari says mildly. "But damn, girl."

"Blow me, Augustine," Maren says, dropping onto the edge of the bed.

Ari's only reply is a lurid, crooked smile that makes Maren immediately regret her choice of words. She wonders dully if she should be feeling heat in her cheeks, a blush on her skin, but instead she's just *cold*. With a bone-deep weariness that seems to radiate from her like the chill in the air, she climbs into bed and immediately wraps herself within the blankets.

"I've got to stick some stuff on you," Ari says, holding up what Maren's tired brain catalogs as some kind of electrode, or reader. She's not sure. She knows jack shit about the living body.

"Fine," Maren murmurs, letting the blankets fall from her shoulders and leaning back instead, hands at her side. She stares up at the ceiling and clutches at the sheets, pressing her lips into a thin line and swallowing. If her heart was even capable of it, she has a feeling it would be racing.

The small, sticky pads are cold as Ari places them carefully along the lines of Maren's body. Instead, however, Maren is aware of the heat of Ari's hands, of the sear in her fingertips when she presses them into Maren. They're like points of light that dance along Maren's skin, and she finds herself wanting to roll over into the touch, to chase those sparks and gather them up within herself, tuck them into her core.

She stays still, stares at the ceiling, and breathes a ragged *in out in out* through her nose.

—

The number of times Maren remembers jolting awake from a nightmare outweighs the number of times she can remember drifting off to sleep by an unhealthy margin. She springs from technicolor horror, hands grasping at her in that shattered, in-between world, into the dark of waking. The cording tangled around her doesn't help, the heavy plastic lines trailing out to a laptop that Ari had left on the dresser to record whatever the heck the electrodes were supposed to be reading.

Perhaps in another time, in another world, Maren would say it's the least restful night of sleep she's ever had. Unfortunately, she's had several worse nights recently, to say nothing of the times she'd spent the dark hours of the day tucked uncomfortably into chairs in her mother's hospital room. She'd been growing like a weed that fall, her limbs coltish and her height sudden, and that had made it even worse. As her mother's body had failed, hers had decided to go on a hormone binge.

Blinking sleep from her eyes for perhaps the tenth time, she stays still for a moment, listening. She's done the same every single time she's woken up, waiting to hear the sounds of Ari stirring. Sometime around three a.m. she'd made a pact with herself that she wouldn't get up until her host did. Although she wants nothing more than to get the hell away from the contraption snaking over her chest and around her head like some demented crown, she also wants to not have to repeat the test. More data can't hurt.

From somewhere within the apartment, Maren finally hears sound. Closing her eyes and letting out a long, low breath, she finally gives herself permission to sit up slowly, knowing that her head will take a moment to spin like a top before she gets her bearings.

Another oh-so-fun side effect of being skewered through the *ka* by a bit of someone else's.

Peeling the electrodes from her skin feels like trying to rip tape off paper. No matter whether she goes fast or slow, they take the top layer of her with them. Gritting her teeth and squeezing her eyes shut she muscles through them, eager to be free of the tangled vines she's currently ensnared in.

When she goes to rinse her mouth out in the ensuite, she finds a husk staring back at her, high cheekbones and fever bright eyes, angry red welts where she'd yanked the electrodes from the thin skin over her too-prominent ribs.

It's easier to just turn the light off and retreat to the bedroom, to swaddle herself in her sweater and leave the room behind entirely, snagging the laptop on the way out. It comes unplugged much easier than she had, and a fully irrational spike of jealousy punches through her.

Ari is in the kitchen, wearing a sweatshirt that's too big on her and purposely worn through in places. Maren can only assume it costs a small fortune.

"Breakfast again?" Maren asks, depositing the laptop on the counter and eyeing the pancake griddle Ari is poring over like an especially complicated bit of math.

"Don't get too excited," Ari says to the pancakes, spatula held at the ready. "These are from a box, and I felt that I should feed you after subjecting you to extra medical tests. I'm about out of things I know how to make."

"What would we have done if we'd stayed together? Existed on take out and frozen food?"

"This is Manhattan, *everyone* subsists on take out." Ari looks up at her with one cocked eyebrow. "Imagining a domestic future for us, Ren?"

"Not in this universe," Maren mutters. "I take it even if I force you to look at the test data right now, you'll need to crunch numbers and do doctor-y things."

"Correct. And there's a lot of data to doctor. Trust me, I'd like to get to it as soon as possible. In the meantime, I'm feeding my patient."

"Aftercare usually follows something a bit more fun," Maren grouses. Ari's responding grin is prurient. "Fuck, I need to keep my mouth shut."

The grin goes downright carnal. Maren glares at Ari in return with every last ounce of frustration in her body.

"Watch the pancakes," Maren says, straightening up

206

and stalking off towards the windows.

The small figures weaving and trailing through the city several stories below seem to be a mix of service industry workers who haven't been given the holidays off and hungover revelers heading home after parties that went so late as to push into the next day.

Raising her eyes to the building across the street, she finds herself staring directly into another apartment, this one dark. There's a man standing in the window, staring straight at her. In the half-light he looks gray, almost flattened against the world. His clear eyes burn, though, haunting strands of muted metallic dragging from the whites as he inclines his head slightly.

He looks like a skull on fire. Maren's hand goes to her chest, feels her lungs and ribs contract and her heart thunder like a sluggish beast waking from sleep. She gasps, eyes wide, choking a breath in and then out.

A hand settles on her shoulder. She whirls without thinking, stumbling in her current stiff state, latching her fingers onto the outstretched arm like a vice. Something rises in her, tries to fight its way out of her chest, and when she locks eyes with Ari for a brief, awful moment, something deep within her wants to reach out even further. Wants to lock hands around her throat.

Ari's wide eyes aren't shocked, just confused. Imploring. Her jutted-out chin and raised eyebrows are an unspoken question.

Maren looks back across the street to find the window empty and the dark apartment deserted.

"Sit down?" Ari asks. When Maren turns back to her, Ari's confusion has turned to concern. "I can feel your pulse."

She nods down at where their arms are pressed together. Maren snatches her hand back, feels the heat of Ari's skin pull away from the chill of her own. Whatever had tried to claw its way out of her seems to be silent and quiet, gone as quickly as it had bloomed, the empty space replaced by the thudding of her pulse and what little air she can pull in.

Maren sits like a stone thrown to the ground, plunking down on the low bookshelf under the window. Ari eases down next to her, and Maren belatedly realizes she's holding a heaped plate of pancakes and two forks in her other hand.

"Sorry," Maren says.

"It's alright," Ari answers, not even bothering to ask what on earth Maren would have to apologize for.

"I thought–" Maren starts, and then stops, taking a fork from Ari instead, shaking her head at herself.

"You thought what?" Ari asks.

"It's not important."

"Maren. Don't lie to me."

The frustrating truth is that Maren has no reason to hold it back from Ari.

"I thought I saw a man across the street with glowing eyes. Or something. I sound insane, sorry," Maren says.

"You're going through some shit," Ari says with a small one-shouldered shrug. She places the plate down between the two of them, the warm steam rising to Maren and bringing the smell of sugar, flour, and honey. "Do you know what *fractio panis* is?"

"Breaking bread," Maren translates, having to dig deep back to her college Latin classes.

"Yes. Breaking bread. It's a Catholic myth that their god broke bread with his followers to symbolize them all becoming one body. They still do some version of it at their services," Ari says.

"And you know this because?"

"I like learning about different faiths," Ari says. She wrestles one pancake from the stack, cutting it cleanly in two with her fork. Taking one half for herself, she nudges the other towards Maren. When Maren looks up at her she nods towards it. "That half is yours."

Maren skewers it perhaps a little more forcefully than she needs to. Holding it up to mirror Ari's own position, she knocks their halves together.

"*Prosit*," Maren says, which earns her a lopsided smile from Ari. "Thanks for breakfast."

"Of course," Ari says. "Under this roof, we break bread. We're one mind. You don't need to lie to me, and we'll figure this out."

Maren looks away, back out the window. The man remains gone, even though that dread she'd felt at seeing him is still swirling sickly in the pit of her stomach.

# CHAPTER 16

## *Burning Up*

"I have checked, re-checked, and triple checked the toe tag, and yes, this is absolutely Thabit Bell," Tad says, standing at the head of the stretcher he's just wheeled into the greenhouse, Oscar hot on his heels. "I *know* that this is him."

"The totaled state of the body also helps," Oscar says.

Maren looks up from where she's going over paperwork one last time to shoot Oscar a sidelong glance. He has the decency to look chagrined.

"Thank you for doing that, Tad, that's very helpful," Maren says. Considering this is their first cremation since Mr. Augustine — and first *sanctioned* one in even longer — they're all being rather hyper aware of who's going into the retort this afternoon: Thabit Bell, lifelong member of one of the ancient cults that's ok with cremation. He'd died in a wreck a week prior that had thrown him from the car, destroying his body. He'd been left with horrible molting bruises covering most of his skin and a patch on his hip where the road had degloved his body down to the pelvis, chipped bone and muscle showing through. Maren wasn't sure of all the accident details, just had taken inventory of his corpse to verify the coroner's findings, but it was brutal in every sense of the word. Not only had it been a violent death, but he'd been young — one semester away from graduating high school. Getting him into the suit that his parents had hoped he would wear to graduation was a sadly difficult process.

Light flurries goose the glass around them with a tiny, icy sound as Maren carefully opens the cardboard coffin on the stretcher, revealing what's left of Thabit. The tag that's currently tucked into his suit pocket does indeed bear the correct name, date of birth, and burial method — *whole body cremation, urn entombment*. Maren clips it onto her clipboard, and then signs off on the paperwork before handing it off to Henry for his assent.

"These are always tough," Maren says, the words meant for Oscar and Tad but said to Thabit's bruised face. She'd been able to settle his floppy hair over some of the worst damage to his skull, but it hasn't done anything to disguise that Thabit had not known peace in his last moments. "You don't need to feel like this hasn't affected you. It has, and it's allowed to."

She finally looks up at her two apprentices, both of them meeting her gaze with somber steeliness.

"He was young, and the death was senseless. Hopefully his passage through the afterlife is gentle," Maren says. The sects and cults that allow cremation have a slightly different approach to the afterlife, one that puts heavy emphasis on the idyllic Elysium and much less on the trials and tribulations before it in Duat.

"I'm sure," Tad says with his usual shining sincerity, and Maren gives him a small smile before replacing the box top.

"Why don't we go get Thabit's family?" Henry asks, giving Maren a backward glance as he herds Tad and Oscar out of the greenhouse and up the stairs to the main level of the House, leaving Maren, Thabit, and the snow. She looks up through the glass roof to the pale gray sky beyond, the clouds thin but unceasing. Closing her eyes, she takes as deep a breath as she can muster, trying to force the cold from her core. It's become a habit, trying to get rid of the ever-present chill that seems to have settled into her body. She takes another breath, smelling burning dust and the last clinging earthy smells of the greenhouse's original function. Below both is a hint of decay — Thabit. He's been refrigerated, but nothing ever really halts decay fully.

The door opens, a soft creaking, and Maren opens her eyes, squaring her shoulders and turning to the group coming in, her consoling, professional smile firmly fixed on her face. Thabit's parents are first through, two people approaching middle age, his father pale and starting to gray and bald, and his mother a good head shorter than her husband with bouncy curls the color of the night sky. They're both clad in somber blacks, their faces blank. Not carefully, as if to hide their feelings, but in a way that Maren is familiar with — an inability to quite know what to feel about the situation. Behind them comes a grandparent, a hunched woman leaning heavily on a walker that has a small handbag hung off one side, and a teenage boy carefully helping her. He looks very much like the pictures of Thabit in life she's seen, close-cropped dark hair and honey brown skin not too dissimilar from Maren's own. He has a riot of freckles dappled over his nose and cheeks, and they make him look even younger. It's a quiet, subdued little procession, brought up by Henry who carefully closes the door behind them.

"Hello," Maren says, extending a hand for Thabit's parents to shake. She'd met them once before, when they did intake forms, but it had been a brief thing. She's used to consulting with clients through the whole process of readying a body for burial, but these types of cremations are short, with no oils or texts or grave goods.

"This is Thabit?" His mother says, carefully and tentatively putting a hand on the box like it might explode.

"It is," Maren says with a nod. "You're welcome to see him."

"I can't see my baby like that again," his mother murmurs, and Maren nods.

"Do you have any words you'd like to say?" Henry asks, but the family stays mute, a few people shaking their heads.

"The funerary service was lovely," Thabit's father says at long last. "I don't think I could say anything more."

"Don't feel like you need to," Maren says. "Even though Thabit will be gone, you can always speak of him, and to him. There's still time for words."

"The last time you say someone's name is when they truly die?" The father asks.

"Yes," Maren says with a smile. "As long as you speak Thabit's name, he's with you."

The father nods at that, drawing an arm around his wife, and she leans into him, dry but wide-eyed.

Maren opens the retort door, a gust of heat blooming from the pre-heated chamber as Maren and Henry carefully load Thabit. The door shuts, leaving only a small circular window for viewing, and Maren steps to a tablet mounted on the machine. It displays a simple white screen that only has a handprint outlined.

She can't stop the brief shock of chill through her body when her mind forces up the memory of Casper Augustine touching that same panel.

"Will one of the family be starting the process?" Maren

213

asks, swallowing hard.

"Yeah," someone says, and it takes Maren a moment to locate the voice. It's Thabit's younger brother, with his freckles and downcast eyes. He clears his throat and raises his gaze. "I want to do it."

He shares a tight, almost desperate embrace with his parents before walking to Maren, his back ramrod straight. He's gangly, hasn't quite grown into himself yet, and he's already as tall as Maren. She meets his eyes with grace, and he stops next to her.

"All you have to do is place your hand here," she says, indicating the touchscreen.

"Ok," he says, and then heaves a deep sigh. "Ok, I can do that."

He raises a hand, long-fingered with bitten nails and a cut on one knuckle that's already scabbed over, closes his eyes, and presses it forward. The screen flickers to green the moment he touches and he leans into it, letting his head fall.

The machine, which had been humming lowly as it heated, now flares fully to life, the nondescript rush of a furnace filling the space. It overpowers the *ti-ti-ti* of the icy flurries on the glass, wrapping them all in the sound.

In a sudden hurry the boy scurries away, making it to the doors before doubling back to collect grandma. Henry leaves with them, a protective hand on the boy's back as he helps his grandmother back towards the elevator. Maren moves to stand with Thabit's parents, a respectful step to the side.

"What cult do you belong to?"

The sound of a voice through the rush of the cremation machine catches Maren off-guard, and she turns to find

214

Thabit's father and mother with wet eyes.

"No specific one," Maren says. The closest she'd gotten growing up was Selene's general appreciation for the minor household deities.

"Do you believe in Elysium?" His father speaks again, his voice rough against his tears.

"For Thabit, of course," Maren says. It's the same answer she always gives, regardless of her own beliefs.

Thabit's father nods, sniffing, and holds his wife a bit tighter. She buries her face into his chest and Maren looks away.

"Would you like time alone?" Maren asks.

"No, please stay," the mother says, her voice muffled in her husband's suit jacket.

So Maren stays, watching the small circle of flame next to a grieving couple whose child has been ripped away very suddenly and horribly.

—

Thabit's parents eventually drift back upstairs, and Maren promises to stay with their son through the whole process. She checks temperature and time left on the tablet screen, and then sits in one of the chairs pushed off to the side. As she moves further from the machine and towards the single-paned glass the temperature drops, leaving her chillier than usual as she grabs the book she'd stashed in a cabinet earlier and begins to read. It's a cheesy mystery novel, complete with the incredibly smart and quirky main guy and the hot cop he's been forced to work with. She knows that by the eighty percent mark the quirky man will have rushed to the scene of the crime without the hot cop,

215

metaphorical guns blazing, only to get captured and monologued at by the murderer for long enough for the hot cop to make a daring rescue, actual guns blazing.

These paperback mysteries might be formulaic, but they're great reading when she has to kill a specific length of time — a flight, or a cremation. She hunkers down, pulling her dark cardigan a bit further around her, creasing the paperback open to where she'd last dog-eared it.

The scraping sound starts when she's about twenty minutes into her reading. Her unconscious brain identifies it as something thunking inside the retort — perhaps the body coming a bit apart — before the rest of her senses catch up, and she snaps her head up. The sound was too loud to have been in the machine. She's alone in the greenhouse but something sounds like it's dragging through the space, the noise unnerving enough to set her on edge.

"What the–"

Behind her, a hollow, low scream. She spins, standing up so fast she gets a bit of a head rush. For a brief moment she sees that gray face again, the one from the apartment across from Ari's. Gold dust dances in the air, the soft impression of a body.

She blinks, and it's gone.

Her pulse spikes, suddenly pounding in her chest. She freezes, wide eyes scanning the space. There's no one here though, no-one but herself. She moves closer to the cremation machine, into the sphere of its heat, as if the burning boy inside could offer her protection.

"Hello?" Maren says, which she realizes is a dumb thing to say. Of course, no one answers her back. Sticking close to the hulking silver side of the cremation machine, one hand skimming the humming metal, she stands stock still, listening for anything else out of the ordinary.

She feels lightheaded, her breathing too shallow and her heartbeat too fast. She backs up slowly, returning to the front of the room. With a wild, crazy thought, she takes a quick peek into the retort. Luckily Thabit continues resting easily through the small window, his body far enough along that his dark bones are visible. His skull has rolled back, and the empty eyes and nose glow a white-hot orange against the char coating the curve of his bones.

A skull on fire.

The warmth of the crematorium is flung from her body in one horrible moment, something unseen slamming into her. With an aborted cry she stumbles back, trying to catch herself on the smooth metal of the cremation machine as the ground races up towards her.

She is so, so cold. She shakes, hair rising on the backs of her arms, her fingers and toes going numb as she curls in on herself on the ground. Her breath comes rapidly again, puffs of crystalline fog.

There is an ice pick in her brain, wedged in her skull, a sharp, screaming pain. She feels like she wants to throw up. Her eyes are wide and unseeing.

Something *pushes–*

The world drops away.

A room of heavy wood and art, books absolutely everywhere. She raises her eyes. There is a figure there.

It reaches out, palms towards her. Something glimmers in — on? — the figure's hands.

A galaxy of lights surrounds them, distorting the world, making things swim in and out and pop in her vision.

The hands connect with her chest.

217

Her heart sobs, stutters, and, in a rend of absolute pain, stops.

Water rushes up to her. The roaring of a river–

No–

Hands on her shoulders, shaking her.

The rush of fire.

"*Nykara!*"

She gasps, eyes opening and spine arching, breath screaming from her body. Above her, the world swirls. As she adjusts she realizes it's the snow, falling softly to the glass roof of the greenhouse. The whining hum of the cremation machine still powers on. The floor is hard and bitter beneath her, and her teeth chatter. Her chest feels like it's been ripped open.

Henry is leaning over her with wide, concerned eyes, his glasses pushed up onto his head.

Maren curls over onto her side again with another sob. Her tears are hot against her frigid skin.

"Are you ok?" Henry asks urgently, pressing a hand to her forehead. "Do I need to call–"

She shakes her head *no no no* because she doesn't trust herself to speak. Henry stares down at her with grim concern.

"Can you walk?"

Another *no no no*, her hair pulling against the rough cement below her.

She is rolled, and then, with a lurching sensation, she's rising through the air. Henry's arms are strong around her body, and he lays her out on the stretcher that had transported Thabit not that long ago. Curling tighter around herself, she knows she will never feel warm again in her life. Her tongue is numb and metallic, her heart dancing drunkenly in her chest.

Lights pass, rooms change, her vision swimming. Before she can fully track their passage, Henry is helping her into her office chair, wrapping a throw around her shaking shoulders.

"I'm going to find more blankets, and get you something warm," Henry says, and then vanishes, leaving her alone in a room that should be incredibly familiar but feels wrong somehow. Everything glances across her vision strangely, unnaturally, the blanket weightless around her.

A strand of her hair rises, then another. Curls hover around her head.

"No," Maren says as she realizes what's happened, where she still is. She's still under, in that strange place between life and death that she's seen more than enough of for a lifetime.

She needs to survive. She needs to stop this.

Forcing her body to stand is agony, her muscles screaming, stretching over a skeleton made of fracturing glass. Her head swims, fresh tears pricking at the corner of her eyes. She makes it, though, hunched over but technically standing up. The blanket slips from her body and she's hit with another blast of icy air. She closes her eyes, tries to remember what coming out of this has felt like before.

A name. She has to remember her name.

"Maren." It sounds like the peal of a golden bell. She reaches for it, towards the light and the warmth singing along the tone of her name. She forces the cold current down and away from her body, letting it slough off her skin and untangle from her hair.

With a gasp, she opens her eyes to find herself standing up straighter, her hair hanging around her face. She blinks a few times, still cold, still in pain, but getting better. The world seems real again, the warmth of her office a familiar cocoon, a home away from home.

Very carefully, she kneels to the ground and then crawls across the old wooden floor until she reaches the fireplace. With shaking hands she unwraps a starter from the pile in the basket next to it, tossing it into the cavernous space on top of the logs. She pulls a long match from their holder beside the basket, the bright cherry head a brilliant, incredible color, and strikes it on the slate of the hearth. It roars to life and she leans into it, staring into the warmth, needing it all around her.

The match quivers in her unsteady grip, but she holds it to the starter long enough for flames to claim it, small at first and then consuming more and more, the wood catching with a smokey popping, the scent of pine and camp filling the space. She lets out a long sigh, letting her head loll onto her chest. The match drops onto the hearth, burning out into nothing against the dark stone, and she gathers her blanket back around her.

She savors the heat of the fire against her skin like the lifeline it is. Gradually — too long — her heart returns to a gentle, even, rhythm.

—

When Henry returns with tea, he doesn't ask her why she's sitting on the floor dangerously close to the fire, simply sits down next to her with a whole serving tray. He's put together a sandwich, some cookies, and a pot of tea, from which he pours them each a cup. The minty heat of the tea sears the back of Maren's throat, and it feels like living.

Henry offers her a cookie, holding it up in silence, and she takes it, slowly taking small bites until all that's left are crumbs on the lap of the blanket.

The quiet holds for a while longer, until Maren clears her throat.

"Thabit?" She asks. Her voice sounds like sandpaper rubbed over fractured glass.

"Oscar and Tad will collect the bone fragments and process them once the retort cools down, they're watching over the last few minutes of the cremation now," Henry says. He doesn't look at her.

"Thank you," Maren says, and takes another sip of too hot tea.

"Nykara," Henry says quietly. "What the fuck is going on with you? Are you dying?"

"I–" Maren starts, but then frowns, realizing she doesn't know how to answer that question. She sure as shit hopes not, but she has part of a vengeful man's soul caught in her chest, and that piece seems to want to take her down by frying her heart from the inside out.

"Oh fuck," Henry says, and puts his head in his hands. "Nykara, you *cannot* die on me. You are forbidden from doing such a thing."

"I'm not trying to die to spite you," Maren manages.

"What is it? Cancer? Some disease I've never heard of? Poison?"

"Who would be poisoning me?"

"I don't know, these things happen. If I need to solve your murder, at least give me a head start."

221

"There's nothing medically wrong with me," Maren says. A sip of tea. "I think."

"That's vague, just so you know."

Maren sets her tea down, swallowing hard, and then turns to Henry a bit, keeping the plush blanket wrapped around her as tightly as she can.

"This is going to sound beyond delusional," Maren says.

"That's fine," Henry says, eyes wide. "I'll take *any* answer out of you, even one that's 'my heart is giving out because I've started doing coke.'"

"You think I'd really do cocaine?" Maren says, taken aback.

"No," Henry says, serious as death. "Answers, please?"

Rip the band-aid off.

"I have part of someone else's soul in me," she says.

Henry stares at her for several long moments, blinking. He puts down his tea without looking, raises a finger and opens his mouth, decides better of it, and lowers his hands to his lap. A second attempt at saying something gets as far, and he makes a *hmmm* noise.

"You're haunted?" He asks at long last.

"I suppose," Maren says. "That sounds horrible, though."

"I just found you passed out, barely breathing, with blue lips on the floor of our crematorium. I think *horrible* sums it up just fine, thank you."

"Sorry about that," Maren says. "We think it's Mr. Augustine, and I'm wondering if being that close to the cremation machine made him act up."

"Mr. Augustine? You have a piece of that old robber baron in your soul? Gods, that's horrible."

222

"It hasn't been fun," Maren says with a heavy sigh.

"And who's this *we?*" Henry's eyebrows are both furiously creased and lifted in surprise, producing a rather deranged look behind his glasses.

"Oh," Maren says. She really doesn't want to implicate anyone else in this, but she has now gone and stepped in it by using a plural pronoun. Chewing on her lip for a moment, she finally says, "Ari Augustine and me."

"Wow, you're super in bed with that whole family," Henry grouses. "Why the shit didn't you tell me any of this when I asked weeks ago?"

"I didn't want to endanger you by dragging you into it."

"Nykara, you idiot," Henry says. "You understand I'm your ride or die, right? I came to you about the creepy, possibly zombie-related shit going on in the House, and you listened, and then you didn't say anything back to me? I could have been helping this whole time, instead of waiting to find you half-dead on the floor at the feet of a burning body!"

"Head of," Maren says. "Not feet."

"Oh, that is so not the point right now," Henry says, brows fully furrowed. He picks up his tea to sulkily take a sip, glaring at her over the china rim. He pulled out the good tea setting for this occasion, although Maren has no idea why. The gold rim glints in the firelight, making the whole cup look rather sparky.

"I really didn't want to pull you into this mess. I mean, whatever bit of his soul I'm carrying around is clearly trying to kill me, so why include you?" Maren says.

"But you'd include Ari Augustine?" Henry says, his tea still raised protectively to his chin.

"I knew her from before, and she's good with

223

necromancy," Maren says. "It was convenient."

"You never told me that story," Henry says softly. "How you know her. She's your ex?"

Maren's heart sinks even lower. She didn't realize she hadn't dished that amusing story out to Henry yet — *hey, our new client? Totes used to bang one of his daughters.*

They could have laughed about the absurdity of it over lunch, crammed into the kitchenette down the hall, Henry with reheated leftovers and Maren with a salad from the bodega down the street. The exact image blossoms in her mind, made out of so many memories just like it, shared lunches and shared stories. She doesn't know how to tell this particular tale right now, in this space.

"I just," Maren says, voice low. "I wanted to protect you. You'd already seen the video."

"You didn't, and you don't need to," Henry says. "You left me out in the cold."

"I know," Maren murmurs.

She picks her tea back up, fiddling with some of the filigree on the handle as she takes several small sips. The steam dampens the tip of her nose, warming it further. Wanting nothing more than to look away into the fire, she resolutely refuses to, holding herself to look her actions in the eye. Henry's dark eyes are luminous behind his glasses, golden in the firelight, capturing the flame. He is lit up from the inside, indignant and righteous, and Maren feels like utter shit.

"Did you know about the video before I showed you?" Henry asks quietly.

All Maren needs to say is *yes.* A simple, single word. Instead, it sticks on her tongue, and her silence is an even worse answer.

224

"Finish your tea," Henry says, voice flat as he puts his own cup down. "I'm going to go check on Tad and Oscar."

And then he's gone. Maren hates herself in that moment, and when tears come for a second time, they are not a surprise.

# CHAPTER 17

## *The Library of Irene Lucanus*

Ari keeps Maren updated through the week as she picks apart the data she'd siphoned from Maren's mostly-sleeping body. By the end of the week, all Ari can figure is that Maren has an abnormal REM state, awful oxygen and pulse stats, and some incredibly strange brain activity going on. Specifically:

*Ok but no lie I think these activity patterns are previously unseen and unknown to medical science. Wild!*

Maren texts back *your bedside manner remains awful, Dr. Augustine.*

As she's packing up her phone rumbles in her pocket again. This time it's a simple *meet here?* with an address uptown. Considering her Friday night plans before this mostly skewed towards hiding at home, she has no reason to turn Ari down.

The address turns out to belong to one of the stately apartment buildings that line the west side of Central Park, all heavy stone and arching windows. Ari's standing outside, puddled in light from the lobby, her breath puffing out in steam. When she turns to look at Maren as she approaches her eyes are briefly luminous in the dark.

"Who lives here?" Maren asks, looking up at the expanse of the monolith towering above them.

"I grew up here," Ari answers. "Mom still lives here."

"Can't believe I didn't know anything about your super-secret life as a rich bitch until now," Maren murmurs, and she meets Ari's gaze with a twist to her mouth.

"In your defense, I was extremely cagey and secretive about it," Ari says. "Shall we?"

Maren had expected a doorman. She's instantly proven wrong, however — there isn't one doorman. There are two.

The lobby is opulent bordering on tacky. There is marble in several different shades everywhere, and wood so rich that it probably costs more money than Maren will make in her whole life. In addition to the two doormen, there's also a small man standing guard at the heavy wooden desk.

"Good evening, Ms. Augustine," the man behind the desk chirps, and Ari tosses off one of her disarmingly charming smiles in response as they glide through the lobby. Maren is extremely glad that she's spent years dealing with wealthy people, allowing her to school her face into a mask of bored calm and not the gob-smacked, open-mouthed pose that's hovering just behind the façade.

Thankfully there is no elevator attendant, so they're left in peace to push their own buttons. The elevator's doors are burnished brass, incised with an art deco design that flows through into the boxy interior, and the buttons, although highly shined, show signs of thousands upon thousands of fingers having pushed them through the years.

They rise to the ninth floor, Ari getting progressively further into her coat as they go. By the time that the door opens onto a hallway with a disorientingly-patterned white and black hall runner, she's covered in collar up to her nose. The hallway smells like a hotel, some kind of commercial cleaning product overlaid with a floral scent that's coming from the alarmingly large flower arrangement hulking on a delicate console table between

227

the two elevators. Maren expects to be led down the hall, but then she takes full stock of her surroundings and realizes there are only three doors in the whole hall — one to their far left marked with *STAIRS* in elegant, bold lettering, and the other to their far right showing a similar sign that says *REFUSE*.

Maren did not realize rich people took out their own trash. She wonders if Casper Augustine had ever opened that door in his life, or if there had been a cavalcade of maids to do it for him.

The last door is painted a shiny black, wide and solid, with an honest-to-gods brass door knocker in the center of it. The heavy metal shows the image of an ibis head, its long beak holding the round knocker itself. The eyes are studded by green jewels that catch the soft, yellow light of the hall and glimmer. As the years have passed the brass has started to oxidize, and now it's a dim, dark color. Against the wide door, it looks almost otherworldly.

As much as Maren would love to know what the knocker sounds like, Ari instead produces a totally normal keyring from her pocket, undoing both locks. The door swings open with a simple touch, opening up into a second long hallway that Ari shuts them into. Unlike the space they'd just left, this one doesn't feel particularly closed in, the moonlight trickling in from the rooms around them. For a fairly confined place, there is an airy sensibility. There's heavy paneling here too but it's been painted a soft white, and the marble floors have been covered by a golden-green carpet. It looks much more lived-in than the communal hallway.

"Welcome to Casa Augustine-Lucanus," Ari intones solemnly, throwing her arms wide to show it off, even though she's still rather turtled into her coat collar and scarf. "Yes, the floor is real marble, and yes, I grew up here."

"I'm sure it was a lovely experience," Maren says, and Ari rolls her eyes.

"You're so good at that," Ari says as she turns to start leading them down the hall.

"What?" Maren asks.

"Always saying the right thing," Ari says. "It's a skill I wish I possessed."

"I talk to people all day who are in a rather precarious place," Maren points out. "It comes with the territory."

They pass through a dining room with an opulent crystal chandelier and a living room full of white fabrics that have probably never been sat upon. The whole place looks staged, although Maren guesses that someone, if equipped with the proper budget, could probably live here occasionally.

Maren thinks they've reached a dead end when Ari throws her shoulder into part of what Maren had taken for a wall. Instead it caves in, folding in on the panel next to it to reveal itself as a door. The two panels move along a track, laying flush with the wall. Ari vanishes through the opening into the gloom on the other side, and Maren follows.

The first thing that hits her is the smell of old books. She's reminded of the stacks in the library when she was in college, nothing so old as needing to be kept under glass, but plenty of books that were older even than her parents. It's a round, earthy smell, dust and paper, and Maren takes a deep breath as light suddenly blooms in the room. Ari works her way down the wall, tugging on pull cords to send the sconces flaring to life.

"I feel like I need a pipe," Maren notes. The walls are covered in heavy floor-to-ceiling bookshelves, these ones polished wood instead of the soft neutrals of the rest of the apartment. Beams crisscross the ceiling, squares of brocade showing between them. Despite the number of shelves there are books on almost all of them, only a few left over for knickknacks and small statuary. An antique writing desk with an honest-to-gods quill stands to attention under one of the windows, and a low coffee table gleams with wood polish and an inlaid golden design. Otherwise, the rest of the furniture is heavy and leather. Very executive.

There is something familiar about the room, although Maren can't quite put her finger on it. It nags at the back of her mind as she strips off her coat and hat, dropping them on one of the wingback chairs. Ari pulls out a small laptop from a compartment in the writing desk, plopping down on one of the window seats and popping it open. Maren stares at her for a moment, and the way she's backlit by the moonlight from outside, before she makes herself look away and towards the bookshelves.

Each book bears a label on the lower spine with a grouping of numbers and letters. Unlike every other cataloging system Maren has ever seen, this one is written by hand, dark golden ink on light, tawny paper. It's completely over the top.

"Did the librarian hand-write every single tag?" Maren asks, selecting a book at random and pulling it down from the shelf.

"Gods no, my mother hired a calligraphy team for that. The woman can find the most inane ways to spend all the money in the world," Ari says. She's worrying her bottom lip, typing away on the small laptop.

Maren passes her fingers over the top of the book, the material a buttery leather underneath her skin. There are hieroglyphics pressed into the deep green cover, their metallic ink a bit faded. With a thumb pressed into each one in turn, Maren puzzles out the title, the hard consonants guiding her murmuring.

"Ah," she says with a brittle smile when she reaches the end. It's a copy of the Coffin Texts. That explains the heft and breadth of the book.

She reshelves it, moving slowly down the row with a hand on the smooth wood. Titles jump out at her in English, pressed between ones in Greek, hieroglyphics, alphabets that Maren doesn't recognize. Every once and a while she'll pass a small trinket or piece of art among the books — the stone bust of a woman, her hair done up in an elaborate Roman style, her ears and nose rubbed down. A glass jar with a wooden top that's full to the brim with old subway tokens, the $Y$ at the center of each a small window. A scarab votive figurine under a domed glass cloche, the barest traces of bright paint left clinging to its shell.

"Where did your mom get this collection from?" Maren asks, pausing to smile at a shelf of popular fiction that includes a handful of well-worn Nancy Drew books.

"The books or the random crap?" Ari asks. Maren looks over her shoulder to find Ari looking up at her, soft puzzlement on her face.

"Both," Maren says.

"The books are an assortment of stuff that's been in my family for a while, and then stuff that she accumulated on her travels. The random crap is mostly my dad's, actually. Or, I guess, was. Now my mom gets to have all his worldly possessions." Ari takes a moment to type a few more things into the laptop before scribbling something down in a notebook she's produced sight unseen. "Ok, you start with these, I'll grab a few others, and we'll see if we can find anything about you being a very unhealthy soul jar."

She rips the page out with a satisfying sound, handing it to Maren. It's scrawled with a bunch of call numbers and corresponding titles and authors, roving wildly over the page in a way that pays zero attention to the lined nature of the paper. They seem to be mostly religious texts.

"What's on your list?" Maren asks as Ari takes up a place next to her, one section of shelving to the left.

"Ghosts and shit," Ari says, sticking her tongue between her teeth, already on the hunt.

"Ghosts and shit," Maren echoes with a nod. "Let's hope we find something of interest."

Maren finds herself pulling books from a wide range of eras, some so new that their glossy dust jackets have author blurbs that include the writer's Twitter handle, and some old enough that the pages are heavily yellowed and Maren feels almost guilty touching them. They have titles like *Prayers and Symbols of the Ancients* and *Body and Spirit: Anatomy of the Ka.*

She pulls the books down in twos and threes, depositing them on the coffee table behind them as she goes. One of Ari's hastily scribbled requests makes her pause and grin — *252.35: hieroglyphics??* When Maren locates the book, she finds that indeed, the title is in the aforementioned alphabet. This one takes longer for her to figure out, and she stands, carefully working through the individual characters inside the cartouche as Ari works quickly next to her, flitting around the shelves like a small bird,

232

alternating between standing on her tiptoes to barely reach a book on the top shelf to crouching down on her haunches to sort through volumes on the lower ones.

"*A Study of* Ib *and* Ichor," Maren reads, before flipping it open to find that not only is it totally in English inside, it was also written in the 90s — millennia after people stopped writing in hieroglyphs in their everyday lives.

"Is that the one that I couldn't read the title of?" Ari asks.

"Yeah. It's about the circulatory system, but through a view of godhood," Maren says.

"Sounds like riveting reading," Ari says, not looking away from her stretch of books. "I grabbed anything that fit all the keywords I needed. We'll see if anything is useful."

They finish their respective stacking of books in a comfortable silence. Maren marvels briefly at how easily they've found themselves fitting back together. Moving around each other is surprisingly easy, and soon Maren finds herself curled up under a blanket in one of the squishy, squeaky leather chairs across the book-strewn coffee table from Ari. She's cracked open a large book about the different parts of the spirit and is balancing it across her legs.

Maren knows the spirit like she knows the back of her hand. She had it drilled into her head for years as an apprentice, and now helps make sure that all the bits and pieces that make a soul a soul are taken care of in the afterlife. She mouths them to herself as she runs down the list with a finger, skin against the rough, aged pages.

*Khet.* Not actually part of the spirit, but rather a body. However, with no body, no spirit could exist. An anchor for the spirit to walk this world.

233

*Sah*. The spiritual body. A body for the afterlife, a ghostly mooring point.

*Ib, ba, shut, ren* — heart, self, shadow, name. Everything that makes a person a person. When Maren had first started her apprenticeship Mr. Valentine had made her really think about each one in turn, not just in the abstract but what they meant to her — her own heart, her sense of self, the shadow that followed her, and her given name.

"You ever realized you nicknamed me 'name'?" Maren muses. Her family and friends have always used her full name, but Ari saw fit to nickname Maren from the moment they met.

"Hmm?" Ari asks, clearly deep into whatever she's reading.

"Each part of the soul has a name, beyond being the *ka* as a whole. *Ren* is the bit that refers to your name," Maren says.

"How accidentally witty of me," Ari says with raised eyebrows before returning to her own reading.

She'd spent a lot of time thinking about her name when Mr. Valentine had charged her with that self-reflection. Maren Nykara. Maren isn't particularly unusual, the female form of a common Roman name. She'd had plenty of classes as a kid where she had to go by her first name and last initial to make up for its frequency among her peers. Nykara though — her surname is as old as their gods, their ancestors, and their dead. It had come out of the golden sands and black plains when Ra was still newly born, and it had survived until now, and would continue onwards. It had always been a point of pride for her father, that he bore a true *Kemet* name. If the last time a name is said is the true death of a person, then the ancient world lives on through

234

her own name.

Maren looks up at Ari, blinking to adjust her vision from close book page to distant figure. Her socked feet are up on the table, and she has some medical journal propped up in her lap. Her bun is being pushed up onto the top of her head against the cushions, her chin tucked into her sweater, and she looks exceptionally comfy.

"Find something?" Ari asks, flicking her eyes upwards when she realizes she's being watched.

"No... I'm reading stuff I already know," Maren admits. "It's weirdly comforting."

"I get that," Ari says with a small shrug up into the cushions. "When I used to get stuck and frustrated in med school, I'd go back to some of the easy stuff just to remind myself that yes, I did in fact know something, even if I didn't know that thing I was working on."

"I still can't believe you went to med school," Maren says. "What kind of doctor are you, anyway? You're so cagey about it."

"I'm doing a fellowship in ophthalmology currently," Ari says, her gaze dropping downwards once again.

"You want to be an eye doctor?" Maren asks. It seems so pedestrian.

"I *am* an eye doctor," Ari says with a shrug. "Keep looking. I'm reading a very interesting article about the role of the heart — spiritually and physically together — in mental health, but I don't know if it'll be of any use."

"I'll take anything at this point," Maren says.

"I gotchu," Ari says, and dives back into the journal.

Maren sets aside the rather rudimentary spirit book, and instead dives into a small, slim volume specifically on the fracturing and coming together of the soul around the

235

process of loss of a living *khet* — the transition between life and death. It's a strange thing to think about, even though she deals with it daily. Maren has made a nice little wall around that exact moment, when agonal respiration gives way to silence, and an uneven heart rhythm shifts to asystole. She knows all about what happens afterwards. Her clients come to her already dead, body systems and functions resolutely shut down. It's a much easier view of death. Maren has experienced loss of life in the immediate once before, and it is not a process she's interested in repeating.

"Hey," Ari says after a while. They look at each other over the coffee table, and Maren notices the tired lines creased around Ari's eyes and mouth. Her lower lip is chapped and bitten, and there is something bitter in her eyes.

"What's up?" Maren finally asks. "Find something good?"

"No, still not. The only thing I've found is that we can solve this problem by killing you," Ari says.

"Let's not," Maren says archly.

"No kidding," Ari says. "No, I wanted to ask you something. My sister is getting married."

"I know," Maren says.

"I need to bring a date," Ari says, tossing her book down on the coffee table.

"Need to?"

"Phaedra told me she doesn't want me coming alone."

"So find someone to bring," Maren says.

"Are you purposely being dense?" Ari asks. Her voice is quiet but fierce. "I know you're smarter than this."

Maren sets her own book down. She meets Ari's gaze

for a moment before she stands to take one long step over the narrow coffee table, coming to perch on the arm of Ari's chair. The other woman watches her the whole time, wide eyed, lips pinched together. She almost looks like she's in pain, trying to keep something at bay.

"I'm being purposely dense," Maren says. She wakes up shivering now. Takes showers hot enough to strip her skin a ruddy red. The fact that it's winter is only adding to it. Sometimes her heart will be so slow and so tired she's afraid she might just die right there, in the prep room or the parlor, or while feeding Miu.

There's terror growing in her too, there's no doubt about that. She has no interest in dying young, of following in her mother's footsteps. Miu can sense either the cold or the terror, and when Maren is home now the cat rarely leaves her side, winding around her feet, riding on her shoulder, splaying across her lap. Maren will press a hand to her small body through her long fur, and feel the rumble of her purring, and it's always both calming and frightening.

She doesn't want to leave the world cold and alone. However, she's also aware that she's dying.

"Why?" Ari asks.

"Because I'm giving you an out," Maren says. "Considering my current state."

"I don't want an out," Ari says. "I took an out before."

"You did," Maren says. Ari had been the one to call, had been the one to tell Maren it was over. Maren had thought she loved Ari, and Ari had thrown it back in her face without even offering up a reason. "And maybe one day, before I die, you'll tell me why."

Ari is leaning close to her, radiating heat that Maren

desperately wants to sink into. She won't meet Maren's eyes.

"Come to the wedding with me," Ari says in a rush, the words bursting from her all at once, no time to take them back or turn around. She blushes, spots of color high on her cheeks, but she doesn't look away.

"No," Maren says.

"Come to the wedding with me, Ren," Ari says, a little thunderstorm of coiled energy. "You're fucking dying, let me dance with you one more time."

Maren feels the intensity of the words like a solid thing. Something in her brain is frantically telling her to lean back, drift away from this sunspot of a girl sitting next to her.

She has no idea what to say in this moment, this strange moment where Ari is glowing, almost as if there is godhood in her, seeping from the cracks and crevices in her skin. No idea how to say no to that request.

"No, Ari," Maren says. Ari's face stays stuck in a mask of frustration for a heartbeat before her shoulders drop and she lets out a long breath.

"I'm going to fix this," Ari says.

"Then we should probably get back to reading," Maren says.

———

"Ok, found something," Ari says. They've been in the library all weekend, picking through a hundred years and more of scholarship and pop science. Maren is spread out on a couch and Ari is sitting on the floor, hunched over a book on the coffee table. Take-out cartons cover whatever

238

bits of the table aren't covered in research materials, the air smelling slightly of the noodles that Maren had just picked at.

"What is it?" Maren asks, hanging over the edge of the couch, her own book sliding across her lap far enough that she has to reach out to quickly catch it, crinkling one of the pages a bit. Maren winces, carefully setting the book closed behind her body.

"We have to do a kind of reverse summoning, for lack of a better word, along with–" she shuffles through legal pad notes, frowning when she can't find what she needs before locating it underneath the catalog laptop. "Ah ha — ok, we need to redo the anchor points in the summoning circle as well."

"I thought you said never to open the milk container," Maren says. She's trying to keep her heart rate normal, not let it spike in excitement. Every little spike of her pulse lately has terrified her, her throat constricting, her hands shaking. The stairs out of a deep subway station have become her greatest enemy. As long as no one is looking, she's even been abusing elevator privileges at the House to keep her heart rate down and her oxygen levels up.

"Gods, no, not that one — we'll refresh the other three." Ari gives the paper a bit of a shake, clearing her throat. "Blood from the known vein, wine and honey from the cradle. So, your blood, and then some local honey and wine."

"That part is easy. But I've never even done a normal summoning, let alone whatever a *reverse* one entails," Maren says.

"I'll guide you through it. Instead of summoning a spirit from outside yourself, you're summoning the one within

239

you. I'm hoping it works. As far as I can tell, it's only been done a few times in some fringe psychiatry," Ari says.

"What if we rip my own soul out?" Maren asks.

"Uh," Ari says. "Don't worry about that."

"Lovely," Maren mutters.

A beat, and then–

"Do you think my dad was murdered?" Ari says, voice low. Maren hears her shift before she's aware of the smell of Ari's shampoo — lemon, ginger — somewhere near her head. Ari must be leaning against the couch. Maren rolls her head to the side and finds Ari dangerously close, all luminous eyes and stray brown hair.

"Maybe," Maren murmurs. "His spirit certainly seems vengeful enough. The cremation could have covered something up. Sometimes I swear I've seen his death in my dreams, but that's probably just my brain firing off randomly."

"Did you see him before the cremation?"

"I did. His body was intact, but there are certainly ways to kill someone without obvious violence."

"Great," Ari says with a heavy sigh.

"Does it matter if someone killed him?" Maren asks.

"No," Ari says. "It matters *who* killed him."

They sit in silence for a moment before Ari lets her body slip further towards the floor, scrubbing at her face with ring-studded hands.

"You think it was someone close to him," Maren realizes. "How long has this been bothering you?"

"A while," Ari admits. "I think my mom did it."

Maren furrows her brow, tipping her head to the side. Before she can question how Ari got to that particular conclusion, a heavy door opens somewhere deep within the

240

apartment.

"Who's that?" Maren asks. Thin, distant voices find their way to the library through the thick walls, two new denizens of their research cocoon.

"Mention the cat and it will come jumping," Ari says, brittle and bitter. "How would you like to meet my mother for real?"

Ari stands up, holding out a hand to Maren to help her stand. As always when their skin comes into contact, Maren wishes she could capture some of that roaring heat for her own shrunken, chilled body. She finds herself reluctant to let Ari's hand go. When she doesn't drop it Ari simply leads her along, their fingers linked until they're out of the library.

They come face to face with the newcomers over the dining room table, Ari and Maren standing on the living room side and the other two people on the kitchen side. Maren instantly recognizes both — Irene, as Ari had predicted, and Phaedra. They're both bundled up still, coat collars turned up over scarves, shopping bags on their arms, cheeks and noses bitten red.

"You're home," Ari says.

"I got in this morning," Irene replies, her voice a strange melodic sound, cold and distant but lyrical. "I take it you're the one who's been leaving books all over the library?"

"It's good to see you," Phaedra says with a small, loose smile in Maren's direction as Ari and her mother quickly devolve into bickering over the state of the library.

"You as well," Maren says congenially as Ari and her mother continue to peck at each other, now moving into the kitchen, leaving Phaedra and Ari alone in the chilly, sparse

241

dining room. "How's wedding planning going?"

"Almost done, thank Juno," Phaedra says with a heavy sigh. "I've hated this whole damn process. I'm paid to plan events but finding myself in the position of planning something I'm paying for instead is just the pits."

"I take it it's going to be large?" Maren asks.

"Massive." Phaedra shakes her head, finally dropping her shopping bags onto the smooth expanse of dining table. "The guest list is alarmingly long."

Phaedra braces herself on the back of a chair, her knuckles pale with tension, her engagement ring a deep blue void. The stones and metal of the band glint sharply under the light of the chandelier above their heads.

Maren is drawn to that ring. She's not sure why, and it chews at her. She frowns, crossing her arms and trying to remember what she's missing. Perhaps it's as simple as having seen it that first day she saw it, a horrible day thrown clear off its axis, the world tilted and wrong.

"Ms. Nykara?"

They both turn to see Irene, her head stuck out of the kitchen.

"Ma'am?" Maren asks, standing up a bit straighter under her strange glowing gaze. Wherever the girls got their eyes from, it isn't Irene — her eyes are a dark, deep brown that seems to suck light in.

"Ariadne's let me know you've had dinner, but would you stay for coffee and perhaps dessert? We bought some pastry from Zabar's while we were out," Irene says.

"That would be lovely, if it's not too much to impose," Maren says. She almost hopes it is an imposition, if Ari's reckless conviction of her mother has any truth to it. She'll take the out if it's given.

242

"Of course not," Irene says with a wave, vanishing back into the kitchen. Maren stares at the slowly swinging door, back and forth, before she realizes that Phaedra's gaze has returned to her.

"What are you two up to in the library?" Phaedra asks, voice even.

"Just some general history," Maren says. She's not interested in Phaedra knowing the details, especially after their strange conversation during Saturnalia.

"General history," Phaedra muses. Her knuckles tighten on the edge of the chair another degree, her french-tipped nail digging into the plush back.

Maren just offers her a warm, detached smile, lowering her arms into a less threatening clasp over her stomach. The show of obsequiousness doesn't seem to do much, however, and Phaedra's frown deepens. Maren's starting to get concerned that she might poke at Maren's rather flimsy answer when the door swings violently open, revealing Ari with a ceramic platter, standing in mid hip-check. A french press and several elegant, tall cream mugs are clustered in the center, surrounded by more than just *some* pastry. Really, it's more of a full mountain range around the coffee.

Ari sets it down with a clatter, dusting off her hands. She beams serenely at Phaedra for a moment before shoving a whole rugelach in her face, munching happily.

"By the way," Ari says through a mouthful of dough and filling, "I'm coming to your wedding — which, duh — but stag."

"Of course you are," Phaedra says with a heavy sigh and tired eyes.

243

—

Maren has to make a concerted effort through dessert to not stare openly at Irene. It's hard, considering that Ari's now put the idea in Maren's head that her mother is a murderer. As Maren had remembered, Irene's demeanor isn't particularly murderous, or even cold — mostly just even and deep, with occasional peaks of exasperation at something one of her daughters has done or said. Mostly Ari.

Choosing to listen more than speak, Maren leans back against the overstuffed living room couch and contributes little to the conversation. It ranges wide, although the bulk is about the upcoming wedding, which Maren has learned is much sooner than she had expected — only a few weeks from now, and just a few floors above their head, in the cavernous penthouse ballroom and terrace on the top floor of the building.

"Ms. Nykara," Irene says, picking slowly at a black and white cookie, "if you don't find it too forward, how did you end up in your profession?"

"I was recruited by *Hemet* Thais Cooper, who presided over your husband's funerary service," Maren says. "She thought I would be an excellent fit at the House of Five Gates."

"Mmm," Irene hums in the back of her throat, breaking off another tiny piece of cookie. "It's interesting, I always assumed that embalmers and support staff at Mortuary Houses had some connection to the funerary industry; in the family, or some such."

"Most do," Maren admits. "But not always. My two apprentice embalmers both came from an open posting.

244

Neither of them was related to the industry before they set foot in the House."

"And you find they do good work?" Irene asks.

"Excellent work," Maren says.

"You trust them?"

"Implicitly."

Irene makes that humming noise again, placing what's left of her cookie down on her saucer and taking up her coffee instead, swirling it slowly around in her mug before looking up at Maren. Something catches in Maren's throat, and she shudders out a small breath as her heartbeat speeds, her blood rushing under the suddenly piercing dark gaze of Irene.

"Oh Gods," Phaedra mutters, setting her own mug down with a clatter, using both hands to frantically type on her phone. "Felix is wondering if we can do cream linens now."

"I emailed him specifically about that," Irene says, her attention gone from Maren as smooth as a knife, focused fully on Phaedra. Just as quickly as the strange feeling had come, it slips away.

"I know you did," Phaedra bemoans. "What would cream do that eggshell wouldn't?"

"Well, I suppose the slight bit more yellow might be nice," Irene murmurs.

"Mom, no," Phaedra says, exasperated.

"Let's never get married," Ari mutters, scooting closer to Maren so that she can be heard.

"Completely fine," Maren agrees automatically. "Wait."

She turns towards Ari, raising an eyebrow, and finds that she's on the receiving end of one of Ari's cut grins. The fact that it brings the briefest spark of heat to Maren's cheeks seems impossible.

# CHAPTER 18
*Patéras, Anakaléo*

"Maren?" A knock at the door. When she looks up from her desk, she finds Henry hovering on the threshold to her office.

"Hey," Maren says, wearily leaning on the desk. "What's up?"

"Thais is here to see you," Henry says. "She's up in the salt cellar."

Maren's weariness morphs into tired confusion alarmingly fast, her mouth tugging down at the corners. Thais isn't scheduled to be in until next week, when their first funerals of the new year are scheduled. With the long President's Day weekend coming up, people have planned funerals for when they know people will have the days off.

"She's early. And she didn't tell me she'd be early," Maren murmurs, wrapping her cardigan tightly around herself. She's taken to wearing more and heavier sweaters, wishing that this whole disaster had come at the height of summer instead of the dead of winter. "Did she tell you?"

"No," Henry says with a shake of his head. He holds the door open for her and she shuffles out after him.

"Did she say why she's here?" Maren asks.

"Also no," Henry says, and then, after a pause, "you're getting worse."

"I think I have a solution," Maren says. "Just working on getting a few things together."

Ari had briefly played around with delaying their

attempt at evicting Mr. Augustine until Dies Wadi, on the assumption that trying to do anything with the dead, piecemeal or whole, would be much easier during the ancestral celebration honoring their dearly departed. Unfortunately, with Maren mostly reduced to a walking corpse, cold to the touch with a stuttering heartbeat, she'd just as quickly dismissed the plan. They'll do it this weekend, a month from the last day of Dies Wadi, a date that might not have anything to do with anything but that Ari had called *auspicious*, so they're going with it.

"It better be a fast solution," Henry grouses as he stabs the button for the elevator. Although he and Maren are still on uneven ground after her collapse, he's softened a bit in the last week as she's slipped further and further.

"It should be," Maren says, holding her head as high as she can.

She leans against the wooden-paneled side of the elevator, letting her body sag into the polished surface. Against all odds, she's found herself missing the spikes of her heart rate, this horrible plodding rhythm in her chest a maddening, slow moving reminder that she's currently toeing the line between life and death *very* closely.

The elevator gives a pleasant ding and the doors slide open, the top floor silent and warm from the heat rising from the bottom floors. Henry stays back, and Maren throws him a confused look over her shoulder.

"She said just you," Henry says.

*Well, fuck*, Maren thinks, but she gives Henry a tight-lipped smile and heads for the salt cellar.

The attic is alive with dust motes floating serenely through the golden light of the late afternoon. In the dry, arid space Maren feels slightly warmer, as if she's stepped into a sun-soaked desert halfway around the world. Floorboards creak under her shoes as she crosses the space, towards the hunched form near a far coffin.

Thais is sitting on the edge of one of the limestone slabs, carefully brushing natron away from one of their current clients. The cartouche that has followed this particular body through its stay at the House is familiar to Maren by this point in the process – Sekhmet Morrison, neatly painted by hand in dark ink on a long page of heavy paper attached to the outside of the coffin.

"I can't tell — is she too young or too old to look this good?" Thais asks, smiling gently down at the exposed face of Sekhmet. Her dark skin in life has darkened even further after death, her skin smooth and pulled, her lips still showing fullness despite the desiccated nature of her immediate environment.

"Too old," Maren says, sitting down on the other edge of the slab across from Thais. "If I didn't think it was horribly uncouth, I'd ask her husband where she had the work done. It's very impressive."

"I'd say," Thais says, letting her eyes hover on Sekhmet for a moment before brushing salt back over her face, just as gently. The disturbed particles send a fine mist of salt into the dry air, smelling of decay and oils. "Help me with this?"

They replace the cover of the coffin, Maren struggling much more than she likes, trying to keep her breathing as even as possible, not wanting to rouse any suspicion in Thais.

"It's so good to see you," Maren says with a smile much more at ease than she feels. Thais showing up unannounced is a very strange development. "What brings you out here early?"

"You, actually," Thais says, staring Maren down with a calm smile. She takes Maren by the elbow, pulling her towards the visitor bench under one of the windows. Maren sends up a silent prayer to any god or goddess who may be listening that Thais can't feel the chill of her skin through her multiple layers. She makes sure to sit as far from Thais on the bench as she can, just in case.

"Me?" Maren asks, frowning. She would hope that if Henry had called Thais here to sic her on Maren, that he would have at least owned up to it in the elevator. He's not great at keeping things from Maren, and he'd seemed just as surprised as Maren at Thais' arrival.

"You," Thais confirms with a gentle tip of her head in Maren's direction, sending her gold-capped braids spilling over one shoulder. "And something I heard about you."

"I'm fine, trust me," Maren assures her, trying to keep her voice as even and pleasant as possible.

"I'm sure you believe you are," Thais says. She holds Maren's gaze, stern eyes and arched brows. "But you would be wrong. You know — I know you absolutely do — that you cannot bring necromancy into this House."

Maren stares at Thais for a moment, thrown a whole loop by her words.

"Necromancy?" Maren says after a beat. "Death magic?"

"Do us both the favor of not playing dumb," Thais says, her words sharp but her tone rather kind. "What on earth made you turn to necromancy? You know it's forbidden within the sanctuary of a Mortuary House or Complex."

"That's not specifically codified anywhere in our religious texts," Maren points out, shoving her hands into her sweater pockets to keep them from visibly shaking.

"That's because nothing is *specifically* codified anywhere," Thais says, raising one eyebrow. "My role would be a lot easier if it was, but instead we've got a dozen or more texts crammed and cobbled together in various files on my tablet. It's part of the beauty. What is not is necromancy. Even if you want to argue a technicality, I'm arguing morality. It's an ugly art, death magic. It will consume you, eat you up. Let the dead lie, Maren. We guide them to rest, not raise them."

"I know," Maren says quietly. She licks her dry lips, dropping her gaze. When Thais reaches out to raise Maren's chin back up with one long finger, Maren jerks her head back up instead, quickly, before Thais can touch her bare skin. Thais frowns, her eyes slowly taking in Maren's face. She knows what Thais is seeing, what horrors she's cataloging — hollow cheeks, bruised eyes, lips that have started to tint blue even behind the lip color Maren had heaped on this morning and reapplied at least three times since.

"It's already gotten its claws in you, hasn't it?" Thais asks, mournful. "My darling, no. You cannot walk this path and survive. Even if you were to survive, it will be a half-life, drained of your warmth and chasing spirits that can't actually help you."

"Thais–" Maren starts, if only to knock her out of this cavalcade of terrors. But Thais continues.

"And," Thais says, and here her voice finally hardens a bit, "I do not want to have to remove you as *Sesheta* of this House."

Silence. A cold pit yawns in Maren's gut that has nothing to do with her current status as somewhat haunted.

251

"I would hope that you wouldn't do such a thing without a review board, *Hemet* Cooper," Maren says. Her words are clipped, careful.

"I would never permanently remove you without a full review, I'm not a monster," Thais says. "But I would place you on temporary leave while the investigation progressed."

"Well, lucky for both of us, you have nothing to worry about," Maren says. She wants the smile on her face to be tight and pointed, a sneer, a *how dare you*. This is her House, and hers alone. But she forces that smile down, wearing one of general congeniality instead. Lets her eyes open wide, innocent; rounds her face as much as possible under current circumstances.

"I don't?" Thais asks.

"You do not," Maren says, standing, brushing a bit of salt dust off her slacks that had found its way there while she was sitting with Sekhmet. "Whatever you think may be happening, you're unfortunately misinformed, and I'm so sorry that someone had you laboring under that delusion. I'm just under the weather, sadly. I was an idiot and didn't get my flu shot this year."

"Really," Thais says, very clearly not making it a question. "And as to what you admitted to earlier in this conversation?"

"I don't believe I admitted to anything. We simply discussed orthodoxy held in our holy texts. Or lack thereof."

"Careful, Maren," Thais says, narrowing her eyes.

"I always am," Maren says, and it's not placating. It's a promise, all edges and armor.

252

—

"Glad you're home," Maren says shortly as she blazes past Ari and into her apartment.

"Uh, yes, so good to see you, too," Ari says, closing the door. "What's got a bug up your butt?"

"Thais is going to remove me from my position if we don't fix this issue right now," Maren says, unloading wine and honey from her bag she'd picked up at a farmer's market on the way there. "How are we getting my blood?"

"Just a finger puncture, but take a step back for a second — Thais, like *Hemet* Cooper? She's going to remove you if we don't de-spirit chunk you?"

"Yes, that Thais. If I don't stop 'walking the path of necromancy,'" here Maren hooks rather passive-aggressive air quotes around her words, "she will fire me."

"She can fire you?" Ari asks, picking up the wine to take a look. "I'd pour us a few glasses but... uh. So. I don't want you dying, right?"

"Unfortunately, she can start the removal. And correct, me not dying is an important part of this process," Maren says, frowning. "What exactly do you have in mind for that?"

"I'd like to insert an IV into your arm," Ari says, and Maren gets the feeling she's putting on her Dr. Augustine tone. "It won't hurt too badly, and it will allow me to administer medication if you have complications."

"Complications," Maren echoes. "So you'd like to pre-wire me for the possibility that you have to pump me full of something to keep me alive?"

"Basically," Ari says with a shrug that's more casual than the situation calls for. "Just long enough to make sure you don't die, then we can get you to a hospital."

"And we tell them what?"

"Haven't gotten to that part yet," Ari says brightly. "But anyway, I don't want you drinking because it's a contraindication to the meds I've got, and I don't want to drink because you don't want my hands shaking when I stab you."

"Lovely," Maren says, pinching the bridge of her nose. "This sounds awful."

"I have very high hopes, actually," Ari says. "I'm just being careful."

"Cool," Maren says, and takes a deep breath. Her heart rate has been ping-ponging all over since her conversation with Thais, and she knows she needs to attempt to get it at least under control. "So, should we do this?"

"Yeah," Ari says, mirroring Maren's breathing. "Let's get set up."

The rug in the guest room is pulled away with a dusty flourish, and they drop to the ground to set about pulling out and refreshing the brass reservoirs.

"Leave that one in," Ari says, pointing to the first one that Maren had pulled at. "That's the milk."

They free the other three from the floorboards, setting them in a line in the center of the summoning circle. The incised brass glints lowly in the light from the table lamps.

"Ok," Ari says, setting down the bottles of wine and honey. "Take all this, prick a finger you don't use too often, and squeeze it into this."

Maren holds out her hands to accept the grab bag of materials that Ari tosses her way — one of the canisters, a small piece of cylindrical plastic that looks like it might have come from the inside of a pen, and a sterile wipe.

254

"I take it this is to prick my finger?" Maren asks, holding up the strange plastic thing.

"Yeah," Ari says, distracted. She has her tongue between her teeth, concentrating on getting the top off one of the canisters. "The top twists off."

"You sure about that?" Maren asks, picking up her own canister and looking at it with some trepidation.

"I meant the lancet," Ari says, nodding at the bit of plastic. "Twist off the circular bit and stab yourself."

"Your bedside manner remains astounding," Maren murmurs. Bracing herself, she pops up the small handle on the canister and uses it to put some force behind her efforts to twist the top off. It does her the bare minimum honor of budging a hairsbreadth before resolutely sticking, the smooth copper making it hard to get a hold of.

"Ah ha, take that!" Ari crows suddenly. Maren looks up to see that she's managed to get a canister open. Ari peeks into it, giving it a small sniff. "Ok, this one is wine."

"How did you—" Maren stops suddenly when the top of hers gives way all at once, with enough spin that Maren can't keep a hold on it and it goes clattering to the floor. Peering into the dark interior, she finds it stained a dark, dull color, almost black. There's some hint of dried flecks of something hovering around the edges, and it takes a second to realize it must be blood. Or was blood. Perhaps a very long time ago.

As Ari pours out a bit of wine into her canister, the brief splash a strange sound against the heavy metal, Maren twists the top off the lancet as instructed. A small metal point greets her, glinting sinisterly.

"Don't forget to sanitize the finger first," Ari says without looking up.

Right. Clamping the end of the lancet in her teeth, Maren rips open the single-use pack and swabs the pad of her left pinky, figuring that she probably uses that finger the least. Reclaiming the lancet in her hand, she takes a deep breath, and, setting the needle tip against her skin, pushes down in one smooth motion. The sharp burn of pain comes immediately, localized and more annoying than searing. Holding her finger over the dark hollow, she gives it a squeeze with her other hand. A second bloom of pain comes, and she winces, a small motion, as a few drops of blood pool out of her skin, lazy and thick, dropping into the canister.

"Just a couple drops, right?" Maren asks.

"Yep, that's fine," Ari says. She's got another canister open, balancing it on one knee, the other playing host to the jar of honey. As Maren watches, Ari spoons a bit into the brass vessel, having to use her finger to push it from the spoon. She sticks her finger in her mouth, sucking it off, before shoving it away with the bottle of wine.

Maren swabs off her blood with the wipe, screws the top back on the canister, and then sticks it into line with the other three. They stand proud and aged in the center of the summoning circle, the antiquing on the brass more pronounced now that their hands have been all over them. Four jars in a line, not unlike canopic jars in a way.

"I've got to go grab some more stuff, if you want to put them back," Ari says, voice full of forced levity as she gathers up the honey and wine.

"Sure," Maren says. The minute Ari's gone Maren swears the temperature drops a few degrees. She shivers, sticking her chin in the scarf she had come wearing and hadn't bothered to remove, before slotting the canisters back into their spots. As each one falls flush with the wood of the floor, Maren presses a cold hand over the top, closing her eyes and mouthing *please*. She doesn't have any prayers or incantations, doesn't know any benedictions for this moment, but she knows this is far, far from the first time in history that someone has meant please as a prayer, and it won't be the last time either.

Wrapping her scarf around her neck one more time, she slides to the middle of the circle, letting herself relax as much as she can, letting her spine compress and curve. Her heart is a sluggish, heavy drumbeat in her chest, even but slow. Except for the lingering sting of pain in her one finger, she can't feel much of her far extremities. The cold seems to have finally wrapped itself around her bones, fused to her ribs, penetrated her heart. When she lets out a long, shaking breath, she almost expects to find her breath steam in the cold air.

She realizes, with a distantly growing hum, a white noise ringing in her ears, that she is terrified.

Ari returns, this time with a mishmash of medical supplies and candles. Maren tracks her movement as she puts the medical equipment down, and then sets a pillar candle at each cardinal point, right over the tops of the canisters.

"Ok, now the fun part," Ari says, sitting down in the circle facing Maren. "I know you're going to hate this, I'm sorry. You're right-handed?"

Maren nods, holding up her right hand. Ari gives her a rueful smile before taking Maren's left instead, pulling her arm towards her, turning it over. Maren lets her, lets her push up her sweater sleeve, lets her warm fingers explore her cold skin. They're like pinpoints of light, sunshine through tree coverage, warming her skin in bits and pieces.

"Make a fist," Ari says, voice low, and Maren does so. "Ok, this should work."

"Make it quick," Maren mutters.

The warm press of Ari's thumb in the crook of her elbow is replaced with the sudden chill of another alcohol pad.

"Shit," Ari mutters.

"I do *not* want to hear that," Maren says.

"No, it's whatever, I just forgot to put gloves on. I washed my hands, I promise," Ari says.

"I promise to not sue you for malpractice when I get a blood infection if you get me through this alive," Maren says.

"Gee thanks," Ari says. "Ok, get ready, a small prick–"

Maren resolutely doesn't look, instead choosing to stare at the top of Ari's head. She's pulled her hair back, the clean line of her part tight to either side of her head.

The punch of the needle comes with a press of sharp hurt, like the lancet, but larger. It tightens her muscles and she licks her dry lips, trying to keep her breathing even. Just as quickly as the needle has come, it's suddenly gone. There's a brief clink of metal on plastic, and Maren looks back down to find that Ari's somehow removed the needle and ditched it in a bright red sharps container to her right.

Next comes a strange clear plastic band-aid, placed over the site where the needle had gone in. Maren realizes that whatever has been left behind is still in her, and when she gives her elbow a tepid, timid bend, the bandage pulls but nothing blossoms into pain.

"Huh," Maren says as Ari attaches some kind of plastic valve to the other end of the bit of translucent tubing that's

258

now protruding from her elbow.

"Ok, so here's the deal," Ari says, looking up at Maren. Her eyes are big, very close, and creased with concern. She swallows so hard that Maren can actually hear it. "We're going to go back under. I'm also going to give you this."

Here she fishes around in her pocket before she comes up with a heart monitor that she clicks onto the end of Maren's left pointer finger. It takes a second, but then it dutifully starts a read out of her heart rate on the small screen.

The dull, dark numbers show 58.

"That's bad," Ari says, pointing at it.

"Thank you, I'd figured," Maren says. "You were saying?"

"I'm going to be monitoring your heart rate. I've got two drugs with me — one will help restart your heart in the event of full cardiac arrest, one will put your heart back in the correct rhythm if it gets too out of control." Ari's holding up two small vials, both of them totally unassuming, the liquid inside clear and the labels simple black text on white.

"Hopefully we don't have to use both."

"We can't." Ari's eyes are luminous with worry. "They contraindicate each other. So let's hope either your heart stops and I just push the epinephrine, or the antiarrhythmic does its job and keeps your heart beating."

"Or, we can hope for neither," Maren suggests.

"Yeah, that would be aces if neither happened," Ari says. "But I'm prepared for the worst."

Silence descends upon them for a moment. Even the sounds of the city seem tiny, horribly far away. Everything seems to be fading away.

Ari's face goes through a complicated number of emotions, finally settling on something akin to *contorted*. Her mouth is scrunched to one side, pressed away from the center line of her face, tugging her nose with it. Her brows are creased together, almost screwed up, and it's too much to look at, so Maren looks away. She stares down at the cannula in her elbow instead, concentrating on what might shortly be her lifeline to the living.

"Hey." Ari's voice is soft, gentle. "Ren."

Maren looks back up at her. Her features have relaxed, but there's still worry in her eyes. She's leaning very close, one hand on Maren's knee, palm up. Without much thought, Maren puts a hand over Ari's. Their fingers lock together.

"You don't have to do this," Ari says. "I mean, you do. We do. But I want to give you the chance to back out."

"So I can wither away and die?" Maren asks. "No. We're doing this."

"I'm scared," Ari says. "Is that horrible of me? I'm not in danger here."

"I'm terrified," Maren admits.

"Maren," Ari says, bringing her other hand up to cup Maren's face. Maren closes her eyes, shutting out Ari's too-close eyes, leaning into the heat radiating from her palm.

"You're so warm," Maren murmurs.

Ari makes an aborted noise, something choked at the back of her throat.

"You're sure?" Ari asks. She sounds far away.

"Yes," Maren says.

"Let's light the candles, then," Ari says.

They rise together, Ari passing Maren a box of matches

to work with. This part Maren knows from various salons, knows how to draw upon the protection of the gods through flame. She remembers the prayer for this, the words to say.

Ari flicks the overhead light back off, the room lit only by the golden spill from a side lamp.

Two matches are struck, hiss to life.

They bend, reach for fresh candles, press fire to wick.

"Pluto, Lord of All, come with favor and joy. I summon you." Ari's voice is even.

"Serapis, Lord of All, come with favor and joy. I summon you." Maren's own voice seems hollow to her ears.

Their words weave, layer of invocation over layer of invocation. Tongues of flame reach for the ceiling, stretching up from the Underworld.

"Mors, come with favor and joy. I summon you."

"Anubis, come with favor and joy. I summon you."

They settle into their places at cardinal north and south. This time, though, they sit closer, knees almost touching. Ari has the two vials close at hand, syringes for each.

"*Patéras, anakaléo,*" Ari says. "You have to say them this time."

Maren takes a deep breath, closes her eyes. She rolls the words around in her mouth for a moment.

"*Patéras, anakaléo,*" Maren repeats. The words seem to hum in the air for a moment, and then they drop into the current.

Maren hadn't thought she could physically get any colder, but she's proven wrong. Now her breath is coming out as fog, when she can manage a breath through the chattering of her teeth. She steps into the room of shattered light and books and realizes where she is.

In her own summoning, the room is clearer. Maren feels like she walks on solid ground.

Familiarity greets her — the writing desk. The leather. The books, the notepads, the dim lights. The subway tokens in their jar.

When she faces Casper Augustine, he is a cracked husk, skin gray and shattered in places. One eye glows, and smoke blooms from the places in his skin where his body has broken open.

The other eye is hazel, a deep green-brown that's now as familiar to Maren as this room.

He reaches for her, a snarl contorting his face, and Maren lurches forward as pain explodes in her chest. Stumbling towards him, she feels like a fish on a line, thrashing at the end of a lure as pain ruptures through her. Her blood boils. Her bones turn to ice. When she cries out, it's with a sound that she knows she could never make in the living world, high and horrible and utterly inhuman.

"*Throw him out.*" Ari's voice, from within her.

Somewhere, far away, in another life, hands clasp her own. The warmth of the first true day of summer.

"*Push,*" Ari says. "*You can do it.*"

In the library, Maren closes her eyes, banishes what is left of Casper Augustine from her sight, and reaches deep. Reaches past the pain consuming her bit by bit, reaches deep into the ice coating her own soul. Her breath stutters, her heartbeat erratic and wild. Her chest feels like it's on fire, a punch to the ribs, and Maren gasps, tears prickling at the corner of her eyes.

Casper closes the gap between them and closes his hands around her heart.

She is no longer sure she knows what lives beyond pain.

"*Maren*," Ari says, and it is a command.

So she rises to the occasion and reaches back. Grabs that star-shard of another eternal soul, the wandering point of a constellation that has become trapped in her own orbit. She closes around it, pushing against the horrible throb of pain in her whole body, pushing against the feeling like she is about to shatter.

She cries out, a sobbing sound wrenched from her lips, tears coming easy now, brought on by pain swirling and rampaging through mind and body alike.

Her hair lifts around her. An electric storm, a summer thunderstorm, crackles at the back of her tongue.

Clutching Ari's hands with everything she has, she takes a deep breath, finds it pushed back out in another lurching sob, and then takes another deep breath.

Takes the cold air into brittle lungs.

Presses her whole spirit, her whole soul, all of her *ka* against the wrongness in her heart.

And pushes.

# CHAPTER 19

*Thais at the River*

The door opens.

Maren turns, expecting Ari. Instead, standing cloaked in the light behind him, Casper Augustine enters the library, whole and alive, although his edges fray and pulse in time with his heart, beating so loudly that Maren can hear it.

There's no pain, however. Everything seems muffled, like the city under heavy snow.

She wonders, distantly, if she should be afraid of this strange wave of a specter. For some reason, she can't quite manage the emotion. Or any emotion for that matter. When his eyes sweep past her, they don't linger. He can't see her. Frowning, she creeps closer to him, winding around the back of the couch.

Between one step and the next he stutters, stops, and then slings forward, a badly processed graphic. It's like he's moving through time differently than Maren, and she shadows his idiosyncratic path as he heads for the writing desk under the window. He picks something up — a letter opener. Or rather, what Maren had always thought was a letter opener. Instead, when she slides up close to Casper, she sees that it's actually more of a small dagger, delicately inlaid and bejeweled, the blade in need of a polish and the grip an equally dull copper. Instead of the shabbiness taking something away from the blade's beauty, it seems to enhance it, making the stones shine all the more.

Casper tosses the dagger, flipping it, catching it by the blade. He stares out the window in front of him, letting out a long sigh. Maren moves a bit further around him, watching his face fractal and shift, shadow and sunlight together. She tries to find Ari in his features, but it's hard with the way his whole being seems to have entered a liminal space it can't quite snap out of. Perhaps the nose? The ears?

The door opens a second time, and they turn as one.

Maren's eyes snap wide.

Where there should be another shadowy, fraying figure, there's instead a solid mass of popped galaxy lights, stars and haze spun tight together. The distortion moves with the figure, and when it says something, the sound comes out as a strange, unearthly noise, a harsh wind through trees edged with steel.

"How?" Maren says out loud, and her own voice sounds fine, if a bit distant.

"I'm not interested in having this conversation again–" Augustine is cut off by the figure raising its hands, long fingers curling into claws.

A sadness crosses his features. He slumps suddenly against the desk.

"Enjoy living with this," he gasps.

The dancing overlay of impossible lights where a person should be pushes their hands forward, rushing Casper. He starts choking before the person gets there, making the desk rattle apart for a moment, pieces and parts spinning outward and then returning. He clutches at his chest, his breathing horrible and gasping.

What little color had bled into this world starts to drain away from him.

The static figure reaches Augustine, reaches out, places one of those hands full of hatred on his chest.

Maren doesn't know what happens next, because the pain that explodes behind her eyes is so sudden, so horrible, that her vision drops white and she screams, the sound wrenched from her chest. Her whole body is on fire, her skin flaying, her blood boiling. If she has a heartbeat, she can't make it out; it's either too fast or too slow.

She is on the floor. Her screaming won't stop, tears running hot down her face. She is dying.

She's not supposed to be doing that. This is supposed to fix that.

*Don't you dare, Maren Nykara.*

She's not sure if she actually hears the words, or if she imagines them. She decides to cling to those words all the same. Cling to the last two bits. She knows those sounds, syllables, letters. They're hers. They belong to her, belong to her spirit and her body.

So she lets the pain all the way in.

Her scream changes. It's no longer the pain forcing the noise from her, but rather, her own breath pushing the agony from her lungs. She is not dying. Her soul is hers, whole and total, and she remembers that through the pain, through the blinding lights consuming the space.

One last push, her ribs breaking open, a piece of soul flung from her chest, somehow brighter than the pain.

She finds herself tumbling away, the floor beneath her gone. In that free fall, she lets the fire and the wrongness trail away, wicking away from her skin, dancing off the ends of her fingertips.

Cold hardwood meets her back with a sudden snap. She's having trouble breathing. There's a face, briefly, above hers.

Then, there's nothing.

266

—

It was impossibly cold. The kind of cold that snapped at you, over and over again, followed you inside, left you no respite. It had been like this all week, the chill having settled over the city last weekend. The weather casters had all been beside themselves, breathless with the promise of a *polar vortex.*

Maren hated it. Normally, thinking about the weather wasn't a habit she cultivated. It just wasn't worth it. New York was cold, New York was hot, it was everything in between. She'd made peace with that as a little kid, and nothing had ever challenged that. Except for this new, horrible frozen tundra that had found the city a great place to set up shop.

Maybe it was the anger that had been growing in her. There were days when she'd find herself on the floor, not knowing how to get up. Days where she'd start to walk and didn't stop until long after she should have. She had gone walking today, had walked down the High Line, then back up partially, and then taken a rickety pair of clanging metal stairs down to street level. She was probably putting herself in massive danger of frostbite, but she was also pretty sure that she hadn't gotten any yet.

The streets were mostly empty. Not shocking, no one could possibly want to be out in this. Maren didn't want to be out here either. It had just seemed like the best use of her time.

Her mother was dead. This was also not shocking, as Selene had been dead since Maren was twelve. Maren had been there, she would know. Would remember, carrying

267

that horrible day with her forever. It had gotten better on and off, but then everything got suddenly horrible again on anniversaries like this one, or important days. When she had moved into her dorm freshman year, after she had said goodbye to her dad and Fiona, promising them that she was right as rain, she'd closed the door, slid down it, and cried. It had been such a perfect picture, them moving her into this cramped space that she shared with another human being — terrifying — and yet it was also *wrong*. She loved Fiona, honestly. It was just that Fiona wasn't Selene.

Walking down the street, head bent against the cold as if that would somehow protect her from the temperature, she gritted her teeth and let her hands clench and unclench in her coat pockets. She'd pulled out her parka for this particular jaunt, some animal part of her brain awake enough in there to keep her from freezing to death.

The river surged along up ahead, the surface a cracked, splintering mess of gritty looking sheets of ice. The Hudson was gross on all days, this day no less so.

She stopped at the edge of the West Side Highway, gave it a few seconds of contemplation, watched a couple of taxis go by, and then plunged onto the asphalt, running full tilt into the wind, streaking across the street with little care for such things as crosswalks. A cab whistled by behind her, horn blaring long and loud at the girl making the dumb decision to run across a divided highway, but she ignored it, making a beeline for the other side of the street.

A thin layer of frozen snow greeted her on the walking path along the river. It swirled around her booted feet, a brittle sound against the leather as it pelted into her. She had lost feeling in her nose. It had felt cold when she'd started, then stung with the icy temps, and finally burned.

That was the last time she remembered being able to feel it.

"That's probably bad," she muttered, removing her hands from her pockets and clamping them over her nose, the rough wool of her gloves rubbing her skin and not doing much. Taking a deep breath, she stuck her bottom jaw out and blew hot air into her cupped hands, shivering a little bit.

Up ahead, the river seemed to be singing some strange, siren song. As she watched the chunks of ice slide past, she found herself drifting closer and closer to the water, towards the planter set in front of the railing separating her from the water.

The flowers were, very appropriately, totally dead and mostly covered in a sad combo of ice and snow. It all matched her mood pretty decently — a strange, cold, all-consuming void with brief moments of crystal clarity that somehow didn't make things make any more sense. It was miserable feeling like this. She didn't like feeling like winter was constantly living inside her head any more than she liked actually being out in the hideously bad weather.

A barge of some kind drifted by. For one brief moment a man stared at her from its deck, strange and gray with too-clear eyes, but she ignored him in favor of hefting herself up onto the edge of the planter, taking a delicate hop over the dead plants and landing, slightly precariously, on the far edge. The bricks were icy, and she found herself bracing her body against the railing to keep from spilling either back into the dirt or pitching forward into the water a decent drop below.

Braced on the railing, the metal cold enough that she could feel the radiating chill through her thick gloves, she stared, unblinking, down into the gray water. An eddy was

269

caught just below her perch, swirling around and around and around. Somewhere overhead, a gull let out a sheer call into the open air.

It was a dumb thing to think, a childish thing, but she missed her mom. Plenty of people had told her that it wasn't childish, and even if it was, she was basically still a kid, but she didn't feel that way. Almost ten years had passed, and somehow the wound still went back and forth between a hardened scar and a fresh gash right down the center of her chest, her own heart on display for her to see hurting. She sniffed in the cold air, frowning down into the water. She couldn't still be a kid, so she couldn't still feel like this. There had been a moment, last year, where she thought maybe she had finally found someone outside of a therapy office to talk to about it, but that hadn't panned out. The girl who she'd stupidly fallen head over heels for at a dumb party wasn't around anymore, and Maren couldn't mind. Or maybe she could, but she didn't want to mind. So she avoided it.

Tipping a bit more forward, she hung her body further over the railing. Her hands were starting to cramp against the cold of the metal, and there was a voice echoing, quiet, in the back of her mind — what if she did let go? She didn't think she actually ever would, but the voice was there all the same. A strange voice, coming from everywhere and nowhere at the same time.

The water wasn't a pair of open arms. It was a yawning maw. All the same, it was something that could hold a person, pull them down, take them apart. It seemed to open, seemed to glow darkly, calling to her.

She leaned forward. Her fingers strained.

"Please tell me you're not planning on jumping," a

voice said.

Blinking slowly, her eyes stinging, Maren turned towards the sound. There, standing a short way away, was a woman. She looked strange, most of her outfit hidden by a giant parka that went all the way down to her knees, but Maren could still tell that whatever was under the totally normal jacket wasn't standard. The edge of a skirt peeked out from under her coat — or maybe it was the hem of a robe. There was gold woven in her dark hair, the dozens of small braids playing host to metallic thread. The deep, rich blue of her coat stood out against everything, all of her looking like it was cut from some other cloth and hastily stitched into this tapestry.

Behind her, a few people were walking up a dock, a procession of quiet, somber folks in black and grays. A funeral, Maren realized suddenly.

"I'm — I'm not going to jump," Maren said. She found that she meant it.

"Good, because I just came from one funeral, and I don't have another one on the docket for today. Which is good, it's bloody freezing," the woman said. "How long have you been out here?"

"You were at a funeral?" Maren asked, leaning back a bit.

"Yep. That's what I do," the woman said.

It took Maren a moment to realize what the woman meant — she was a priestess. That was what the hints of strange robes were all about.

"You're, uh... in service to Serapis?" Maren said, struggling to remember the exact wording for the priests and priestesses who lived their lives to shepherd people safely into the afterlife.

271

"That's rather overly formal, but yes," the woman said. "I'm *hemet*. *Hemet* Thais Cooper, to be exact."

She stuck a hand out, her warm brown skin ungloved. Maren stared at the hand, not sure quite what to do with this woman who had appeared suddenly like a ghost and was now offering a hand to shake.

"You're going to have to come down. My hand is freezing," *Hemet* Cooper said.

"Yeah," Maren agreed, and, minding the icy lip of brick she was standing on, hopped back down to the ground, hurrying through the cold air over to the woman to clasp her hand, giving it a shake much firmer than she felt.

"What's your name?" *Hemet* Cooper asked as she pressed that hand to Maren's back, guiding her towards the crosswalk, joining them up with the group of people that Maren realized must be the mourners from the funeral. They were all different ages, their only linking characteristic that they all were dressed in whatever dark clothes they'd had in their wardrobes.

"Me?" Maren asked, and *Hemet* Cooper nodded. "I'm Maren Nykara."

"That's an old name," *Hemet* Cooper said with a smile as the light changed. Maren scrambled into the crosswalk after her, realizing that this woman was even a bit taller than her and had longer legs.

"Yeah," Maren said. "My dad's proud of it. It's an unbroken line back to the ancient world."

"It has to be strong to have pulled that off," *Hemet* Cooper said.

"I guess, if a name can be strong," Maren said. The bleak openness of the West Side Highway had given way to the cozier, more hemmed-in neighborhood of the West

Village, rows of brownstones and pre-war buildings rolling by as they walked under the cover of skeletal trees.

"Names can certainly be strong," *Hemet* Cooper replied. "Keep that one close."

Maren nodded, a bobbing motion.

"Yeah," she said. "I will."

—

Everything hurts.

Not just in a sore way, or an aching way, but in a super unpleasant stabbing fashion that seems to be attacking her whole body. Her chest is the worst of it, and every breath is agony. And even below the pain, under her skin, there is a strange feeling.

Maren lets out a low moan, tries to shift, and immediately regrets it. Taking a moment to take the deepest breaths she can manage with her ribs in open rebellion, she tentatively, carefully, reaches out with one hand. The pads of her fingers skim over soft cotton — a sheet. She's in a bed. Based on the weight on top of her, she's under the covers, tucked in tight.

As much as the thought frightens her, she knows she has to open her eyes. She has no idea what she's going to see. Although her memory is a hazy fog at the moment, there are enough pieces of the last twenty-four hours that she unfortunately needs to contend with the fact that she might actually be dead. What a shit death, though, to be in this much pain. The fact that she has to breathe also seems to be a tick in favor of being alive. Not blissfully alive — too much hurt for that — but alive nonetheless.

She swallows hard, squeezing her eyes shut. Taking a

273

moment to count to ten in her head, taking more of those shallow-deep breaths, she finally cracks her eyes open. Some small part of her mind had assumed that she'd be assaulted with light, but instead, she's in the semi-darkness of a late winter afternoon, the lights in the room off. The ceiling is beamed and white, nothing particularly distinct. Taking a rather painful minute to slowly rotate her neck, her eyeline drifts down from the nondescript ceiling to a soft taupe wall, and then a now-familiar set of drawers.

This is Ari's guest room. She's in the bed with the summoning circle at the foot. And she is, as far as she can tell, not dead.

The minute all of these thoughts collide in her idled, dizzy brain, she realizes what the strange feeling under the pain is.

It's warmth. Her own skin, radiating heat.

Her pulse picks up, but it doesn't frighten her for the first time in what feels like an age. It's the normal thud of her heart, clean and even. With a stuttered breath, half pain, half amazement, she rolls onto her side, blinking sleep from her eyes and staring into the room. The last light of the day is curling through the gauzy curtains, a beautiful golden spill. She closes her eyes, squeezes them up tight, and then opens them again. The room hasn't changed — the dying sunlight is still gorgeous, dust motes drifting lazily through the air, in and out of sunbeams.

She has a brief spike of a worry, a shot of adrenaline, that this could be a dream, the last bit of electrical impulse thrown off by her dying brain, but then she realizes that the IV is still in her arm, now squished under her a bit. Shifting, she frees it from the space between the bed and her chest, following the clear line up to where someone has hung a banana bag off one of the knobs on the wardrobe next to the bed. The sluggish drip feeds down towards her, presumably trying to get her back on her feet.

Careful of not only the IV line but also every other part of her aching body that's in pain — so, all of it — she very gingerly pushes herself up on her elbows. Her head spins with the effort, her ribs screaming as she curls up, stretching out a spine that feels like it might snap if she goes any further. She freezes, panting, afraid to move more.

"Ari?" She calls into the quiet. Her voice comes out sounding like she's been eating glass, raw and red. Gently clearing her throat, she tries again. "Ari?"

For a moment, nothing. And then, the sound of feet on the floor, bare skin slapping the old wood as someone jogs in her direction.

Ari appears in the doorway in a flurry of wide eyes and concern, projected so fiercely and wholly that Maren swears she can feel the waves of it from across the room. They stare at each other for a moment, Ari looking like she's seeing a ghost, and Maren with tears prickling in her eyes from the pain.

"I need to lie down," Maren croaks, and then inches back down into the comforting cradle of the bedding. Ari is at her bedside in an instant, very carefully taking a seat on the edge of the mattress. For a few long heartbeats Ari just hovers, and then she reaches out as if approaching a wild animal. Her fingers capture the hollow of Maren's wrist, pressing into the skin, and the point of contact sings between them. No longer a brand of sun in the darkness, Maren rises to her, both of them warm and whole.

Ari looks up at her, through where some of her hair has

275

fallen across her face. The fine strands are a limp mess but it doesn't matter. She looks like a painting to Maren in that light, lit from outside and in.

"I'm not dead, right?" Maren rasps.

"No, no, you're alive," Ari says in a long breath. She scrambles for something on top of the chest of drawers and slips the finger sensor back onto Maren's hand, watching it for a moment, her shoulders relaxing with each thump of Maren's heart. A smile creeps across her face and she says, low and quiet, "71."

Maren lets her eyes close, lets her face mirror the smile that she knows is still pressed into Ari's.

Raising the arm that isn't currently playing host to several medical devices, Maren holds her hand out to Ari.

"Thanks for saving me," Maren says. Ari's fingers brush her own, linking their hands together.

"You saved yourself," Ari says.

"Pretty sure I didn't keep my own heart beating while I was under," Maren says. "Did my heart stop?"

"Not totally. You for sure got a wackadoodle rhythm going that I had to fix, however."

"Is that accepted medical terminology? Wackadoodle?"

"Afib," Ari says, and Maren can hear the smile in Ari's voice. "That's the accepted medical term. But wackadoodle is a close second."

"Ok," Maren says. She can already feel sleep tugging at her again, her half-broken body ready to not feel anything anymore. In her foggy, warm state, she feels almost recklessly light. "Get down here."

"You're sure?" Ari asks. There's surprise in her voice.

Maren nods against the pillows. A breath, then two, and then, the mattress shifts, dips, and Ari lays down next to her, curling around one side of her. She fits her head into the flat of Maren's chest under her collarbone, and Maren wraps her arm around her, resting her palm against Ari's back. Under the covers, with the heater on, it's perhaps too hot for them both in the bed, this close.

Maren doesn't give a shit. When Ari squeezes Maren's body with her own, Maren squeezes back.

# CHAPTER 20

## *Hunger*

The pain is worse the second day. Ari drugs her up with some NSAIDs from her medicine cabinet and they manage to get her sitting up. Maren stays hunched over, panting with the strain. Once she gets herself into one position, getting herself out of it and into another proves to be exceptionally challenging.

"I don't understand," Maren mutters, sitting up against the headboard so that she can slowly eat a bagel sandwich Ari has put together for her.

"Your heart nearly stopped," Ari says. "And if I had to guess, I think you went pretty deep. Your body is reminding itself that you're alive."

"So what, if I hadn't pulled back, I could have just faded away into the underworld?" Maren asks.

"Yeah," Ari says. "Although I wouldn't have let that happen. I was working on keeping you alive on both the body and soul side. I had a hold on you."

"Thanks," Maren says.

"Stop thanking me," Ari says with a wide smile.

Maren stares at her, at her wide eyes and messy hair, and chapped lips, and thinks about kissing her. It's not a particularly weird thing to think, she's thought it before in her life. But she hasn't had a thought like that in years and years. It was so easy when they were young, almost conspiratorial in their physical need for each other.

Now, she just wonders what would happen if she turned

her head sideways and brought her lips to Ari's. Start it all over again. Leave a door open for Ari to break her heart again.

"I'm going to have to go home," Maren says.

"I'll take you," Ari says.

Maren should say *no, no, I can get home on my own.* It would be the easy thing to say. But the easy thing to do would be to let Ari take care of her.

"Only if you feel like it," Maren says.

"Of course I do," Ari says, a simple thing, no hesitation.

"Ok," Maren says, and then stops herself from saying *thank you* yet again.

Walking to the front door of the apartment makes Maren consider just lying down in the middle of the hallway floor and never getting up again. Dying slowly on the floor would certainly be less painful than her current situation. She's just narrowly escaped death, however, so she plows on, Ari's arm linked in hers so that she has some stability.

"I'm excited to meet Miu," Ari says as she locks the door behind them.

"She can be a little skittish around new people," Maren cautions. "Especially since she hasn't seen me in a few days."

"Just watch," Ari says. "I'm the cat whisperer."

"Hmmm," Maren says, because she highly doubts that, and also using actual words at the moment seems impossible.

Against all odds, Maren's legs protesting the whole time at being made to move, they make it outside. Stepping outside into the wintery weather the last few weeks has been a horrible, draining experience for Maren, the frigid air driving the chill within her even deeper. She still braces for it as the door swings open and an arctic blast of wind howls into the vestibule, carrying them out into the morning. The sky is crisp and clean and blue, and Maren lets out a long steamy breath from her chattering mouth. It certainly hurts, especially when she tenses up against the temperature, but it no longer feels like a dirge. It's just winter. Her nose and cheeks prickle with it, and she scrunches her face up, enjoying the feeling of having normal blood flow again. What a strange thing to no longer take for granted.

"Cab," Ari muses, as if there was even any other choice with Maren in her current state. Still supporting Maren, they take small steps to the edge of the sidewalk. While Ari thrusts a hand up and out in an attempt to reel in a taxi, Maren leans against an ancient *Village Voice* box to avoid falling into the sludge at the curb.

She takes a moment to just *look*. The world seems brighter somehow, like she'd already started slipping behind a darkening veil that she's sprung free of. Even though the snow has been reduced to a gross gray-brown slush, she still stares around with wide eyes, taking in every little grungy bit of the block. Icicles on creaking old fire escapes, pigeons cooing with every head bob as they putter here and there underfoot, an overflowing trash bin on the far corner. She feels like she's home again.

"I don't enjoy being an invalid," Maren murmurs after Ari's helped bundle her into the back of a cab. She rests her head against the window, enjoying the feeling of the chilled glass against her warm temple.

"Don't worry about it," Ari says, brushing the comment away. "I promise I'm ok doing this."

"No, not that," Maren says. "My body was failing me, and now it's semi-useless, and I just want to get back to feeling normal."

"Ok, that I understand," Ari says. She smiles softly over at Maren. She's wearing a striped scarf that she's wound around her neck enough times for it to stack all the way up to her chin.

They ride in silence for a while, the city slipping by in bits and pieces, clipped blocks and rapid turns. It's late enough in the morning that commuters have started up the morning rush hour, and their cabbie seems to want to avoid it all by taking every side street and corner he can. Maren has to pull her head away from the window; there's so much stopping and starting that she keeps bumping her temple into the glass. She rubs it in slow circles after the last bump, wincing at the stress that raising her arm produces in her upper back.

"Did you... uh, see anything?" Ari asks after a few more blocks. "On the other side."

Maren captures her bottom lip between her teeth, chewing on it in thought. A distant memory stirs in her mind, fogged and fractured. It's hard to wrap her head around it, to really get a good handle on what she saw while she was slipping towards the underworld.

"I did," Maren says, slow, words methodical. "But I don't know what it was."

"It might take a while to come back to you," Ari says. "Let me know when you remember."

"I will," Maren says.

She remembers the library. Remembers the paneling and the books and the furniture not quite fitting together correctly, light moving strangely. What she can't dredge up is why she was in the library, or if anyone was there with her. She thinks there must have been, but then again, the library isn't a place of singular sanctuary or solitude to her, so there's no guarantee that she isn't just remembering the half a dozen times she's been there in this real world.

The small TV mounted on the back of the front seat drones on through the same few things over and over again, ads and weather and small bites of news that aren't linked to any lodestone of time. Maren watches it out of the corner of her eye, feeling horribly like she's forgetting something that she has to remember. In one of the ads, three people stand in front of a painting at a museum, backs to the camera, and Maren fiddles with a loose button on her coat. The plastic is smooth under her fingers, real and solid.

Three people. She wasn't alone in the library. Two other figures stood with her.

"Maren?"

Dragging her gaze away from the back of the seats, Maren finds that Ari has started to open her door, one leg halfway out of the cab already as she shoves her wallet back into her purse. A frozen swirl of air seeps in from outside, scattering prickling cold across Maren's exposed hands and face.

"Sorry," Maren says, scooting across the bench seat to push herself up and out into that chill. The air wraps around her, but she shoves her hands into her pockets and dips her chin into her coat, refusing to let it settle into her soul. Not again, not anymore.

Her fingers are stiff as she fiddles with her keys, letting them into the vestibule of her building. It all feels so normal — standing on the delicate mosaic tile, fighting with her persnickety mailbox to get it unlocked. Ari stands at her shoulder as she wrenches a few envelopes out of the tiny box, a relic of an era when letters and postcards were small and not legal-sized envelopes. Maren's acutely aware of her, this sudden addition to a routine that she's been doing for years now.

Up two flights of stairs, pain with every slow lift of her legs. The wooden treads creak under their feet, worn down by thousands of steps over the years. Maren has a brief flicker of worry about what Ari is going to think of Maren's tiny apartment, but then moves past it. Ari had seen Maren's horrible college apartment, a crowded three-bedroom furnished in half flat-pack and half dumpster; certainly her current digs are a step up from that.

And so, when she opens the door, letting it swing in, she steps aside, letting Ari cross the threshold first. She watches the set of Ari's shoulders, the line of her neck down into her spine as she looks around, scanning the space as it welcomes her in.

The door shuts with a heavy, metal thump. Maren stands by the door, not taking her eyes from Ari until the telltale jingle of name tags heralds the arrival of Miu.

"Hey," Maren says. Without thought, out of habit, she makes to bend down to pet the cat, and immediately regrets it when it sends pain searing through her. "*Shit.*"

With Ari's help, she plops herself down on the floor, legs outstretched. Miu walks back and forth between her legs, bottle brush tail held proudly high. Not interested in sitting still, Miu accepts a pet or a pat on each cross. Maren's grin grows, and she curls over Miu, doing her best to ignore the sharp protests of pain her back fires off at her.

"I take it this is the famous Miu," Ari says. Maren looks

283

up, nodding. Taking a more refined path to sitting on the floor, Ari sits next to Maren and offers a hand to Miu. The cat stops her back and forth across Maren's legs to give Ari a cursory glance, her yellow eyes slits as she examines the proffered hand. She sniffs the air, and then scoots closer to Maren, wrapping her tail around herself and purring against Maren's leg. Ari barks out a startled laugh.

"Told you," Maren says.

"I'll win her over, just you wait," Ari says.

They sit in silence, there on the hardwood, the apartment dark and cool around them, Maren running her hand over Miu's fluff. When Maren looks up Ari is backlit by one of the living room windows, the dim winter light catching on the burnished russet of her hair. Seeing her silhouetted like that, her features hooded and flat and color popped around her edges, tugs at something in Maren's mind, but she can't quite reach it.

—

Ari has to help her back up off the floor. It takes a while, Maren's body screaming in protest at every infinitesimal movement where she must support her own weight.

"You went harder than I thought you did," Ari says as Maren flops onto the sofa, letting her head tip back so that her neck doesn't have to bother with doing any work. "I mean, it was… a lot. You were a lot."

"How so?" Maren asks to the ceiling. The couch cushion next to her dips, and a second later familiar paws patter onto her thigh. She puts a hand on Miu automatically, scratching behind her ears and earning a chattery stanza of small meows in return.

"Well. I don't know what you were doing down there, or where you even got to, but you went gold."

"I don't know what that means," Maren says, rolling her head to the side so that she can see Ari.

"Your eyes went gold, like mine do. But you were... I don't even know how to describe it. I mean, I do, clinically. You went into afib, fell on the floor, your muscles all spasmodically, involuntarily contracted. You looked like you were going to break. Your spine was off the floor, like a span." Here Ari pauses, rolling words around her mouth, looking away from Maren for a moment. "It looked like you were being tortured."

"Yeah, that tracks with how I'm currently feeling," Maren says.

As much as she could have done without that information — that image of her body pushed so far past its limits that her heart was sounding a death knell against her ribs while she rose from the floor in sheer pain — she knows it's now going to stick with her for a while.

"I'm sorry this happened," Ari says.

"You helped, not hurt," Maren says.

"None of this would have happened if my dad hadn't landed in your House," Ari says, letting out a long sigh.

"No, I suppose it wouldn't have," Maren says, slow, methodical. "But what's done is done, and we've come out the other side. It's ok."

"You're too forgiving of me," Ari says. Her voice is quiet and scratchy.

"That's for me to decide," Maren says, raising her head to look Ari square in the eyes.

A pause, and then–

"I miss him," Ari blurts out. "Is that horrible? I do. He was *such* a dick. Do you know we were estranged? And not because I was gay, but because he thought I was dating 'below my station'? He didn't give a flying fuck about the gender of the person I loved, just that they were a normal college kid. The man still believed in arranged marriages. But I miss him, all the same."

Maren holds a hand out on the cushions between them, palm up, fingers extended. Ari looks at it for a moment before she closes her own hand over Maren's, sealing their palms together. Maren gives a squeeze, a soft smile.

"You are allowed to miss him," Maren says. "Often in death transgressions are forgiven by the living."

"I don't want to hear that," Ari says. "I don't want to hear from *Sesheta* Maren. I know you're so fucking good at that, but that's not the you I know. Besides, I can doctor myself well enough."

"I only know how to do death as *sesheta*," Maren says, calm and quiet.

"What did you do after your mother died?" Ari asks.

Maren could certainly continue playing her role, could make something up about how she grieved. But she doesn't remember what she did, and even if she did, she's certain it wasn't anything good.

"I woke up," Maren says simply, instead. "I had fallen asleep in her arms one night. We'd made dinner and she couldn't eat anymore at that point, so she was napping on the couch. My father and my aunt and I ate around the coffee table. None of us wanted to get too far from her. She'd been slipping further and further, more with each day. Not fading, per se. More... withering. She was still there, still a defined space, but there was less and less of

286

her each day.

"I woke up thirsty in the middle of the night, and I realized something was wrong when her arms didn't feel right. She was stiff. I guessed what had happened, I knew what was coming. And then... I don't know. I remember almost nothing of the next week. My first firm memory afterwards was the boat ride to Staten Island. It was impossibly cold, and I insisted on standing up on deck in the open air. The wind was so intense it felt like it was stripping the skin from my bones. I cried a lot, daily sometimes. Every little thing set me off, when I realized my mom wasn't there. A tough problem on my homework, not being able to braid my hair correctly. My dad tried hard, but it wasn't like he could heal me from the hole she left in my life. And after a while, like I was a pebble in the waves, the edges rubbed off and it became softer in my mind."

"You got over it," Ari says, *sotto voce*.

"No, never," Maren says, shaking her head. "The days between missing her just increased. But there are still times when I miss her terribly. I missed her the day we broke up, both because we broke up and I needed someone to talk to, but also because I realized that I never came out to her. I mean, I don't know if I even fully knew. I was twelve when she died. But I cried that day, and the day I graduated. Every birthday is hard, hers and mine, and the day she died. But you learn to know the pain. It gets familiar."

"I'm sorry," Ari says.

"Don't be," Maren says. "I'm sorry you're having to cope with this now. Your relationship with your dad complicates it."

287

Ari scoots closer, resting her head on Maren's shoulder. Miu gives her a wary side-eye but doesn't move, purring protectively on Maren's lap. Maren drapes an arm around Ari's shoulder, wincing when it pulls all her muscles just a bit too much for her current state of health.

"I'm sure that if Duat is real, his heart is being eaten right now," Ari says venomously. "Hope it's a juicy snack for Ammit."

"She's probably enjoying it as we speak," Maren says.

"Good for her," Ari says confidently.

"You can miss him," Maren says. "There's nothing written that says you can't."

"I know that logically," Ari says. "Doesn't mean I can rationalize it emotionally."

"I hear that," Maren says.

Ari scoots closer, fitting herself into the hollow made by Maren's outstretched arm and the side of her body. Something moves automatically in Maren's body, lets her roll her hips so that she can bracket Ari's body with her own. Miu squawks at being moved, but the minute Maren is settled again, the cat curls up in the crook of her bent knees. Maren lets her head come to rest on Ari's, turns her face into it, inhales.

For a long time after they broke up, Maren had remembered what Ari smelled like, her shampoo a sharp smell of salon chemicals and her skin doused in some kind of fruity body wash. Ari's shower had been a riot of colorful products, and Maren remembers having to hunt for one that didn't smell overwhelming like a fruit basket every time she'd stayed over. The finer points of those smell memories are gone now, given away to the visual memory of the thousands of bottles in the shower. She'd

288

almost expected Ari to smell like that still, but she doesn't. Instead, it's that tang of ginger and lemon and honey.

"Your hair smells like you wash it in tea," Maren murmurs, her eyes closing.

"That sounds nice," Ari says, fatigue trickling through her own words. "But I don't."

"Figured," Maren says. "Not much of a cleaning agent."

Ari snorts out a quick punch of laughter, the corner of her smile warm against the juncture of Maren's neck and shoulder. To feel both of them warm again, Maren giving as good as she's getting, is like waking up to a brand-new sunrise. It's the most beautiful thing Maren has ever felt.

Without thinking, she turns her head that last little bit, lets gravity pull her, and drops a kiss on the top of Ari's head.

Something in Ari's posture stiffens. Maren's eyes snap open, her pulse suddenly racing with the realization of what she's done.

They pull away from each other. Ari's eyes are wide, ringed by day-old makeup, and there's a crease of confusion between her brows. It yanks at Maren's heart and she swallows hard, balancing herself on the couch with the arm that had just been holding Ari.

Those two impossible words are on the tip of Maren's tongue, simple and horrible and impossible all at the same time. A basic, *I'm sorry*.

Her lips part. And then Ari dives back in, pushing her body against Maren's, every possible plane pressed together. Maren lets out a little *oof* when her sore ribs wail at the sudden weight, but she ignores the spike of pain in favor of tangling her hands in Ari's sleek hair, pressing her palms flat against the sides of her head.

"You were about to apologize," Ari says, and she is so, so close, a blush blossoming across her cheeks and the bridge of her nose, her eyes impossibly large and luminous. "Don't you fucking dare."

"Ok," Maren says, and kisses Ari. Lets it all drop, lets it all in.

Ari makes a noise in the back of her throat that Maren remembers, and presses impossibly closer, lips on lips, Ari's hands gripping Maren's shoulders like her life depends on it.

"*Ribs*," Maren manages to wheeze out between kisses.

"Sorry!" Ari says, breathless, pulling back for a moment before diving back in. She kisses ferociously, hard and punishing and unforgiving, like she never wants to stop and they don't have enough time in the world. Maren loves it, revels in it, pulling Ari's head back by her hair to tip her chin up.

*Hunger*. Maren remembers this, remembers starving. A yawning need that she's always felt with Ari. It used to make her feel powerful, but now there's something desperate about it instead. A pleading for something more. It's a thunderstorm, when all she wants is a calm sea.

# CHAPTER 21
## *Sesheta Maren Nykara*

Although it's not her proudest moment, she sits in the shower. On a step stool from the kitchen, but still sitting. She just can't be bothered to stand, not with the way her body is currently feeling. Although the sharpest aches and pains have faded a bit, a dull roar at the back of her mind, the general whole-body soreness is still out in full force.

She lets her head hang, her arms braced on her thighs as the warm water sluices over her skin, a warm embrace after months out in the cold. Drips of water roll down the tile as steam rises around her. It feels like renewal. Her body melts under it all, burning muscles and taut skin, and she welcomes it as she's welcomed few things before in her life.

The fact that she's not dead, and no longer dying — or, at least, no faster or more actively than usual — is a relief, but in a simpler way than she'd expected. She's heard stories about people with new leases on life, people who radically alter their paths after nearly dying. None of that kind of upheaval appeals to her. All Maren wants is to get back to work and get back to normalcy. She knows that she may never have normalcy, not really. There are too many facts and conjectures in the way of a quiet life for her now. A possibly-murdered man walked himself to her crematorium, got in, and bathed himself in fire, all post-mortem. No answers have surfaced, just more and more questions. Who could have murdered Casper Augustine, if he even had been murdered, and then who urged his spirit to get up and walk, all the way to its possible final death? Maren has a feeling the image of him shuffling to the retort will be popping up in her nightmares for a long time to come.

She'd love to have answers, would love to know if Ari's mother really did it. She seems so incredibly ordinary for someone who might have committed murder.

Maren watches the water swirl down the drain, around and around, and closes her eyes, letting out a long breath. Ultimately, it doesn't matter. It can't matter, because otherwise it will eat her up inside. She could compartmentalize it, she supposes, tucking it away in a safe corner of her mind.

Or she could let it go. She opens her eyes. Droplets of water fall from her outstretched fingertips, joining the rushing river at the bottom of the tub.

Stepping back over the edge of the tub is as painful as getting in had been. She lets out a little groan of relief when she's finally standing on the bathmat, the humid air clinging to her damp skin, almost claustrophobic. Wrapping herself in a towel she stands there for a few moments, taking deep breaths and generally dripping everywhere. When she finally moves, it's to the sink, where she has to wipe off the mirror to get at her reflection. She's been avoiding staring at her own face as much as possible lately, and she can't say she enjoys the image that looks back at her. Although her skin has a livelier tint to it again, and her eyes no longer look like empty pits, she's still too skinny. She lost weight during this mess, and her cheekbones are too prominent, her chin a bit too much of a point. She wants to be able to look in the mirror and not wince at what she sees.

Ruffling as much water out of her hair as she can with her shoulders and arms as sore as they are, she leaves her reflection in the bathroom, turning off the light for good measure.

Ari has moved while Maren was in the shower. She's rolled over and spread out, taking up a fair amount of the bed, arms and legs akimbo. One side of her face is mashed into a pillow, and her hair is a disaster. Last night, slowly and gently in light of Maren's pain, they'd remembered each other. It hadn't felt like the homecoming that Maren had needed it to be. They'd both been closed off, unwilling to make anything more of it.

Taking a moment to watch the soft rise and fall of Ari's back in the early morning light, Maren bites her lower lip, worrying it between her teeth. She wanders closer, letting her knees thump against the edge of the mattress. One sleepy eye lazily opens, blinking up at Maren.

"Time izzit?" Ari mumbles.

"6:30," Maren answers.

"Work," Ari sighs, closing her eye and turning her face fully into the pillow.

"Yeah," Maren says.

It seems strange to just be returning to work like this, after she's upended and restarted her life all in one weekend. But in reality, it's just another Monday that she's still alive for, and that means she needs to go into the House and work on evening out the relationships she's been gleefully ruining for the past few months.

They stay like that for a moment, both still, before Ari flops over onto her back, staring up at the ceiling, hair dragging across her face. She tries to blow some of it out of

293

the way before giving up and yanking it away instead. The stark strands fall to the white pillow below her.

"I… feel the need to say something, but I don't know what to say," Ari says. Maren's lips twist into a frown, and she carefully sits on the edge of the bed, mindful of her aching joints.

"About yesterday, or the day before?" Maren asks.

"Yesterday. I have plenty of words about the day before, most of them expanded versions of 'thank fuck you're not dead,'" Ari says. Her face takes on a rueful cast, something in her brows and the corners of her mouth. In the dim light of a barely-risen sun, she looks almost ashen.

"I feel it too," Maren says quietly.

"I don't want to feel it," Ari says. "But I also don't know what the alternative is. I don't know what we're supposed to feel like."

"I'm not sure we're supposed to feel any particular way," Maren says with a shrug. Ari's still staring at the ceiling. "Hey."

"Hey what?" Ari asks.

"Can you look at me?" Maren asks, rounding the edges of her voice.

It takes a moment, but Ari rolls onto her side, propping her head up with her hand. The tight material of her crimson shirt pulls across her shoulders, a pop of color in the desaturated dawn.

"It's me," Ari says. "I can't maintain meaningful relationships."

"You have meaningful relationships," Maren says. "Your sister, Roger and Juni, your friends."

"I've never had a romantic relationship last longer than a year, though," Ari says.

"Same," Maren admits with a bitter grin. "Including, you know, us."

"Good to know we're both shitty at this," Ari sighs, flopping back down.

Maren wants to pettily point out that Ari was the shitty one. Instead — "I can't imagine that anything we've been dealing with lately is helping."

"Yeah," Ari says. "I mean, my dad's still dead. But you're not dying now, so that's nice."

Maren stays silent, watching Ari for another moment before standing with a grimace. Her skin has dried and the chill is starting to prickle it, gooseflesh rising on her arms.

"C'mon," Maren says, extending a hand to Ari. "Pretty sure we can get through the week."

"You say that, but who knows," Ari says. "After all, this week is going to be its own kind of special stupid."

"Busy week?" Maren asks as Ari grabs her hand, hefting herself out of bed mostly under her own power, which Maren's sore arm is eternally grateful for.

"I'm on a four-day-twelve-hour shift this week due to a bunch of scheduled surgeries, and the wedding's on the weekend," Ari says. "Busy is an understatement."

"Oh shit, I forgot," Maren says, honestly surprised and aghast, because she has never made a habit of forgetting anything, especially anything important.

"You had other things on your mind," Ari points out.

*Don't say it–*

"I'll go with you," Maren blurts.

Ari stares at her, blinking and wide-eyed as if Maren had slapped her. Maren supposes it was sort of a verbal slap.

"You're sure?" Ari asks, hesitant and quiet.

"No, but that's ok," Maren says. "I'd... I'm interested in dancing."

"Ok," Ari says with a slow smile. There is something bright in her face again, the sun behind her eyes, and Maren finds herself smiling softly at her. Ari reaches out, resting a palm over Maren's even pulse through the column of her neck, and then darts in to press a kiss to Maren's mouth. Her lips part in surprise, an inhalation, and then the kiss is over just as fast as it started. Maren licks her lips, swallows hard. She wants nothing more in that moment to reach out to Ari, to tumble back into bed, to forget the world. But neither of them can. Not now, possibly not ever.

———

The House is quiet and empty when she gets in. The basement door swings open on its normal squeaky hinges, and she has to scramble for the alarm panel like always — it had been installed slightly too far from the door to take a leisurely walk over to it. With the insistent beeping silenced, she stands in the dark of the hallway and takes in a deep breath, closing her eyes for a moment and centering herself. She's been so tied up in her own head, hands bound by binding of her own making, that she hasn't felt at ease in the House like she normally does.

It smells like dust, and old wood, and under it all, decay and spice and oil. It smells like home.

A deep breath in, bringing it all into her lungs, and out. Greeting the House, sharing the air it holds within its walls.

She refuses to take the elevator, climbing to the second floor on sore legs instead. It's exhilarating though, knowing that the burn in her body is just an ache, that her breath and heart remain stable and even as she makes her way upstairs. She leaves her jacket and bag in her office and collects a box before heading down the hallway to the room at the front of the house.

Everything is exactly as she'd last seen it. She assumes, anyway. Tad and Oscar's side of the room could be a differently arranged hurricane than usual, and she wouldn't know. To her, it just looks like the usual bomb went off.

She falls to her knees in front of the old fireplace, opening the slide-topped wooden box she'd brought with her from her own office's fireplace. Pulling a long match from the box, she strikes it and holds it to the wick of each pillar candle in turn until they're all lit. She lights the few smaller candles on the mantle as well and then flips on Henry's desk lamp, leaving the space illuminated only by the low-wattage bulb and the cascading firelight.

Lastly, she pulls the good tequila and two shot glasses from the bottom drawer of Henry's desk, regarding them with a critical eye before realizing that first thing in the morning is probably a terrible time for alcohol. She puts them back in the drawer and sits behind his desk instead, brushing down the front of her blouse and taking a deep breath. The specifics of what she's going to say to Henry are a bit washed out and undefined, but she's not worried about that. She's good on her feet. Mostly, she just wants to make this go away, wants everything to return to a sense of normalcy.

She doesn't realize she's dozed off, her head pillowed on her crossed arms, until someone is lightly shaking her shoulder. She raises her head slowly, almost shyly, blinking up at the two people standing at her side. Henry is looking at her with some degree of concern, Thais behind

297

him with her mouth pressed into a thin line.

"Gods, I'm so sorry," Maren says, huffing out a small laugh. "I was waiting to chat with you."

"The candlelight is a nice touch, very romantic," Henry says. "But unfortunately I just got a call, and we need to be on standby to receive a few bodies. Can it wait?"

"Sure," Maren says, even though she wants to say no. "A few?"

"Three," Henry confirms, somewhat gravely.

"Same family?" Maren asks, although she has a feeling she already knows. A sad nod from Henry confirms it, and she sighs, sweeping some of her curls out of her face and back behind her ears.

"I'm going to go get ready for intake," Henry says. He hangs his coat on the rack by the door and then he's gone, Maren's plans derailed. Instead, she finds herself face to face with Thais as the other woman perches on the edge of Henry's desk. She's still bundled in a coat, a toggle parka complete with fur-lined hood, as if she's about to embark on a journey into the arctic unknown.

"You're here for the funeral this afternoon?" Maren asks.

"I am," Thais says. "And because I wanted to see you. I didn't like where we left our conversation last week."

"I didn't either," Maren says, leaning back in the desk chair.

"This is your House, absolutely. I would never seek to change that, and frankly, cannot, considering you're the rightful owner according to the state. I also know that it's your home, and it would be a cruelty to take it away from you. However, I also want to make it abundantly clear that even though it is not strictly written anywhere, necromancy is a morally forbidden issue that should never darken the doorstep of any Mortuary House or Complex. The House of Five Gates will be your House as long as you see fit to keep it. But if I need to, if your behavior continues, I will make a recommendation that either Mr. Archer-Manius or Mr. Hadley be elevated to the rank of chief embalmer. It's for everyone's protection — including yours. I'm not well-versed in spirit or death magic, but I know enough that it would be disastrous to let you continue working that close to souls if you're dipping your toe into a well that has no bottom."

"Neither Tad nor Oscar is in any way ready to take on the role of *sesheta*," Maren says.

"I'm sure they could handle it if they needed to," Thais says, her fingers interlaced around one of her knees. Her nails are painted a lovely deep copper, flashing brightly in the morning light.

"Trust me when I say that I'm not looking to divest myself of my title," Maren says.

"I figured," Thais says. "I've never seen someone jump at the ability to step into these shoes like you have. I can't imagine you'd want to throw it away so quickly, and for so little."

"Thais," Maren says, sighing heavily, and she leans forward. "It's fine. You don't have to worry about me, I promise. While I appreciate you wanting to protect the souls we're charged with, know that we're aligned on that. It's not just my job, it's my purpose. What I did — and it is past tense — was to assist one of those souls. I swear by the Gods."

Thais stares her down for a moment, hovering above Maren a bit like a specter. The firelight warms her dark skin, edges her in a sharp golden glow.

"You lied to me," Thais says. It should be an accusation, but it's more a simple truth.

"I did," Maren says. "And I'm telling you the truth now. What I did, I did to save someone."

"Death magic doesn't save people."

Maren knows there's no way she'll ever convince Thais, even though she wants to. There's a part of her that wants to stand from her chair, of height with Thais, and let her know everything, every last seamy detail of just what necromancy is capable of, from death to life. She doesn't, though. She carefully wraps all those words up and puts them to rest at the back of her mind. Instead, she takes a deep breath, never looking away from Thais' black eyes, and leans back once again, letting the chair tip a bit.

"I'm not sorry for what I did. I *am* sorry for worrying you. And everything is in the past. I'm here, completely present, and ready for the funeral this afternoon," Maren says.

"Alright," Thais says after a pause. "I hope I'm not misplacing my trust in you, Maren. It would break my heart."

"You're not," Maren says, shaking her head and swallowing hard. "I'm still with you."

"Good," Thais says. Her face softens, a smile brushing across her features. It warms something in Maren, that same part of her that feels like utter shit for doing all of this in the first place. She realizes, almost distantly, that it's probably what's left of her moral compass.

There's a knock, and they both turn to see Henry in the door, looking tired already.

"They need your signature," Henry says, nodding at

Maren.

"Yes, of course," Maren says, standing. "We're all good?"

"We're all good," Thais confirms, and gives Maren's shoulder a squeeze on the way by.

Henry keeps sneaking looks at her out of the corner of his eye as they spiral down to the basement.

"You're looking better," he says finally. "Less corpse-like."

"Thanks," Maren says with a quirked grin.

---

The funeral that afternoon goes off without a hitch, and they bid farewell to the man who found his way into their care after a skiing accident. As always, Maren watches them push away from the dock and into the slipstream of the Hudson, safely at the end of the pier and bundled up against the wind tunnel the river always provides.

With three new bodies in the House, the week goes from a sleepy sendoff of a few funerals to a busy dash to get the first steps of the mummification process done on their new clients. Even though Maren had said that neither Tad nor Oscar was ready to be chief embalmer, that doesn't mean they're not perfectly capable of working with supervision. They each take one of the bodies, rotating them across the two steel tables in the prep room. As is often the case with multiple deaths in the same family at the same time, they'd died in a vehicular accident — a small plane crash, in this case. A mother, father, and teenage daughter. They'd left behind two older children, twin boys safely away at college. A sister of one of the parents had done the intake to spare hauling the boys home just for this, which in a way, Maren is thankful for. She can't imagine the pain those two must be going through at the moment.

They spend the days in the basement, working against time before returning the family to cold storage each night. Maren gets home at the end of each work shift smelling like new decay and general viscera. They're having to do a fair amount of work on the bodies, as they'd suffered extensive damage in the crash. Usually the most destruction that Maren has to repair is her own from cutting open the torso to remove and treat the organs.

By Wednesday night she knows she's not going to have any free time to sneak away from work and attempt to wrangle a dress of some kind for the wedding. While she does own quite a few nice, professional dresses, none of those are even remotely close to falling under the header of black tie. And so, she calls in an eleventh-hour assist — or rather, texts in one.

Thursday rambles past, and then Friday. She finds herself ending her first week fully back in the driver's seat of her life standing on the steps of the house with Oscar, Tad, and Henry, Maren locking up behind them all. The gold hieroglyphs on the door glint in the sulfuric glow of the streetlights.

"Drinks?" Henry suggests. "We've had a bit of a week."

"Maren's had a few weeks," Oscar says.

"You have been in and out," Tad agrees. "How are you feeling?"

"Much better, thank you," Maren says with a small smile. "And I'd love to join you for drinks, but I have a date with my stepmother."

"Nykara," Henry admonishes. "On a Friday night? We need to get you a girlfriend before you morph into an old lady in front of our eyes."

"Having a significant other does not preclude aging," Maren says. "And also, I'm someone's plus one for a wedding this weekend so Fiona's brought me some dresses to try on."

"Oh man," Tad says, raising his eyebrows. "How did we not know? Are you going to tell us everything about her?"

"No," Maren says. Truth is, she's not sure how much there is to tell. With how busy both of their weeks have been, Maren hasn't seen Ari since Monday. They've texted — or rather, Ari has texted in vague semi-hysterics and Maren has texted back encouraging emojis — but she hasn't even heard Ari's voice in the last five days. After what they've been through in the last few weeks, it's a sudden, visceral change.

"Fine, keep your secrets," Oscar says. "But we're going to get drinks."

"Well deserved," Maren says. "Someone have one for me."

Waves and pleasantries are exchanged and then Maren's off like a shot, hailing a cab in the interest of getting back to her apartment as fast as possible. There's a good chance that she'll still be a bit late returning home and that Fiona will have beaten her there, unfortunately.

Sure enough, Fiona is standing on her front steps loaded down with several bags, all bearing names of various stores that are a step above what Maren would have expected.

"Gods, Fiona, what did you do?" Maren asks, agape, as Fiona crushes her into a hug. Her ribs twinge a bit but the

303

aches and pains from last weekend have luckily receded immensely, helped along by painkillers.

"Had fun," Fiona says conspiratorially. "Also everything you don't pick is getting returned, don't worry. And I brought some sandwiches for dinner!"

"You are my knight in shining armor," Maren says. "I would have shown up to this wedding in a little black dress I've worn to several dozen funerals if it wasn't for you."

"Can't let that happen," Fiona says, holding up the bags triumphantly.

The various dresses get laid out on Maren's bed, Miu immediately hopping up to do a thorough inspection of the merchandise.

"Miu, you cannot shed on these, they're being returned," Maren tells her, as if that will stop Miu from picking her favorite to sit on.

"Here, come join me and shed on my nice white shirt," Fiona says to the cat, picking her up and kissing the top of her head. Miu immediately hunkers down, as Fiona is one of her approved people from whom she'll accept affection.

Maren grabs the first dress at random and heads to the bathroom. The minute the door is shut, Fiona hollers after her.

"So, who is this person you're a wedding date for?"

Of course. Maren doesn't have a good answer for that. She wishes she does. Gods, she'd take an answer from Fiona on that front. But if she doesn't know, Fiona certainly doesn't know.

"An old friend," Maren yells back as she shimmies into the first dress. It's a slippery satin, with a sort of slinky old-Hollywood glam to its cut. The silver material is gorgeous, impossibly smooth under Maren's palms, but it doesn't feel particularly like her, and, more alarming, it shows off the angry points of her hips and ribs. She turns her back on her reflection, opening the door just wide enough to grab another dress from Fiona.

The second one ends up being a floor-length shift with an attached cape, the yoke a glittering fantasia of traditional beading — there's even a scarab crawling over one shoulder.

"Too on the nose," Maren pronounces when she decides she can at least show Fiona this one. "Also, thank the Gods I don't have to dress like this on the daily."

"Could you imagine trying to keep all of that cream clean in a Mortuary House?" Fiona asks, looking somewhat queasy at her own suggestion.

"It would be physically impossible," Maren says. She sweeps over to the bed, the trailing fabric behind her making her feel like a queen while she sizes up the remaining possibilities. There's a gown with a larger skirt, but it's an overly heavy satin in a floral pattern, so she passes. Another one is a quite basic black gown, which Maren supposes will probably be a good runner up if nothing else works. She picks up a lightly-sequined violet gown, eyeing the spaghetti strap top, when she notices that it had been covering one last dress.

Deep emerald velvet is spread across her comforter in a perfect column. Tossing the shimmering dress aside, she holds up the last gown instead.

"Oh wow," Maren says.

"That one is a whole look," Fiona says sagely with a nod.

It is. The dress fits like a glove, molded to her body the minute she tugs the zipper into place. It falls down the lines of her body, leaving her arms bare, and rising to her neck. With the thick fabric, she looks whole, not a spindly mess of almost-death.

"Ok," Maren tells her reflection before opening the door for the last time.

"Oh yes, yep, that one!" Fiona says, giving Maren a double thumbs up as she stands in front of the full-length mirror next to her closet. In the soft, neutral tones of her room, Maren stands like a bronzed statue, the jade of the gown saturated and rich.

"Absolutely," Maren says, doing one slow revolution in front of her reflection, watching the smooth whisper of fabric against the ground.

"Well, whomever this old friend is," Fiona says, "they might just fall in love with you tomorrow."

"I'd be surprised," Maren says.

"I wouldn't," Fiona says, and then, "sandwiches?"

# CHAPTER 22
## A Golden Wedding

Maren has been to a fair number of weddings in the past few years, mostly college friends and a few people from high school who she's stayed in touch with, and they've all tended to follow a standard structure: the marriage certificate is signed, and then a procession is lead to the party location, usually a park or someone's backyard. They're fun, easy celebrations, joyful feasts where most of the budget has gone into the food, the long tables watched over by silent *lars*. Dancing goes on long into the night, the party thriving on the cheer of the bodies moving on a laid-down dance floor.

She knows the minute she steps into the lobby of the Augustines' apartment building that this is not going to be one of those weddings. The certificate was signed somewhere tucked-away, and guests are to arrive straight to the dinner part of the evening. The lobby has even been decorated with massive, extravagant vases, resplendent palm fronds, wheat sheafs, and lilies bursting from their mouths. The ones on either side of the reception desk reach to the height of the smiling doorman behind the desk, even though they're resting on the floor. A calligraphic sign in brilliant gold ink welcomes Maren to the marriage of *Ms. Phaedra Lucanus Augustine and Det. Felix al Waset Perry*. This too has sprigs of wheat bursting from its back, carefully attached to the easel holding the sign.

"This is… a lot," Maren murmurs as another doorman

presses the elevator call button for her.

"It's the Augustines," he replies easily, a breezy smile on his face.

The elevator doors open into a receiving hall, populated by a couple signing a guest book placed on a vintage table. In the candlelit hall, it takes Maren a few steps to recognize one half of the couple.

"Detective Choi," Maren says, surprised.

"Ms. Nykara, nice to see you," Choi says, standing up straight and returning her smile. She places a hand on the back of her companion. "My husband, Arda."

"So good to meet you," Maren says, exchanging a handshake with Choi's rather broad husband. His smile is just as wide, his eyes sparkling.

"This is Maren Nykara, the chief embalmer of the House of Five Gates," Choi says.

"Oh wow," Arda says, nodding along. "What a job that must be."

"It's a privilege to serve Serapis and the dead," Maren says, and Choi smothers a laugh at the canned response into a cough behind Arda.

"I bet, I bet," Arda says.

Maren's saved from figuring out a reply to that by the room they've just stepped into. The ballroom at the top of the building is an impossible space, made even more impossible by the current decorations. Round-topped windows reach up two stories, providing a light-studded panorama of the city at twilight, the sun leaving the sky smudged a deep purple. The glass is bisected by a colonnade that plays host to carved bookshelves behind each pillar, stocked with old books. With the wood paneling, it feels a bit like the library. However, the fresco arching over their heads is a stark departure from the sedate feeling of the library — Bacchus, larger than life, is surrounded by freewheeling maenads, the feast gilded onto the ceiling beyond any mortal celebration.

"Damn," Choi says thoughtfully, her eyebrows raised. Maren follows her line of sight to where a dance floor has been placed in the center of the room, long tables arranged on each side. There are smaller versions of the floral arrangements from downstairs on the tables, and the light here is low as well. Instead, candles flicker in long lines down the table runners, and uplighting in a brilliant gold has been placed around the room, warming the walls. People are already sitting at the tables, the string quartet in the corner going at it as one adventurous couple glides across the dance floor.

The dance floor that, it would also seem, appears to be lowly glowing with LEDs.

"I do not want to know how much this all cost," Maren murmurs.

"I kinda do," Arda says, enraptured.

"Well luckily, we have our best bet at figuring out the cost right here," Choi says, jerking her head in the direction of Maren.

"I have no idea how much anything cost," Maren says.

"Yeah, but Ariadne will absolutely tell you if you ask," Choi says.

"I don't know about that," Maren says. Choi raises her eyebrows at her.

"Emerson, come check this out!" Arda calls from where he's moved a few steps away, pointing at one of the tables. It would appear that the place settings are also no-holds-barred over the top.

"Duty calls," Choi says, saluting her with an easy grin. "You're on the case of the overpriced wedding, detective."

Maren has no intention of figuring that out. Choi can ask her partner if she really wants to know. Unless, Maren realizes, somewhat horrified, Felix doesn't know how much this whole shindig came in at, either through purposeful or accidental ignorance.

Wandering the other way around the room, Maren peeks at place cards as she goes. There had been a long sign by the entryway detailing what table everyone was at, but she's having more fun figuring it out this way. Plus, she guesses that she's probably seated at whatever table the family's at, even though that in and of itself is an alarming thought.

She passes what feels like a hundred names she's never heard or seen before in her life, a few names she knows from the pages of glossy magazines, and two that she actually knows — Roger and Juni. Maren realizes that this wedding would probably be a lot more fun with some of the Catholic high schoolers in attendance, but she assumes none of them have been invited, sadly. She bets they can cut a rug, in that wild way only teenagers can.

Her own place is indeed at the table with a bunch of names that seem suspiciously like family — Augustines and Lucanuses. Someone has also insisted that she be addressed formally, *Sesheta Maren Nykara* in looping calligraphy heralding her seat. She almost resists rolling her eyes at it. She's been hearing her title a lot lately, and it just reminds her each time how ceremonial and parochial her job is in a lot of people's minds. Mostly it's doing just garden variety embalming and dealing with all the entrails that come with that.

310

"Well, hot damn on toast."

Maren turns at the sound of Ari's voice. She's standing a few feet away, having come in through a side door that Maren can see tucked just behind one of the bookshelves. Like the room around her she's bathed in gold, her slim suit a heavy silken material embroidered with large blue and white flowers, an abstract fall of a spring scene across her body.

"You look lovely," Maren says, blinking a few times to make sure Ari's real, here and now. Her hair is done up away from her face, wrapped into a bun at the back of her head and secured by a golden hairpin.

"Who cares about me," Ari says, drawing closer and gesturing to all of Maren with her half-empty champagne glass. "My Gods, can I make a suggestion? Drop the corporate office drone wear and the dead people and become a fashion model. You wore so many basic jeans and t-shirts in college! A crime. I'm calling the police. Have you seen Detective Choi yet? We can turn you into her for being *too* hot."

Maren can feel a blush rising up her neck and warming her cheeks, can't hide the small grin that tugs at her lips.

"I'm pretty sure being attractive isn't a crime," Maren says. "And thank you."

"We're going to eat, and dance, and then I'm going to take you downstairs and show you my childhood bedroom, in a totally non-creepy way," Ari says.

"Is that a good idea?" Maren asks with a frown.

"What part?" Ari's close enough now that Maren can see that her eyes have gone a muddy amber in the light, the gold sucking the green overtones from her irises.

"The sex part," Maren says.

311

"I mean, who knows," Ari says with a shrug. "But I'm two glasses of champagne in, and you're gorgeous, and I know if nothing else we have great sex. So, indulge me for one more night. We can figure us out in the morning."

"Ok," Maren says. She's heard worse plans in her life, and Ari looks incredible.

"Thank Gods," Ari says, and then flags down a passing server to get Maren a flute of champagne of her own. "*Prosit*, hottie."

"To a long and happy marriage for Phaedra and Felix," Maren says, clinking her glass to Ari's.

"They can get there all on their own," Ari says. "So I'm going to be selfish — to us, and unfucking ourselves."

"I like that," Maren says with a smile, taking a sip. Whatever it is, it's good, and probably out of Maren's price range.

A cheer goes up from behind them, and they turn to see a crowd has gathered around the door.

"That'll be the newlyweds," Ari says.

"Shall we?" Maren asks, offering an arm to Ari, who takes it with a grin. They lean together, walking across the glowing dance floor to slip into the gathered well-wishers and guests.

———

"I'm stuffed, I can't move," Ari moans, leaning back in her chair. Maren grins at her, wrinkling her nose, and leans in close, braced against the long table.

"You owe me a dance," Maren says.

"Do you even like to dance?" Ari asks, rolling her head towards Maren.

312

"With you, yes," Maren says. She's feeling emboldened by the atmosphere around her, people laughing and talking, the clinking of glasses and tableware. The dance floor shimmers almost hazily in the dark room, bodies swirling past as people kick off shoes and raise their arms above their heads.

At the center of it all are the bride and groom. Maren keeps catching glimpses of them through the dancing, locked in their own little gold-tinted world. Felix, wearing a simple black tux, has been easily outshined by his bride, even with his flashy cufflinks and watch. Maren has seen plenty of interpretations of the traditional orange for a bride — washed out pastels, deep oranges that might as well be red, sometimes nothing more than gold jewelry with orange stones. Phaedra, on the other hand, has leaned hard into tradition, and is wearing a flame-colored gown, a strapless column dress that makes her look like she's on fire, so simplistic that she seems all the more regal for it. She's even gone for a crown of laurel leaves and zinnias the same bright hue as her dress. She paints an amazing picture, something out of an excavated mosaic from ancient times. A myth, sprung to life from the ground up. Her smile is impossibly wide, her eyes fever-bright, her gaze locked on Felix as his is on her as they spin each other around.

Maren stands, holding a hand out to Ari.

"Yeah, who am I kidding, I'm not passing this up," Ari says, taking Maren's hand and hauling herself to her feet. "I am, however, losing the shoes. You too, Sasquatch."

"My heels are comfy," Maren says.

"You're so tall though," Ari huffs as she uses her free hand to wrestle her stilettos from her tortured feet, the

313

straps leaving red indents behind.

"Fine," Maren says with a smile, kicking her own pumps under the table. Hopefully no one drunkenly walks off with them.

Stepping onto the dance floor throws strange shadows up against them, the golden glow under their feet otherworldly. Here, in the mass of bodies, the room is warm, closed in against Maren's skin.

"I can't believe all this," Maren says, just loud enough for Ari to hear over the music.

"The dance floor might be a bridge too far," Ari says. "Or maybe not far enough. I'm going to get married on top of a pool and have synchronized swimmers underneath doing a light show."

At Maren's scandalized expression, Ari throws her head back in a crow of laughter. A few strands of her hair have slipped free, curling down her temples and brushing against the cut line of her jaw.

"Please don't," Maren says, even as she starts swaying to the music.

"I'm kidding, Ren, don't look like I just threatened to shoot a puppy," Ari says. "I have no idea what I want my wedding to look like, just not like this."

Hands raised and eyes closed, Maren lets the sound pumping from the speakers crest over and through her. It reminds her of the cascade of lights and noise and beats filling the clubs they used to go to, weekend after weekend, before they'd go home and tumble into bed and go their separate ways in the morning. When she opens her eyes it takes a moment for her mind to catch up with what she's seeing, the two versions of Ari overlaid briefly in her mind's eye.

314

One, in a sequined mini, head tossed back and hair flying, the other, in this gorgeous suit, shimming to the music. She stutters as they realize into one figure, one person, and Maren watches Ari as she moves with the beat, shoulders and hips and long fingers. Her jewelry glints in the lights, the embroidery of her suit catching and sparking in the golden haze.

"You look like a goddess," Maren says, leaning in close.

"That's rather sacrilegious of you, *Sesheta* Nykara," Ari says back, closing the space between them. She throws her arms over Maren's shoulders, pulling them close, and this is more of what Maren remembers, no air between them and alcohol making their blood sing. It's hot and claustrophobic, and Maren presses into it all, her body somehow still knowing how to move with Ari's in this singular space. Her hands automatically fall to Ari's hips, squeezing her, the silk of Ari's jacket smooth under her calloused palms.

For a few moments, heartbeats, a stretch of breaths, it's just them, and then they bump into someone, jostling them out of the reverie they've fallen into. Ari laughs, leaning back to look up at Maren, and they move again, around and around.

The song changes, and then again, and again, and each time they adjust slightly so that they can match the thrum of the music and the pulse in their veins. The music gets slower and slower, and they sway together, anonymous in the bacchanalia.

"I'm glad I got my dance," Ari says, low.

"Me too," Maren says into a smile.

It's only when there's another song break that Ari slips

315

away, holding their hands up, fingers laced together, and tugs Maren back towards that far corner where she'd first appeared like a specter.

"Where are we going?" Maren asks as soon as they're far enough from the DJ to be able to hear each other again.

"I told you," Ari says, eyes alight in the dark. "I'm going to do unspeakable things to you in my childhood bedroom."

"Still weird," Maren says with an easy grin as Ari shoulders the corner door open.

"Don't worry, my mom redecorated the minute I moved out. It looks like a hideously bland guest room," Ari says. "I promise you won't have to stare at any *Bend It Like Beckham* posters mid-orgasm."

"Oh my gods," Maren says, pinching the bridge of her nose with her free hand, Ari tugging her down a flight of stairs. In stark contrast to the refined space of the penthouse ballroom the stairs are normal access stairs, the dull safety lighting strangely green after the light upstairs.

A few flights down dumps them in the long corridor outside of the Augustine apartment. Maren's pondering where on her person Ari could have possibly stashed a set of keys when she simply opens the front door, throwing it wide and striding into the entry hall, her bare feet padding across the marble tile.

"Someone's going to steal something," Maren says with a raised brow.

"No one would think to in this crowd," Ari says, turning to walk backwards a few steps, waggling her hips suggestively as she goes. Maren grins at her, speeding her pace up so that she can crowd into Ari's space, bracketing her hips with her hands again. Ari tips her head back to

316

meet Maren, the kiss strangely sweet for both the occasion and them.

The second one is more their usual bruising style, lips parted, Ari's hands cupping the side of Maren's head, pushing her hair back away from her face.

A voice echoes through the cavernous apartment. They both still, turning their faces towards the noise.

"What?" Ari mutters, eyes narrowing.

"Told you," Maren says a bit breathlessly. "Robbers."

They can't hear the words, but there is a lilt to the voice that makes it sound borderline hysterical, a rising cry.

"That does not sound good," Ari mutters. She hurries in the direction of the living room, Maren hot on her heels.

The library door is cracked open. They pause just outside, Ari stooping a bit to peek through, Maren looming over her head to get a good view.

It takes a moment for Maren to place the figure beyond the door before the layers of navy and white cream give it away. It's Irene in the high society maven gown that Maren had seen her in earlier, when there had been speeches at dinner. She lets out a long sigh and moves to sit on the edge of the writing desk under the window, giving Maren a clear view of the other occupant of the room.

Her flower crown has fallen askew, dipping to the left slightly, but her flame-colored dress is still a vision. Phaedra's makeup, however, is a straight-up disaster, mascara running down her face where tears have tracked down her cheeks. She smudges the whole mess further as she drags a hand across her face.

"Stop it," Irene sighs, crossing her arms. They stare at each other for a beat, and then Irene lets out another, more exhausted breath. "I'll call the makeup artist back in here, don't look at me like that. I'm not going to send you back to your wedding looking like that."

"Even if I knew he would have spit on today," Phaedra says. Her voice is broken glass, shards of hurt. "I still miss him so *much*."

"I do too," Irene says. "Every single day."

"We could have called him back," Phaedra says.

"No, we couldn't have," Irene says.

"I know, I know," Phaedra says. "But *Gods*, it's killing me, like something's eating me from the inside out. I just — I shouldn't have — I overreacted and thought of Felix and it was so stupid and *ugh–*"

Irene is saying something but Maren doesn't really hear it, because Phaedra turns to Irene, and reaches out with her hands, palms up, curling her fingers in anguish, her wedding ring a sapphire beacon on her finger.

And Maren remembers.

The memory suddenly flares to life at the base of her brain — the static starburst figure doing that same thing, in this same space.

Phaedra, draining the life from her father.

Maren is dully aware that she's sliding sideways, into Ari, as the memories weigh her down, her world tilting with her.

"Ren!" Ari hisses, supporting as much of Maren's weight as she can. "Snap out of it!"

Phaedra and Irene turn towards the door as Ari pushes Maren back to her feet. She stumbles a step but plants a hand on the wall and takes a deep breath, centering herself in the hurricane of the memory crashing down on her all at once. She stares at Ari with wide eyes, mouth open in soft shock, and Ari looks back at her, clearly confused.

The door peels open all the way. Irene Lucanus stands in the space, all perfect dress and perfect hair with a rather large jade skeleton key necklace resting at the juncture of her collarbones. Her shrewd brown eyes scan the scene and then she turns, sweeping back into the room to perch on the writing desk again.

"Join us, girls," Irene says, turning to them once more. Phaedra looks a wreck of shock and sadness and Ari goes to her immediately, carefully pulling her down onto the couch and wrapping her in a blanket. Maren is left standing on shaking legs behind the opposite sofa, hands braced on the wooden spine on the back of it.

"What did you hear?" Phaedra asks with a sniff, leaning into Ari.

"Nothing," Ari says, shaking her head and holding Phaedra tightly against her shoulder. "Phaedra, don't cry on such a day."

"Technically as it's my wedding I can do whatever I want to," Phaedra says with false cheer.

"That's a racket," Ari says. She turns to her mother, raising her eyebrows, a storm brewing behind her eyes. "Can we actually call the makeup artist in here?"

"How much did you hear?" Irene asks, and Maren sucks in a breath.

"Oh," Ari says, frowning. "Really, nothing."

"Maren, would you give me a moment with my daughters?" Irene asks.

"No." The word is out of Maren's mouth before she can stop it. Her heart feels like it's beating a million miles an hour again, making her jittery, weightless. Her mouth is dry, her lips parted. "No, I can't. What did you do?"

"I don't know what you're referring to," Irene says

319

blandly.

"Ren, drop it," Ari says.

But she can't. Because she has her answer finally. Phaedra did this, Phaedra started all of this. And Irene has known the whole time.

She rounds the couch, eyes locked on Irene, head held high.

"Phaedra killed him," Maren says. She hears a sharp intake of breath from behind her, and she can't tell if it's Ari or Phaedra. "And you *knew*."

"Not only do you have no proof, but what would you do with that information?" Irene says, tone even, as if they're discussing the weather. "We've gone from paying off the police to having them married into the family. No charges would ever be brought."

"That can't stand," Maren says.

"It will," Irene says with a small shrug.

"I won't let it," Maren says. "She *murdered* him. Someone has to know."

"Well then," Irene says, and heaves a sigh.

Before Maren can even think, can even react, Irene reaches behind her, grabs something that glints in the light, and then shoves it forward.

The punch is hard, knocking the wind from Maren, and she takes a step back. When she looks down, she finds that Irene's fist is still pressing into her stomach. Strangely, she seems to be holding the hilt of something, the gems glinting in the light.

And then Irene yanks her hand upwards, and Maren feels like lightning has exploded under her ribs, the pain immense and so, so sharp. It's a living fire burning through her torso.

320

"Oh," she says, the sound little more than a breath forced from her lungs by pain and the strange sensation that something is impossibly loud.

Someone is screaming. Maren isn't sure who. She reaches out to grab onto the bookshelf closest to her, her hand grasping for purchase on the polished wood. Gravity wins out, however, and she tumbles to her knees, Irene moving away from her. A few books come down with her in a shower of flapping pages, and then a glass jar of something that shatters the minute it touches the ground. Shards of glass fly across the floor from the epicenter, coins rolling around and around, coming to settle among the glass and blood.

There's a lot of blood. Maren looks down as she kneels. It's pouring from her stomach, staining her green gown a deep crimson, almost black. She's not sure if she should press her hands to the wound or keep them away. Some part of her brain is screaming at her, telling her this is no time to debate this, but another part is weighing the pros and cons of both quite thoroughly.

Hands on her shoulders. A body behind her, warm and weighted, and she sighs, slumping against someone's chest. It feels nice, the brush of sun-dappled warmth at her back. She lets her eyes close. It's hard to be here, to be present. She can't seem to pull air into her lungs. Those hands move to her stomach, pressing against the strange slash that's appeared there, and Maren winces at the sudden pain.

"Ren, no no no, Ren, Maren, please don't — please — Phaedra, call a fucking ambulance *right now*." It's Ari. "Maren, listen to me, ok? I'm going to lay you down, I need to try to stop the bleeding — Mom, give me that fucking pillow. *Give it to me!*"

Her voice is powerful, surrounding Maren, holding her tight. Ari clamps a hand over Maren's wrist, a whisper of a memory that now seems a lifetime ago.

"*Mom!*"

Maren's hand closes over something on the ground. It's round with a raised edge, the metal cool under her feverish palm. Perhaps a coin. She closes her hand around it, presses it into her skin.

"Maren," Ari says, and Maren slips into the current.

# CHAPTER 23

## *Coin*

"Caramel?"

Maren blinks in the twilight darkness, letting her eyes adjust. The world around her is grand and immense and she can't quite take it all in, so instead she presses her palms down on either side of her legs, against the smooth, cool stone of the bench she's sitting on. It's a slab of something, honed to a flat slate texture.

There's a hand in her peripheral vision holding a wax-paper-wrapped piece of candy.

She turns to find a familiar face smiling at her. The last time she'd seen that face it was desiccated and a deep brown, stained with oils and pine tar. Here, it is full of life, plump cheeks and a pointed nose, her eyes a clear brown.

"They're salted," Mrs. Colvard says with a smile.

"Thank you," Maren says, taking the caramel and carefully prying the sticky sweet from the translucent paper before popping it in her mouth. It does indeed greet her with a tang of salt, but the taste is strangely muted. She frowns.

"Give it a bit, you'll adjust," Mrs. Colvard says, closing her small handbag and setting it between them. It's simple and black, the same as her sensible dark tweed dress with matching blazer and black kitten heels. The only part of the outfit with any levity is her reading glasses, a bright pop of red hanging around her neck on a chain that seems to be made of mismatched plastic beads — butterflies, black letters on white backgrounds, emojis and flowers. It looks like it might have been a gift from a child. She peers closer and her suspicions are confirmed by a few of the letter beads: *WORLD'S BEST GRAMMY*, each word punctuated by a bubblegum pink bead shaped like a watermelon slice.

"That's sweet," Maren says around her caramel, gesturing to the glasses chain with her wad of wax paper.

"Isn't it?" Mrs. Colvard says, smiling with pride. "My youngest grandchild — Sofie — just loves beads. She made it for me a few years back."

Maren dimly remembers that there had been a young girl at Mrs. Colvard's funeral, bedecked in multiple homemade bead-based pieces of jewelry.

"You're dead," Maren notes, frowning.

"So are you," Mrs. Colvard points out.

Maren swallows some of the caramel, looking up and around at the place she's found herself in. It's almost night, a slip of crimson orange lipping one edge of the horizon, and there are stars hanging above their heads. There are so many it's almost dizzying, a hint of the edge of the galaxy visible in a way that Maren has never seen outside of photos.

The topography is strange, unlike anything she's ever seen on earth. An unmoving, unbent river stretches past them, its surface roiling with fog. As she watches, stars drop into the mist, glowing and vanishing. On the other side of the river are the rolling, wind-swept hills of a high desert. Ancient bridges link the two sides, all of them full of foot traffic. Between the stone bridges are skeletal ships moored at the edges of the river, some unfelt wind filling their golden sails.

When she turns, she finds herself staring up into a city

324

built into mountains that rise above their heads, snow-capped in the far darkness. Dark metal lanterns light up tier after tier, buildings and tombs carved through the rock face.

Maren stands slowly, open mouthed and staring around at the scene. It feels like something out of a fairy tale, or, she supposes more properly, a myth. She closes her eyes and takes a deep breath in through her nose. Beyond the tang of the caramel at the back of her throat, she can smell pine, and ocean air.

"This is Duat?" Maren asks.

"It is indeed," Mrs. Colvard confirms with a nod. "The first gate. I hope you brought coin for the passage across."

"Why are you still here?" Maren asks, perching back on the bench and looking at Mrs. Colvard with some degree of trepidation. "We buried you months ago."

"I appreciate the concern, but don't worry about me," Mrs. Colvard says, waving a nonchalant hand at Maren. "I'm just waiting on Carl. My husband."

"Oh," Maren says. "Is that going to be… a while?"

Maren is finding her terminal professionalism is failing her. She's had no experience asking ghosts of former clients how long they're planning on sticking around before their significant other kicks the bucket.

"Not at all," Mrs. Colvard says, shaking her head. "Frankly, I'm surprised I went before him! The man's been slowly dying for *years*. And then flu season comes around and poof! I lose my head in a week. But he was going quite downhill, even more so than usual, so I think he'll be by soon. I promised him I'd wait right here."

"That's very kind of you," Maren says.

"No point in doing the afterlife without him," Mrs.

Colvard says with a warm smile. "It's nice to have someone to explore with."

"It is," Maren says, staring out into the mist. Something beyond that river is calling to her, singing in her bones.

"You should go, though! No need to stay and babysit me," Mrs. Colvard says. "You're equipped, surely, being *sesheta* and all? Have all the gods' and goddess' names?"

"I do," Maren realizes, but only because of her profession. She's come here with nothing but herself, which is strange. Certainly if she had been buried already, which she should have been for her full spirit to be here on the banks of Duat, she would have maps and lists of names and snacks at the very least. But she has nothing, except for her person and the two items in her hands.

Two items. Maren stares down into her palms, upturned to the almost-night air. One hand holds the crushed-up wax paper wrapper, and the other holds an old Subway token, from before they switched to the swipe cards. She remembers them from when she was a kid, how people's wallets would jingle every time they needed to pull them out at the fare gates. Selene would give her one, and she'd be able to push through the turnstile on her own.

"How weird," she murmurs. "I don't have any grave goods."

"That is strange," Mrs. Colvard confirms, a worried crease appearing between her wrinkled, white brows. "Here, let me give you something to take with you."

She retrieves her handbag, opening it with a clean click, and, to Maren's amusement, starts pulling rather large items out of it. Tins of fancy chocolates and delicate cookies, boxes of tea and coffee.

"I — I don't have anything to carry it in," Maren says.

"And it's your food, you should keep it."

"Ms. Nykara," Mrs. Colvard says, pausing to lay a comforting hand on Maren's arm. "Let a grandmother feed a youngster one last time."

"Ok," Maren says, one corner of her mouth twitching up at being called a *youngster*.

"Besides, I think I have — ah, yes!" A dainty clutch comes out of the bag next, a black satin-clad tube with gold and red accents, the clasp a jewel-eyed scarab. "My daughter-in-law clearly thought I would need something fancy for any parties that might pop up in the afterlife. Ha! Turns out she was wrong about why I'd need it, but was right about needing it all the same."

The clutch comes open in Mrs. Colvard's hands and she unspools a golden chain shoulder strap before packing the space with chocolate and a few muffins, each one wrapped in the same translucent wax paper as the caramel. Next are a box of scones and a jar of some kind of preserves, complete with silver knife. For good measure Mrs. Colvard also tosses in a few more sweets.

"Here you go," Mrs. Colvard pronounces, holding it up for Maren, proffered with both hands. "*Now* you're ready."

"Thank you so much," Maren says, swallowing hard around a lump in her throat. "I don't know if I can ever repay you."

"The dead don't keep track of debts," Mrs. Colvard says with a wink. "Now get a move on, enjoy!"

"I hope Carl shows up soon. Or — uh," Maren peters out, not sure if that's wishing death on someone.

"He will," Mrs. Colvard says. "Maybe we'll see you past the gates."

"Maybe," Maren says, and then, swinging the clutch

across her chest, she picks up her velvet skirts in one hand and uses the other to wave backwards at Mrs. Colvard as she heads off.

As she draws closer to the misty river, she can see that each boat is flat-bottomed in the deathly clear water, each bow carved into the shape of a jackal head, the eyes glowing golden in the foggy darkness. She stops near the edge to inspect the stone under her bare feet, finding it as carved as the bench she'd been on. This whole world seems created by hand. Glancing back and forth down the wound of the river she can see people boarding boats and crossing bridges, all of them with packs or purses or bags.

When she looks ahead of her again, she finds a pair of legs have stopped in front of her. She raises her gaze as she rises to find a man standing there, clothed in shapeless, unbleached linen, a jackal mask obscuring his face. The smooth black of the mask has the same glowing golden eyes as the prows of the ships on the banks. The edges of him shudder and whisper strangely, curling dark smoke weaving into the air from his skin, catching the light from the lantern he's holding up.

"Bridge or boat?" The man asks, his voice slightly muffled behind the mask but otherwise sounding strangely normal.

"What's the difference?" Maren asks.

"Have you passed beyond the last gate?" the man asks.

"I just got here," Maren says.

"Boat it is," the man says, and then holds out his hand. "Payment, please."

Although it feels wrong to part with it, this singular thing that's made the trip from the world of the living with her, she knows she's not getting across the river without it.

So, with her lips pressed into a thin line, she reluctantly drops her subway token into the waiting hand.

"Second on the left," the man says, jerking his head in the aforementioned direction of one of the boats and then walking off, towards the next soul standing on the banks of the river.

She boards the correct ship on a gangplank carefully balanced between the bank of the river and the rail of the ship. Another jackal-headed man blocks her path, both hands palm up and out to her.

"A name," he says.

"Manifold of Forms," Maren says, naming the first gate goddess. The air sparks and shimmers around them, and the man gives the briefest of nods before stepping aside, letting her hop down to the dark planks of the deck. Crossing to the front of the ship, she stands at the rail and stares out to the desert beyond the river. A few other souls putter about on the boat, but none of them approach Maren, and she doesn't approach them.

The fog swirls around them, a breeze creeping over the wooden deck. Maren looks up at the full sail, and then, with a creak, the boat casts off from shore and begins the journey across. She looks back down, over the edge into the water, but can't see how deep it goes or what lurks at the bottom. Stars fall past them as they glide along an unseen current, each one vanishing into the darkness.

Although she has no way of knowing for sure, she has a feeling they're souls, although she's not sure which way they're going. Just arriving, or departing to the depths of a second, forever death? She squeezes the wooden railing under her palms, frowning.

She can't remember her death. The last thing she

remembers is kissing Ari in the tacky marble entryway of the Augustines' apartment. After that is a simple blip of black, like she'd fallen asleep before waking up on a bench next to a dead woman. There's no memory of her heart stopping, her breath ceasing, her own embalming and burial. Had the House done that all, or had they not been able to? Maren should know that bit, as her spirit decayed in pieces, dropping away into the underworld bit by bit until, at last, her mouth was opened at her funeral and her spirit was finally able to walk here in Duat with a light heart. She should be equipped with her own bag of grave goods, not just a clutch full of some sweets from a kindly old grandmother whose family was overly generous during her burial.

She thumbs at the cool, smooth satin of the clutch, frowning at it. Not a single text has come with her, either. She never would have made it past the first gate before being devoured if it wasn't for the fact that Mr. Valentine had drilled the names of every single gate god and goddess into her head during her first year of working for him. She's poured over funerary texts with Thais for years, Pyramid and Coffin and Coming Forth By Day. If it's luck that's brought her here with that knowledge even though she wasn't buried with it, she's the luckiest son of a bitch this side of Elysium.

Elysium. She stares back out into the desert, the unrelenting undulating sand under the cover of night. Is it beyond the desert? Or is this just the first gate? Technically the second, she supposes, as the first is the easy one — a coin for the ferryman. That's done and behind her.

Leaning on her elbows on the railing, she closes her eyes for a moment, savoring the wind in her hair, and thinks back to that last memory, a small smile hovering on her lips.

—

The sun does not fully set, but it also doesn't rise. The sky stays a star-studded twilight as she disembarks on the other side, the sand swirling around her bare feet. At the bottom of the gangplank she hears the jackal-headed man from behind her.

"A name," he says again.

"Watchful of Face," she says into the dry air.

She turns to thank the ferryman but the words die in her mouth, alarm bells ringing in her head.

The river and the mountains are gone. There's nothing but endless desert, the sand bleached of golden contrast in the bleak darkness.

For the first time in her afterlife, Maren feels a spike of panic.

"Fuck," she says, and scrounges around in her clutch to find another caramel. This one tastes better, saltier and sweeter, and she sucks on it with concern as she starts walking again. She wracks her brain, dredging up every tiny piece of information about Duat she can remember from the Book of Gates. The first one was getting on the damn boat, the second was getting off. It had passed so fast, and those were the easy ones.

"*Fuck*," Maren says again, this time through a sticky mouthful of caramel. The third gate is the one with the lake of fire. There are spells that a priest or priestess could perform to ensure safe passage for a soul over the underworld's worst superfund site, but considering she has no memory of her life after her death, she has no idea if Thais had done so. She hopes so, but there's no guarantee. She's not going to be super-excited if she has to muscle across the lake somehow.

Something whispers in the back of her mind that there's no escape. She walks faster.

Even though it's night the sand is still warm under her feet, and she pushes along, steady steps through an unforgiving desert. She hadn't even thought about what a horrible place Duat was supposed to be, only listened to that siren song in her blood that had beckoned her forth. Now she's stuck in the middle of it, praying that she doesn't die a permanent, second death on these sands.

Occasionally she'll pass a small, skeletal shrub, but otherwise she doesn't see anything else that might have once been living. At the crest of every rolling dune she crosses her fingers, but when she stands on each spine, the breeze whipping sand around her ankles and tugging at her dress, all she sees is more desert.

It goes on and on, the sun never rising, never setting, the desert unrelenting. She doesn't sleep, doesn't tire. She walks with only her increasing anxiety for company.

It occurs to her after what feels like several days have passed that she could be going the wrong direction, or be going in circles. While no one is really buried with a compass or a GPS, people do go into the underworld armed with ancient maps. She squeezes her eyes shut for a moment, letting out a brief noise of frustration at the back of her throat, before stomping down the other side of the latest dune, half sliding. The only saving grace of the whole mess is the even air temperature, neither warm nor cold. Considering her outfit is currently a heavy, high-necked, sleeveless velvet gown, it's another stroke of luck.

During the first days she tries to keep her dress clean, stopping to brush grains of sand from the fabric, but gives up after a while. There's no use fighting fate, and right now fate is the sand caked to her dress up to her shins. It weighs her down a bit, and she realizes if she was smart, she would have asked around on the opposite bank of the river for someone who had been buried with scissors to take off the bottom bit of her dress. She doesn't even have anything to pin it up with.

Her anxiety is tinged with a non-specific grief. Her mind wanders. She forces herself forward, towards Elysium.

Her calluses are probably developing calluses, step after step against the rough ground. Her feet are sore. She's cursing the gods for coming up with such a hideous excuse for an underworld when she drags the back of one of her hands across her forehead and it comes away damp with sweat.

She stops dead. The air has heated, the temperature ticking up. There is sweat beading her skin. Something smells vaguely of sulfur.

If you had asked her even an hour ago if she'd ever *run* towards a fire lake she would have laughed. Now, however, she hitches her skirts up to her knees and launches herself in a sprint towards the heat. She breaks across the top of a dune to find a glow on the horizon. Taking a brief moment for a victorious fist-pump, she plunges back down, sand flying behind her, perspiration collecting in the hollow of her collarbone.

*Lake* turns out to be the wrong word, perhaps something lost in translation, or something that's shifted in the environment over the millennia since people started writing about Duat. Instead, it's a snaking raw, red wound across the desert, slithering between the hills and dunes. The slow-moving dark magma on the surface is wrinkled with breaks of bright red. A volcanic river that crystallizes its own banks, making them slick and deadly superheated. Around it, the desert glows like a flame.

In the center there is a small temple, the pylon out front some Hellenistic mishmash of odd designs. It stands on an island of glass, looking oddly humble to be here, in this otherworldly desert.

Maren creeps closer, wary of the fact that each step takes her further and further into the heat. She's sweating freely, her dress heavy against her damp skin, and faint flickers of pain are dancing at the edges of her vision. Stopping a good twelve feet from the edge of the river, she finds her body doesn't want to go any further. Each time she sucks in a breath of air it feels like her last, drying her mouth and making her throat burn. There's certainly no way she's making it across that mess if she can't even get close to it.

She backs up a few feet to a safer distance, putting her hands on her hips and taking a good long look at the river with narrowed eyes. She doesn't see any obvious way across, nothing that could be used as a bridge, no islands of glass close enough to hop from one to the next. And even if that was an option, she's barefoot. Her skin would boil off in seconds. Every option she comes up with is even less pleasant than the last.

There's a very real fear gathering at the back of her mind that something had gone seriously wrong in life, and she's unembalmed and unspelled, bereft of any offering that could assist her in this brutal place. None of that explains why her spirit has made it here intact, but that just unfortunately adds to the strangeness eating at her.

Pacing back and forth along the bank, she chews on a fingernail, weighing her fairly non-existent options. Stopping to peek back over her shoulder, she stares into the darkness of the pylon. Even though the desert is lit by the river, the glow doesn't touch the deep void of the opening of the temple. There's something in there, and she'd bet it's where she needs to go.

Resuming her pacing and her nail-biting, she goes through everything one more time. The scrub brush around her will be of no help, burning up immediately. Her own skin will fail her even faster. She's not in a hurry to wander the desert forever, because she knows eventually something will find and devour her. There's no part of Duat where being devoured is not a concern. The only safe haven is Elysium, on the far side of this extended horror show.

"Screw you guys," Maren mutters. "The afterlife is miserable. I hope you're listening. This whole place is the pits. Who makes an afterlife like this? What if someone isn't buried properly, but led a virtuous life? You just *kill* them? The game's rigged."

The desert does not say anything back to her. The only noise is the rustle of wind and the strange low rumble of the river of fire.

"What a joke," Maren says. She's always thought of herself as fairly driven, but evidently just three gates into the underworld and she's met her match in some slow-moving lava. It's a horrible feeling and she drops to the sand, sitting down and glaring at the river. "I hope one of you is listening."

She balances her head in her hand, her elbow digging into the side of her knee, and she sighs, slumped. The heat is still intense, but she has no reason to move. If she's going to die here, maybe she should just throw herself into the river and be done with it. Although that does sound like a miserable death. Perhaps it would be better than being torn apart by demon jackals or hyenas.

"Just… someone help," Maren says, letting her head drop, her curls sweeping across her face.

———

Another day passes. She stays there on the sand, hot and grimy and sweaty, and doesn't even bother moving. The debate between being torn apart or burning to a crisp fades to a low drumbeat at the back of her mind. A strange calm settles over her. A stasis.

Perhaps she will just waste away to nothing here and become part of the sand, one day churned into glass by the molten snake that stands in her way.

———

On the third day, a strange noise makes her look up. She finds that part of the pylon at the gate has been obscured by tree clippings, dumped into the river to be devoured. Even as she watches fire springs up the leaves and branches, pulling them along and down, destroying them with unchecked power. As the burning boughs pass, Maren finds herself staring at a figure in the doorway, a woman dressed in muddy pants, a long-sleeved shirt, and a welding mask. The figure brushes her hands together, and then turns around.

"Wait!" Maren hollers, scrambling to her feet, waving her arms over her head. The figure stops, taking a peek over her shoulder. She stills, almost impossibly, touching a hand to the bottom of her welding mask like she means to raise it.

And then she's gone, back into the darkness, fleeing.

Maren drops back to the sand, letting herself flop all the way down, the sand warm against her cheek. So this is how she dies for a second, final time — the first real challenge of Duat, all because she hasn't been taken care of after death, all for something totally out of her control. Rolling onto her back, sending a spray of sand across her body, she stares up into the ever-evening sky. The stars twinkle overhead, as if winking at her, and she closes her eyes and presses her fists into them.

Her only oasis is that soft memory of Ari kissing her under golden lights.

# CHAPTER 24
## *The Third Gate*

She lies in the sand, unchanging, eyes shut, grief simmering, until wailing cries break the silence of the desert.

Sitting up so fast that if she were still alive she would have had a massive head rush, she scrambles to her feet, yanking her dress around when she finds herself half-tangled in it. It's a horrible howling noise, high pitched and sorrowful, echoing across the dunes. As she listens, eyes wide in fear, more calls join the original group, more and more, growing and growing, closer and closer.

*Move*, something in her brain snaps at her, and she goes.

She needs something to protect her, right here and now. A quick half-turn sends her stumbling in the sand before her eyes land on one of the dead bushes. Racing towards it, she skids to a stop and, using one foot and both hands, wrenches free the longest branch she can find. It's a light brown, bleached by some unseen light, and it's blessedly solid. It'll do.

She fumbles open her clutch next, dumping the muffins out and abandoning them to the sand so that she can wrap their wax-paper packaging around the end of the stick. While leaving food behind isn't something she's in a hurry to do, it's not going to matter much if she dies in the next five minutes.

The animalistic lamentation draws closer. Taking a quick peek over her shoulder to find herself still alone for now, she runs towards the river. The heat hits her like a blast furnace, her skin blazing and lips peeling as she gets closer. Sweat runs down her back, down her legs, and she ignores it, scooting ever closer to the lava, one step at a time. Sand scorches her feet, her body feeling like it's starting to curl up on itself, burnt and boiled. Sweat drips into her eyes, clouding and stinging her vision. Her breath is rough, the heated air a supernova of pain at the back of her throat.

She can't walk another step, or she knows she'll burn. With a cry of anguish, she thrusts the branch as far from her as she can get, straining and reaching, tipped forward on one foot like a dancer.

"Please," she whispers, her throat wrecked, tears joining the sweat.

A rush of movement catches her eye. There, over the top of the dune to her left, a pack of jackals. They look normal enough, sooty gray and sandy brown, large ears twitching. But, horribly, their eyes glow. That yellow-brown is a terrible, iridescent gold, like the wings of a beetle. As they slink closer she can see their teeth are bared, and their wailing has stopped, replaced by the low rumble of a communal growl. A group hunt.

"Please," Maren murmurs, closing her eyes. "Dua Anubis, I have entered the gates to your realm as I watched over them in life. Do not let me die here upon the banks of the Lake of Fire. Help me past the Third Gate."

The brush of a breeze, the air cooling around her just a fraction, soothing her skin.

Something within her rises.

A hiss from her other side. The pop of fire catching. Letting her eyes open, she looks away from the approaching jackals and down her arm, down the length of the branch.

The wax paper has finally caught, close enough to the heat at the edge of the river. With a cry of triumph she spins around, squares her shoulders, and walks out of the shimmering air, towards the pack gathering near the skeletal shrub she'd ripped her weapon from. The branch blazes in her right hand, and with her left, she digs into the clutch and whips out the knife that Mrs. Colvard had given her. Holding it as she'd hold a scalpel she lets it fit comfortably into her palm, and she walks to meet whatever her fate may be.

The growling sets her teeth on edge as she gets closer. She watches as the jackals hunker down, hackles raised, bodies coiled to strike. As she sweeps the branch in front of her, a few of the front ones back off a step or two, hackles raised. One of them, a smaller one, makes a move around her unprotected side, leaping at her. She can't pull the branch around in time but she flips the knife in her hand, a solid, steady, hammer grip, and thrusts it up to meet the jackal at the apex of its jump, throwing as much strength into her arm as she can.

The jackal twists in midair, trying to avoid the blade, but Maren goes with it, slicing open its neck as it falls towards her. With a horrible screeching noise it tumbles to the sand, blood pooling from its throat. It starts to unspool, gold mist rising from it, smoking black, and she stares in open surprise as it comes apart before her eyes.

Her pause is a mistake. Two of them jump from the other side. She notices them just in time, rolling aside with a punched cry, coming down on both knees in the blistering sand. More advance on her, and she has to give

340

ground, back towards the river, her back heating further with each hurried, clumsy step. Stabbing out with her right hand, she catches one by surprise, scorching fur and earning another unearthly yelp for her troubles. She manages to singe another jackal, and, sweeping the branch around, strikes a third one on the back swing.

One charges her with a blood-chilling snarl, and she bares her teeth back at it, cutting widely across her torso and taking the creature across the eyes with her knife. Like the other one, it goes down in a heap, golden dust spilling from its stilled body.

"Keep them off for one more moment!" Someone bellows.

Maren chances a quick look over her shoulder to find that the woman in the welding mask is back. She drops to her knees and hands on the porch edge of the temple, as if she's going to drink from the river. As Maren watches, spots in the lava begin to glow, stepping-stones linking the shore and the island.

Breathless, she turns her attention back to the jackals, knife dripping with strange, foggy black blood. It curls up from the blade, and she switches her grip again, holding it reversed across her chest, armor and weapon alike.

With a deep breath, her throat wrecked, she lets her soul rise as she had learned to do in life, lets everything go. Lets her own spirit bleed and burn bright, stretching to fit every last atom of her body.

"I have entered the gates to your realm as I watched over them in life," she repeats, feels the branch as an extension of her arm, and the flame bursts bright, a bonfire licking down the wood. With a cry, she launches it into the middle of the pack, sending them scattering in a chorus of

341

whines and yelps. A few of them come towards her, and she swings low to catch another one across the throat.

A weight hurtles into her from her blind side, sending her spilling across the sand, knife knocked from her hand. The jackal bears down on her, and she clamps a hand across its face, another one under its head, arms screaming as she wrestles with it. Claws rip at her shoulder and she cries out in pain, using all her strength to throw her knees into the jackal's belly. It bleats, falling to the side, and she scrambles away from it, grabbing for where her knife has landed a few feet away in the burning sand. Her hand closes around the handle just as the jackal crashes into her again, throwing itself across her back. With a grunt, she rolls over, and they come apart.

Springing up, she stares the animal down, knife raised, blood streaming down her shoulder. When she tries to move that arm, she finds it useless with pain.

A hand finds hers, squeezes tight.

"Run!" The voice from before says and Maren stumbles into a turn, the other woman already running towards the river. Maren sprints after her, still holding tight. A path has formed across the lava, broad rectangular stepping-stones that glow a pale, warm light against the sinister red cast off by the lava. With her heart hammering against her ribs, Maren plunges into the simmer.

The heat doesn't hit her. Instead, the air is cooled, and the scent of flowers floats around her.

"Give the name!" The woman yells.

"Hostile of Face," Maren gasps as she sprints.

They hit the glassy shore and leap from block to block, having to unlink hands. Maren doesn't think, just throws her weight from one stepping-stone to the next and the next, until she's on the solid ground of the temple, and she's pitching forward into the dark.

"Watch the stairs!" The woman yells, but Maren has already found them. The first hit sends pain ripping through her shoulders, and she yells out in the darkness, her bearings gone and her balance lost as she tumbles down the stone steps. Each thud against the stairs is new agony and she lands at the bottom in a heap, breathing hard and whimpering.

Hands roll her over, and she finds herself looking up towards the elegant, richly decorated barrel vault ceiling of a villa. The woman appears over her, welding mask pulled up to reveal a face that's familiar to Maren in a way that sends one final punch to her gut.

"Mom?" Maren gasps.

Selene gives her a rueful smile in response.

—

The villa turns out to be a massive antechamber full of plants and fountains, the floor tiled with such artistry that Maren can't imagine that mortal hands had ever made it. Selene helps her up, Maren in so much pain she can't tell where her body begins and ends, and they limp to a low bench under a lemon tree. She slumps down on it as Selene prods and maneuvers her in a way that gets her to lay out.

"Stay here for a moment?" Selene asks, and Maren nods weakly. It's not like she has anywhere to go, nor is she in any shape to.

She does roll her head to the side to watch her mother walk away, past a few other souls milling around by a fountain fed by water so clear it almost looks like a mirage.

Her mother. She looks exactly as she had when she had died, her dark hair cropped in a clean pixie cut, not a single extra line of age on her face. Maren's brain is having a hard time processing it.

Selene returns with a small wooden bowl, a winding trail of vine carved around it. She kneels next to Maren, closing her familiar brown eyes. Maren can just see into the bowl, cupped in Selene's hands and full of flowers floating on that strangely clear water from one of the fountains.

"Proserpina, I give you my service so that you might give me this salve," Selene says.

"Huh?" Maren asks, and Selene opens her eyes, smiling softly.

"You'll need to drink this," Selene says, holding up the bowl.

"Fuck," Maren mutters. Just pushing herself up onto her one good arm is agony, and she can feel tears welling at the corner of her eyes again. Selene lifts the bowl to her mouth, tipping it, and Maren gulps down whatever it is, only slightly aware that maybe she shouldn't be drinking or eating anything in the underworld, especially when provided in Proserpina's name. It goes down blissfully easy though, tasting of lavender and rose and honey, and brings with it a soft warmth under her skin. Laying back down with a sigh, she lets that feeling spread through her, banishing the hurt from her soul.

"Give it a few minutes," Selene says.

"I can't believe you found me," Maren says to the ceiling.

"I think you found me, more like," Selene says. "There are multiple ways down to the fourth gate, and you happened to pick the way that went past me."

"Are all of them that hard to get through?" Maren asks, dreading the answer.

"Yes," Selene says.

"Oh thank the Gods," Maren says in relief.

"But you should have been given spells to get across. That's what I used to get to you," Selene says. "Were you buried improperly?"

"I don't remember," Maren says. "But I have to believe so at this point."

"That's not good," Selene says.

Slowly, feeling emboldened by whatever she had drank, Maren carefully sits up. Her aches and pains are slipping away and the gouges in her shoulder from the jackal have healed over to pink, fresh scars. Rolling one of her feet, she can see that her blistered soles are even healing.

"That's some good shit," Maren says, turning to Selene and looking at her properly for the first time. She's wearing overalls with a flannel thrown over them, a pair of dirty gardening gloves tucked in one pocket. She's ditched the welding helmet, although she seems to be wearing a pair of mean, steel-toed boots caked in soil.

"A perk of the job," Selene replies, reaching up to tuck one of Maren's curls behind her ear.

"What is your job?" Maren asks. "I didn't realize the dead could have jobs."

"Oh, sure," Selene says. "Ferrymen, gate guards, clerks, the list goes on. I'm a gardener here in the fourth gate."

"You always did love your garden," Maren replies softly. She revels in the strange sensation that she doesn't have to mourn that. Her mother is here.

"I still do," Selene says, and then, after a pause.

"Darling, you're much too young to be here, what happened? Please tell me the cancer didn't turn out to be genetic."

"No, no," Maren says with a shake of her head. "Can you not see what goes on in the mortal world?"

"Not really," Selene says. "I'll get snatches every once and a while, but that's it."

"I didn't have cancer." Here Maren pauses. "Honestly, I can't remember what did kill me."

"Oh, honey," Selene says sadly. "I'm so sorry. Having that knowledge is such an important part of this life."

"I suppose it's ok. I mean, I'm dead. Not much I can do about that," Maren says with a shrug that feels fake.

"You don't have to try to just get past it," Selene says.

Maren doesn't know what else to do. Push it away, push it down. She can't bear to spend her death mourning the life she's lost. Can't bear to dwell on the heartbreak of that last remembered moment with Ari. Can't bear the memories of Henry. Or Tad, or Oscar, or the House.

Or, most heart-jerkingly at the moment, Miu.

"Oh no," Maren says quietly. "Who's going to take care of Miu?"

"'One who mews'?" Selene asks.

"My cat."

"Oh honey, I'm sure someone will welcome her with open arms. Your father, maybe?"

Her father. Her throat constricts.

Maren has now wrenched open an old wound, ripping his daughter from him as his wife was ripped away — too young, and painfully. A melancholy gathers at the edge of her mind, swirling depths that she doesn't want to fall into. She sits up straight, forces it to the back of her brain, turns away from it. She won't let it claim her.

"So what is this place?" Maren asks instead, voice wavering as she gazes around the villa hall. There are antechambers around the perimeter, shadows spilling from their wide, tall doorways.

"This is the Fourth Gate," Selene says. "Honey, if–"

"It's a massive improvement over the last one," Maren says. "Which was weirdly terrible compared to the others."

"They're all terrible, in their own way," Selene says with a sadly calm expression Maren recognizes from her own face. "If you try to pass the First Gate without coin or bribe, you'll be thrown over the edge. Stepping onto the unknown of the ferry is too hard for some people. And if you're found wanting, the edge of the river on the Second Gate side might never let you reach it. The Third Gate is just transparently the worst."

"What trickery does this one have up its sleeve?" Maren asks, gazing around the luxuriant growth around her.

"Some people find that they can't bear to leave this safety after the desert. So they linger here, wasting away, until so little is left of them that they can never pass on and never reach the Fields."

"But you work here?"

"I've passed through the last gate. This is just my office," Selene says. She reaches out to tuck a piece of hair behind Maren's ear, and Maren closes her eyes for a moment, savoring an interaction she hasn't been able to indulge in for half a lifetime.

They sit in silence for a moment, Maren watching the souls here stride across the tiled floor. Some of them do seem faint, their edges misting as the jackals had in their deaths. Some are dressed in outdated fashions, and one,

347

now little more than a breezy haze of gold and black fog, looks to even be wearing a Victorian dress.

"Maybe some people are ok hanging on to last moments of beauty and never knowing the full afterlife," Maren murmurs.

"I think they are," Selene says. After a beat, she continues. "It's so good to see you, you know? I mean, it's horrible, for you to have been taken from your mortal life so soon and so young, but, selfishly–"

She reaches out again, cupping Maren's cheek in her hand, and Maren leans into it, meeting her mother's gaze. Fine dark hairs fall across her forehead, her skin a smooth, even, deep tan. Her doe eyes meet Maren's, and she smiles, dimples appearing at the corners of her mouth.

"What did you do with your life, sweetie?" Selene asks.

"Grew up and dedicated myself to the dead," Maren says, reaching up to place her hand over Selene's. "I am — was, sorry — was *sesheta*."

"My goodness," Selene says with raised eyebrows. "No wonder you were able to make it so far even with an improper burial."

"Yeah," Maren says. "I didn't come into this totally blind. And thank you for saving me back there."

"That's what moms do," Selene says. "Come on, I'll show you around."

Selene leads her through the incredible gardens — flowers in every color, tall palms, fruit trees so laden that their boughs dip towards the tile floor. The clear fountains sparkle in the sunlight filtering in through the clerestory windows high above their heads. Everything looks like it has been touched by the gods, unfurling in full finery. Around every tree, behind every bush, there are souls

348

reclining and drinking and laughing. Rosemary and jasmine perfume the air, their blossoms tucked into every planter that Maren can see.

"You tend to all of this?" Maren asks.

"I do," Selene says with a small, proud smile. "I almost wasn't able to leave here, I loved it so much. But I asked Proserpina for guidance and knew that I would be able to come back here as its gardener if I continued onwards. Come on, I'll show you the lakes."

Maren had forgotten about the two lakes of the Fourth Gate. She frowns, following after Selene, unsure where they've hidden a lake in this villa. Selene leads her to the outer edge of the room, where she finds she can peek through into the antechambers as they pass. They're muddled, lit with low, glowing light, and her eyes can't quite adjust to get a handle on what's inside. Selene doesn't duck into any of them however, and instead heads for the far point of the gardens. As they come around a thicket of palms and jasmine, she finally sees where they're headed — another set of stairs, these luckily lit properly by tall pillar candles standing sentry on each stair, one to the left and one to the right. Passing below the engraved stone lintel, Maren immediately feels a chill, deepening with each step. By the time they reach the bottom of the stairs, goosebumps have raised on her bare arms.

The hypostyle hall that yawns in front of them is immense. Maren thinks that it's flooded, until she steps to the edge of the path that runs along the wall and sees that it's instead a low pool, only a few inches deep. Small, gold mosaic tiles glint at the bottom, lit by balls of soft white light that float freely among the spates of paper reeds that burst from the water's surface occasionally. When she

349

looks to the stars she finds she cannot see the ceiling, the gloom such that the pillars holding it up simply vanish into the dark.

Down the middle of it all, wide blocks are set into the water, almost flush with the calm surface. They extend far out, far enough that Maren can barely make out the doorway that sits opposite the one they're now standing in front of. It looms large, and the sudden shiver that passes through Maren has nothing to do with the temperature of the room.

"That's the doorway to the Fifth Gate," Maren says, pointing into the shadows.

"It is," Selene says with a nod. "You'll have to pass between the Lake of Life and the Lake of Uraei to get there."

"Let me guess, it's treacherous?" Maren asks with a sigh.

"No, not for all," Selene says.

They stand in silence for a moment. Unlike the sounds of the garden — laughter and clinking cups, the fall of water and the rustle of leaves — it's almost alarmingly silent in the hall. No souls dwell here like they do in the massive space upstairs. Maren is starting to understand how people may pass through the luxury of the gardens, come down here, and immediately nope back up the stairs to the sunshine and drinking. Even though eternal life is just across the lake, it's foreboding in this endless waste.

Plus, that's to say nothing of what's standing between a soul and that eternal life in the Fifth Gate.

"You said you asked Proserpina for guidance," Maren says. "How?"

"She's in the antechamber on the north side of the hall,

350

first one after the steps up to the Third Gate," Selene says.

"Just hanging out?" Maren asks, raising an incredulous eyebrow. She can't imagine that the Queen of Duat finds the time to chill in a garden for all of eternity for shits and giggles.

"In a fashion," Selene says. "We can head back up, I do have to get to work. But after that, stay and have a drink with me?"

"Of course," Maren says, a soft smile blooming on her face.

They head back up the candlelit steps together, one foot after another.

# CHAPTER 25
*The Lake of Life*

Maren does not make it to Proserpina's antechamber. Instead, when she parts with Selene at the top of the stairs, a tugging feeling at the back of her mind draws her to the south side of the gardens. Passing below a beautiful tree of red blossoms, she finds herself pulled towards one of the middle antechambers instead.

She stands in the tall, squared arch, bracketed by pillars carved with scenes that she recognizes from the Book of Coming Forth by Day. She lets her eyes adjust in that liminal space, staring into the dim glow.

Unlike the rich tiling of the space outside, in this much smaller, square room the floor is a single sheet of marble lit by some unearthly glow the color of firelight. Her first steps into the room echo off the walls, the background noise of the gardens fading.

In the very center of the ceiling there is an oculus, providing a perfect view of the night sky through it. Below that, standing proud, is a larger-than-life statue of Anubis. Carved from a black stone that seems to absorb what little light the room provides, the only color comes from a few cursory, brief details done in gold paint — his eyes, the four bands around his arms, and the sun disk that brackets his jackal head. His feet are placed directly on the floor, no plinth to elevate him, and people have left him offerings: flowers and laurel crowns, jugs of wine and honey, springs of evergreen and stalks of wheat. They encircle the statue, some propped up on his ankles, prostrate and clawing up towards him, silently beseeching.

Maren has come empty-handed. Or, not quite. Popping her clutch open, she takes out two caramels. Unwrapping one for herself to eat, she leaves the other in one of Anubis' outstretched hands, standing on tiptoes to reach his palm.

She crushes the wax paper between her own hands as she slowly chews the dense, sweet stickiness, wondering what she should say. He might have helped her back there in the desert, but she's not sure. Maybe she'd just been standing close enough to the river of lava long enough for the wax to catch. Truthfully, she's never really prayed to any of the gods or goddess before and meant it. When she was younger, she'd prayed to the household *lar* because it was expected of her, rote and easy, and with no meaning behind it.

She settles to the ground, sitting cross-legged and ruminating while she finishes her caramel. The salt and the sweet seem to have more of a taste now, and she wonders if she's already adjusting to this strange place.

Running a hand through her tangled hair, she lets out a long sigh. Now that she's no longer in imminent danger of dying, the grief and heartbreak are swirling back, shot through with some strange amazement at seeing her mother again. It tangles in her gut — the grief of her death, the sorrow of that last remembered kiss with Ari. It hurts to swallow, her throat tight.

"I honestly don't know what to say," she admits eventually. Her voice echoes softly in the dim room. "It's rare I'm at a loss for words. But I guess I'm much better at comforting other people than myself. That's what I've done in life — served you. I hope I've done well, and led people properly into Duat."

She pauses to scratch at her nose for a moment, thinking of the bodies she's had in her care over the years.

"Even Casper Augustine. I did what I could. Unless I fucked that up too."

Another pause.

"*Did* I fuck that up?" Maren murmurs to herself, staring down at her hands where they're clasped in her lap.

Anubis doesn't respond. Maren can't blame him; he's probably got much better things to do than answer lamenting souls via statue.

For a long moment, Maren just breathes in and out, even and rhythmic. Something warms her skin, wets her eyes, and she has to swallow hard. She realizes, horribly, that she's feeling guilt, and a sense of loss because she will never be able to find out who his murderer was, or how Casper had risen after death and been able to climb into the retort on that horribly rainy day.

The thoughts tumble through her head, a mess of needy frustration. Snowballing, they gain other facets — loss and worry. Anhur and Fiona. Henry and Thais.

*And Ari. And Ari. And Ari.* The thought bounces around her head like a funeral dirge.

"Oh fuck," Maren says tightly, and then looks back up at the statue. "Dua Anubis, if you did help me once before, help me now. I can't suffer an eternal life with this pain. Take it away and let me have the peace of the Fields."

Nothing happens. Maren feels tears roll down her cheeks, and she chokes out one small sob. After a while her legs start protesting, throwing up pins and needles that make no sense in death but still seem to happen all the

354

same. She struggles awkwardly to her feet, turns her back on the statue, and crosses back into the sunlit gardens, wiping tears from her eyes.

—

Selene finds her at the end of the day, when the sunlight has started to dim to the rainbow hues of a sunset. Maren has tucked herself into a small table in a shaded corner of the garden, and she watches as the trees and shrubs come alive with thousands of tiny pinpricks of light, illuminating the space as the sun fades.

Maren looks up when a glass of deep red wine is placed in front of her. Selene smiles down at her, taking up the empty seat opposite Maren with her own glass.

"Oh sweetie," Selene says with a frown. "Were you crying?"

"Yeah," Maren says. She sees zero point in lying to her mother when they're both dead.

"Who do you miss?" Selene asks.

"Everyone," Maren says heavily. "Dad, and Fiona. And, uh, Henry."

"Henry?" Selene asks, raising an eyebrow and grinning in a small private way. Maren can't help the answering brittle laughter.

"The Administrator at my House. He's gay, I'm gay, tough combo for a relationship between us," Maren says.

Silence follows this, and Maren realizes what she's just said. She stares down into her glass and then picks it up, tossing back a hefty sip and not meeting Selene's eyes. She expects a burn, having just chugged a decent portion of a glass of wine, but instead it goes down like honey, rich and bodied and so aromatic that it seems to flush her blood with the taste.

"Ok, so no boyfriend or husband to miss," Selene says after a beat. Maren finally looks at her, and finds that she's looking off into the distance, tapping her chin like she's thinking. "Gosh, this explains why you liked that one show so much — what was it called? The fantasy series with the bad production value?"

"Xena?" Maren chokes out with wide eyes. She'd watched reruns constantly in the hospital with Selene.

"That's the one!" Selene says, snapping her fingers. "I mean, Lucy Lawless is quite gorgeous, and she did show off a lot of leg in that."

"Mom," Maren says. She can feel a blush rising to her cheeks.

"I get to embarrass you again now," Selene says. There's a slightly evil twinkle in her eye. "Get ready for an eternity of your mom refusing to drop you off around the corner from school."

"Oh fuck," Maren says, but there's a levity at that, the idea that even if she has lost everyone in her life, she has instead recaptured the love of a mother who left the mortal world too early.

Selene's grin fades to a soft smile, and she reaches out, placing a hand over Maren's on the table.

"Do you miss someone else?" Selene asks.

"I do," Maren says. "But I don't know what I'd call her."

"Well, if you miss her, she's at least a friend," Selene says.

"She saved my life. Although I guess that's moot, considering I managed to kick the bucket anyway a week later."

"Tough timing."

"Extremely," Maren sighs. "We dated in college, briefly. I guess we were just reconnecting."

"What's her name?" Selene asks.

Maren takes a deep breath, closing her eyes, remembering the last time she's said the name out loud.

"Ariadne," Maren says.

"Let her live in this space through you," Selene says, giving Maren's hand a squeeze. "And one day, she will join you here. Everyone does."

"Unless Ammit eats them," Maren points out.

"I can't imagine that anyone you would love would be wicked enough to have their heart devoured," Selene says.

Maren wants to say *I don't love her,* but she finds the words stuck in her throat, can't get them past her lips, so instead she stays quiet. Even if Ari does find safe passage to the Fields, would it even matter? She could die decades from now, perhaps long-married to a wife with a whole family of her own. There's no reason why she'd hang around a former college fling for eternity.

"So what happens after this?" Maren asks. "I pass through the Fifth Gate and do get to see you again, right?"

"Of course. I live in the Fields, I can see you as often as you'd like," Selene says.

"Crazy," Maren murmurs with a small smile. Considering she'd never fully believed in Duat, it had never occurred to her that she had a future with her dead mom.

"I'm glad you turned out beautifully, even though I only had half a hand in raising you," Selene says.

"Me too," Maren says with a small smile.

357

"*Prosit*, my darling," Selene says.

Their drinks clink cleanly together in the garden, the stars of light around them reflected in the glass.

—

"You'll be fine," Selene promises Maren at the top of the stairs, brushing the last of the sand off Maren's dress, sending grains of it scattering across the beautiful tile work. "It's an easy trip across the Lake, I promise."

"I'm sorry you can't come with me," Maren says. Selene's presence seems to be the only thing keeping Maren upright at the moment, weighed down by the spirits of the living as she is.

"You do have to do this bit by yourself," Selene says. "But! I'll see you on the other side. Assuming you don't get your heart devoured."

"Yeah, I'll try to avoid that," Maren says. "Not my idea of fun."

Selene tucks a lock of Maren's hair behind her ear again, smiling up at her. Maren fights down the urge to reach out and cling to Selene.

"You'll do beautifully," Selene says. "I know it."

"Thanks," Maren says, ducking her chin and grinning.

Standing on her toes, Selene takes Maren's face in her hands and drops a kiss on her forehead before pulling back.

"Breakfast tomorrow?" Selene asks.

"Absolutely," Maren says, before sweeping Selene into a long, crushing hug, the silence between them easy. Her mind screams to not let her mother out of her sight, this woman who slipped through her fingers when they were both too young, but a saner, cooler head reminds her that this is forever. They have all the time in the universe now. All Maren has to do is get to Elysium.

358

They part ways there, Maren taking a deep breath and then trotting down the wide steps to the hall below. Cautious of the fact that she's not equipped with spells or prayers that could be helpful, she instead takes out her silver knife again, gripping it hard before sucking down a deep breath and taking her first step out onto the lakes. The stepping-stone under her is steady, and she takes another step, and another, and each one holds. Raising her head high, she relaxes her defensive posturing and strides towards that last gate, shrugging off the low light and chill that seeks to slow her down.

She's made it halfway across when a ripple to her right catches her eye. Freezing and raising the knife again, she slowly turns her head to find the source of the movement.

A worryingly large cobra is moving languidly out of the water, coiling up with its head reared back and wings wide. Maren, who has never seen any snake outside of a zoo, let alone a fuck-you-sized venomous one, finds herself frozen with fear. With scales a deep navy and burnished gold, and a heat shimmer in the air behind its head in the shape of a sun, the snake looks exactly like something out of an ancient painting. It's the kind of curving figure that would be displayed front and center on the crown of a pharaoh.

A low humming hiss rumbles from the snake, and Maren realizes her hands and feet have gone numb, her breathing so fast that she's hyperventilating.

*A Name.* A voice from everywhere at once, echoing and twisted, the words running together in a strange tonal melody.

"Sharpest of Them," Maren whispers.

*Look into your life.* The voice seems to echo in her very bones.

Maren has no idea what that means. The snake stares her down, lightless eyes a void that gives nothing away.

They stay locked like that for long enough that Maren's hands start shaking.

Then, very slowly, cautiously, the cobra tips its head to one side, almost like it's indicating the water on the other side of the walkway.

Frowning, Maren takes a quick peek down towards the Lake of Life.

"Oh," Maren says, frown deepening. "Like, look into the Lake to see my life?"

If snakes could nod, it would look like whatever strange and unnatural head bobbing this cobra is currently doing.

"You're not going to devour me while my back is turned, right?" Maren asks.

The snake looks taken aback.

*That is not my purpose*, the voice says.

Great," Maren says, and then shoves the knife back into her clutch. Scooting over to the edge, she stares down into the still waters. Nothing seems to have changed, the tiled bottom even, nothing swirling in the water. She crouches down, her dress pooling around her, and she carefully dips a finger into the water.

A flash of memory across her tongue, the taste of the sweet holiday bread her mother used to bake during Saturnalia. She dips her finger again, and this time it's a smell — the floor cleaner that her elementary school had used. One more, and a brush of music, a single bar. A lullaby that Anhur would sing her when she was young.

She stands up, takes a deep breath, and hops off the stone into the few inches of water.

There is the tiniest, briefest moment of cold, and then

the world fades away.

She is a young child, snuggled up under a bright green and purple comforter covered in cartoon dinosaurs, and Anhur's voice is low and lovely as he sings her to bed. Maren wants to hear it all it, and she forces her eyes to stay open, fixed on her father's face, but it's so warm and cozy under her dinosaur blanket, and she's so tired, and she finds herself drifting, even as frustration screws up her face at not being awake to listen to the full song.

There's a knock on her door. Popping one headphone out, she sits up straighter when both her parents come into her room. They both look strange, a cast to their features that Maren doesn't like. Closing her math textbook, she shuffles her homework away to clear a space for them to sit. They're holding hands, so tight that their knuckles have paled, spots of near-white on their tan skin. They look her dead in the eyes, somehow gathering the strength to not shy away from telling their child that one of them is dying, and Maren's heart seizes and then runs.

She finishes putting the dishes away, tossing the damp towel in the direction of the laundry room before walking slowly, quietly to the living room. Her father is watching TV, and her mother is asleep on the other couch. Maren hates that she has to make sure that Selene is still breathing but is relieved when she can see the shallow rise and fall of her chest. Someone has tucked a blanket around her, but her arms lay on top of it, her wrists and elbows all bony protrusions. The life has been sucked from her and her face is a mess of hollows and hard edges, a fine film of hair over her head doing nothing to hide it. Maren goes to her, and, feeling young and stupid and afraid, clambers up next to her, tucking herself against her mother. Anhur watches her do it but says nothing. In the strange hours of the morning, Maren will wake up to the cradle of her mother's arms, that rising and falling chest stilled, and she will wail and scream and have to be pulled away, hot tears burning down her face.

It is snowing in Washington Square Park. Maren stares up past the fur lining her hood, sticking her tongue out to catch a few flakes. A couple of kids are already gathering up what little snow has stuck to make snowballs and are pelting each other with them, laughing uproariously. She should really get to class, but instead, something makes her reach down, pick up her own handful of delicate snow, and, with a quirked eyebrow, select a target. Aim, fire, impact.

The snowball throwers have a party. They invite Maren. There is a girl there, dancing on a sofa in a bed sheet toga. She is a goddess of old, godhood leaking from her eyes, smearing through the air, and Maren kneels before her.

Maren and the girl with the godhood stay together for a while. They're bad at it. They're good at the basal parts, the parts that don't include talking, but they're horrible at figuring out how to communicate with each other and to say what they're really feeling. They do not last.

Maren's mother has been dead for eight years. She stands at the edge of the Hudson on a bitterly cold winter day while Serapis beckons to her from the water. Instead, she takes the hand of one of his priestesses, and follows her Home. She has been wandering for so long. It is a relief to find her House.

She has a job before she graduates from college. She is smart, and she likes what she does, and she listens and learns and molds herself into someone a little less angry, a little less wild, and learns to be the person that her clients need her to be. One day, she comes in early, standing on the threshold, keys in her hand, and stares into her space that, since midnight last night, is now officially in her name. Triumph — or something close — blooms in her chest. This is hers, she's done this. Mr. Valentine has trusted her to be the next leader of the House.

There are other women. None of them last either. She's still very bad at communication. Instead, she has friends. There are dinners with Henry and Taner, there are bad movie marathons with the snowball-toga party group from college, there are drinks with Tad and Oscar, and she knows laughter and warmth, but sometimes it is a little bit surface, a little bit at arm's length.

A man is in her cremation retort, his skull aflame. His daughters are on her stoop, golden light in their eyes. His heart is lodged in her own, and one of his daughters is trying to figure out how to rip it out and entangle their hearts instead. They get halfway there.

The woman with the godhood is a vision on the glowing dance floor, and every time their eyes catch there are almost sparks, something calmer now, something older and more even, something that can be nurtured and brought forth, day by day.

She is grown, and there is a knife lodged under her ribs, and her blood is on the floor, and she is dying in the cradle of Ariadne's arms.

—

Maren is sitting on one of the stepping-stones between the lakes, and she's breathing hard. Taking a moment to

363

come back to herself, she scrambles backwards, dragging her sodden skirts and spilling water everywhere, desperate to pull her whole body from the Lake of Life. Taking long gulps of that cold air, she rubs a hand across her suspiciously blurry vision and finds her hand comes away wet with tears. Pulling herself as close together as she can, she wraps her arms around her wet legs, her teeth chattering, and she presses her forehead into her knees.

*A life well lived*, the voice says. Maren isn't sure she agrees.

The soft sound of scales on stone is prelude to the cobra dropping back into the water, and then the only sound is Maren's own breathing and clicking teeth. She's alone with all of the horrible thoughts that come with having to speed-run her own life, complete with that last moment that her brain had carefully kept tucked away. She had been murdered.

Strangely, she can't remember the pain of her death. That was gone from her final moments. Instead, she remembers the heat of her body frantically trying to keep blood in her veins and breath in her lungs. It was like she had plunged into a sudden fever, every system on overdrive. That strange, bejeweled knife of Irene's had slid through skin and muscle and organ just above her navel and traveled up at an angry, ugly angle, ripping through her until it hit a rib and could go no further. Without conscious thought, she places a hand over the spot of the injury, although in death she is whole and unharmed, even her dress in one piece. Well, slightly singed, dirty with sand, waterlogged, and ripped a bit where the jackal had gotten to her shoulder. But no knife damage. It's unmarked by whatever had transpired in life.

Finally, for the second time, she knows who killed Casper Augustine. His own daughter had pulled the life from his body with the force of a necromantic power that shouldn't exist. Ari had told Maren once that everyone *could* do necromancy, if they had the right tools and the wherewithal. And yet somehow Phaedra had walked the surface of the earth with no summoning circle, holding immense power and doing the unthinkable.

Because of the godhood in her veins. The same golden light Irene had also passed down to Ari. She wasn't just a necromancer — she was semi-divine.

This whole time, and Maren had known none of it.

*Don't lie to me, Maren*, was evidently not a two-way street.

She doesn't want to go forward. She wants to flee this place between two lakes, away from what she had seen, and return to the garden villa. She doesn't care that she'll eventually waste away, forever stuck in some strange place that is neither life nor death, but rather one of the gateways into Duat. She understands now what Selene had meant when this place wasn't transparently horrible. What had her mother seen? Whatever it had been, she still had the stubbornness to look her life in the face and walk towards it, towards an eternity of living with the memories of what had happened in her life.

Selene was always so strong in life. Maren remembers that most about her mother, that she had raged against the disease for as long as she could, and then refused to die hooked up to machines. Maren remembers her as strength personified in that moment.

Maybe it was resignation. Acceptance of what was coming and understanding she had no strength to change

365

her future and her fate.

Perhaps that was its own moment of strength.

Maren curls herself further up, tears still tracking down her face. They fall, dripping onto her dress and her chest. The only good thing in all of this is that the mystery of Casper's death had been solved.

"No," Maren whispers with a frown.

That wasn't her original mystery. It was only the secondary, after the fact of his cremation. After he had stood and, on dead feet, walked himself to the cremation machine in the greenhouse. Someone had gotten him there, through spell or ritual or puppetry. There had been so much power there, necromancy thick enough in the air to choke the life out of the security footage.

Phaedra's power had only cloaked her own figure in Maren's mind. She could only project her magic from herself, not smoke out the whole world with it.

Ari, though. Ari had shrugged off her power like a bit of dirt on a shoulder, casual and unconcerned. She'd said that necromancy could kill. Known things that Maren didn't think anyone really knew. Tried to keep Maren from pushing the issue moments before Maren's life had been taken — by Irene. Irene who had covered for Phaedra.

She can't bear it, this thought of an ultimate lie.

Maren springs to her feet, sodden skirts wrapped around her legs. Hitching them up, she runs. Her bare feet slap the stepping-stones, a wet echo around the hall. Her breath comes short, and she flies.

Not towards the gardens, though. She craves the peace of the Fields of Elysium like the very air she breathes.

# CHAPTER 26
## *Hall of Ma'at*

The ancient, heavy doors are made of simple wood. Maren barrels into them, shoving them open while she yells the name of the Gate Keeper into the still air.

And abruptly stops.

The space beyond the door is a simple office hallway, complete with a few plastic waiting room chairs. It's so utterly ordinary that Maren is thrown. She puts a hand out, holding herself up on the wall while her world settles into the strangely normal place.

All of this makes the massive pylon on the far wall stand out as brightly as if it had been made of neon. The grooves in the columns on each side are bejeweled with rich lines of painting and hieroglyphs, the lintel similarly adorned and unnervingly gorgeous. As Maren draws closer, she finds that the story carefully placed into the stone is a mishmash of two familiar ones. Bearing the general look of the extravagant illustrations of the Book of Coming Forth by Day at the height of its usage and respect, it shows the journey of two men from childhood, left on the banks of the Tiber. However, instead of Romulus and Remus ending up split — one dead, one founding Rome — they stride through Duat together and end up in the Hall of Judgment, their hearts weighed as one against Ma'at's feather by a group of gods and goddesses. She marvels at it, mouth moving silently as she translates what she's able to of the hieroglyphs.

367

Someone clears their throat. Maren squeezes her eyes shut for a moment but does not jump, instead lowering her gaze to find a man standing in the doorway, holding what appears to be a tablet.

For a single heartbeat, she thinks he's another soul, dressed simply in loose pants, a long-sleeved crewneck, and rather intense sneakers, all in a perfect black, his hair buzzed short. But his dark skin looks like the smooth surface of a statue, broken only by golden freckles, and as Maren's eyes adjust to the dim space beyond him, she sees godhood. It seeps out, light from his eyes and mouth, his nails, everywhere that his skin is thin and can't quite contain the glowing gold swirling within him.

It is a very hard thing not to gape at Anubis. Maren manages it by the barest of minimums, a mere moment from letting her jaw drop open in surprise. Instead, swallowing very hard to try to wet her suddenly very dry mouth, she inclines her head, pressing her hands together in a gesture of sublimation.

"Dua Anubis," she says. Her voice stays strong, does not waver. She does a mental fist pump.

"*Sesheta* Maren Hatt Nykara," Anubis says in answer, his voice strangely normal. Maren had expected something booming, all encompassing, perhaps from everywhere at once like the cobra in the lake. Instead, he sounds human.

"That's me," Maren says.

"I know," Anubis says, raising one carefully sculpted brow. "Follow me, please."

He turns on his heel, vanishing into the dim space beyond the archway. Maren stands stunned for a moment before hurrying after him. The room beyond is much closer to the hall with the lakes except here she can see the walls

368

and ceiling, even if it does soar far over her head. The rows of pillars on each side of the hall terminate in what Maren thinks are strange sun disks, until she gets closer and realizes that they're deep hurricanes, lightless black, their interiors a brilliant gold and lit with candle flame.

At the far end of the night-dark room is a window. Or, no, Maren realizes as she gets closer — not a window, but some strange moving image without border or crossbar, a square hole in the wall that doesn't seem to be an actual reflection of what's on the other side. A TV screen, almost, showing a field of swaying golden wheat under a perfect blue sky.

In front of that stand three divine beings. Maren's steps falter for a moment before she stops in front of them, her lips now parted in open wonder.

Anubis stands to one side, still holding his tablet. On the other side, Ammit emerges from the shadows and Maren clamps her jaw shut, trying to avoid meeting the goddess' eyes. A creature of nightmare to scare children straight, the reality of her is somehow more horrifying than anything Maren had been kept awake by at night as a kid. Something about her doesn't move correctly, her edges flickering and dragging, her swamp-water eyes narrowed to slits in her crocodile head, the dark scales shifting and transitioning to a mane and rippling coat. Her paws are impossibly large, studded with claws of obsidian, her lashing tail a scaled mace.

"Don't mind Ammit," the third god says, almost offhanded. "I can tell you right now you're not getting your heart devoured."

Maren turns her gaze towards the speaker. The man is of average height and build, sporting an artfully trimmed black and gray beard and long hair that he's bundled up at the back of his head and secured in a golden modius. At first Maren thinks he's wearing ill-fitting clothes, but then she realizes that the strange sweater he's wrapped in from the backs of his hands to his neck is made of cream bandages, as are his pants. His feet are as bare as hers.

Most arrestingly, what little of his skin is visible is crisscrossed by golden seams, as if he was once broken and then put back together with melted metal.

And, alarmingly, this is the third time in her life she's seen him.

"You're Serapis," Maren says.

"Indeed I am," he says, taking the tablet from Anubis and flicking through something on it.

"Uh," Maren says intelligently, before taking a deep breath and diving in headfirst. "I have come before you, master of my own heart, and brought what is right to you. I have committed no crime in the face of what is right. I have done no evil. I have not…"

Maren trails off. Anubis has crossed his arms over his chest, looking bored, and Serapis seems to be paying more attention to the tablet than her.

"You said I wasn't getting eaten," Maren points out. Her heart is hammering in her chest. She *has* to make it to the Fields.

"Oh, you're not. Please, continue. I find that some people still find peace in the reciting of anti-confessions," Serapis says, not unkindly.

"But you don't need me to?" Maren asks.

"No," Serapis confirms, and then holds the tablet out in one hand, screen up. Above it, projected like something out of a science fiction film, two holographs appear: a heart and a feather. As Maren watches, the feather slips down through the air, falling back into nothing on the screen of the tablet, and the heart stays, rising high.

"See," Anubis says with a shrug. "You're good, *Sesheta*."

"But," Maren says, narrowing her eyes. Something seems wrong here.

"But," Serapis echoes. "You asked something of one of us, and he's more than happy to give it to you, should you do something for him first."

*Oh shit*, Maren thinks. She'd asked for a few things.

"Is this about wanting to know about Mr. Augustine? I never actually voiced that," Maren says, wondering if gods can read minds.

"What?" Anubis asks, confused. "Knowing what about who?"

"I wanted to ask you if you could tell me if a soul had passed into the Fields, so that I could ask him something," Maren says.

"Ah," Serapis says. "You seek information about Casper Augustine. You're a regular Nancy Drew, you know."

"You know who Nancy Drew is?" Maren asks.

"Edward Stratemeyer *is* dead," Serapis says simply. "To answer your question, yes, in part. Mr. Augustine's heart did make it to this hall, but with no body to carry on, he had precious few options. He came in here riding a charred skeleton that could barely walk."

"And then Ammit devoured what was left of him," Anubis says.

Maren's eyes widen, and something drops in her stomach.

371

"So I did fail him," Maren murmurs.

"No, *Sesheta*, you did what you could, and that is to be commended," Serapis says. "He failed himself in life by choosing to live as he did. The man is gone from existence."

"But if you want, you can still get a degree of revenge, I suppose," Anubis says. "You've asked three things of me since your death — safe passage through the third gate, to not live in pain, and to make it to the Fields."

"I did," Maren says slowly.

"Great. One's done, and we can take care of the other two," Anubis says. He takes the tablet back, typing something in and smiling up at Maren with a rather disarming number of teeth.

"Are you going to... erase my memory?" Maren asks, worrying at her hands.

"No, nothing so draconian," Anubis says. "I need you to destroy three people for me. One task for each request."

"Destroy?" Maren asks, taken aback. "I don't kill people. Not for anything."

"You now know eternal life in Elysium exists, so don't think of it as a real death," Anubis says as another figure walks out from behind one of the columns. She's shorter than the rest, a rather small woman with absolutely huge hair, half of her dark curls piled on her head and half of them loose down her back, all of it woven through with various colored strings that gleam when they catch the light. She's dressed as simply and monochromatically as the other two, wearing a flowing dress in a basic gray that hides her figure. However, the godhood bursting from her skin hides nothing.

She stands on her tiptoes to peek at the tablet, Anubis

tilting it a bit so that she can get a better look.

"Huh," she says, squinting at it.

"Proserpina, Maren," Anubis says, gesturing between Maren and newcomer. "Maren, Proserpina."

"Oh I know you," Proserpina says, delightedly. "You're Selene's daughter. Honestly, the best gardener I've had in at least five hundred years. Gods bless that woman, she's a keeper."

"Thank you?" Maren says with a frown.

"So," Anubis says. "Here's the deal: you know who Hecate was?"

Maren wracks her brain and comes up empty.

"No," she admits.

"No worries, she's obscure. Minor three-faced goddess of the underworld back in Classical Greece, got associated with Isis and faded away over the years. She wasn't much of anyone, but she had a child, who had another child, and so on and so forth, and they all had a shred of her power, and got kind of dickish about it. Because it upsets my natural order, which I am not about, I need her offspring dead so that the line ends and we can all move on with our lives."

"I'm not killing anyone," Maren says again. She's not in a hurry to go toe-to-toe with a god — even worse, *her* patron god — but she's already dead and she's not going to go back as a ghost to slowly suck the life from three separate people.

"You are, though," Anubis says. "Because you're uniquely positioned. And then you get to live with your grief, but not here. In the mortal realm. And when you die, hopefully this time of old age, we'll promise you the Fields."

The words are strange to Maren's ears. They don't sit right. She chews them over, her frown deepening.

"You're sending me back," she says at last.

"Not me," Anubis says, and then points to Proserpina, who gives a little wave. "She is."

"We love Anubis for a lot of his amazing gifts, but resurrection is *not* one of them," Proserpina says, giving Anubis a pat on the arm.

"I... I don't want it," Maren says. She doesn't want to be resurrected. She's dead. She died. It happened. Now she wants to move onto the Fields and live in eternity, guilt and feelings be damned. Her heart was weighed and found light, and therefore, she is owed Elysium.

"Well, if you don't kill them, you'll find yourself right back here in thirty days," Anubis says.

"I give you my word that you will still be granted entry to the Fields," Serapis says.

"I'm not... I can't," Maren says. Her heart is beating fast, her breathing coming hard. She just wants to pass on. The Fields are calling to her, an ache in her breast, and she wants to continue through. She has a breakfast date that she wants to keep more than anything else in the world, mortal or dead. "You tried to make me do this before, didn't you?"

Serapis just levels her with a cool gaze.

"It's true that this is not our first intercession with you," he says.

"You wanted me dead," Maren says. "That day — you wanted me to kill myself."

"We were planning on sending you back. It seemed like an opportune time to end Hecate's line, what with your recent break up," Anubis says.

The sudden awareness that closes in on Maren is like a vice, choking the air from her lungs.

"Oh no," Maren says, taking a step back. "Absolutely *fucking not*. I am not *murdering* those three. Please, send me onto the Fields, I beg of you, I'll live with my pain–"

She tries to take another step backwards, away from the horrors unfolding before her. When she tries to move, however, she finds herself stuck fast, her feet unable to go anywhere.

"I won't do it," she says, raising her voice over the rushing in her ears.

"You have to," Serapis says gently. "You know them. You can do this. One even dared to take your life from you. We can end all that."

"No." The word is small, and far away, and bleak with grief. "No, I won't. I can't. Please, please, don't ask this of me. Don't make me do this."

"It will be easier in the long run," Serapis says, drawing close and placing a hand on Maren's arm. She wants to jerk away from him, his gray-green-gold skin unnatural this close, so inhuman.

She is choking on air, unable to center herself.

"It's alright, duckie," Proserpina says softly, also coming closer. Maren is glowing with their golden light.

"Oh, and please don't kill yourself, we'll just send you back again," Anubis says. "Good luck."

"Fuck you," Maren spits at her patron, her god, and then Serapis is stepping away, and Proserpina is pressing her forehead to Maren's and murmuring low words, prayer and incantation and more.

# CHAPTER 27

## *Dies Wadi*

She comes awake aware of the cold and nothing else. It's beyond anything she's ever felt before, even when she was dying. It's within her, and outside her, and she is made of it. She cannot move. She tries to take a shuddering breath and finds she can't.

And then the fire starts.

It rips through her, and although she tries, she can't scream as flame consumes her body, her muscles and bones and heart. She raises stiff arms, clawing at whatever is around her, animalistic in her thrashing. Panic grips her like a vice as she meets resistance everywhere, limbs and back crashing into hard walls that have her held tight.

There's something in her throat. She can't breathe. Rolling onto her side she gags and coughs and chokes until finally a clot of blood expels itself from her mouth. She spits more blood after it, letting it come in painful waves, emptying her stomach and throat until it hurts, the metallic taste making her gag anew. In the total darkness she can only feel it, tacky and lukewarm as it coats her arms.

She has to escape. She has to get out. How did she get here?

Squeezing her eyes shut and pressing a fisted hand to her temple, she tries to remember what had happened, why she's in such pain, why every breath is agony, why she feels like she's defrosting from being frozen solid. Pins and needles rake across every limb, her head splitting with knife-pops of color.

Her eyes snap open when the memory hits like a crashing wall of water.

Her life has been returned to her, and she hates it, deeper than she has ever hated anything before.

Forcing herself up onto her elbows, she tries to sit up and slams her head into the top of what she's realizing is a small box. Panic grips her anew, and she can't stop the scream that rips from her body. She slams the heels of her hands into the top of the box until they sting in pain, over and over again, but it doesn't budge.

In one last fit of terrified desperation, she throws her feet out, slamming into the wall at the far end of the box.

It budges, ever so slightly. She freezes. Forces herself to calm down. Take gulping, horrible, painful breaths of frigid air. Reaching up, she braces herself on shaking, bloody arms, and then throws her bare feet at the far end of the space again.

A crack of light appears as her feet sing in pain at meeting the unforgiving metal. It's gone just as fast as it had come. She wants that light back more than anything in the world.

Each stomp on the door is agony. She doesn't care, goes again and again, until finally—

The door comes open all at once, light and warm air filtering into space so quickly that for one moment she's blinded.

Pushing herself out in a frantic flail, she falls from the space onto hard ground a few feet below, gasping in pain as she goes down on a knee, bracing herself on the metal wall behind her as fiery hurt explodes in her legs.

She pulls a deep breath into her lungs and the familiar

smell of decay, oil, and cedar hits her.

The House is dark, only the barest hints of sunlight seeping in from the greenhouse, still slumbering. She's in the hall outside the prep room. Grabbing onto the door of the open mortuary cabinet behind her she drags herself to standing, anger propelling her. Using the wall to keep herself upright, she moves jerkily towards the elevator, using a knee to jam the call button. When it comes she stumbles into it, making the ride on hands and knees before forcing herself to stand again.

With more effort than she's ever had to expend before in her life, she makes it to the bathroom outside her office. The floor-length mirror on the far wall instantly reveals the sorry state she's in.

Her hair is limp, skin sallow. She has blood everywhere, half of it dried from her stomach down, staining her dress dark and making the velvet stiff, and half of it shining on her upper body. Feeling stronger by the minute she wrestles her body from the ruined gown, letting it drop heavily to the ground. The old dried blood continues under the dress, stuck to her skin in flaking smears and splotches.

She freezes with a hand hovering above her stomach.

Her knife wound, the one that had killed her, is sealed with molten gold, as Serapis had been stitched back together. She runs a palm over it, feeling it flush with the skin, and finds herself shaking with rage.

"How dare you," she hisses to her reflection.

Not wanting to spend any more time in a House dedicated to Serapis and Anubis than she absolutely has to, she turns the shower up to a scalding temperature and lets it burn away the blood, lets it ruddy her skin. She drips

378

water all the way to her office, where she fishes an emergency outfit of leggings and a t-shirt out of her bottom desk drawer, pulling them on and then rattling around in her top drawer in search of keys and money.

Instead, her hand closes around a small plastic dinosaur in a sweater, tossed there a few months ago and forgotten.

Maren sets it gently on her blotter and stares down at it. She swallows hard, can't stop the haze of tears that washes across her vision. She remembers the leather of the booth under her hands, remembers the warmth of the restaurant, the winter world locked on the other side of the fogged windows. Remembers the spiced aroma in the air, the gifts, the drinks, the people, one in particular–

Anger flares at the base of her skull anew and she turns her back on it, returning to the drawer until she fishes out what she needs.

As she steps across the threshold of the House into a crisp, brand-new day, she feels the pull of the wards that she and Felix had laid down all those months ago. They sing to her, but they let her pass. She's alive again.

She can't have been dead for too long, as spring clearly has not sprung yet, the trees still skeletal and ugly, gray lumps of slush and snow still dotting the curbs and sidewalks. It's surreal to feel a real temperature again, the wind brushing across her exposed nose and cheeks as she power-walks to the main avenue.

The cabbie that picks her up does not question why she's dressed like an insane yoga teacher with bad hair at six in the morning, or why there might still be a bit of blood on her, and for that she is grateful. When she sees the date on the screen in the back of the cab and learns that just shy of three weeks have passed, she can't stop the

379

hysterical laughter that bubbles out of her. An extended vacation, that's it. Shit, she'd spent longer backpacking around Europe between high school and college.

She catches the quick eye-dart that the driver fixes on her in the rearview mirror, but he doesn't stop and throw her out of the cab for giggling like a maniac.

There's a man setting up a cart on the corner of her street, and she nearly bumps into him as she stumbles out of the cab, still laughing softly to herself. A garland rings the open door of the cart, wheat woven with violets and jasmine, winter hothouse flowers.

"Sorry," Maren says, hoping out of the flower seller's way.

"Flowers?" The man asks with an ear-to-ear smile.

"No, I'm — oh my Gods," Maren says, and then the laughter starts again, and she has to double over and hold herself up on her knees, nearly hacking up whatever else is left in her system.

"Are you alright?" He asks, reaching out like he wants to help Maren but clearly too concerned about her to fully close the gap.

"It's February 13th," she wheezes. The man can only nod in mute confusion. "Of fucking *course*."

She's been resurrected on the first day of Dies Wadi. No greater irony has ever been known to history, certainly. She wouldn't have been venerated this year anyway, considering she very clearly had *not* been buried, but still. It's the heart of the matter.

The man watches her with open worry as she giggles her way to her building, wiping tears from her eyes as she opens the front door. She makes it all the way to the door of her apartment before she realizes that she has no idea

380

what she's going to find beyond this door. All of her bills are on autopay, but she'd died. Her things could have already been moved out, her apartment put up for sale, and her electricity cut off.

She just wants to be home, surrounded by the familiar. She wants — no, needs, to be sitting in front of the fire with Miu purring away in her lap.

Her keys still work. When she steps into the cold interior of her small home, she flips the light switch to find that the power is still on. She turns the heat on next before dropping her keys in the bowl on the low table by the door, a practiced motion. She's home, and everything is exactly where it should be. She's starting to realize that everything surrounding her death is just a little wrong, a little off. Something about the whole timeline of events feels strange.

She wanders a few steps into the apartment, the wind languishing in her sails as she realizes that she has no idea what to do next. Home or not, she doesn't have any plans beyond this spot in space and time.

Sitting down heavily on the end of her couch, she stares into her dark kitchen. Someone has cleaned it, there are no dishes in the sink or on the counter, and Miu's bowls are gone.

"Miu?" Maren calls, realization settling heavily on her shoulders. Standing with some effort, she opens the cabinet reserved for the cat food to find it empty. The litter box in the hall closet has been similarly removed.

Miu isn't here. Maren doesn't have the first clue where she may be, but clearly someone came and got her and all Miu-related items for the time being. It's another oddity.

Maren sits back down, putting her head in her hands

and letting out an exhalation that turns into a breathy, drawn out, *fuck*.

She prides herself on always being able to move forward, always being able to find her way out of a problem. But now, back alive, of all the injustices and insanities in the world, she finds that she has no heading and no map. The compass in her mind has been smashed and she feels like she's moving backwards now. Anger bubbles in her and it fights the exhaustion tooth and nail, all of it tangling up into a paralyzing mess.

—

"Maren!"

Someone is knocking on her door. Pounding, actually. Maren sits up stiffly, rolling a crick out of her neck and blinking sleep from her eyes. She realizes slowly she's in her apartment. Sunlight is filtering through her windows, perhaps nearing solar noon. Pressing cold fingers into her neck to relax it — she must have fallen asleep in an awkward position — she shuffles towards the door.

Through the peephole she spies Henry, looking like the human equivalent of a wind tunnel, and Felix, who is looking somewhat more subdued but still concerned.

Right. This makes sense. She had, after all, been dead. Henry showing up at her door when he'd found a bloody, empty place where a corpse had been in cold storage is one of the more coherent things that has happened in Maren's life — or lack thereof — in a while. She rakes a hand through her now dried-stiff hair, her curls matted down on one side, and takes a deep breath to steady herself. Truthfully, she has no idea what to do when she opens the door, but she also can't *not* open the door.

One lock at a time, chain last. The click of the knob turning. The two dumbfounded faces standing on the other side of the door jamb.

"Holy shit," Felix muses, eyes wide.

Henry charges forward a step, and then pauses, evidently thinking better of it, before carefully embracing Maren in a gentle hug. She stands still for a moment, blinking in confusion, until something bubbles over inside and she hugs him back, clinging to him like a port in a storm, balling her fists into his jacket.

"You're not dead," Henry breathes.

"No," Maren says. "I would say that reports of my death have been greatly exaggerated, but, uh, they weren't."

"Luckily, you got better," Felix responds, dry as the desert. "Let's take the conversation out of the hall, shall we?"

Although Henry lets her go so that she can shut the door after them, he hovers close to Maren's shoulder, eyes constantly darting to her, taking stock of her. Making sure she's all there and all real.

"Just to get everyone on the same page, I have no idea what to say here, or to do, or exactly how this happened, although I have an idea," Maren says, clasping her hands together. "So, to start off, can I suggest alcohol?"

"Please," Felix says.

"Tequila," Henry says at the same time.

"Can do," Maren says. She feels impossibly awkward futzing around in her kitchen a few short hours after being brought back from the dead, but she doesn't know what else to do. Acting like nothing out of the ordinary has transpired is the very easiest course of action. That, she knows how to do.

They crowd around her small bistro table, Henry pouring out shots that are rather generous for a pre-five p.m. world.

"I'm extremely relieved, but also very confused," Henry says, holding his shot up and then downing it so fast it sends him into a minor coughing fit.

"Me too," Felix responds brightly before taking a more restrained approach to his own drink.

"Great, at least we're all in the same place," Maren says. When she tosses her shot back, she expects to feel the warm spread of alcohol through her body, down her legs and arms, but for some reason she doesn't feel much of anything.

"So," Felix says. "How was your trip?"

"You cannot just ask that," Henry says, leveling a pointed finger at Felix while pouring another shot for himself with his other hand. "You cannot *just* — do you know, Nykara, that this man gave me his card when we… when we did your, uh, *intake*, and said, and I quote–"

"Call me if anything weird happens," Felix cuts in.

"Yes, that," Henry says. The second shot he drinks at a more manageable pace, setting the glass down rather aggressively. "'Anything weird.' *Anything weird.* What a horrid thing to say when your friend has just *died.* It was so calm."

"The tux probably didn't help the image," Felix muses.

"Oh yeah," Maren says with a frown down at the table. "I ruined your wedding banquet."

"You didn't do shit. My newly minted mother-in-law did that all by herself," Felix says.

384

"Let me guess," Maren says, sighing heavily. "Nothing has been done."

"Gods, no. You think I'd arrest the matriarch of the family who's paying me off to clean up the trail of destruction they leave?"

"Why in all of the mortal world and Duat have you married into that family?" Henry demands.

"Money," Felix says with a shrug.

"Because he loves one of them," Maren murmurs.

"Pedestrian, but true," Felix says. "Irene is still happily unincarcerated."

"Even though she murdered me," Maren says.

"I mean, technically, you are sitting here, very much alive, and speaking to us, so you've kinda let her off the hook yourself," Felix points out.

"Do you seriously deign to suggest–" Henry says.

"Did you just say *deign*? Who says deign in normal conversation?" Felix says.

"That's not the point!"

"I didn't really suggest anything at all–"

"Oh *yes you did–*"

"Gentlemen," Maren says calmly. The two men at the table quiet down and sit up a bit straighter.

"Sorry," Henry says with a deep sigh. "I don't know how to process any of this, at all."

"Neither do I," Maren says, leaning on the table with crossed arms. "To answer your original question, Felix, my trip was fine. Great, even. Honestly, being dead did not suck. But, through circumstances that I can't even begin to untangle, a handful of meddling gods decided to resurrect me."

"At what cost?" Henry asks. "Going by myth, the gods

385

don't do things out of the charity of their own heart."

"No, they do not," Maren sighs. She swallows hard, digging her fingers into her arms and closing her eyes. No one speaks, letting the silence that Maren had started drag on. Her breathing is ragged, and she has to clamp down on something inside her that seeks to rise up.

"Honestly, can I check something out?" Felix asks, already standing. "Call it professional curiosity."

"Do whatever," Maren says, flapping a hand in his direction.

Felix grabs his bag from where he'd dropped it on the couch, bringing it back to his seat and rooting around in it. Maren has a feeling she knows where this is going, so she turns to Henry instead. He looks drawn and poleaxed all at the same time, a complicated mess of emotions impressed on his face, lining his brows and the corners of his mouth. She reaches out carefully, slowly, giving him time to pull away, but instead he flips his hands palm-up, so that Maren can slide hers over top, clutching his wrists. Clamping his own hands over Maren's arms, he lets out a long sigh.

"I'm sorry," Maren says.

"You better be," Henry says. "You scared me so badly. I came into work this morning — which I was not giving myself off because Dies Wadi sucks when your friend is recently dead — and found blood smeared everywhere and you missing. Don't ever do that again."

"I can't promise I won't, but also, I assume there's a low chance of a repeat performance," Maren says with a wan smile. "I'm sorry that I kept you in the dark, locked you out, and didn't let you help. Ride or die, right? Well, 'die' successfully carried out, now let's ride. For a month, anyway."

This is greeted by silence, confusion coloring Felix's features and horror dawning on Henry's.

"Oh no, no ma'am, that is *not happening*–"

"Henry," Maren says. "You said it yourself, the gods don't do things for shits and giggles. I mean, they do. But in this case they absolutely expect something in return, or I'm shuffling off the mortal coil again."

"Fuck," Felix murmurs. He's pulling his travel summoning kit from his bag. "That blows."

"You have the *worst* way with words," Henry bites at Felix with a glare before turning back to Maren. "What do they want? We can figure it out. You let me help this time, and we can do anything."

"Not this," Maren says quietly, melancholic. She sneaks a peek at Felix, squeezes Henry's arms tighter. "Not here."

Understanding flickers in Henry's wild gaze. Felix, with a practiced casualty, eyes them both. He's paused with that long-necked lighter in his hand, his golden bowl and vials already set up in front of him. Maren can see now that it's cheap and modern, probably from some overpriced home store.

"We're not doing this again," Maren says, standing up. "Clear the *lar* off — he can go on the mantle — and let's set this up properly."

Felix looks mystified, but he gets up with Maren, collecting *lar* and incense burner alike. Maren claims a piece of chalk from the small magnetic blackboard on her fridge and returns to the table.

"Phone," Maren says, holding out a hand to the two men. After a brief moment, Henry scrambles for his, unlocking it as he hands it over. Opening the compass app, Maren drops the phone in the middle of the tabletop, letting it swing for a moment before it settles on the cardinal directions.

"Ah," Felix says. "I see you subscribe to the Ariadne Augustine school of an overabundance of caution."

"Considering the last time you did this I ended up with a bit of someone else's soul stuck between my teeth, yes," Maren says primly as she draws a wide, arcing circle around the wooden top of the table, placing a single tick mark for each direction. The chalk bumps and scrapes over the wood grain, scattering dust through the sun-lit air.

"You're making a summoning circle," Henry murmurs, clearly entranced and a little horrified.

"Yup," Maren says distractedly.

Using the phone as reference, she marks off *septentrio* and *auster*, *subsolanus* and *favonius*, cramming her handwriting down as small as it will go in chalk, careful curves of words under their respective tick marks. The only sound in the apartment is the scratch of the chalk, everyone silent as she works. Once she's done, Felix replaces the offerings and bowl of charcoal, brandishing the lighter.

Maren rounds the table, standing north to go with Felix's south. Henry moves back a step, although a glint of worried interest remains in his eyes.

"Shall we?" Maren asks.

Felix lights the bowl in answer, the fire roving across the coals, orange flame licking into the air. The smell hits Maren immediately, the harsh chemical tang ugly against her memory of burning pine at Ari's apartment.

"*Anakaléo,*" Felix intones, the word clearly alien in his mouth, a later-life addition. "I call to see the spirit of Maren Nykara."

Nothing answers. Felix frowns.

388

"I'm not dead, I have to do it," Maren mutters, and then, "*anakaléo.*"

Easier that she has ever known it, she drops into the current. The thunderstorm snaps inside her, welcoming her home. Gravity floats upwards, her curls air-bound. She lets herself drift, gives herself into the flow of this liminal place between life and death, and opens her soul.

The feeling starts in her core. Incredible warmth, a dusty wind over a dry desert, sunlight bleaching the earth. It feels like home, something known, welcoming her with its heat. When she looks down at her hands where they're braced on the table, bracketing the word s*eptentrio*, chalk dust on her fingers, she finds that she's glowing golden. It's a strange imitation of the godhood she had seen in the Hall of Judgment — a weaker version, but still present. Light peeks from around her nails, the tips of her long fingers, all the places where her skin is thinnest.

"Well shit," Felix says, his voice floating and airy, far away.

Maren pulls back easily, returning to the surface with a gulp of breath.

"What in all the Fields was that?" Henry asks, doing an admirable job of keeping his voice even.

"I had no idea you could call yourself," Felix says. "Are you... haunted? By yourself?"

"No. Anyone can; Ari taught me how. This is unrelated, I'm–" Maren stares at her fingernails. The light seems to have vanished. She swallows hard. "I'm carrying godhood."

"Because you were brought back to life," Felix says, raising his eyebrows.

"Yes," Maren says.

389

"Why?" Felix asks. "Or are you waiting until I leave to tell Henry? You're welcome to lock me out of the loop, but of the three people in the world who know you're no longer dead, I *do* have the most knowledge in this department."

The awful part is that he's not wrong. While Maren seems to have picked up some tricks from Ari that are above his head, that doesn't change the fact that he's been dabbling in the world of the supernatural for much longer than Maren's scant few months.

"I..." she starts, chewing on all of the words she could say. "For my own protection I can't share that information with you at the moment, Detective Perry."

"Cool. Also bullshit," Felix says gamely.

"If we need your help," Maren says, "I will ask it of you. In the meantime, I think I have a date with Henry."

The realization is sudden and horrible. She has a date. *Had* a date. She chokes out a small breath, as if she's been punched. When they had parted, Selene had assumed she'd be seeing Maren shortly, judged pure of heart and just and sent to the Fields. Maren had assumed it too. Nothing strange should have happened. She should be having breakfast with her mother right now. She blinks frantically a few times, swallowing hard against the tightness of her throat.

The remnants of the burning coals crowd her senses.

"She thinks I'm gone forever," Maren murmurs, tears blurring her vision and throat suddenly raw.

—

The House is dark and quiet when she gets in the next

390

morning. Outside is a bright, fresh day that she instantly hates. Knowing the House would be deserted for Dies Wadi, it had seemed the best place to come. The idea of languishing in her apartment day in and day out until she dies again sounds like a kind of horror she's not willing to ever look directly in the face.

Plus, Henry had given her a day to collect herself, promising to meet her here for the full story this morning.

Various parts of the House whisper and pull to her now, threaded cords that seem hooked to her heart. It takes her half an hour of wandering around, up and down the stairs in a dull plod, to realize they're all the places where death touches the House most directly: the salt cellar, the temple, and cold storage. All of the places spelled and blessed by Thais once a year, the day after Dies Wadi ends. Maren has knelt at those door frames with her year after year as she spoke lowly in a language that still sounds alien to Maren's ears sometimes. Every time she steps across them now, she thinks of the necromantic wards she invited into this House, and each time she realizes more and more than they're almost one and the same.

Eventually, she settles into the salt cellar with one of her stashed paperback books. Bending the cover open and laying back on an empty, sun-warmed plinth, she spends a few hours ignoring the enormity of everything by reading about a CIA agent tasked with shadowing a buxom Egyptologist exploring the Nile Delta.

The wrath and depression that have dogged her steps for the past twenty-four hours fade into the background, like distant thunder. She doesn't think about the godhood newly coursing through her veins, which are also once again newly flush with regular old blood. If she ignores the strange taste of a storm at the back of her throat, she can pretend like everything is normal. She would do this more often when she was younger, when Mr. Valentine was still *sesheta* and she had more free time. It's an easy nostalgia.

When someone knocks on the door — Henry, no one else knows she's here — she squeezes her eyes shut for a moment before sitting up slowly, rising back into the unfortunately real world.

"Maren?" Henry calls.

"Yep," she answers as he slips through the door. She's clearly not the only one feeling out of sorts. He's wearing a t-shirt and his hair is free of its usual product, flopping across the top of his glasses.

They both fiddle awkwardly in the silence for a moment before Henry lets out a long, heavy sigh.

"Can we talk somewhere less arid?" he asks at last.

"Yeah, sure," Maren says.

He offers her a hand up, and she seizes it, letting him pull her to standing.

The visitor's couch next to Henry's desk is bathed in the same warm sunlight, slanting in perfectly through the tall windows and layering across the leather and throw pillows. They both sink into it slowly, maintaining a respectful distance, and for long heartbeats they say nothing.

"If I ask you to start at the beginning, will you?" Henry asks finally.

"When I died?" Maren asks, and then bites down on her lip when Henry winces. "Sorry."

"It's fine," Henry says in a way that clearly means *it is not fine*. "But yes, that bit. And, uh, I guess if you left anything out or lied about anything when you told me

392

about what happened with Mr. Augustine as well."

"I... I don't think I did," Maren says. "Well, not at the time. The short of it is that Phaedra killed their father — although I don't know why — and then Irene Lucanus killed me."

Henry blinks frantically at her for a few moments, gripping the tassel on one of the sofa cushions like it's his own link to life.

"I gathered, after what you said yesterday. We didn't know before. Detective Perry gave no explanation when he brought you in," Henry says finally.

"Did you do an examination?"

"No." Henry shakes his head. "I left you in that drawer and couldn't bear to look at you."

"And you didn't start embalming me? Why?"

"Perry asked us to hold off until he could, uh... finalize the official story."

"Ah," Maren says coldly. "I'm assuming he was going to fish me out of the East River at some point in the future and no one would think anything of it. Much better than finding me dead in the apartment of an extremely wealthy and powerful widow."

"I don't know," Henry admits. "But that sounds plausible. He was the one who sent me that recording, a few months ago. The one of the morning of Mr. Augustine's cremation."

"What?" Maren asks, mouth twisting in confusion.

"Yeah, and then he told me to drop it when he brought you in."

Maren sinks back further into the cushions, knitting her fingers over her stomach, feeling the rise and fall of her body as she breathes. She can't help the broken snort of laughter that escapes her, barely avoids rolling her eyes.

"He didn't know, the idiot. He found out that Phaedra killed her father when the rest of us did. His own fucking wedding," Maren says.

"This was clearly a very interesting wedding banquet," Henry says drolly. Maren grins up at him from where she's gone into full recline, watching as the sunlight fractals through his glasses.

"You could say it was–" she starts.

"*No*–" he huffs.

"*–killer.*"

"You're awful. I don't like you joking about your own death. What would you say if Oscar or Tad made a joke like that about one of the clients in our care?"

"You know I'd tell them not to. The difference is that this corpse is walking and talking and making her own self-deprecating jokes."

"This is all terrible. I hate it. I mean, I am so, so glad to have you back. I'm still processing it, of course, but–" something in his voice breaks, and he presses his lips together thinly, swallowing thickly.

Maren knows what she must tell him, even though she knows it's the cruelest thing she could say to him. Just alluding to it yesterday had seemed to crack something open in his chest.

"But, not forever," Maren finishes. "Just thirty days. Or, I suppose, twenty-nine now."

For a moment Henry is so still he looks like a statue, a body frozen in the sun-lit time of this room.

"I don't understand," he says carefully. Maren stares up at the ceiling for a moment, taking a few deep breaths, before she raises herself back up to sitting, struggling through the overstuffed pillows. Bracing herself on flat palms, she stares through those warm rays between them and tries to smile — and fails miserably. She can feel the lopsided grin falling away before it's even fully formed.

"I have a month," she says.

"I understand that thirty days make a month," Henry says, biting the words out. "I just thought, yesterday, that we'd have *time*. That we could try to figure something out. You have... you have the single blink of an eye!"

"That's truly more correct that you could know," Maren says. The godly fucks who have cursed her have probably taken *longer* blinks.

"What do we need to do? We have to start planning now."

"Henry, no."

"I did a little bit of research when Felix gave me that tape. We serve in the House of a God, certainly we can reach out to Thais."

*"Henry–"*

"Or maybe–"

Maren reaches out, secures his hands in her own, holds them up between them, building a bridge across the golden light of the sun.

"There is no fix for this," Maren says.

Henry stares at her, eyes wide, lips parted just enough for breath. Something twitches in his brow, at the corner of his mouth. The age lines around his eyes seem to stretch, pulled taut by barely held back emotion.

"There is always a fix," Henry says finally, low and raw.

"I will not claim three lives just to save my own," Maren says. "I was charged with killing three people."

"The gods would never ask that," Henry says. "That's *ghastly*."

"And yet, that's exactly what they did. So unless your plan includes either taking on the gods or committing murder, I'll be dead again soon."

"Can it be any three people?" Henry asks. "I could think of three people we could kill."

"While I appreciate the enthusiasm, no. It has to be three specific people." Maren takes in a deep breath, pulls back into her corner of the couch. "Irene Lucanus. Phaedra. And... and Ari."

"Why those three? I mean, I suppose two are murderers. Don't tell me Ari's killed someone too."

"I don't know for sure, but I'm worried she's the one who cremated Mr. Augustine," Maren says. Now that she's said it aloud, given it voice, the idea feels dangerously real.

"Oh my Gods. They're all terrible."

"They're also all descended from a goddess, which is actually why I have to kill them. To restore the natural balance of death or something."

"This all sounds like something out of a myth," Henry says.

"Everything about the last month of my life has been mythic," Maren replies with a small shrug. "Or, everything about my death."

Henry leans forward, pinching the bridge of his nose and letting out a long sigh. His hair hangs down, curling around his ears, and Maren swears she can see individual strands of it moving in some unfelt breeze.

"So you're dying again," Henry says to his lap.

"I am," Maren replies gently. "But my mother's there, Henry. I won't be alone. And I already died once, how hard can a second time be?"

He looks up at her, wan and drawn, and when he tries to smile he fails just as spectacularly as she had.

"Don't die just for your mom," Henry says.

"I'm not. I'm dying to save three lives," Maren says.

"They're horrible people! Fuck, Nykara, one of them *murdered* you."

"Not lost on me."

"But you're fine with this?"

"No."

"Then why? Who cares about a single one of them?"

"I do," Maren admits, voice small and brittle, and it's a horrible thing to realize.

# CHAPTER 28

## *Three Lives*

Maren and Henry use the holiday-emptied House to reorganize things, digitize files, and clean out the storage room. When he's not around, she'll read, devouring books out of a stack that she liberates from the back of her closet.

She only goes home to sleep. It doesn't feel like home. She's living in the strangest place she ever has, both alive and dead. Shrodinger's *sesheta*. Worse still, she knows her world is about to get even smaller, because Thais is coming into town and Oscar and Tad can't know what's happened. Evidently, they're under the impression that she's missing.

She'd laughed bitterly when Henry told her that. Instead, she misses them — all of them. Her coworkers and friends, her family. Her father, who can't know she's alive again. Miu. Evidently the cat is doing alright at Henry's but is still spending most of her time hiding under beds.

Maren cannot bear to see her only to lose her again.

Mostly though, she reads to avoid having to think about anything. She camps out in the salt cellar, in the back garden, in the parlor. On the last day of her freedom, before the hubbub of the House returns post-Dies Wadi, she reads on the grand main staircase, arms braced on her legs and book split open at the spine, as always. A mostly-empty mug of coffee has gone cold next to her, although the thick, rich smell of it remains in the air, seeping into the pages of the book and the skin of her hands.

She's just finished a chapter when the front door creaks

open.

Maren feels her before she sees her. Feels a seed of power pushing up against the well of godhood in her own body. It's small, but it's there — a spark that can occasionally ignite a fire that roars through a forest.

When she locks eyes with Ari, it's like they're standing across a battlefield from each other. Maren's heart has jumped to her throat, and she can feel the start of a tremor in her hands.

"Maren?" She asks, the color drained from her face. There is gold flecked in her eyes, and even though Maren knows why she's never seen it before, it's hard to believe that she ever missed the godhood in Ari.

"Sorry, I didn't hear the bell," Maren replies, more shakily than she wants to. "Come on in."

Ari steps across the threshold like she's possessed, staring at Maren with too-wide eyes.

"You're not dead," Ari says quietly.

"No," Maren says. "I'm not."

Looking directly at Ari is difficult. It feels like there are two halves of her warring, one that wants to rush to her and one that's reminding her, coiled and cool, why Maren has been brought back. Reminding her of exactly what she suspects Ari of having done.

"I watched my mother gut you," Ari says. "I tried to save you."

"Thank you," Maren murmurs.

"Don't thank me," Ari says, and then takes a few shaky steps into the front hall. "Your pulse stopped under my hands. I failed."

Maren has to tear her eyes away from Ari, carefully shutting her book and setting it down on the steps. To delay further she places the mug on top, flattening the abused, curling cover. She can hear Ari draw closer, knows the squeak of the bottom step as well as she knows her own name. When she does finally dare to look up again, Ari has crept close. She's paused a few stairs down from Maren, looking like she's approaching a wild animal.

She is the creature of myth that Maren had first seen. There is gold in her eyes, sun under her skin, an unnatural current that races through her. The last daughter of a goddess. Maren feels like she may choke on it all.

"You lied to me," Maren whispers.

"I didn't," Ari says, frowning. "I never did."

"By omitting that much of the truth, you *did*. You said anyone can do necromancy–"

"Anyone can."

"No, not like you. Not like Phaedra. Not like your mother. What you have is godhood."

Silence greets this. Maren watches Ari swallow hard and then take a deep breath.

"You know," Ari says finally, quietly.

She wants to throw Ari out of the House, to shut the door behind her and lock it, to take this final day of peace for herself. But part of her, something wedged so far back in her skull it's almost silent, wants something very different.

"Did you burn him?" Maren asks.

"What?" Ari breathes.

"Did you cremate your father?" Maren asks.

Ari presses her lips into a thin line, the gold in her eyes blazing.

"Don't you fucking dare," Ari says. "I did *nothing*. I would never do something like that."

Maren doesn't see a lie in that fiery look. Neither does the godhood within her.

"Then who did?" Maren asks. "You have so much power, you could have snapped your fingers and made it happen."

"I don't know if I could have. I do know that I didn't do it, and never would. Fuck off, Maren. You know who did? My piece of shit mother. Which I found out right before she pulled me off of your *corpse* and threw me out of the apartment."

The morning plays back through Maren's head in slow motion. Every single memory made, everything that had been said and done.

"You were meeting her that morning," Maren murmurs.

"Yeah," Ari says. "But she botched it and left some of him behind, which is how you got screwed up."

"Because the dead don't like water."

"No, they do not."

Silence swirls around them, so thick in the air it's almost claustrophobic.

"You promise," Maren says, staring down at Ari. Not a question. A demand.

"Swear to the Gods," Ari says. The golden light snaps between them, shimmering with power and truth. "Can we talk?"

"Yes," Maren says hoarsely.

She leads Ari all the way to the top floor of the House, past offices and storage, heading for their rarely-used terrace.

The doors come open a bit easier under Maren's hands than she wants to think about. It's easier to believe that perhaps Henry had opened them recently, or even Oscar or

Tad, than to wonder on the strange power in her body that lets her see and feel things that she couldn't before.

A gust of wind greets them, scattering a few very dead and soggy leaves across the brick floor.

"It's finally getting warmer," Maren mutters. She crosses to the railing, bracing herself on it and turning her face up towards the sun, closing her eyes. There's a very good chance that she'll never see the true sun again soon, and she wants to soak up as much as she can.

"Winter has to end at some point," Ari points out. Maren feels her slot in next to her, and when she cracks one eye open Ari is leaning on the railing on her forearms, hands clasped tightly together. She's staring out at the city, a strange look of wistfulness on her face.

"Yeah, it does," Maren answers.

"You're... you're not wrong," Ari says. "In regard to your first point. I withheld a truth from you. It's just... what I do. Growing up I learned that it was easier to live up to the lowest expectations and fly under the radar. My mom and Phaedra think I have my head in the clouds and don't really care about necromancy, because I didn't want to get wrapped up in their special brand of tortured codependency that comes with being the last descendants of a goddess. She gave me the offering vials I use when I turned thirteen with the hope that I'd get into it. I told her I threw them in a closet and forgot about them."

"But you didn't."

"Oh, I threw them in a closet, but I didn't forget about them. The minute I had my own place I carved that damn circle into the floor myself. They've both walked over it who knows how many times, and they've never sensed it. I have it crisscrossed with so many wards I don't know if they'll ever notice it."

"Paranoid."

"Oh, totally." Ari turns a rueful smile on Maren. "But the less everyone knew, the better. The less I got wrapped up with my family, the fewer things they could hold against me. Until my dad figured out I was dating you."

Maren's heart drops into the pit of her stomach.

"He knew about us?" She asks. "I was the one who caused your estrangement?"

"No, the only person who caused that is him. He was a bigoted, wealthy old man who couldn't comprehend of a world beyond his ivory tower penthouse. He married my mother because he wanted her family's money as well. She married him because he could give her children that might pass on her godhood. It was a marriage of grandeur for both of them," Ari says, detached. "He wanted me to marry just as filthy rich, to the point where he didn't want us dating. I wanted to introduce you to them. Instead, he told me to break up with you or he'd kick me out."

They sit in silence for a moment, Maren breathing deeply to calm the tremor that she can feel building in her hands again. It's taken more than a decade, but she has her answer. She'd been on the wrong side of a black or white choice between a girl and her family. She'd thought about this moment for ages, figured she'd feel triumphant, know that she was the bigger person.

Instead she just feels sorry for what Ari had been asked to do.

"You don't sound bitter," Maren says eventually.

"I don't have time to be anymore," Ari says. "I have new things to be bitter about in relation to my family. Namely that they're a bunch of murderers."

403

"It's a tough look," Maren murmurs.

"Understatement," Ari grouses.

"Why are you here?" Maren asks.

"Felix gave me a key."

"How did *Felix* get a key?"

"I think Henry gave it to him. They're in some kind of weird tug of war over everything surrounding... that night."

"Oh great," Maren mutters. "I want that key back."

"That's fine," Ari says, producing it from her pocket and setting it on the stone railing. "I uh... I came to see you."

Maren finally turns to Ari, confusion pressed into her brows.

"Me? I'm dead. Technically, at least."

"Hence why I came to see you," Ari says, voice small. "I wanted to give you your due before Dies Wadi was over."

She pulls two more items out of her jacket pocket, placing them on either side of the key. The small tableau wrenches at Maren's chest and hurts to look at, makes her feel like she's coming apart at the seams.

They're offerings. For her. Items to continue nourishing and entertaining her in the afterlife.

A tin of loose Rooibos tea and a tiny dinosaur in a sweater. This one is a blue triceratops in purple knitwear.

Maren turns away, draws herself closed, crossing her arms tightly against her torso and pressing her chin to her chest. She's shaking like a leaf, breathing hard enough to have just run a race. Her vision narrows, tunneling in on her even as the godhood in her surges, screaming to be free. To wrap its hands around the neck of the woman at her back.

It flares within her like a brand, as sharp as a knife.

"Maren?" Ari sounds far away. "Maren — *what*–"

The sudden sear of Ari's hand on her arm yanks her back into herself so fast she sobs, sagging a bit. Ari is there to catch her and help her down carefully to the dirty ground, kneeling next to her and pressing a hand into her back. It forces unnatural warmth into her body, making her borrowed godhood sing and cry. Something sparks between them, a thread of godhood between two beings who haven't met in eons.

"How?" Ari breaths.

"That's how I'm back," Maren gasps.

"The gods brought you back," Ari says, the realization ringing hollow in her voice.

Maren just nods, clearing her throat and wiping at her eyes.

"They did," Maren confirms.

"And in exchange?"

Maren doesn't answer. Ari moves like a cat, down on all fours, hunched in front of Maren. When she takes Maren's jaw in her fingers and raises her head, her eyes are wide in terror.

"Maren," Ari's voice is urgent and steeled. "*What in exchange?*"

"They promised me Elysium," Maren murmurs. "So I could see my mother again."

"If you did something they wanted." Ari's fingers are tightening, and now she's the one shaking.

The woman with the godhood in her veins would understand intimately that the gods do not give gifts idly.

"Three lives in exchange for me," Maren says at last.

The fingers drop away. Maren looks up as Ari slowly sinks the rest of the way to sitting on the cold bricks.

"What three lives?" Ari asks. The urgency is gone from her voice, replaced by a deep dread.

"Your mother's. Phaedra's," Maren says, swallows painfully. "Yours."

Unbothered, the city goes on around them. The breeze carries a faint scent of brine and wet pavement. The sound of car horns, footsteps, doors opening and closing. The backfire of a cab and the answering bark of a dog.

Upset by the wind, Maren's hair snags in her eyebrows and a few strands of Ari's come loose from her bun.

"We can get through this," Ari says finally. Her voice is almost too quiet to be heard over the city.

"Not both of us," Maren says. Ari doesn't even bother with a reply, must know the truth as well as Maren does.

—

"I should bring Miu back," Henry says as he sets his bag of groceries down. He's taken to shadowing Maren, helping her with small tasks when he's not at work or at home.

"No you shouldn't," Maren says, hunting through her own bag to fish out a bottle of wine. Picking up what she's putting down, Henry checks the cabinets until he finds two wine glasses.

They sit together on the edge of the couch, looking out the window into a clear, crisp day. They're in the roller coaster of late winter-early spring, that strange time when the weather has very little idea what to do and can't stick to any discernible pattern.

"Wine's good," Henry murmurs.

Maren makes a noise of agreement at the back of her throat, even though in her own mouth it tastes flat and simple. The smell and taste of the honeyed wine from the Third Gate still sticks to her tongue in dreams sometimes, so whole and real that she's woken up a few times assuming she's dead.

She's been dreaming of Duat, the good and the bad, of what Elysium might hold for her. The longer she's thought about it, the more people she realizes she'll see — family, friends, former clients. What she'd experienced with Mrs. Colvard and her mother is the tip of an iceberg that she knows is drifting out in those open fields, just waiting for her.

"You should get home," Maren says after a stretch of silence.

"I know," Henry says. "But you're dying."

"No more than usual," Maren says.

"Way more than usual, actually," Henry says. "Just because you're whole and healthy right now doesn't mean anything. This reminds me of the way my grandmother died — took a fall, fractured a hip, got pneumonia in the hospital, and that was it. The doctors would keep us updated, how many days they thought she had left."

"I'm terminal," Maren says bitterly.

"Yeah, you are."

"Nineteen days."

Maren stares down into the deep red of her wine, swirling it around a bit and watching it circle the glass. When she was younger she'd always thought that red wine looked like blood, but she knows better now. Knows the consistency and the color is all wrong.

"I just can't believe there's nothing to do to save you," Henry says suddenly, the words rushing out.

"There's no way my life, which technically already ended, is worth three other lives," Maren says.

"I like you better than any of them," Henry mutters, taking a sulky sip of wine.

"Yeah, well, I'm not interested in getting into murder just because you happen to be better friends with me than them," Maren says. "If you brought in an embalmer, would you do my funerary rites at the House? I don't want Oscar and Tad to have to do them, but I'm also not interested in my soul ever darkening any other House's doorstep."

"That's awful."

"I mean it. You kept me as a popsicle for a couple of weeks, so it wouldn't be the first time my dead body was under the protection of the House."

"Why are you being so calm about this?" Henry grouses, putting his wine down on the windowsill and turning to her. There's an angry pinch to his face behind his glasses, thick brows bent towards each other.

What he doesn't see is the raging and crying she's been doing in private. Does not know that she stays up late at night shaking, her mind incapable of dealing with such an unknowable situation. She's been stuck in her apartment with nowhere to go and no one to run to, stuck in a swirling hurricane of her own anguish and the borrowed godhood making her borderline superhuman.

"What other choice do I have?" Maren asks. "I'm not killing anyone, so I will die again in nineteen days. That's it. End of story. I'm asking you the cruelest favor ever, I know. But I want to be able to trust that my body is cared for, and there's no better place I know for that than the

House. Call someone in... I can recommend some names. There's a woman in Los Angeles I really respect."

"I want you to know that I deeply, deeply hate this. All of this. This conversation, this situation, everything. It's awful," Henry says. "But yes, fine. We'll care for you in death as you cared for us in life."

"Thanks," Maren says, picking his wine glass back up and handing it over. "And thank you for sticking with me."

"Ride or die," Henry says with a deep sigh. "*Prosit*, bitch."

"Ride *and* die," Maren says with a knife-wound of a grin. "*Prosit*, asshole."

Their glasses ring through the quiet of the apartment, their wine sending red slashes of sun across the floor and walls.

# CHAPTER 29
## A Knife in the Dark

Eleven days left.

Her phone rattles on the table with a text.

*Come over.*

It's from Ari. Maren gives her phone a cursory glance before tossing it next to herself on the couch, text unanswered. She focuses on the mind-numbing reality show she has playing on TV instead, every so often shoving a forkful of pasta in her face. Her phone buzzes with texts a few more times during the episode, but she doesn't even bother looking at them.

Exactly an hour later, the first phone call arrives. Fifteen minutes later, the second. Fifteen minutes after that and–

"What?" Maren answers around a mouthful of now-cold noodles.

"*Come over,*" Ari says on the other end.

"No," Maren says with a heavy sigh. "There's no reason for me to be around you. We don't even know if this godhood in me won't murder you the minute I see you."

"*We also don't know if it* won't," Ari points out. Maren glares at the TV. "*Ren, get your ass over here. I have a surprise.*"

"Are we entering the part of my impending second death where you shower me in overly-expensive gifts?"

"*No, and we never will, as that is both gauche and pathetic. This is a surprise I have spent no money on.*

*Although if you want it to be, take a cab and I'll pay for it.*"

"I'll take the subway," Maren says.

"*Great!*"

"Fu—" Maren pinches the bridge of her nose, realizing she's agreed by accident. "Ari, I can't. It truly could be dangerous." There's a reason why Maren hasn't seen Ari since that day at the House. Many reasons.

A long sigh comes from the other end of the line.

"*I did not want to have to stoop to outright manipulation, but—*"

Maren listens with growing confusion as something jostles and rustles in Ari's background. There's a bit of a scuffle ("*Ack, no, don't—*") and then—

"*Say hi to your mom, you fluffy assassin,*" Ari grouses.

A single squeak is the only warning before Ari yelps in pain, shortly followed by a dull thud and the sound of tiny paws skittering away across a wood floor. Maren has a hand over her mouth before she can stop herself, eyes wide and suddenly wet. Her throat feels tight, something rising in it that she won't name.

"You have Miu?" Maren asks. She doesn't try to hide the warble in her voice.

"*Uh, I mean, she is currently in my apartment, but 'have' implies a slightly warmer relationship than the one we're currently nursing. We're working on it. I think,*" Ari says.

Something in Maren breaks open.

"I'll be there as soon as I can," Maren says.

Her mind moves faster than her trip, spinning and weaving between a jumble of thoughts that knock around in her head as rhythmically as the sway of the train. She grips the bar in the middle of the car like a lifeline,

411

chewing on her lips, staring at the people around her and not seeing them at all.

She can't see Miu. She has to see Miu. She could kill Ari. She could kiss Ari.

Being dead again would be so much easier. Her whole life feels like a splinter right now, stubborn and refusing to budge while causing more and more pain.

"You should smile," a man remarks as he slides onto the train. When Maren looks up at him from beneath a heavy brow, there is something in the set of her face or the intensity in her gaze that makes him retreat, warily backing away. He gives her one more glance over his shoulder before heading for the opposite end of the car. In his absence, she can see her reflection in the dark window of the train.

Gold rings her pupils, spreading across her irises. The barest hint of a skull shadows her features, burnished and burning.

"Fuck," Maren murmurs, squeezing her eyes shut and hunkering down in her coat.

In. Out. In. Out. Calm the buzzing in her mind to calm the glow under her skin. She won't let herself open her eyes and stare at her dim reflection again. Instead, she keeps her head down and eyes closed until Ari's stop.

Maren doesn't look at Ari when she answers the door. Instead, she pushes past her, staring into the apartment with wide eyes. The space is largely the same as it was a month ago, still a strange mix of eclectic decor and furniture that seems to have little in common besides being 'cool.'

The one new addition is hunkering down on the bookshelves under the windows, ears flat to the sides and tail flicking from side to side, a void of light with two

412

narrowed yellow eyes.

"Miu," Maren breathes. The tail stops twitching, the ears swivel forward. Miu raises herself up on her front legs and, with suddenly giant pupils, pushes off from the bookshelf in an impressive flight path, bounding the rest of the way to Maren.

She's on her knees immediately, hunched over with hands buried in Miu's long fluff, whole face pressed into her back. The beeping from below is sudden and peppery, an annoyed chorus that would like to know *where* Maren has been and *why* she has been made to suffer the indignity of all these strangers and their homes in the meantime.

"Hi Miumiu," Maren whispers, rocking back onto her heels and gathering the cat up into her arms. Miu hunkers down in that protective circle, purring as loudly as her little body can. If Miu has any thoughts or qualms about the godhood in Maren, she doesn't seem to want to share or act on them.

"Man, you are really not a dog person," Ari remarks from above them.

"You can like both," Maren says. "But Miu's been through a lot with me."

Even when Ari walks away, Maren doesn't bother moving. She stays like that, curled around Miu until her legs start to go numb and she knows, grudgingly, that she needs to move. Not wanting to put Miu down, she instead rises still holding her, a fluid motion that should have made something crack or hurt but doesn't seem to.

Ari is sitting on the couch, scrolling through her phone. Maren just stares at her for a moment, the way the light of the afternoon catches on her auburn hair, the spatter of freckles across her olive nose and cheekbones. She can feel

413

that single iota of godhood in Ari that makes the air around her shimmer with a drop of power. The godhood in her rises in response, but she tamps it down with an angry hand, holds it fast.

"Thank you," Maren says.

Ari looks up at her with that crooked smile. Maren's chest tightens.

"I wasn't ready to let you waste away without at least seeing Miu again," Ari says. "I know you can't see your family, but at least you've got Miu."

"I didn't want to," Maren admits as she drifts towards the couch. "I was scared to. I'm going to lose her all over again."

"Not if we find a way to fix this," Ari says with a loose-limbed shrug that does very little to hide her hardened expression.

"We can't," Maren says. "We've been through this."

She perches carefully on the arm of the sofa, staring down at Ari past Miu's fluff. Ari puts her phone down, swiveling on the cushions to face Maren. There is something deadly serious in her gaze.

"I know if you don't kill my family, you end up dead again. What happens if you *do* kill us?" Ari asks.

"I live," Maren says. "I don't want that. I would not be able to live with that kind of guilt."

"I wouldn't ask you to live with it. Did they say you had to kill us specifically?"

"Among other words, yes."

"What others?"

"Destroy. End your line. Mostly kill, though. This is an insane conversation to be having."

"Oh, a hundred percent, but my undead girlfriend is

414

sitting on my sofa, so who cares at this point?"

Maren narrows her eyes, purses her lips.

"Sorry, were we dating again?" Maren asks

"I guess technically we never defined that before you got stabbed," Ari muses. "The undead part stands, though."

"That is true," Maren admits with a sigh, scratching Miu under the chin. The purring rumbles on. It's the calmest Maren has felt since she woke up in the pitch black of the morgue drawer.

"I like one of those phrases though — 'end my line'," Ari says.

"That's still killing," Maren says.

"Not necessarily," Ari says. "We can work with that."

"Did you have me come over to reunite me with Miu, or to pick my brain about the exact wording of my one-sided deal with the gods?"

"Bit of both," Ari admits. Maren just shakes her head in response.

—

Maren finds herself still at Ari's that night. She and Miu have spent the afternoon and evening in each other's back pockets, both seemingly unwilling to leave the other's side.

"How do you get cats to like you?" Ari muses from the other end of the sofa. She's deferred to Maren's tastes and there's a nondescript home renovation show on the TV in the background, volume low.

"Some are more social than others," Maren murmurs, a hand pressed into the fur of Miu's back as the cat slumbers next to her.

"Ok, but how do I get Miu to like me?" Ari asks.

415

"That's an uphill battle. She's still wary of my parents and Henry."

"You should have seen Henry and I trying to get her into the carrier this morning."

Maren grins softly in the dim apartment. She can imagine it pretty well, but still would have enjoyed seeing it in person.

"Maybe she'll warm up to you. Would she — will she stay with you?" Maren asks, not looking at Ari.

"For now, sure," Ari says. "You can too, you know."

It's much easier to stare at the TV and not look over at Ari.

"Ari, please don't offer me a future when I don't have one to give in return," Maren says. "Remember: ten days."

"I'm not. I'm offering you a now."

Maren finally tips her head to the side, rolls her gaze towards the other figure on the couch. Ari is curled up as tightly as Miu, wrapped in a blanket with only her head poking out. In the strange evening light, a gray-blue that's half TV and half distant streetlight, her eyes spark and her temples glow. Maren can feel her heart beating in her chest, running gold with ichor. Where Maren has started to feel like her skin doesn't fit correctly, her body unable to fully contain what she's been given, Ari's godhood sits comfortably within her.

As she watches Ari dripping faded, glittering gold power, her own snaps at the base of her skull like the twang of a bow string. It so badly wants to be let loose and fly.

"I can feel it bleeding through," Maren says in answer. "There's something unnatural in me that wants to snuff out the answering power in you. I have to keep holding it

416

back."

"That tracks," Ari says. "The gods want me dead. I'm surprised they haven't just killed me, honestly."

"If myths have taught us one thing, they rarely intervene directly. Nothing like a nice afternoon of fucking with the mortals instead."

Ari snorts, a smile twisting across her lips.

"Ain't that the unfortunate truth," Ari says. "Bastards."

"I think I told Anubis to fuck off," Maren says.

"Rightly so." Ari pauses, leveling her with a hard gaze. "Will you let me offer you tonight? Tomorrow? The nine days after that?"

"You want me to die on your sofa?" Maren asks dry as desert.

"Did you have somewhere else picked out?" Ari asks, unflinching.

"I... I did not," Maren admits. "I haven't thought much further than talking with Henry about my embalming. Which actually presents a good point. I should probably just go croak at the House, then no one has to move me."

"Morbid, but weirdly prudent."

"That's basically my whole MO."

"At least stay tonight?"

Ari pokes one hand out of her blanket cocoon, pressing it into the space on the cushions between them. Maren stares down at it, where the golden dust settles at her cuticles, setting off the deep navy of her nail polish.

"This is a truly terrible idea," Maren sighs.

"Perfect!" Ari says with a blindingly sunny grin. "I'll get the guest room set."

—

For the first time in her re-life, Maren goes to bed with Miu on her feet and wakes up with her in the same spot. It feels more like a rebirth than the actual one she'd experienced. It feels correct.

Just like every morning for the last three weeks, she rises from bed with an unnatural grace, nothing stiff or sore, no smudges under her eyes or sleep to blink away. She hates it. She would give anything to feel like her old self again.

Maren slips into the clothes Ari had found for her the night before — loose jeans that probably puddle on Ari but hit Maren right on the ankle, and a garishly green sweater that is, all things considered, extremely comfy. She yanks a hand through her hair with a silent *sorry* to her abused curls. Miu finally rises into a stretch on the bed, rather pointy mouth open in one of her lazily giant yawns.

"You live a charmed life, Miu," Maren says with a small smile. Miu just plops her butt back on to the comforter and gives her a few slow, sleepy blinks in return.

The smell of spiced coffee leads her to the kitchen. Ari is there, holding a cup of coffee and staring at the opposite wall in a way that suggests she's seeing right through it.

"You're awake," she notes distantly.

"I don't need much sleep these days," Maren says. "You look like you do though. Did you sleep at all?"

"Uh, loosely," Ari says, turning to Maren. She's a sleepy mess of undone hair and bloodshot eyes. She'd clearly tried to pile her hair on her head in its usual style, but it's come loose and is sliding down the back of her skull, leaving a knotted mess at the nape of her neck. Her bangs are a frizzy disaster and she's wearing mostly what she was yesterday — she just seems to have swapped her jeans for bike shorts at some point.

"Loosely," Maren echoes, raising her eyebrows. "You trying to race me to the grave?"

"I appreciate how cavalier you're being about your own death," Ari says with a tenuous grin.

"I have no idea how to process it, so I'm defaulting to gallows humor," Maren says. "You should get some sleep. It's still early enough."

"Not yet," Ari says, pushing herself off of the counter and shaking her head.

"Yes yet?" Maren suggests.

"I had a thought that I've been working through."

"Oh no."

"Oh yes." She crosses the kitchen to lean against the island, close enough to Maren that she can feel her godhood swirling. She tangles it between her fingers and closes her fists around it, swallowing hard.

"Can we at least get you somewhere soft in case you pass out?" Maren asks.

"I will submit to that. The other mug is for you, by the way," Ari says, nodding towards the twin of the one she's holding, slowly steaming next to the coffee maker.

"Thanks," Maren murmurs, carefully collecting the warmth in her hands, clasping her palms around it and savoring the temperature. It smells like Saturnalia.

They end up across the dining table from each other, Ari slouched with her feet up on a second chair and looking like death warmed over. Maren takes a third chair and Miu a fourth.

"What if we could end Hecate's line without also ending my family?" Ari asks, her last word vanishing into

419

a yawn.

"That's one and the same," Maren says.

"Not necessarily. I made an interesting discovery the night of my sister's wedding."

"Outside of her being a murderer?"

"Amazingly, yes. When, uh… when you and that knife came into contact–"

"When I was stabbed. Let's cut the euphemisms, Ari."

"Heh — cut — but sure. When you were stabbed. By my mother. The raging shitstain of a human she is… anyway, I digress. I noticed that I could suddenly feel every single piece of your soul in a way I never could before. Normally I'm aware of the threads and parts of a soul that are woven together only in the abstract, and mostly as a whole. I can feel when something's *wrong*, like when my dad was haunting you — my *Gods* I am so sorry, my parents are the absolute worst — but not the individual shards. Not that clearly. But the minute it was in you I *knew* what your soul looked like, and how the parts made up the whole. You were pinned in place, perfectly preserved."

"Like a dead bug," Maren mutters.

"Nothing like that," Ari says, shaking her head as violently as she can in her currently sleep deprived state. "It was — *you* were gorgeous. And I could feel my mom reaching for you as well. So I gathered up all the bits and pieces of you and pushed them as far and as fast as I could, hoping to get you into Duat before my mom could do whatever nefarious evil I'm sure she would have tried. She was so, *so* mad, like nothing I've ever seen. When she looked at me I thought she was going to kill me, too."

"That's why," Maren says, tugging at her lip in thought.

420

"I couldn't figure out why I didn't have offerings or spells with me."

"That was a risk I realized later," Ari admits sheepishly, rubbing the back of her head. "It kept me awake for nights. Well, and also your death. But I was afraid I'd doomed you to a second death."

"But I wasn't wholly unprepared," Maren says with a soft smile.

"I did hope," Ari says. "If anyone was going to be shoved into Duat all at once without the proper procedures to prepare them and still survive, it would be you. And you did. In fact, I did such a good job that look at you, you're alive again!"

The grin on Ari's face is so unnecessarily pleased that Maren gives in and finally rolls her eyes.

"Yes, yes, very good," Maren says. "We're lucky your mother didn't try to summon me back to... I don't know what she'd do."

"Destroy your soul," Ari says simply. "And oh, she did. She was already trying as she was kicking me out and Phaedra was still screaming her head off. But she couldn't find you. I thought maybe it was something I did, but now I'm wondering if it was because the gods had other plans for you."

"I'd put money on option two," Maren sighs. "I do owe you a thank you, though."

"Eh, please don't. I didn't know if it would work. It was an act of desperation with pretty much no thought behind it."

"It still kept me from being double-killed by Irene."

"True."

A beat, Ari chewing on her lip in thought.

"That's why she made him walk, by the way. My dad. She's big into destroying souls these days."

"Lovely woman, your mother."

Ari just answers with a bitter scoff.

The silence they lapse into is comfortable, buoyed by the city around them and Miu's sleepy purring from just below the tabletop. Maren takes a long, slow sip of the coffee, letting the clove and cardamom swirl at the back of her throat.

"You mentioned a plan," Maren says, staring down into her steaming coffee. "Does it have to do with the knife?"

"It does. Also, sidebar, really kicking myself that we didn't know about a knife that could hold a soul in place to piece it apart when you had that extra piece in there."

"That would have been incredibly handy," Maren realizes. "Although you would have had to stab me?"

"Correct," Ari says with a bob of her head. "I'm willing to bet it might work with a superficial wound though."

"Painful," Maren says.

"But also not dead," Ari points out. "If I hadn't pulled so far back from my family's weirdness my mom probably would have taught me about ancient shit like that knife."

"We also probably would have had a very different outcome to where our lives are intertwined."

Ari smiles at her, something soft and sleepy and undone that tugs at Maren in a way that has nothing to do with godhood warring against godhood.

"We would have," Ari agrees. "I do know this, however — the godhood in me is, like your borrowed bit, a distinct part of my soul. That my mom managed to impart to me as a kid."

Maren stares across the table at her, white-knuckling

her mug as the last piece slips into place.

"No," she says.

"What?" Ari says with a frown. "You don't even know what I was going to ask."

"I am not going to let you set yourself on fire to keep me warm. I'm *dying*."

"Yes, which I'm trying to fix. Or, at least push that date back by a few decades. Let's do this. That godhood you've got lets you do all the same nasty shit we can do, and that includes destroying souls. Or, in this case, part of one."

"No way are you giving up a part of yourself to possibly gamble on my life. We have no idea if that would work. It probably wouldn't. I'll just be dead, and you won't have your power anymore."

"So?"

"It's who you are," Maren says. There is a note of hopelessness in her voice.

"People change," Ari says.

"Not like this." Maren stands, the chair scraping across the floor behind her. It hurts to swallow, and her heart is beating too fast behind her ribs. "I won't destroy that part of you that's Hecate."

She turns away so that she doesn't have to see whatever no-doubt-crestfallen expression Ari is sporting. Halfway across the room, Ari's voice finds her.

"Think on it, Maren," Ari says. "Please."

She doesn't stop. She won't turn back.

—

She's still at Ari's the next night. And the next. And the one after that. As the days tick down, something starts

423

coming loose in Maren, and the ironclad compartmentalization she's been working on for the past almost-month starts to fail. Everything around her is a terrible, perfect reminder of what she's losing in a few short days. The city that has borne her across her whole life. The father and stepmother she hasn't even been able to see. Henry and Miu. She drifts, panic seizing her in quiet moments, only for her to be slammed back into her body by the godhood that's rising in her further and further every day. Sleep abandons her almost totally. Food doesn't taste right. Wine is like ash in her mouth. Agony and rage come too easily. She's worried it will consume her and finish the job she won't do.

But at the same time her new world is beautiful. The sun and the moon throw light across every atom of her universe. She stands at the wide windows of Ari's apartment and watches single bits of dust caught in the air. When she reaches out to touch the glass, her skin sings with the stories of every person who has lived here through the century of the building's existence.

They don't talk about Ari's plan any further. When Ari goes to work during the days Maren devours her books, working through them with a level of discipline that only comes from knowing exactly how many days you have left on earth. The pages whisper to her, the words dancing across the rough paper, each letter inked with passion.

One day, she walks straight to Union Square and then back down to Tribeca and doesn't tire. She's torn between exhilaration and horror. This borrowed godhood is like an overloaded reactor, propelling her further and further ahead until it will, very suddenly, drive her into the earth.

That night, when she walks in the door, Ari is already

there.

"I'm dying," Maren says.

"Yeah?" Ari asks, rising from the couch in confusion. "We know that."

Maren is breathing fast. Depression and mania are both fighting for control of her mind.

"Knowing and realization are two different things," Maren says as Ari comes to stand in front of her.

Ari must see something in her expression, because they meet in the middle. Maren knows this is wrong, that this will only deepen the hurt more, but she needs this now. She needs Ari's body against her own, needs to feel something human with the last little bit of her own humanity. They leave a trail of stripped clothing in the hall, falling into bed in the dark of Ari's room.

Every place they come into contact is a prayer, deeper than their skin, their blood, buried in their bones. With the godhood coiled in both of them any touch seems to fall into a chasm, bottomless and impossible. The hunger becomes ravenous, an unrelenting craving that dances between them.

—

"I have to wonder how this is going to work, considering my soul's already been to Duat once. Think it still has to decay away, or will I just pop right back into the Hall of Ma'at?" Maren asks to the ceiling of Ari's bedroom after. The sheets are in disarray, both of them lying side by side and loose-limbed.

"You're sure they'll let you back in just like that?" Ari asks.

425

"They promised me they would."

The bed shifts, Ari's power coiling around them as she raises herself up onto an arm. Her hair spills over her shoulders, the long, straight strands feathered across her skin and bedding. Maren lets her eyes linger, lets her gaze trace the long line down her throat and arm to where one of her hands is gripping the navy sheets, godhood and nail polish and thin rings all glittering together.

Maren rolls onto her side in response, placing a hand on Ari's shoulder and lowering her back down to the bed, her hair coming to rest around her head like a sun disk in the last light of the day. Straddling Ari's hips, Maren braces herself over her, staring down into those wild hazel eyes. Gold flecks dance in them, and when Ari juts her chin out it comes with a grin that's too brittle to be anything but broken.

"I can see it in you," Ari says. "More than I've ever seen it in my mom or Phaedra. It's like your body can't contain it."

"It was never made to," Maren says. "Where do you see it?"

"I can see it here–" Ari reaches out to press her thumb into the space at the corner of Maren's eye, making something within her wail at the touch. She drags her thumb down to Maren's mouth, pressing into the bow of her lips. "And here. Your fingertips and your toes, the space over your shoulders where you skin presses close to the bone. It's honestly the most gorgeous thing I've ever seen. It's massively fucked up that something so beautiful is straight up murdering you."

Maren lets out a long breath before she very carefully places a hand over Ari's heart, letting her eyes flutter

426

closed as Ari's whole soul comes alive under her, burning bright like a falling star.

She knows that part of that is Hecate's power, the power of a lineage carried down from a goddess thousands of years before the two of them ever came together in this place.

"What if they don't honor the promise?" Ari's voice is little more than a whisper.

The thought is like ice in her veins and she sits back, swallowing hard.

"I want to say they have to," Maren says.

"But they don't actually have to. Nice afternoon activity, right?"

"Fuck," Maren says, rolling away from Ari and staring at the far wall. The mattress dips and sheets rustle in the dark as Ari comes to wrap her up in her arms, pressing her skin to Maren's. Maren leans into it, barely able to hold onto the power that wants to destroy the goddess at her back.

"Let me set myself on fire, Ren," Ari whispers into her ear. "It might save you."

"We don't know that," Maren murmurs.

"No, we don't. But I won't be able to live with not trying. Don't leave me here without at least exploring the possibility."

There are tears tracking down Maren's cheeks. Ari takes her chin in her fingers, turns it slowly so that she can press a kiss into one of the trails. It only hurts more, and Maren shudders out a sob, doubling over on herself.

She has no control over this anymore. She can't pretend it's going to be ok. When she'd first been brought back, she'd been so *angry*. She'd wanted to get back to Duat so badly, to just be left alone in her death. It's been harder and harder to latch onto the strange peace though. There is something wild and untethered in her soul.

"I only have two days," Maren gasps.

"Let's see if we can find at least a few more," Ari says.

Maren lets go in a way she has only once before in her life, letting her soul push at bounds it's always known. Ari pushes right back, the rising fog after a thunderstorm, blanketing the world in its own quiet power.

"Ok," Maren says, and Ari knots a hand in her hair and presses her face into the crook of Maren's neck.

# CHAPTER 30
## *Hecate Trimorphe*

Maren feels like a specter as they stalk down the hall towards the library. The apartment is awash in gray and blues in the dark, stripped of color. The shadows stretch until they're all one but Maren is able to peer through it, watch as dust motes swim in the night air and catch the light of the moon as if the sun was high in the sky.

She follows the golden smudge of Ari towards the place where she died, their hands linked as Ari leads the way like a herald. Maren stares at their intertwined fingers, Ari's dusted with shimmer and Maren's own glowing like she's dipped them in stardust.

The carpet in the library has been pulled up, no doubt thanks to all of the inside of Maren that ended up outside. It's revealed a gorgeous floor inlaid with delicate wooden designs, clearly well-trod-on over the years.

What really draws Maren's eyes, however, is the summoning circle. It's as large as the one in Ari's apartment, but unlike the rough wooden carving of that one, this one is delicately inked in golden paint, elaborate designs and Greek calligraphy woven around it. At each compass point there is a tall, brass hurricane, and when they draw closer Maren can see that in addition to the pillar candles making their home within them, the holders are also playing host to honey, milk, wine, and blood.

"She was trying to summon you," Ari notes, annoyance coloring her voice. "Well, fuck you mom, not this time.

Honestly, considering how fresh this stuff is, the last time she tried she was probably looking in the wrong place."

"Can't find a soul in Duat if it's hanging out in the West Village instead," Maren remarks dryly.

"Alright," Ari says, rattling around in the writing desk. She comes up with the dagger, the hilt glinting in the light of the candles.

Maren feels it like a punch in the gut, remembers how it had sunk into her, ripping apart skin and muscle and everything beneath. For one moment she feels like she's reeling, but then Ari is there, her hand gripping Maren and holding her up. Maren closes her eyes, takes a deep breath in, lets that golden godhood flood her and steady her. When she opens her eyes again, Ari is holding the dagger out to her, hilt first.

Taking it in her own hand feels strangely anticlimactic. Nothing comes alive under her hand, nothing changes. She hefts it up, giving it a flip and watching it spin through the air before catching it. It's perhaps heavier than she'd expected, but that's it. Otherwise it's just rough under her palm, the hilt as inlaid with wire filigree and cut gem as it is.

"So," Maren says. "Where exactly would be the best place to stab you?"

"I can't say I'm much of a trauma surgeon," Ari says as she shrugs out of her coat and tosses it aside, squaring her shoulders. "But there's no good place to get stabbed. I think our best bet is over the top of my shoulder, which will avoid a bunch of bits that bleed a lot. Just don't hit my rotator cuff. I'm too rich to not be able to play tennis."

"You don't play tennis," Maren says.

"Caught me," Ari says. "Just injecting a little levity into

the situation before you, you know, *stab me*."

"We're doing this as safely as possible," Maren points out.

"We're actually not," Ari says. "As we're not doing this in a hospital. Or anywhere even remotely sterile. I'm guessing you know how to suture, but not how to stop me from bleeding out."

"Uh. We're not taught to suture like medical professionals are. It's... cosmetic," Maren says with a wince.

She chances a look up at Ari. Her face is a strange twist of messy emotions and golden haze. There's fear, carefully shut behind hard eyes, and that lopsided grin of hers. Maren tears her eyes away and reaches out to her, wrapping her hand around Ari's shoulder and pressing her thumb into the joint.

Letting her hand slide down to Ari's wrist, she closes her fingers around her pulse point to feel the thump of her heart under her skin.

They're so close, sharing the same air, sharing the same heartbeat, and when Maren raises her eyes to Ari's face again, she finds them stuck on her lips, chapped and bitten as always.

"One last one for the road?" Ari asks.

"Yeah," Maren says quietly.

It reminds Maren of their first kiss, a little sloppy, both of them shaking a bit, not quite as coordinated as they'd like to. It's fear making them buzz now, not alcohol, but Maren feels as off-kilter as she remembers. When she pulls back, she watches the light in Ari's eyes, remembers how she thought that Ari looked like something ancient and powerful all those years ago.

431

Turns out Maren was more right than she knew. Maybe, in that first sweet, fleeting moment, somehow her mind had let her see Ari's true nature.

"I'm ready," Ari says, breathless. "I mean, I'm not, but fuck it, let's do this."

"That's about where I am," Maren admits.

"Cool," Ari says. "*Anakaléo,* Maren. For luck."

"*Anakaléo,* Ariadne," Maren says as she forces her arm to move, lets the godhood trapped within her burn bright and hot and guide her hand and the knife clasped in it.

—

Maren can see Ari.

Every piece of her soul is singing, rising on the river, golden ropes twisting around the blade of the knife currently in Ari's shoulder. Even the blood that runs down her bare skin shines metallic, ichor and iron.

Her heart, her shadow, her body, and spirit and name all rise to Maren, calling out to her own soul in return.

And there is one extra bit, a key that seems to lock it all together.

"Working?" Ari grunts out, her nostrils flaring. One of her hands is currently gripping Ari's shoulder, her weight leaning into her good arm as she pants and keens, noises that the humanity hiding in the back of Maren's brain wants desperately to soothe.

"Yes," Maren says, and the word rumbles up from deep inside her.

Something in her reaches forward and pulls the key from the lock so sharply and suddenly that it makes Ari cry out, her knees buckling and her forehead coming to rest on

432

Maren's shoulder. Her breath is hot and wet against Maren's neck as she chokes out something that might be words or might just be heaving sobs.

Giving another tug, Maren works to bring the key to the surface, to let whatever power is within her wrap its hands around it and separate it from Ari like a splinter. With one last languid pull it comes free from her soul and body.

"Oh fuck, *fuck*–" Ari gasps, and the next thing Maren knows they've tumbled to the floor, Maren on her knees over Ari where she's crumpled on the ground, her eyes open wide and perfectly golden. Her head tips back, her mouth wide open in a silent scream.

The key hovers just above her lips, made of golden mist and shadow. Maren holds out a hand for it, lets it drift to her palm as her eyes flutter closed. She can feel the heat and the power woven into it, all that's left of a goddess long lost to memory and worship.

She closes her palm as if to snuff out a candle. The key meets the godhood in her and shatters apart.

Opening her fingers slowly, she watches as golden sparks drift towards the stars, faint and pale and fading in the dark. Entranced, she lets her head tip back further and further until all she sees are the shadows spread across the elegant ceiling.

Ari reaches out, closing a slick hand around Maren's wrist.

"Ow," she grinds out.

Something within Maren snaps, retreats, and she yanks the knife out, stumbling back and falling onto her ass, one hand bloody and one sweaty. The blade clatters to the floor like the ringing of a bell.

"Shit," Maren says, breathing hard as she comes back to

herself. Ari sits up slowly, levering herself up on her good arm, her other one cradled against her chest. She's bleeding more than Maren feels particularly comfortable with, the blood dark in the low light. "Shit, I'm so sorry — are you ok?"

"I feel awful," Ari says. Her voice is an absolute wreck, and she coughs, doubling over in two. "Oh wow, this is all incredibly painful. Did you pull the knife out? You did. Ok, that's not the best thing in the world, but I think we can manage."

Maren crawls over to her, holding her head up gently in her hands. Her eyes are a warm gray in the dark, human and bright, the gold flecks faded and gone. Every breath she takes seems like absolute agony, the air flowing through her sounding so painful that it makes Maren wince.

"Are you..." Maren asks, searching Ari's face for any traces of anything out of the ordinary.

"Dying? No," Ari rasps, shaking her head. "I don't think so. But I did just have magic ripped out of me. Shit on a stick, this is beyond painful. Is that what you felt like after I yanked my dad out of you?"

"Phrasing," Maren says.

For a breath, the only sound is Ari's horrible, labored breathing, and then she laughs. Maren cracks a grin too, can't help her own laughter, although it fades the moment Ari starts coughing again. Maren carefully gathers her up, wraps herself around Ari like a bandage.

"I should put my arm above my head," Ari says. "Hand me my jacket?"

"Ok," Maren says, scooting just far enough to help Ari prop her arm up on Maren's shoulder. She lets her head drop, her hair falling across Maren's lap, and Maren presses the coat into her shoulder to stop the bleeding, kissing the top of Ari's head over and over again as something blooms in her.

Maren has no idea if this counts, if this will save her, but it worked. She'd held Ari's godhood in her hand and snuffed it out, and Ari had let her.

They stay like that until Ari is able to stop sobbing and coughing, while her breathing evens out to something less terrifying. Ari mumbles something into Maren's sweater and Maren can't help the smile she presses into Ari's hair.

"I missed that," Maren whispers.

"Sorry," Ari blubbers, lifting her head. "Do you think–"

The sconces flare to life around them, bathing them and the mess around them in warm light that sends the shadows skittering.

Maren looks up sharply to find Irene Lucanus bearing down on her, golden fire in her eyes and her hands outstretched, palms up. Maren knows that posture, and it sends her heart lurching into her throat. The world slows.

Once again, the fire in her rises as she does. As if possessed, she grabs the dagger and stands in one smooth motion, advancing on Irene to meet her halfway, knowing there are sparks dancing in her own eyes.

Before Irene can close her hands, can start to drain Maren's life from her, Maren drives the knife down through Irene's left palm, all her strength behind it to push it through skin and bone, watching through a golden haze as Irene gasps, falling to her knees at Maren's feet, a red river pulsing from her hand as her fingers twitch.

"Who are you–" Irene gasps out, but Maren silences her with a hand to her forehead.

She knows how to do this now as she picks the lock

435

around Irene's power and pulls it from her body, yanking it from the weave of her soul and crushing it to dust in her hand. It's not like Ari's, not like that golden, brilliant light. It's twisted and darkened and brittle, but powerful in a way that fights against Maren as she closes her palm.

The godhood in her is stronger though, and she curls her fingers shut with a sharp breath. The second key of power crumples to nothing and falls to the floor like sand.

Irene stares up at her with wide eyes, horror stretched across her features. With a snarl, she spits in Maren's face.

Maren reels back, blinking as her vision clears.

And finds herself staring at the last face of Hecate across the room.

Phaedra lets out a whimper, and then faints to the floor in an unceremonious, crashing heap.

—

"She's coming around," Ari says. She's crouched down next to Phaedra, one hand checking her pulse and the other holding her jacket to her still-bleeding shoulder.

Frankly, it's one of the stranger scenes Maren has ever seen.

The fact that Irene is still kneeling at her feet, cradling her hand to her chest and breathing like a wounded animal is just making everything even more insane.

"I'm glad she's alright," Maren says automatically, and Ari looks over at Maren with her eyebrows raised.

"Thank you, *Sesheta* Nykara," Ari says, dry as the desert. "You would think that now that you've stabbed me we'd be past all your pleasantries."

"Sorry," Maren says. "I uh… don't really have any

words for what's an incredibly fucked-up situation."

"A first, for sure," Ari says.

A hand slick with blood latches around Maren's arm, and she turns to find Irene pulling herself up. Scooting away, Maren yanks her arm free, glaring down at the woman who murdered her.

"Stay away from me," Maren says, pointing the dagger down at her.

"Do you have any idea what you've *done*, shade?" Irene seethes as she pulls herself to standing on a chair. "This is why I wanted to find you and destroy you, so that you couldn't come back to haunt and kill my family."

"I'm not a shade," Maren says, frowning. "And I haven't killed anyone."

"You have, though," Irene says. "You've killed almost all of what remains of our line."

"Yeah, and she's going to need to do it to the last third," Ari says, standing and glaring at her mother. "And I can vouch for her not being dead."

"She's playing a trick on you," Irene says, although she doesn't take her eyes off of Maren.

"She's not," Ari says.

"What–" Phaedra murmurs as she stirs, opening glazed eyes. With the very sudden lack of Hecate's magic in the other two, Maren can feel it stronger in Phaedra, somewhere between Irene and Ari.

"Hey," Ari says, helping Phaedra into a sitting position. "Take it slow, there you go. Do you know where you are?"

Phaedra nods, blinking a few times like she's just come out of a cave into the sun.

"Mom's place," Phaedra says, and then her features crumple as she surveys the scene in front of her.

Maren feels her body automatically straighten, hands clasped in front of her, something ingrained in her at this point.

However, no amount of hospitable posture is going to help the fact that she knows there's blood smeared across the floor and through the summoning circle. Nothing's going to help the fact that the dagger is still in her grip, two people's blood on her. Nothing to get away from the fact that Irene is bleeding onto the sofa she's using to help herself stand.

And nothing to help the fact that Maren should be dead.

"My Gods," Phaedra says, voice small. "I — I don't — what happened?"

"It's a long story," Ari says. "C'mon, let's get you up and out of here."

"Don't you go anywhere," Irene says like the edge of a knife.

"Fuck off, mom," Ari says.

Instead of responding, she turns to Maren again, and the hatred Maren finds in her eyes is so deep that it hits her physically.

"You will die a final time for this," Irene says.

Maren just stares back and has nothing to offer.

—

Ari calls a car for Irene, sending her down to the lobby with a tea towel wrapped around her hand.

"You better fucking say you stabbed yourself opening an avocado," Ari says.

"You're a disgrace to your family and your history," Irene snipes.

"Oh well," Ari says, and then slams the door in her face.

"What happened here?" Phaedra pipes up from where Ari has installed her in the dining room. "Someone has to explain *something*. Gods, this is beyond anything — how are you *alive*?"

"Like I said, long story," Ari says. "And we will tell you. But right now you need to trust me and let Maren do something."

"Do what?" Phaedra asks, voice flat.

"Destroy your godhood," Ari says, coming to sit down next to her. Phaedra turns to her and the color drains from her face.

"Oh no," Phaedra whispers, and she reaches out to grab Ari's hands in her own. "Ariadne, what have you done? I can't feel you — did you—"

Ari nods, and Maren feels like she's eavesdropping as something sad crosses her face, fracturing her features for a moment that breaks Maren's heart.

"It'll save Maren," Ari says quietly, giving Phaedra's hands a squeeze. "She won't have to die again."

"So she really is alive," Phaedra says.

Something passes between the two sisters, old and deep, worn and unspoken and unknowable. Phaedra reaches up to brush some of Ari's hair behind her ear and then leans forward, whispering something to her. Ari's only response is a tight nod.

"I know you'd do anything to have Felix," Ari says. "I know you *did*."

"I did," Phaedra says. She stands slowly, letting her sister's hands fall away as she faces Maren. She takes a deep breath, closing the distance between them before

439

leaning in close, her lips a heartbeat from Maren's ear.

"Do you love her?" It's said so quietly that it's almost lost in the roaring of Maren's pulse.

Her breath catches in her throat as her heart stutters.

"Yes," Maren replies hoarsely. She probably always has.

"She loves you more than you'll ever know," Phaedra says.

Maren nods, trying to swallow down the hurt in her throat, trying to take deep breaths to fight against the tears that Phaedra's words are bringing up.

"I know," Maren says.

"Good," Phaedra says, and then steps backwards, giving Maren a quick, tight nod.

"Just like that? You're sure?" Maren asks quietly.

"No," Phaedra says. "But I wasn't sure when I killed my father either. I did that for Felix, for us. I'm willing to let you do this for her. At least this way no one else has to die. I'm tired."

Maren can see it on her face, can see it in every line and shadow around her features. She looks exhausted.

"I am too," Maren admits.

"I told you not to get involved in necromancy," Phaedra says with a sorrowful smile.

"You did indeed," Maren says, returning the strained expression.

"I can feel the godhood in you," Phaedra says. "It wants to reclaim you. Don't let it."

She extends an arm to Maren, palm down, her sapphire ring glinting under the lights.

# CHAPTER 31

## *The Gardener's Daughter*

The rain wakes her up from a brief slumber.

She rolls over in the dark, staring at the glow of the clock on the bedside table.

Two minutes to midnight.

She sits up, scrubbing at her face. The glow seeping from her settles in the air, and it makes her skin feel like it's too tight, makes her feel like her whole body doesn't fit.

One minute to midnight.

Ari is sound asleep next to her, chest rising and falling, Miu between them. Ari's bad arm is on top of the covers, carefully wrapped up over the stitches she'd had a friend do to keep it off the record.

If Maren is going to die, she doesn't want to leave the corpse for Ari to find next to her in bed.

She slips out from under the covers carefully, gliding down the hallway through the apartment. She's not surprised when she hears the light patter of Miu following her. When she steps into the living room, she finds a figure standing in front of the wide windows. Raindrops roll down the glass and catch some of the golden glow coming from the woman.

The woman turns as Maren approaches, leaving what seems almost an afterimage in the dark, godhood smudging through the chilled air. There are flower buds woven into her curls.

"Dua Proserpina," Maren says with a small bow.

"Hello, Maren," Proserpina says with a warm smile. "I see you were able to complete your top-secret mission."

Relief hits Maren square in the chest.

She can't stop the sag in her body, her knees suddenly rather jelloid. She throws a hand out to hold herself up on a nearby chair back, palm pressed to the cool leather as her heart thunders. Miu weaves between her legs, pressing close and warm.

"It worked?" Maren asks quietly. Her eyes are damp.

"Oh, it did. Very Gordian Knot of you. Serapis was impressed," Proserpina says, waggling her eyebrows. "I always love seeing what ingenuity mortals can come up with. A deathless existence is the death of innovation, I always say. As much as I'd love to reward you for it, I need to take that all back."

She gestures to Maren in the dark, her hands dragging and leaving golden comet trails.

"Please," Maren whispers, pushing off of the chair and closing the distance between them on shaking legs. She only stops when she's close enough to see the gold and kohl around Proserpina's eyes.

"Let's make this as easy as possible — hands up please." Proserpina gently guides her hands into place, palms up, before pressing her own hand into Maren's chest and pushing. Maren gasps at the feeling, the starbursts and sunspots of heat that rage through her as Proserpina pulls something from her. Looking down through watering eyes, she sees it start to form, running from her face and hands, pulling away from her skin like grains of sand and swirling into her upturned hands. It takes the shape of a feather, a gauzy plume that seems to be both gold and black at the

442

same time.

"Serapis?" Maren asks, breathless as she starts to feel her humanity rush back to her, settling like a weight on her shoulders. She welcomes it, crushes it all back into her, reveling at the feeling of her own soul finally being free in her own body and not pushed out of the way by something she was never meant to carry.

"Yes," Proserpina says. "You needed that extra *oomph* of rebirth to get you back here safely. No one does rebirth quite like that man."

"That's an alarming amount of power," Maren murmurs, rubbing at her chest with one hand while the feather slowly spins on the other. "I hated what it did to me."

Everything she did in the library a mere two days ago is something that she knows will stay with her for a long, long time. As Anubis has said, she doesn't have to live with her pain and guilt in Duat — she gets to live with it in the mortal world instead.

"No long-term harm done," Proserpina says gently, although Maren very much doubts that. Extending her hand to the goddess, she watches the last of the glow fade from her hand as Proserpina plucks the feather from her palm and tucks it into her curls. Next to it, the buds in her hair start to unfurl, blossoming into golden-petaled flowers.

The first sign of spring.

"I need one favor," Maren says. "Not a trade, not a prayer. A one-sided favor."

"That's very bold of you to ask," Proserpina says.

"From one vanished daughter of a concerned mother to another — tell Selene what happened, and that I'm ok," Maren says. Something softens in Proserpina's face, a

443

slight uptick to her golden lips.

"As a favor," Proserpina says.

"Unilaterally," Maren confirms.

"I can do that for you," Proserpina says as the first full flower opens in her hair with a shower of gold.

Before Maren can thank her, she hears someone racing up the hall. Maren whips around as Ari appears at the door, sleep-mussed and bleary, breathing like she's just run a marathon.

"You weren't in bed," Ari says, almost accusatory. "I thought — I thought — are you ok?"

"I'm fine," Maren says. She glances over her shoulder but Proserpina is gone, the room still and dark, the rain drumming on the windows

Ari holds out a hand to her and Maren takes it, linking their fingers together.

"You're not dead," Ari whispers.

"No," Maren says, squeezing Ari's hand. "I'm not."

Ari wraps around her, pulling her into a hug, a hand tangled in her hair. Maren presses their foreheads together, lets out a long breath. Everywhere they touch is simple and warm, a quiet, human homecoming.

"Let's go back to bed," Maren murmurs. Ari nods against her, and when she kisses Maren, it's with her crooked smile.

# ACKNOWLEDGEMENTS

Obviously, it takes a village to raise a book, and I would be remiss if I didn't mention this village's incredible denizens. Thank you to Jen Gandrup, Alex Rosenberg, and Josh Sackheim, who served as early readers, sounding boards, and general supporters. Your brunch notes and suggestions were always fun, illuminating, and helpful.

This book would not exist as it does today without the indispensable assistance of my editors. Thank you to Rebecca Brewer for the essential feedback on all things plot, pacing, and character, and to Hilary Doda for slogging through my weird formatting and continual misuse of punctuation. They've shaped this story – literally – in the most helpful ways possible.

To Alex C. for being hype as all heck. To Wendy H. for keeping me on task, on track, and on time-ish. Without their encouragement I'd probably still be staring at a first draft wondering what to do with it.

And last but so very far from least, my family – my mom and dad for their support, Max and Artie for the excellent cat-based inspiration, and my husband David for his heart and drive. When I told him I couldn't write a book, he looked me dead in the eyes and started this all with a dare of a question: *why not?*

Why not, indeed.

# ABOUT THE AUTHOR

Alexandra Martin is a recovering archaeologist who spends her daytime hours producing internet videos. She lives in Los Angeles with her husband and her two extremely fluffy cats. Find her on Twitter and TikTok @almartinwrites.

Made in United States
North Haven, CT
31 October 2024

59660265R00245